THE YOUNG MEN OF PARIS

BOOKS BY STEPHEN LONGSTREET

Fiction

THE PEDLOCKS
THE LION AT MORNING
THE BEACH HOUSE
MAN OF MONTMARTRE
GEISHA
REMEMBER WILLIAM KITE?
PEDLOCK & SONS
THE YOUNG MEN OF PARIS

Nonfiction

THE BOY IN THE MODEL-T
THE REAL JAZZ, OLD AND NEW
A TREASURY OF THE WORLD'S GREAT PRINTS

Plays

HIGH BUTTON SHOES

STEPHEN LONGSTREET

 DELACORTE PRESS / NEW YORK

THE
YOUNG
MEN
OF
PARIS

to no better friends anyplace

LORSER FEITELSON
HELEN LUNDEBERG
HELEN WURDEMANN

*"When God wills, it rains
with any wind . . ."*

CONTENTS

*Leopards break into the temple, and drink
the sacrificial chalices dry. This occurs
repeatedly, again and again; finally it
can be reckoned on beforehand and becomes
a part of the ceremony . . .*
                                    FRANZ KAFKA

BOOK I

Alizarin Crimson

1

THE RUE CAULAINCOURT showed its peeling walls in the strong lime-colored sun, the walks were crooked and climbed steeply. This was the address his friend Dino had given him—in Florence—as a place for a good cheap Paris studio. The front needed repairs and there was a large crack in the sidewalk in which grass was growing. Deo boldly stepped into the doorway and along a short hall. He rang the bell lettered CONCIERGE.

A thin bemused woman, with a head of fine yellow hair in need of combing, red, boiled, delicate-looking hands, appeared from behind a glass door. He smelled sprouts cooking, unaired bedding and the smell of kerosene oil lamps.

"Do you have a studio?"

"We have a big one, we have a small one."

"I'll see the small one." He didn't understand all of the French.

The woman took a large brass key off a board set inside the door. "It's three floors up. You're not a Moslem?"

"I'm Italian. My friend Dino Spinelli stayed here three years ago."

"Before I was here," said the concierge cheerfully. "You look Moslem."

"I'm a Jew. From Leghorn."

"I don't mix in politics. But no Moslems. The filthy Arabs they bring in lambs, they kill them up there and throw the entrails out of the window. The first lamb and it's *le commencement de la fin*."

The stairs seemed fairly clean in the bad light. On the third floor the studio that opened to the brass key had a sloping roof, two small windows, a sagging cot, a wash basin and pitcher without a crack (his respect for the concierge rose) and a small rusting iron stove.

"It is a real artist's studio. Look at the nails they hung the pictures on."

"I believe you."

"You do your own cleaning, and nothing tossed out of the window?"

"Of course not. I'll take it."

He was disappointed. It lacked the romantic flair he had expected from a Paris studio. It was just a shabby room, battered and smelling of stale spilled food, old lovemaking, the gutted melting candle in the wine bottle, the burned-down wick in the tin oil lamp hanging under a smoky spot of sooty ceiling. The concierge warmed to Deo; he had that effect on women. She was charging him two francs less a week than was usual for this studio, she said, handing him the brass key.

"*Bon.*"

Alone, Deo put his hands to his pale brow and hoped he wasn't going to get his shaking attacks. He walked to one of the windows and pushed it open, and up above on the hillside there were houses and gardens, a patch of green trees and old walls. People milled about on the Butte. The air was clear and sweet, smelling of green growing things, old plaster walls, wet earth, sun-toasted brick, freshly dropped horse oranges and a tang of wood smoke.

That's better! He unpacked his suitcase, stuffed the yellow silk handkerchief containing a cluster of gold coins into his back pocket and set out to explore the streets of his new home. He had to stock up on supplies: canvas, an easel, paints, more brushes, and food—and wine.

In the hall he saw a door, the only other one on the

floor. It was half open. A stout bald man, his face concealed under ghastly white stage makeup, was dishing out a stew. He looked up into Deo's stare—he was in his undershirt and a pair of ample checked pants, his braces dangling behind him.

"The new tenant?"

"That's right."

"That calls for a drink, Flinck says. I'm Flinck."

Deo accepted the invitation. A large poodle, dyed pink, was sitting at the small table set for lunch.

"I'm Modigliani. Amedeo Modigliani."

"You look like your name, doesn't he, Baba?"

"The devil I do. I'd rather look like El Greco."

"I never caught his act." The white face broke into a wild grin. "Flinck invites you in. Mademoiselle Baba, Monsieur Modigliani—call him Modi. Looks better on the posters."

The pink poodle barked, holding its paws in front of its face as if in prayer.

"You look cosy here."

"Flinck, the old camp follower, is always cosy. Sit down. Some beef stew? Flinck likes to cook. The meals in the cafés are for people who ruin their digestion. You paint?"

"I try!"

Deo looked over the walls hung with circus posters. He pointed to a figure with a painted face, elongated eyes, red bulb nose, a figure wearing a cap like a sugar loaf and a short gold and red costume over white silk-clad legs. Flinck nodded. "Flinck is a great clown. Eh, Baba?"

Baba barked. The stout man spooned out another plate of stew. "Sit. Eat. Tear off some bread."

Deo was suddenly very hungry. He dipped the good crisp wedge of bread into the stew, he swallowed the pale-yellow wine Flinck poured for him.

"Baba, the young man is an artist. And from where? Italy. Flinck has been all over Europe, head and buttocks—St. Petersburg, Budapest—such women, redheads, not really whores, just bed-happy. And Rome. You can't fool Flinck. He's Flemish but international as bedbugs. Baba, say hello in English."

The pink dog barked in a high key.

"A real Piccadilly how-ja-do-jolly-well hip-hip, eh? Baba

knows people. We're both with the Cirque Medrano this season. You must come. Lautrec used to paint us, and now a young fellow, a Spaniard with big eyes and a cowlick you could wipe plates with. Not you, Baba, keep *your* tongue off the dish. You know Clovis Sagot, the art dealer? No? He used to be a clown too." Flinck gestured, showing the tops of his hands, then the palms. "Not too good, not too bad. But a clown. Now he's an art dealer. Flinck will have you meet him. When Baba asked him why he stopped being a clown he said, 'I love God too much to go to church.'"

"That's a fine stew."

"And why? Garlic! Garlic is the stew's kiss. There used to be a girl Flinck played with in the Cirque d'Hiver, long ago. She became a painter too. Did a high-wire act, fell and hurt her spine, gave it up. She had talent, but a man-eater. Suzanne Valadon. You've heard of her? Her mother once wrote her: 'Don't come home and all is forgiven.'"

Deo sipped his wine and felt the stew settle comfortably in his stomach. "I don't know anyone here."

"A regular man eater, that Valadon. She had a son. Whose, we asked. By whom? Lautrec? Renoir? Degas? Flinck asked her as an old friend, 'Who's the boy's father?' And she grinned. 'They are all such great artists, I'd be happy to sign *any* of their work.' A bitch frankly. You need women, eh? Flinck knows the look. They'll kill you, but I suppose it's as good a way to take a last bow as any. Now clowns, women don't care for them. We're a painted symbol and women don't like symbols. They want reality. Baba, two turns backward from the chair."

The dog did one flip after another, backward, then put out a pink tongue and leered. The clown gave Deo his terrible grimace again. "What woman can do that? At command? But Flinck is keeping you. Must get the rest of my makeup on. Always put on the white when you get up. It attracts attention all day in the cafés, and so people say, 'That's Flinck.' And it's true, it is Flinck. Anything you want, knock on the wall. A pot, a pan, some bread. You look delicate. After the show Flinck will take you around to the cafés. Meet your fellow artists. Old Flinck, they all know his worth."

*

The clown was still talking as Deo went back to his own room. The bed creaked as he lay down. Deep exhaustion and a hollow loneliness overcame him. He dozed, with a great weight in his chest, but he had become used to that. Soon he heard the old clown leave, chatting with Baba down the stairs, voices of children playing under the sycamores and lime trees below. He fell asleep and dreamed of home.

2

"IDIOTA! Don't ever forget it; you're descended from the Spinozas, the great Spinozas who gave the world Signor Baruch Spinoza, he who said, 'All excellent things are as difficult as they are rare.'"

That was his grandmother, an old woman dressed in black who pointed a crooked finger at him from the corner where she sat. Deo was only three years old at the time, wearing sandals, a white linen sailor shirt with a black patent-leather belt. The shirt came down to form a sort of skirt. On the back of his head was a straw seaman's hat. How proud he had been when his mother dressed him.

"*Amore mio,* you mustn't cry when Grandma pinches your cheek."

"I don't like it."

"You're a big boy now, no more the *bambino.*"

Mama kissed him and all his life Deo remembered how she smelled, of sunlight and bath powder and the cooking with which she helped Marie, and a special odor that was *Mama;* like the fruit that came from Sicily—citron and raisins.

La Nonna was very old, full of little naps. There was snow on her head like the pictures in the book with the Alps, and mostly she sat, like a mountain, as wide as she was tall, Deo suspected. Even while seated she leaned on a cane with a golden handle that gleamed like Deo's own tears seen in the mirror.

"So that's a Modigliani?" she said, supporting her heavy dark features on the top of the cane. "*Vita e miracoli!* Amedeo. What kind of a name is that?"

"It means Beloved of God," said Mama, pushing him forward.

"I know that. *Capisco.* Come kiss me, boy, I'll be dead soon and you haven't kissed me yet."

Drawn by the claw, pushed by Mama, he advanced, shuffling his sandals on the cracked marble floor. He offered his face like a sacrifice, a *disjecta membra,* a crybaby—head to one side, tears ready, as if inviting the sacred knife, like when the old rabbi came to kill the chickens for the feast of Passover. That ritual Deo had seen in the yard; the old white-bearded man with his chalk-colored beard stained with blood, the sharp razor-edged, blunt-ended knife in his teeth, while he held a hen between his alpaca-clad legs and plucked the feathers from a spot on the chicken's neck, reciting a Hebrew prayer from between the teeth clenched around the dreadful knife. Then the knife flashed on the throat, the hen danced free among the lilacs, a drunken dance like the coachman Tony after a visit to the wineshop, only the hen was spraying the ground wetly red and it danced on fluttering its feathers and tripping over at last into a bundle of feathers.

No knife touched Deo's throat.

"He's a handsome devil, but puny."

The leathery lips of the old woman brushed Deo's cheek and he lay his mouth against the rough skin and smelled old age, unclean clothes and the Polish brandy ("Grandma likes slivovitz"). He pulled back, but not too quickly. Grandma held the cane like a club.

"Feed him up, Eugenie. There aren't many of us left, you know. We Sephardim are the salt of the earth."

"The Modigliani are a good Jewish family too, Mama."

"Family! *Pazzesco!* They're named after a town. I've seen it, Modigliani, just south of Rome. A few goats, some barefooted monks scratching their ass, and everything in ruins. What's the boy waiting for?"

"You frighten him."

Mama led him away and dried his eyes, and Deo played in

the garden with the bits of broken pottery, red and yellow and blue; the shiny one the coachman called yellow. Anna, the cook's little girl, gave him a blue glass button for his collection.

Deo as he grew aware of things felt sorry for Papa; so fast-moving, always mopping his brow and wiping out carefully the sweatband of his "genuine" Panama hat. And aware he wasn't Sephardim or related to the Kabbal or the Hasidim or the rab-binical great, and certainly not to the great, the glorious Spinoza.

Deo began to understand a great many things. He, Deo, had not been always around, but had been brought down from "above" in 1884. He was the fourth child and the old grandmother—she was a Garsin—would mumble, "The scraping of the pot, the last spoonful, a small coin, a *baiocco*, eh? Who's seen my gold reading glasses?"

The big buildings and the great bell-carrying towers all around were a city, and it was called Livorno. Mama was a Garsin too, before she married Papa. The Garsins had come from Spain ("A black year on the Inquisition and the royal court there; may the holy inquisitors burn forever in Purgatory and be turned to baste on a fire every ten hundred years.").

They had first settled in Marseilles after the expulsion of the Jews and Moors from Spain, and from there the family came to Italy. Of course it took, Deo was told, a few hundred years.

Papa ran a *banco;* later in Paris they would think Deo's father was a banker, but it was only a little broker's office, doing business in what came to hand, and when times were hard, he sold coal and traded in the hides of the great oxen that, when alive, pulled the carts with their solid wooden wheels whose axles sang a sad ungreased song.

"Deo," the old grandmother said, "the child didn't bring luck. The year he was born your husband Flaminio was ruined."

"Not ruined, Mama. Times are hard."

"Don't ask me to pawn my diamond for that *villano*. That's to bury me with."

"Nobody asked for your diamond."

It was a big stone, flawed and yellow, the size of a fly, and Deo as he grew older wondered why a little thing like that could bury anyone. They had buried the canary—he and Anna, the cook's little girl—in the garden themselves, aided by his older brother, Giuseppe Emanuele.

Deo began to gather the family history together the way he collected the colored bits of broken pots in the garden. Grandma often narrated it with ecstasy and disgust.

Papa's parents had once had some money. But they had lent most of it to a Cardinal with red hat in the Roman Curia, Son of a *puttana!* They hadn't wanted to lend, but the Cardinal, described as a very fat man with a fat nose with a wart on it, had made it clear to the Modiglianis that with this transaction they could wink at the law that said Jews could not acquire an estate. The Cardinal had winked again and again and quoted, "Jews are fated to be wanderers on the face of the earth and prohibited from taking root for good anyplace, or to become landowners. *Fiat justitia ruat callum.*" (Grandma may have added the Latin herself.)

The family had smiled too, and sighed and loaned—and put what was left into a vineyard. After hard work it was producing fine grapes. So one night there came two men in shiny leather hats, trailing swords, and they knocked hard at the gates. (Deo shivered to hear Papa retell his version of the story.) They had a legal paper with them and they spit on the freshly washed steps. It said the family had to leave the neighborhood in twenty-four hours, leave everything but what they could carry. "You could hear my mother scream as far as the town well." The Cardinal had a deaf ear to the family's pleas, and his servants beat the messenger sent to him asking for Christian mercy. So they left Rome and moved to Leghorn, and the vineyard was lost and all the money loaned to the Cardinal, for the holy man, *budella e sangue,* died soon after that of overeating a dish of doves cooked in olive oil and tomatoes. His heirs said there were no "records" of any loans that would stand up in a Papal court.

So times remained hard, and now Papa found nothing easy. He sat late at night under the swinging oil lamp with the green shade, and the night insects flew around his bald spot and he kept wiping his face and drawing the most wonderful columns of marks; he said to Deo they were figures, and the credit was poor and the balance was bad and getting worse.

Mama was the strong one, like the old grandmother, who moved away to visit relatives and never came back. Mama sniffed and said, "She was very old. *È finita*, Deo."

Mama (Papa called her Eugenie) knew how to bargain and how to get respect from the neighbors. She had read a great many thick books, and certain yellow ones called Zolas. She quoted a man called Voltaire that Deo didn't remember they'd ever visited.

Papa bowed to Mama's orders. She said he was a dreamer and lazy (*"Per piacere, basta,* Eugenie, not in front of the children."*).

Two brothers and a sister were too many for Deo, and only Giuseppe seemed interesting. "Precarious" was what Mama called their income, which sounded nice but meant no new shoes till spring, no fresh coat of paint on the house, and only Old Marie in the kitchen, smoked by charcoal and olive-oil fumes and given to too much use of garlic. That gave Papa heartburn. Deo would bring him hot water and lemon to ease his spasms.

"I should have as much *denaro* as heartburn."

Mama and Deo went walking along the lane where the shops were thickest, and in the late afternoon you could cheapen a bit of lamb and get a better price on a loaf of crisp bread, Marie walking behind them with her black string bag, fingering her rosary and marking the sign of the cross every time they passed a church and asking forgiveness for having produced an illegitimate daughter.

Mama held her long skirt skillfully, avoiding the old cabbage leaves in the street. "Don't you like to come shopping with Mama, Deo?"

"I like it, but why me? I want to draw."

"You're my youngest. You're in my heart, my last *bambino*."

"I want to go to the river with the boys sometimes and throw stones."

"You're too delicate, Deo. Your chest. I'll have Marie rub it with camphor oil again tonight."

Marie snorted. "I raised seven when married—and one later. Lord keep them wherever they are, and on pasta, *fritto misto*, hot and heavy. It's this fear you have of too much garlic. No germs can get past a boy with garlic in every pore."

"I want to go to the river with the boys. They drown cats."

"I'll buy you some colored pencils, Deo. If you promise not to draw on the house walls."

"Red ones? *All* colors?"

That night in her journal (she showed it to him years later) she had written, "Will Deo be an artist?"

Deo was always making marks on walks, on garden walls, and once indoors. Papa took off his belt and threatened him for defacing the dining room, but Mama stopped that. Now Deo drew on paper; heads of people the way he saw them, staring at him, sitting facing him, making those stupid jokes one makes to children. Yes, to draw was the best of things. And if he did well in school, at the Liceo, Mama had promised him a water-color set with real red-sable brushes. The kind you put into your mouth and made a perfect wet point to draw *putti* with.

When Deo was eleven there was that dreadful time of a strange illness. The darkness of the hot room spun, and his head was tied to a wheel that almost tore it off. Mama in her nightgown stood by the bed with little Dr. Tottini, and it was so hard for Deo to breathe. They had put red-hot stones inside his lungs, and how they got them there he didn't know.

"*Pazienza,*" Mama said.

Dr. Tottini, who blew the silver cornet in the town band, inhaled his cheeks and blew them out and made a hissing sound with very large lips. He said, "Pleurisy."

A cold rain was falling on the blue-purple window glass when Deo no longer felt hot. His lungs seemed to belong to someone else. Mama looked tired and held out to him a black tin shape the size of a book.

"It's German, and the colors are the best, and the brushes are sable."

"Red sable, *Madre mia?*"

"Of course."

He opened the enameled tin and there rows of little square cakes of color with all those fancy names, and sure enough three sable brushes. He picked up the smallest and put the brush end in his mouth. It tickled. He spun the handle and pulled out the brush, his big dark eyes wide and his mouth gaping. Sure enough! A point like a needle!

He began to cough, and Mama said that would do, and put the brush away in the box. From then on he painted and drew, and the hot wind came. Mama and her intellectual friends in the next room with their eyeglasses on long black strings discussed Nietzsche's *Beyond Good and Evil,* and lent each other a worn copy of *Triumph of Death* by someone called D'Annunzio, who— Here the women put their heads together in whispering and Mama said firmly, "It's shocking—*scandaloso* —men and women *what* they do! You'd think a grown man would find better things to do with his time."

"But he describes the passions so well, Signora Modigliani."

"Passions? A lot of fools blowing hard, and getting red in the face trying to get a hernia lifting a skirt."

That's the way Mama talked. No wonder her son Giuseppe was running round with young toughs called Socialists and asking to be elected deputy, making speeches against the Abyssinian war that everybody knew would happen.

The war came in the next year, and strange spicy-sounding places like Eritrea and Somaliland were under the Italian flag. Deo remembered the shouting in the street, drinking wine— Trebbiano and chianti—with strangers, and the coachmen trying to kiss Maria, and getting a thick ear with a soup ladle.

Deo did several large watercolors of the Italian troops under palm trees, and shiny black men with huge saucer lips running away, and lions eating them with relish. But he didn't like landscapes. Faces were better, more interesting.

Life was alive and real. He became aware of Anna in the kitchen—of girls, giggling fools with their pigtails and the habit of looking back over their shoulders and giggling again, sticking their tongues out. *Sciocco.*

The year he was to qualify for his diploma Deo came down with typhoid fever and the doctor said, "It has to be expected, Signora Modigliani; this one is a delicate boy. The Socialists are making a bother about this epidemic, saying it's the tainted drinking water and the back-yard privies, but it's the will of

God; we've *always* had privies—and who drinks water? Let me see your tongue, Deo."

"Your nose, Doctor, is a crimson lake and chrome yellow."

There were times when it was wonderful to be so ill, because there were images you saw when in fever that you never had when up and around. Forms, tones that synthesized into compelling secrets. Great swirling masses of wonderful color, color no paint box could ever reproduce, and the shape of things was stretched and pulled in so many odd and interesting ways. Deo was innately convinced of his genius—who else could have such fever? Sometimes he felt as if floating, usually late at night, warm from the fever and the wind blowing hot from Africa. He would lie there; from someplace in the city came the café sound of music and laughter. The wind in the green hair of the trees in the garden, and the late clop-clop of a horse pulling a carriage from or toward the park. It was a mood so alone, so private, so satisfying for a reason he couldn't give, that later he'd try to make himself sicker just to feel again that floating swimming sensation. It was unlike anything else experienced in the house, or the street, the city, in all of Italy and Europe. Beyond that Deo didn't dare think; it might destroy all this adventuring.

He had what the doctor said was, "Pulmonary complications. A soft diet, an egg beaten in white wine, some chicken."

"I'm not hungry."

"You'll get no strength back if you don't eat."

"I feel strong enough."

Mama rolled her eyes and made a small smile, her special ironic smile she used when Papa said he had a big new deal.

"Strong enough to take lessons from Signor Micheli?"

"I'll drink the egg in wine! Stuff me! *Madre mia!*"

Signor Micheli was one of a school of local painters who were called the Macchiaioli, because a critic had jeered at them as users of *macchie*—patches of color. So they took it as a name.

Signor Micheli, small, pigeon-breasted, pox-spotted, was not a very good teacher. But Deo liked to feel the touch of virgin canvas, so yielding (just like the flesh of Anna, Maria's now-ripe daughter, who helped out in the kitchen and hung the wash in the yard). And the smell of turpentine was good too, like a special piny brandy. Deo mixed his colors with care and he remembered all the rules; the teacher explained to him about primary colors and secondary colors, and how to use linseed oil, and when to add thinner, and *never* to let the brush get dirty.

"Treat color with honesty."

Deo painted the Gypsy boy who swept the studio, sitting in the chair, painted it with a fumbling brush because he didn't know just whose style he wanted to use. Some day he'd have a style of his own, but just now he didn't want Michelangelo's or Titian's or those painters of Napoleon's battles, or of Popes blessing crowds.

One day Deo saw a small glowing confusing painting in a little shop in an arcade. The owner of the shop, picking his nose with a handkerchief, said, "I took it in payment for several frames. It is called Impressionistic and is very fashionable in Paris."

Signor Micheli shouted when Deo mentioned *that* word. "It's not good for an Italian artist to copy the French every time they break wind. We have been and are the greatest artistic nation in the world! You know that, Deo! Now, no more Impressionistic nonsense. Don't draw with your brush. Bind, merge your areas together."

"I like to draw with a brush."

"You be careful or you'll become another Cézanne."

"Who's he?"

Signor Micheli swore at a saint and whispered, "Why am *I* cursed with genius, and so have to teach fools! Cézanne. *Può andar al inferno!*"

"Where can I see his work?"

Deo wondered what the new century would be like. All shiny and glowing with beauty and grace and kindness and the love of man for man, everyone said—even the Pope's *breve*.

Deo was sixteen in 1900, and Giuseppe, a crisp older brother in a working man's jacket with an old hat over his eyes, was hiding the bruise he had gotten at riots in the city square.

He mocked Deo. "There's your new century. Police on horseback beating back the workers, cornmeal going up, salami all goat and candlewax, and the Church in politics up to its moneybags. They made Marconi, the inventor, pay a million dollars for a divorce."

"Respect," said Papa, "for authority."

"You still hope to get Grandpa's money back from the Cardinal's family, *or* the vineyard?"

"Keep your Socialist talk out of this house," said Mama. "Deo, where are you going? Finish your dessert."

"I've had enough. I have to deliver a painting for Signor Micheli to the mayor's office."

"Is it of his piles?" asked Giuseppe. "Our little artist prince will make us all rich with his art. We'll bury him in a marble tomb."

Mama moved the back of her hand toward Giuseppe's cheek. "Big as you are I'll lay you out like *paleri*, I don't like such humor. Save it for your bomb throwers."

"Those are anarchists, Mama. We just want to educate the masses."

Papa said, "For what? To start pogroms?"

Deo felt this was a good time to get away from the table, and he went down the tiled passage and got his cap. Outside he noticed the sky was turning the color of a fine dark grape, and pigeons flying toward their cotes cut across and behind the great church tower and *cappella* where the bronze clangor of the bells was shaking the warm moist air.

Deo crossed to the deserted Foscola stoneyard where they cut breccia marble for churchly building. Behind the yard was a garden of the Muratori family, who lived most of the year in the south of France. It was a rather neglected place, but fine-smelling and silent except for the buzz of insects. Deo let himself through a gate that had buckled and no longer closed. Roses ran wild and the marble statues were worn and flecked, grown with moss. Anna waited for him.

She was fourteen, with a serenity of moral detachment, slim, yet with fine legs, and breasts that would one day match her mother's majestic fonts. Deo always thought Anna looked like a

da Vinci drawing, hair added by Titian—that special gold-red
—and her healthy vulgarity from Tiepolo.

"*Benvenuto.* I saw a rabbit, Deo. Fast little bastard."

Her bare feet were dusty with pollen, and he knew she was
wearing nothing under the overwashed blue gown.

Deo sank down into the tall grass. She sat cross-legged facing
him. Anna was eating a roll with sections of sausage and
tomato-pulp filling. She bit into it with strong wide teeth. Deo
kissed her legs and she laughed and chewed.

"Can't you wait, Deo *mio?*"

"I never want to wait. *Le bonheur semble fait pour être
partagé.* I'm studying French."

She laughed and chewed and mussed his wet black hair with
her free hand.

"You're the most beautiful thing, Deo—I mean that—I have
ever seen. More beautiful than the golden saint in the church,
more beautiful than winning the lottery."

"Men aren't called beautiful, Anna."

He began to fondle and handle her and Anna let the roll fall
into the grass and her mouth was wet. She said softly, "You are
not a man yet, my little rooster, you are a boy. Oh Deo, *amore
mio.*"

"*Bene.*"

"*Benissimo.*"

She lay back, and he kissed her on the mouth still tasting of
food, and he felt his passion rise, his desires spring alive with
fury. They had first made love fully like this a year ago, in a
green ferny summer rain, naked under the stone statue of a
Greek god carrying a huge club. It had been like that all year,
first the full flavor of the gouted agony of desire and then the
fulfillment again and again with the following byplay. All in
the ardor of being young and being aware.

As Anna had said, "After all, we are Italians, and we are the
best at this thing. Who can deny it?"

"Who said so?"

"Father Ambrosi at confession, only he didn't say it just like
that. I got fifty Hail Marys."

His happiest moments Deo had decided were at the full intimate embrace of lovemaking. With Anna he was freely himself, engaged in a combat in which he could not be defeated. It was an escape from the family going downhill into shabby genteel poverty. Loving, holding, panting was his running away from the weakness in his lungs to where he could feel the fullness of being a man, as he did *now*.

Anna stirred beneath him, the wild gold-and-garnet grass was beating around them, Anna's hands were clutched in his hair and his were around her hips.

Yes, the inner darkness fell away, the doubts, the fears of illness, the struggle of life, all would fade. In woman, in women, in Anna was the answer to everything; an answer ennobled by pure sensation.

The sky darkened to deep purple, to olive green, to deep blue, and they were still close together in the grass when it was soot-black and velvety. The first stars came out like fireflies pinned to a backdrop.

"You'll make love with a lot of women, Deo *mio*."

"This is real, Anna—the others are dreams."

"Of course. When it's for pleasure I don't ask you for the wedding ring. Soon I'll marry a cousin, Guido Nardi. He's a fisherman in Sicily. You'll go away to Rome and become a great painter and ride in an autocar, and eat in cafés every night— antipasto of rare things and drink Crema di Timo."

They lay in each other's arms, kissing for taste from time to time, aware of each others thoughts, at ease, sated but not sad. He soon slept. She lay contented, satisfied with her abilities to make Deo happy. Even the most handsome were such little boys.

In some yard nearby a cow mooed, and from the center of the city came the clatter of horses' hoofs, cheers and jeers. It was far off, and from what she remembered of it the new century didn't seem much different than the old one; only Deo was much nicer than the vine trimmer who used to take her behind the garden shed.

Deo muttered in his sleep and gripped her in some troubled need.

3

UNDER HIS WHITE MAKEUP, which he removed after his performance, Flinck looked a lot older to Deo—a bit wrinkled by time. He was dressed in baggy checked pants and a flowing tie, and with a smile he put a large green-glass ring on a finger of his right hand. "Now Flinck is ready to show you Montmartre."

Baba followed them out. Deo smelled the odor of earth and bruised vegetables, the brick dust of the streets. Above, the bulbous shapes of Sacre Coeur reminded Deo of white breasts. They walked, the clown flicking a limber bamboo cane, bowing to people and relating gossip. Deo agreed that the steep street stairs of the rue Muller were indeed worth seeing, and that the tombstones of Montmartre cemetery were fine-looking stones.

"Now, Modi, Flinck will take you to meet the artists."

"Perhaps I should wait until they want to meet me."

"Never hang back. Look around you—what do you see? Painters and *rentiers,* a few drunken *filles de joie.* None of them, Flinck is convinced, were born here on the Butte. You're no more outsider than they are. Baba, *heel.*"

Still, it was exciting walking toward the lights of cafés, the flaring yellow roses of gas jets suggesting comfort and warmth. More exciting than Deo wanted to admit to Flinck—or himself. And no one seemed to worry over costume: blue frieze jackets, corduroy pants (Deo set his heart on getting these), lapeled waistcoats. Flinck pointed out two Englishmen in knickerbockers smoking bulldog pipes.

"Countrymen of Sherlock 'Omes. We'll try the Lapin Agile. Baba likes their music."

"Baba has good taste, I'm sure."

Outside one café, men in wide black hats were shouting at each other about *"l'art pour l'art."* Deo wished he could understand. Their only audience was an Algerian rug peddler with two motheaten samples over one shoulder. Up the hill Deo saw the mechanical gyrations of the Moulin Rouge. The streets were not crowded, but there was a sense of life rubbed smooth.

The Lapin Agile was dingy, in need of paint, with a white fence on two sides. Deo and the clown walked into a low room full of strong tobacco smoke, the odor of alcohol, sounds of earnest or ribald voices, all cemented by music. The tables were half filled with men and women, all seemingly indifferent to the Negro in a fez playing an accordion and singing *Une de Paris.*

"Are they all artists?" Deo asked, smiling.

"Some are, some are not, Modi," said the clown as they sat at a board table and Baba curled up at her master's feet. "But the ones Flinck wants you to meet are not here." He shouted at a passing waiter for a bottle of Grand Roman.

The walls had a few unframed canvases in wild colors and flat tones that intrigued Deo. Two girls, arms around each other, came by. The blond one put a fringe of her shawl between her teeth and smiled at Deo. She said something quickly in city French that he didn't understand.

Flinck shook his head and frowned. "Move on."

The blonde shrugged. "*Un crétin phosphorescent.* A clown with a paunch." She rolled her head at Deo. "Get rid of your fat *père,* handsome, and join us."

Deo laughed. "I promised *ma mère* to take care he didn't get into trouble."

They moved on, swinging soft haunches, eyeing the room like hunting hawks. The singer began *Douleur d'Amour.* Flinck poured the wine into two large glasses.

"You want to meet tarts, you let Flinck know. *Garçon,* two orders of *tripe à la mode de Caen.* At Flinck's age the stomach comes before the bit of slap and tickle."

"Maybe they've frightened off the artists you wanted me to meet."

"You'll meet them, Modi. Ah, there is Max Jacob. He sniffs ether. That one, with the monocle there, staring this way."

"He doesn't paint," said Deo. "And if he does, badly. He hasn't the stance of a painter. His stare has a perverse bias."

"It's poetry with him. Crazy kind, and he's mad for old books. He knows Pablo. Ah, Maxel!"

The bald young man with the strange stare in his eyes focused his attention in their direction. His monocle was in place; the eyeballs seemed to be made from glass and ivory. He came over stiffly, the corners of his mouth smiling as if ready for antagonists.

"Flinck, Baba. Tonight, who are the clowns, who are the spectators?"

"This is Modi, Amedeo Modigliani. He's a Yiddle like yourself. A glass of wine, Maxel?"

"But of course. Amedeo? The Beloved of God. Who named you?"

"Parents are very unkind to defenseless babies," said Deo, letting Flinck refill his glass.

The poet took off his monocle and polished it on a shabby sleeve. "Max, my name, is harmless. It suggests a fat Dutch pork butcher—may my parents forgive me." He looked over the place, filling up now with gayer-sounding people. "Look at us all, in our Garden of Eden."

Deo felt the wine make a mist between his eyes. "Eden is a garden where all the fruit is forbidden."

"Don't remind me. See you again, I hope. . . ."

The platter of tripe was put down by a perspiring waiter.

"I'm moving on to the Austin Fox bar near St. Lazare. You must go there. It improves your English, Beloved of God. All those cockney jockies. But it's better than here where all they argue about is Fauvism, or the rehabilitation of Dreyfus, or who slept with Helen last night."

Max Jacob bowed and went off stiffly. Flinck threw some bread soaked in gravy at Baba. "Let Maxel be a lesson to you, Baba. Never sniff ether. Clap yourself around this tripe, Modi, before it gets cold. Wonderful, eh?"

"Wonderful."

Deo was hungry and there was another bottle. He soon felt the ceiling was moving. It was a good world.

Flinck suddenly stood up, his napkin still stuffed into the waistcoat across his vast chest and paunch. He waved a crust of bread. "*Maitre! Maitre!*"

A short man, his beard touched with copper, turned from the

accordion player and smiled. He came over and shook hands with Flinck, then with Baba's paw. "I must paint Baba; she casts delightful magenta and russet-green shadows."

"May I present, *maitre*, a young artist from Italy, Amedeo Modigliani. Modi, this is Henri Matisse, the wild man who commands the Fauves in art."

"I saw a painting of yours in a gallery in Rome, M. Matisse."

"It's hard to believe. You can barely find one of mine in a gallery here. And beer is thirty centimes a glass."

"If I may," said Deo, digging in a pants pocket, "I'd consider it an honor to buy your beer."

"My boy, some other time. I have to go; there are some crazy Americans, a woman as ugly as a coal mine and big as a manure pile, and some of her family who make no more sense. I really must go. But come and see me at my studio on the Quai St. Michel. Right next to Vanier's bookstore. But only after the working light fails." Matisse leaned down and shook Baba's paw again. "Goodbye, Mlle Baba, M. Flinck, M. Modigliani."

Deo wiped his face with his napkin after the artist left. "He looks like a painter. The point to that beard—like a sword. The mockery in the eyes, as if the world could go jump on itself. And did you notice his hands, Flinck? Not lean or beautiful, but strong and square. Why that man could mold giants, titans. I tell you, he's a great sculptor."

"You're a little too full of wine, Modi. Matisse, he paints."

"He'll sculpt. You'll see. Yes, I am a little drunk and excited."

"Order a bottle of Graves to finish off with, and then Flinck will take you home, your first night in Paris."

Deo was smiling in a silly inexplicable way. He had an edge on—but drunk? Of course not! He turned to watch the accordion player, who was smoking the shortest cigarette stub in the world and closing his eyes to keep out the smoke. Several couples and two *grisettes* were dancing—at least Deo hoped they were *grisettes;* in his imagination *grisettes* looked like that. A glum-looking man with sandpapery Spanish skin, a blue, just-shaved jowl, was dancing with a firm, large, redhaired girl.

"Now that one, Flinck. That's one that I like. The big red-headed girl."

"Ah, Flinck knows her. Julie, that's Julie. Not a tart, but only when you have rested from your journey—and when your place is in better order. *Garçon, l'addition.* Baba, attention."

The pink poodle stood up on her hind legs and barked. Deo rose slowly, hoping with integrity and grandeur. "It's my treat. You've showed me Paris."

"Only Montmartre."

"And Matisse. He is going to be one of the great . . . the hands . . . the beard, broad fingers . . . I want to dance with Julie . . . I will pay."

"You said all that. Flinck pays in Paris tonight. Baba, Deo, march."

"Julie . . ."

Near the door Deo turned and watched the redheaded girl dance in the arms of the Spaniard. She had the long neck, the pensive staring face he desired in a girl. She had firm white breasts, and the yellow dress did little to hide them. The hands were right, too. About women's hands Deo was most particular. Girls didn't have to bathe too often, or change their intimate things every day. But the hands had to be clean, the fingernails cared for. Hands had the distortions and involutions of symbols for him.

"Flinck. Introduce us?"

"To that horse butcher Julie is dancing with? He carries a two-hundred-pound carcass on his back like you lift a brush. The circus buys scraps for our lions and tigers from him. Besides, you're in no condition to dance. Look, you can hardly stand."

"The flesh has its own spirit free of the mind." Either the effects of the journey or the wine, people talking, had done something to his limbs. They felt made of India rubber.

As they left the café an anti-Dreyfusard was punched in the nose, someone began to recite Mallarmé, and a customer shouted for *eau-de-vie*.

Outside the steep slope of the Butte and its streets were lighted by flickering gaslight; lamps illumined some of the bone-white plaster-covered buildings. There was a taste of night, warm as from a steamy field.

Deo slept well and late, and in the morning when the sun was high he went down to the street and found a little color shop. He bought canvas and paints and added to his brushes. The color man threw in an old easel. "I was going to break it up for firewood."

Deo's room was warm under the roof, but it didn't look as dismal now as it had, and he got out his collection of reproductions that he had collected over the years in Italian art schools: of Giotto, Pollaiuolo, della Francesca, da Vinci, Botticelli, Titian, and others. He pinned them around the room and felt alive in a world of his own choosing. Admitting art, he thought, is the most wonderful privilege in human society.

He began to draw heads, half taken from the reproductions on the wall, half expressing a new emotional gaucherie in his feeling about Paris, the people in the cafés. He knew he was enigmatic, lonely, stubborn, but he always was aware of his sensibilities and he was innately convinced of his genius.

In the months that followed Deo became a citizen of Montmartre. In a corduroy jacket and with a slashing long scarf of red and orange wound around his neck he felt properly attired. Modi, the men called him; the girls called him Deo. He had found the local girls to his liking, and in their arms he felt safe and comfortable. Not always the same girl, for he still wanted to meet Julie with the copper-colored hair who had danced at the café. She seemed to have left town.

He became a familiar fixture in the cafés and bistros, in the shops where he bought his bread and cheese, and a herring now and then. Not making too many friends beyond Flinck and Baba, meeting a few young artists, lonely like himself, who drew and painted and as yet amounted to nothing.

Deo's handsomeness no longer attracted comment: Montmartre had grown accustomed to his perfect protrusive nose, those sarcastic eyes, the loud voice singing *Mourir pour la Patrie* in the cafés, his wild laughter with the girls debauching with a skinful of wine. But he also spent a lot of time working on his pictures. Paintings of people sitting in chairs, sometimes with a little smile. As for the streets, a garden, a landscape— that wasn't for him.

"God made the country to grow chickens," he told the girls, "And the city to eat them."

Deo had a harmless wit, a flair for words, but he was not mean or cutting. With his smile it all went over well. No one knew how hard he worked. To the inhabitants of Montmartre —some of them lazy, casual, ironic—he had a kind of archaic honesty; to him, they were all members of an exotic, anarchistic world composed of corrupt desperation mixed with tenderness.

Flinck took him to the shop of the ex-clown Sagot, a big white unbaked bun of a man with a smooth head and neck, a beard, the eyes sunk like blue raisins into his puffy cheeks.

The shop was small and it held unframed canvases by Montmartre artists of no great fame, several old landscape panels that had come from the flea market (and which Sagot swore in a husky voice were from a palace on the Faubourg St. Honore), some battered figures of carrousel horses, inn signs, the figure-head of the American sailing ship *Helen Starkweather,* which he swore was commanded by John Paul Jones. The shop had once been a chemist's; jars of drugs still stood around, and Sagot doctored all his friends—he offered to treat Deo.

Sagot looked at the four canvases that Deo had brought to the shop unwrapped under his arm. They leaned against the wall, the sun shining through the doorway upon them. The big man pursed his heavy lips, pulled on his lower one.

Flinck growled. "Don't try to impress Flinck."

"You've got the touch, my boy. I can always tell. You haven't broken through yet. But you're beating head first on the tent wall. You'll be in center ring yet."

"You'll buy them?"

"Buy them? I haven't sold what I have here yet."

The clown said, "Flinck thought you'd buy them."

"Flinck, you're a man who lives with a pink dog. I don't ex-pect sense from you." The dealer closed his eyes as if in pain. "*Bien.* Ten francs for the one of the yellow-haired girl, and the same—for the other."

"That's my concierge's little boy, Paul."

"He sits with his hands in his lap. You don't paint people walking, or kicking a cat, or pinching each other in the grass?"

"The boy has quality," said Flinck.

"I'm trying to get a monumental feeling into heads and shoulders that some of the early Italian painters had. Their heads stare down from the walls and show art can be ennobled by size."

The dealer held out some tattered franc notes. "Never trust a painter who can talk. Show me some more work when you have new things. And don't spread it around, what I've paid you. I don't want it known I've lost control of myself."

"At these prices," said Flinck, "He'd be ashamed to tell any-one."

In the late afternoon Deo often would wander up the rue Tholoze with its windmill at the top, drink a glass of wine here and there in the bars of the rue Fontaine, recite a little verse, pick out a girl. Walk up to her directly; no use wasting time since she wasn't the one he was looking to set up with for life. Until then no wasted moments; he needed time to paint, to read, to think.

"You'll have a drink?"

"Why not?"

He ordered two drinks and smiled.

"You around here a lot?"

"Enough. You're a good-looking kid. You're not from Paris?"

"I'm Italian. Deo. What's your name?"

"Toinette."

The rest was routine. And as usual. Not deeply involved on either side. No regrets, no tears. Mostly, they were strangers in Paris, from farms and towns, escaping from backbreaking work in fields and cowbarns, becoming laundresses, sewing cloth in backs of shops, slicing cheese, flicking duck feathers. Assembling cloth flowers for hats, boiling food in yellow oils held in copper pots, standing behind counters measuring yards of ma-terial they could not afford themselves. And they brought Deo peace.

Sometimes they were semi-tarts, earning a bit for a farm dowry on the side, walking slowly, hips akimbo, under the lamplight and knowing a room for an hour in an unsavory hotel. But mostly they were simple, lonely, hungry, romantic. They were readers of cheap yellow novels, viewers of poor plays, dreaming of some fantastic luck, an as yet unrealized future. In the end they drifted back to the farms—they told Deo—to marry some sullen peasant and progress into child-bearing with the same persistent regularity of the family sow. If they stayed in Montmartre, they sometimes married junk dealers, small tradesmen, or found themselves in some pathetic fist-flying ménage with sharp-faced men who tattooed on their necks, as they showed Deo proudly, a dotted line and the words: CUT HERE.

The girls were somehow pitiful in the studio at night after the first frenzy had calmed them and flowed away like the past. Deo held their workworn hands; there was not much need for words. Both knew the words would be untrue.

In the morning sun sitting in heaven . . . alone. A girl's narrow head and thin shoulders . . . There was more . . . more knowledge. And less . . . from all he admired. He dipped the brush in a pale emerald green and began to scrum in the background. *All good . . . only good. No exaltation yet . . . Masters, models . . . all and still too close. . . . Come, Deo . . . true Deo . . . full Deo . . . Oh yes, that Italian Jew. . . . Listen . . . Hear the future buzz. . . .*

He stared at the image, touched up the long nose, the side of the cheek. He stood up and bowed and stepped on the smoldering butt and went to find his scarf. The one thing he lacked was patience.

He found the scarf, but did not put it on. Instead he turned an old worked-on canvas around and began to paint on the back. He painted till all light was gone and he fell into bed and slept.

4

HE WAS WALKING, head down, dreaming, near the corner of the rue Bonaparte and the rue des Beaux Arts, following some vague urge to see the house where Oscar Wilde had died. Suddenly, there was a roar of people en masse, the sort of cry that in Paris had shaken kings and generals. A crowd of youths and some fanatical-looking women were surging toward him, lean priests and men with broken chairs taken from café terraces. They were banging into each other, shouting *"Fidei Defensor!"* and "Down with the Black Cloth!"

A man fell at Deo's feet and a policeman began to hammer at him with his folded cape. Cries of *flics* and the name of God were heard. It didn't become any more real. Then a brick just missed Deo's head.

A girl in a catatonic state carrying a great crucifix came up to Deo, her hair hung wildly over an ugly face. She pushed the cross at him, shouting, "Down with the separation laws! Back to Rome! Down with Pontius Pilate and the Rothschilds!"

As always in Paris riots, large stones were flying through the air. Deo fled as several figures in flapping monk's robes began to carry a wounded man from underfoot. A blatant yet melodious chanting filled the streets.

Deo came to a corner and leaned against a lime tree. A plump red-faced man coming from a street comfort station, buttoning himself, smiled at Deo.

"There will be a lot of cracked heads."

"It is a revolution?"

"No, no," said the man, inspecting the gray cloth tops of his shoes. "They've passed the law separating church from state."

Deo fled back to Montmartre, where they didn't care so much for God or state. Better to eye some girl and take her away from under the noses of the caps and felt hats of the café inmates. Better to wander among the accordion players, the *chansonniers* with their songs of Montmartre. He went down to the Auberge du Clou, to the ragpickers from St. Ouen with their donkey carts, went looking in on masquerades and café concerts, to Le Hanneton, a brasserie where the lesbians gathered. He slid past the waiters at the Café Weber, and listened to a few miserable artists who tried to borrow a few francs from him. They told him they *mangeaient de la vache*—were having a lean time of it.

Deo rarely had any francs to spare. His family in Italy was sinking into poverty; what little they could spare, and the very little he got from selling a painting now and then to Sagot or to a shopkeeper, he needed desperately. Sometimes he felt like asking for a few francs himself on a street corner. But as a Spinoza he resisted it.

When Deo went hungry and Flinck was out of the city playing in some country town, and money was low, Deo would get into bed and read *L'Ultimo de Mohecanni* by M. James Fenimore Cooper. Or he drew with the thinnest pencil point and the most graceful line he could produce heads of the local *Vie de Bohème*, the society on the Butte, where they all cursed the *pompiers*, the academicians, and cheerfully poisoned themselves with absinthe if they could afford it. When Flinck returned, Deo sat nights at the circus drawing heads of clowns and riders.

He was having an absinthe on the terrace of the Ami Émile café after sketching at the circus when he met Pablo, whom everyone was beginning to talk about in Montmartre. Deo was watching the waiter, who half-filled a fluted glass with the deadly transparent green poison. ("They distill it from wormwood," Flinck had warned him. "It nibbles away the brain and you end up walking on your heels like a victim of the old *râle*.") The waiter placed a knife blade across the glass, balanced a cube of sugar on the blade, then slowly poured a feeble stream of water onto the sugar and into the glass. The greenish transparency clouded into a green-yellow and became opaque like the skin on a blind man's eyes.

Deo lifted the glass. A short stocky young man in a fisherman's shirt, canvas rope sandals, stood there—he had large dark eyes, oily blue-black hair combed down over one eye. He was watching the color of the absinthe. Under one arm he carried a package of circus posters.

The man smiled at Deo and spoke softly with a Spanish accent. "It's just the color between a flare of gaslight and the pale green of fruit the sun has just begun to ripen. And there's an old whore at the Moulin Rouge has teeth that color."

Deo looked up. "You're Pablo. I saw you sketching the jugglers tonight during the show."

"P. Picasso Ruiz. Some of your things are at Sagot's, that old robber and drug peddler."

"He's the only one who buys anything. He bought one today, so I can stand you a drink."

"I'll have a poison too." Pablo sat down. "Take some of your drawings around to Berthe Weill's shop. She's limited in space, but she buys."

"She's a dealer?"

"A little of everything. Like Redon she sees the inside face of things. Berthe strings a few clotheslines across her shop and hangs up the drawings, and sometimes someone buys. It's better for me than going back to being an Andalusian. You ever hear of Malaga?"

"I've never been anyplace but Italy, and here."

They smiled at each other, and Pablo shrugged his wide shoulders. "It's enough. As Max Jacob says, 'We're making more art here than the world can consume.'"

"I remember Maxel. He was full of ether. . . ."

"He shouldn't go around like that. He'll give poets a bad name. When we take on a few sniffs of the poppy, or eat a little hashish, it's best, you know, to just stay in the studio. If you'd like sometime to join us, we're in the big monster of a building they call the laundry barge."

Deo nodded and sipped his drink. "Doesn't it give you visions? Does drug-taking make the colors better? I hear for epileptics a wonderful eternity lasts five seconds."

"Marvelous. Maybe it could give us visions, but it's not art we're after then. It's a relaxation from the work of painting. Only bricklaying or plowing is harder work."

"Does Matisse join you?"

"Henri! The businessman of painting," Pablo laughed. "And a good one. There's no nonsense about him. You don't see him often in the cafés."

They sat, smelling the circus down the street, two young men with heavy black hair, and the motley crowd passed or stopped at the café to talk or gossip or borrow or attach themselves to somebody. The summer was high, the trees all feathered in heavy boughs of green, and the little gardens were pushing up color. Here and there one of the new autocars chugged, and Mr. Edison's lights glowed dimly.

Pablo began to talk of Pahouin ancestor statues, Iberian wood carvings, archaic Greek sculpture, Ingres' drawings. Deo admitted his fascination with the unpopular past. They scraped up enough coins between them to have another drink, and while the waiter dripped the sugar into the liquid, they talked of Celtic artifacts, Sardinian figurines, Gallic coins. They also talked of women, of love, of the rich, and of the poor. Pablo recalled bullfights, and Deo described the sounds of the sardine fleets blowing conch shells at morning, and the texture of Venetian canals at dawn, the way the tide ran out over rusting chains and long strands of sea moss that swayed and waved, and the world smelled like cold lobster and mayonnaise.

Pablo said, "Come to the studio. I want to show you something."

The Bateau Lavoir, where Pablo lived, was a large building, like a dismasted man-of-war from Napoleon's time. Pablo led Deo through the dark hall and up a few steps into a first-floor room with windows overlooking . . . in the darkness it was hard to make out the edge of things.

Pablo lit two oil lamps. The studio was little better than Deo's room. A bit larger; the usual rusting iron stove ("I burned two hundred drawings last winter to keep warm"), bed, chairs, a screen with some lacy female objects hanging from it. Several huge canvases were tacked to the wall. Mostly they were of pink circus scenes. Lean clowns and thinner mothers, suckling babies, some depraved apes: all done in thin turpentine washes on the rough canvas.

"I've been drawing the circus till I'm fed up with it. But I always go back to this vision of truth in patched tights. But I'm not going to do any more of this." Pablo brought forward two canvases. They shocked Deo. Raw and crude, cruel slashing forms of heads, large blind eyes, a style of crosshatching in paint, a brutal use of pigment to chop out faces, faces like idols rather than human beings.

"It's too new yet for me."

Pablo frowned. "I wanted you to see these. You're stretching proportions, too, in your work. You're frightened of it—but who the devil wants to take *safe* steps?"

"I don't attack this way. I use the round more, the curve."

The door opened and a very beautiful woman came in, her head wrapped in a pale-blue lace shawl. She had dark grace and a special way of carrying her body as if it were too precious, too delicate to trust to ordinary walking. She had a serenity, a detachment, that Deo remembered from Greek art.

Pablo turned to her with a quick smile. "How is our chum, the old sow?"

The woman laughed. "Gertrude never stopped talking, talking, and never made sense. Tonight she was General Grant, she said—only I'm sure that his beard was never so thick."

"Oh, Modi, this is Fernande. This is Modigliani. I was just showing him the new things."

"*La cosa va?*"

The woman slipped behind the screen and began to undress as if Deo were not there, and went on talking. "The Steins are beginning to think they invented you, Pablo, and Matisse too. And *they* discovered America, not Columbus."

"Gertrude will not be satisfied until she's convinced the world she invented art, Paris *and* herself."

The woman laughed—the way Deo liked a woman to laugh —and came out from behind the screen wearing a flowing red robe that opened enough to show her wonderful legs.

"Nobody else could invent Gertrude. You paint, M. Modigliani? I know. Pablo doesn't invite anybody else unless they're Spaniards or buyers." She held out two dusty cakes. "Pablo, I stole these for you. You are hungry?"

Deo said, "I think I'll be going. Pablo, it's like a blow between the eyes, your new work, but now I'm no longer shaking."

"That's too bad. Like the bull growing accustomed to the lousy sword."

Deo looked again at Fernande. He smiled, turning on his charm, but he could see he got nowhere there. This was a ménage that he couldn't crowd into.

Deo walked back to his studio slowly, decided it was time

the art of old men—those ghosts from the graves—was destroyed. And he must get himself a girl, one who would undress
behind a screen and wait in bed for him; not just a hasty collection of ardent thrusts and sated goodbyes. No. Somebody to
love with, and keep, feel close in the night; a love so extended
it was subject to no limits.

The official salon, an academy of rigid painters, still ruled the
fashionable circles, but there was a rising tide of protest. It was
in good taste among the intellectuals of fixed income now to
admire certain of the Impressionists and to make an investment
in Degas and Renoir, both still alive, wrinkled old men. Manet
was almost an old master. Monet, with a beard out of Michelangelo's *Genesis,* was painting water lilies. As for the just gone
Toulouse-Lautrec, Van Gogh and Gauguin, Deo found a select
group of the *avant-garde* writing of them as the tainted saints
of Postimpressionism.

But it was Cézanne whom they—those who cared anything
for the new art—worshiped. Deo ran from collection to collection studying Cézanne's work: how he used the brush; the way
the little flecks of color were put on so mathematically, side by
side in subtle gradations of colors, building up monumental
form into a new order. The old man, Pablo told Deo, had
proudly stated his creed: "To do Poussin over with nature."

Eager young men with paint-stained hands were everywhere
in Paris. Pablo, with his blue period behind him and the old
rose period fading, was working in the tormented slashing savage forms. Matisse painted faces with a green stripe down the
nose, and strange shadows played around his heads. *Color is
emotion. . . . Man's not nature's prerogative.*

There was Pascin—an artist from eastern Europe—with his
paintings of flabby ox-eyed girls in bursting armchairs, falling
out of their soiled underwear. The young Spaniard calling himself Juan Gris seemed to be a poet rather than a man; he always appeared in such a daze. Deo was most amused by Gino
Severini, who wrote all the time on café tabletops, who cursed
the past in good low Italian, and said he was out to destroy the
museums—nothing less.

Then there was a new friend, Constantin Brancuși, burly, hairy, from some place in Rumania. He collected dusty shapes, odd bits of wood and stone, and stood and hammered and carved everything down to the point where it almost lost itself, but stopped at an egg shape, or a thin curved lath. Yet he managed to retain an emotion, sometimes in even simpler forms than Pablo Picasso was trying out on canvas.

As for Deo's own work, he still had a considerable distance to go, but he was satisfied with his progress. There was this painting that he had just completed, of a man playing a cello in a café. *Everything out just a little beyond reality. Stronger reds, rounder curves . . . tangy . . . dark . . . burning . . . the way they used to paint in Venice.*

5

Clovis sagot, the dealer, came to Deo's room, admired the view and pointed out a small painting he might take with him "under my arm."

He squirmed when Deo suggested they seal the bargain with a drink. Sagot was not an easy spender. "I'm not like the big art dealers, Ali Babas and their forty thieves."

Seated in a café, Sagot, with the painting wrapped in an old newspaper and held safe between his fat legs, looked out at the passing people. "Where do they come from, Modi? They all rush here to Paris. The world is in danger of turning over—becoming unbalanced."

"In Paris, Sagot, you have to hold on to your sanity—like your hat on a windy day."

"Modi, there are even Hungarians and Peruvians. I swear it. But buyers? Scarce as virgins at the Quatr'Arts Bal."

"I'm thinking of going," said Deo, watching the dealer reach into a pocket for his purse. "Pablo says it gets so wild they bring out the firemen."

Sagot counted out some coins for their drinks onto the table *soucoupes* and stood up and recovered the paper-wrapped painting. "I don't waste my time or money at balls. Keep paint-ing."

Deo had been feeling the pinch of poverty. Sagot was right; there were few buyers of young unknowns.

Flinck was busy teaching Baba a new trick, "To climb a lad-der, stand at salute while the band plays the national song, the *Marseillaise*, and then run up a little flag with her teeth, fire a cannon and do a double somersault into Flinck's arms."

"The world hardly deserves anything *that* fine."

"Mockery, Modi? That's bad. Baba, turn your back to him."

The night of the Quatr'Arts Bal was a wild one and Deo went without costume—almost all he owned was on his back. It was a big hall that had been fairly well cleaned, and the artists of the Butte were gathered in groups of shouting grin-ning figures carrying bottles of wine and apple brandy, their girls as naked as the police would permit, the models sneering at the exposure of nonprofessional flesh. Deo drank with almost everybody and kissed as many of the girls as he could. Outside in the street they were throwing somebody without pants into a fountain, and the heat and music of the ball were pounding like tomtoms on Deo's head. The cocottes in yellow velveteen and the café habitués grew wilder.

A fat woman in a red dress was making a speech denouncing the members of the Institute, and a girl in a bullfighter's outfit was warding off two bearded young Americans dressed as cow-boys. Deo went to her aid and got punched in the nose.

The girl screamed at him, "Who sent for you?" She threw her vermouth apéritif at him: *"Ventre-St.-Gris!"*

A lean young man in a winged collar, wearing a tailed formal coat, carrying two bottles of Anjou wine, smiled at Deo rub-bing his banged nose.

"Hurt?" The man had pale-blue eyes, a blond-brown well-tailored beard and long pointed mustaches.

"Hurts like the devil."

"Shame to break that very handsome nose."

"How does one know if it's busted?"

"Here, hold the bottles. Let me feel."

"Goddamn expatriates. Why don't they go back where they came from. *Ow!*"

Skillful clean hands, shrimp-pink as if parboiled and smelling of scent, felt Deo's nose, twisted it from side to side with skill.

"Sorry. Nothing broken. It is a pretty one."

"You certain? No damage?"

"Paul Alexandre, Dr. Paul Alexandre. If I say no break, there is no break. And don't drop the wine."

"Thank you, Doctor. I'm Amedeo Modigliani."

The doctor held a bottle of wine up to the gas jet set in the ceiling. "We've finished one Tavel and two bottles of Chateauneuf du Pape. Come and help us drink up these."

The young doctor didn't wait for Deo to accept or reject, but pushed past a Caesar lacking teeth, some Satans in torn red. At a small table sat two girls trying to look bored, throwing back paper streamers tossed at them. Dr. Alexandre set down the bottles in front of the girls with a polite shrug.

"The best I could find, Amedeo. Julie Fouchet and Valerie Bisson. M. Modigliani."

"Bouvil," said the stringy blonde, fluffing up her golden pompadour hairdo. "*Not* Bisson. Couldn't you find any Calvados?"

Deo popped his eyes. "Julie Fouchet," he said as he sat down. "This meeting proves I am not one of life's losers."

"Ah, you know each other," said the doctor, opening a bottle.

"I'm not that drunk," said Julie.

"I saw you dancing at the Lapin."

"That dive," said Julie.

She was even more beautiful close up. Magnificent. Deo repeated it aloud: "Magnificent."

"Rotten ball," said Julie. She moved her head with grace and turned to take the offered glass.

A palsy of love and passion stirred Deo. He felt balanced in some perilous equilibrium. Could such a derangement of emotions really take place? Julie was wearing pale-pink net over almost transparent black lace. Deo smiled. "Your costume— Venus rising from the sea waves?"

"Some idea like that." When she smiled, all her teeth seemed perfect and too white. No wonder, Deo thought, the poets write that after the first love there is no other.

Dr. Alexandre explained. "The girls were at the bar alone—

very lonely, waiting for some one, and I felt as I had this table anyway, they could wait here."

"Very logical," said Deo. "You're a very remarkable doctor."

"Julie has strange friends," said the blonde, pressing against Deo, giving him her stringy haunch and a push of naked elbow in his side. "But I don't care now."

"You've got no self-respect, Valerie," Julie said, drinking.

"You like artists?" asked Dr. Alexandre, opening the second bottle. Some girls nearby were carried out on the shoulders of art students. A man wearing a huge phallus of a false blue nose jumped from a balcony onto a group of people below and they rolled and screamed together.

"Real artists I like," said Julie. "I don't waste my time with a man just because he wears a velveteen jacket and has paint on his hands."

"You're right," said Deo.

"I mean, why are most of them here? For a good time. That's all right, but a real artist if he makes shoes, or pottery, or trains horses, that's worth while. He must roar."

Deo took Julie's arm and pressed it. "I know what you mean. Achilles as a boy was fed the hearts of lions."

"I didn't mean that kind of roar. You paint? Isn't sculpture a higher art? Or an opera tenor?"

He kissed her naked shoulder. She pushed his hands away.

"I never like a man for just looks." She set down her glass and smiled at the doctor. "He's too pretty for me. Valerie, he's all yours."

The band was blaring out an Algerian military march. Couples were trying to form for dancing. Deo moved his chair closer to Julie.

"I don't want Valerie. I love you."

Dr. Alexandre had taken out a pair of gold-rimmed glasses and was looking over the crowd. A large druidic circle of people was forming on the floor, but they seemed to lack an oracle.

Deo leaned over to Julie and put his head on her shoulder. "Will you dance?"

He felt a sudden hard blow on the side of his head; someone angry and strong was pulling him away from Julie, with a grip on his coat collar. Deo whirled around, half rose from his chair and was pushed back. He stared up at the blue-black jowl of a Spanish face. "*Morisco!* Get away from my girl!"

"Don't make a scene, Paquito!" Julie shouted, reaching up, slapping at the Spaniard's arms.

Deo muscled himself to his feet. "Let go of me, you Iberian swine! You horse-beef carver!"

Dr. Alexandre tried to push between them, holding his gold eyeglasses out of reach. "Let's not have all this temper."

Deo felt fire as red whorled patterns formed, pain ran from his groin to his head, and a great rage surged through him as if he had been burned. He rolled his body and broke the Spaniard's grip on his arm. He threw his fist at Paquito and followed with his head, butting into the hard stomach. There was an escape of air, a howl.

Julie began to shout, "Stop it! Stop!"

There was a chair in the air held in the Spaniard's hands. (He was in costume, Deo saw, capturing an image of a hangsman all in black with a black cap on his head.) Then the chair came down on Deo's head and all the light in the world broke up into small splinters and began to push him down, as in the rain of fire in Dante's poem—into a void of silence and fear.

Hooks of pain were boring into his head, and he felt as if he had been in a trance a thousand years. He sucked air, having trouble breathing, and he could feel his heart flapping as if tearing loose. He tried to get more air down, opened his eyes and found he was lying on the dirty floor of a bare room full of folded chairs. Far off someone was singing and a mob of people were crying out and shouting. He lay back in limp resignation.

"Anyway, he isn't dead. I'd hate to explain *this* to the *flics*."

"He has a hard head."

"Don't move, *chéri*. The doctor wants to see if your skull is cracked."

Delicate fingers probed Deo's aching head, "No danger. A bad lump and a darkening bruise. Head hurt?"

"Like a battering ram hit me. I feel crosseyed."

"Double images?"

"A little."

"Take him to La Charité hospital."

Deo got slowly to his feet. He was trying to think, but his thoughts were beating themselves to nothing on the walls. His clothes were in disorder. "No, I live near here. I'll be all right."

"We'll walk you home. Let's go out the back way."

Walking wasn't easy. They made slow progress through an alley and darkness. Deo holding onto Julie and the doctor, the trio reached a winding street with gas lamps burning and some drunkards rolling metal trash containers down hill shouting, "Roll, *chère amie!*"

Julie said, "He's crazy, that Spaniard. Paquito belongs with the animals."

Deo leaned on her a little harder. "He's a big boy."

The doctor shook his head. "A little more of an angle to the blow with that chair and you'd be shipped home on ice. Like a wild boar to a banquet."

Deo turned to Julie. "He's your man? Paquito?"

"How much farther to your place?"

"Two houses down. Third floor. I'll make it all right alone."

Dr. Alexandre said, "Nonsense, we'll help you up."

It wasn't easy. Deo's dizziness seemed to increase. He was having trouble seeing. In the room the doctor lit the lamp and Julie went to wet a towel at the faucet in the hall. She made Deo lie down and began to mop his hurt feverish head.

"It's a beautiful lump. Big as a goose egg."

Deo smiled and closed his eyes. "You ever see a goose egg?"

Julie laughed. "I've picked hundreds of thousands of them from farm nests."

Deo opened his eyes. Julie was bending over him, her breasts hung like mellow moons in space—her head in the glow of the lamp light catching her golden-red hair until each strand was a magic wire, like the halos in a saints' congress.

"You're a damn fine painter," said Dr. Alexandre, standing by the far wall looking at a pile of canvases.

Deo closed his eyes and fell asleep.

6

SETTING UP A ménage in Montmartre's latitudes of intimacy was a simple thing. One ordered, Pablo said, a larger loaf of bread, an extra bottle of wine, and if the girl was dainty, one borrowed a broom, an extra water pitcher, and a basin for her to wash her feet. Most artists who were serious about their work settled in with one woman, fought, made love, howled in agony, laughed a lot. Sometimes they beat each other, bruised flesh, and went cursing down the empty night street when in domestic ferment and revolt. But mostly, Deo knew, when the attraction was deep and true, it worked out as something permanent, or as permanent as anything on the Butte, where extinction, the local philosophers said, was the only full consummation.

The morning after Deo was beaten to a gritty misery by the Spanish horse butcher, he and Julie became lovers.

He had come awake with a dizzy head, feeling a pain in the lungs and an ache in his stomach. The sun was up, but a lumping of storm clouds hung in one corner of the sky, clouds turning from bruised gray to rotten-egg black. Not at all *La Vie de Bohème*.

Deo rolled over on his side with a groan, feeling remote, as if washed up on a rock, and saw Julie in a smock, seated at the table. The open flame of a small spirit burner was flaring up, and Julie with pliers, a soldering iron, and lengths of gilt metal wire was putting together an ornament, a flower shape. He watched her open-mouthed as she skillfully built up a bauble with pliers, wire and the use of the tiny soldering iron. She was very quick at it and engrossed in what she was doing. He coughed, and as she looked up, he noticed how truly exquisite her face was; as if he were just seeing her for the first time.

"You must feel dreadful," she said casually.

"What are you doing here?"

"Dr. Alexandre thought somebody should stay with you in case you started to conk out for good."

"What are you making?" He sat up and looked down at his soiled feet planted naked on the splintered floor.

She answered with a serenity clear of any smugness. "I make flea market junk for Wolowski's shop on the Place du Havre. Gilt-wire flowers, bugs, hearts, anchors."

Deo watched her quick fingers build up another flower. "Is it a living? Making that stuff?"

"Not very much, but I carry my burner, my pliers and soldering iron with me. And I'm free as Marco Polo."

Deo laughed and held his head. "You're a damn artist. But a successful one, Julie. Marco Polo was a bloodsucking businessman."

The girl went to the stove and took some brown tepid liquid from a pot and poured it into a handleless cup. She walked across the room, came over to the bed and handed him the cup.

"Drink this, doctor's orders."

"What is it?"

"Something the doctor wants you to drink three times a day. Some kind of nerve sedative."

"Don't be crazy. I'm fine," Deo tried to stand and fell back onto the bed. Julie laughed, and he liked the way her head went back to one side; she laughed with her mouth and throat and neck and shoulders. "My hero. Drink it or I'll go and leave you alone, hero."

"Our gods, Julie, are no longer Athene or Poseidon—they now make wire flowers." He sipped the brew with obsessive mock refinement. It wasn't unpleasant. "Sit down, Julie. Talk to me. You walk like a cat. I love it."

She shrugged her shoulders and pushed the chair over and sat down. From a pocket of her smock she took out a Russian cigarette, and lit it. She sat there inhaling deeply and blowing out smoke through pursed lips and from nostrils.

"You don't have to worry, or hand me those Athene lines. The Spaniard left for the border when the police went after him."

"I wasn't worried." He put out a hand and took Julie's arm. "Julie, you know how I feel about you. Do you want it simple or with poetry?"

"I don't want it all." She had the instinctive conviction of most Butte girls that they could handle any situation.

"Like the devil you don't. Then why did you stay?"

She nodded, frowned, and looked down at the glowing end of her cigarette. "I knew you'd misunderstand. You were a poor donkey who got hurt. It wasn't my fault, but in a way I suppose it was. My not meeting the Spaniard on the rue Pigalle."

Deo leaned forward from his position at the edge of the bed and put his arm around her as she sat in the chair, and he put his head between her breasts. She didn't have much on under the smock. He sighed and closed his eyes and he spoke in a very low voice as if expecting an exquisite assent.

"Julie, Julie. What else is there to say?"

"You're lonely. You want a woman. That's all."

"Maybe. But I don't think so. Just want to skip all the coercion and lies with you."

"I'm no tart. I don't say I'm a nun from the Church of St. Thomas Aquinas—but I'm no Montmartre trash. I earn my way. I do as I please."

Deo felt her breasts stir, the points alert, the whole intake of breath in her became audible with an immediacy and spontaneity she could not control.

"Julie, stay with me."

"I'm here."

"I mean live here."

"In this dump? Not that my place is any better. Can I ask you a favor?" Her voice had a note of anxiety.

"What?"

"Let me get rid of this goddamn cigarette."

She did, and he kissed her with brutal directness. No time to savor emotions in tranquillity. Julie smelled of Turkish tobacco and solder, and health. She didn't kiss him back. She fought him off, almost casually, and pushed him onto the bed. His head seemed to split open with pain. She walked away as if puzzled and annoyed at herself, stopped at the paintings stacked against the wall, and began to turn them around and look at them, searching for distraction.

"This is all you paint?" she asked, half turning.

"I really have little interest in feet and furniture. The colors are still not clear."

"Thick, aren't they?"

How murky and smoldering the reds and oranges were, how tainted the blues.

Julie shrugged her shoulders and put her hands in the pockets of her smock. "I don't much care for them. But maybe you'll develop. You ever do horses? Or dogs, like the fellows in the Cluny Museum?

"No. Listen, Julie, those are very good."

"I don't know. To me you're not a real artist. They're not really finished."

"They're finished, damn you! You been around the Butte long enough to know what's finished, and what will never be finished. These are finished."

"A real artist—you can almost pick up the fruit in his painting, feel the skin."

He fell back onto the bed. "Go on, make your damn wire flowers. You revolt me. You sound like all the birdbrains peddling painted trays. You're ignorant!"

She turned suddenly serious, bit her lower lip.

"*Popolo grosso, Julie, popolo grosso*—putting art against some fat easy copying of nature."

She turned her back to him and began to weep.

"What have I done now?"

"You lied," she sobbed. "All that fancy talk about love and now I revolt you." She turned around, hair red-gold flying in a cloud of fire, eyes yellow-green, blazing, her hands ending in fists. "What kind of man are you? A girl has feeling, has pride in dressing, feeding herself. Don't shout insults at me."

Deo said softly, "I'm very human, too. Very easy to hurt. So are you. Let's make a truce."

"What kind of truce?"

"We respect each other's art? We admit our love? I'm in pain, too hurt to protest too much."

"It hurts you, *chéri?*" She was leaning over him. "I don't want to hurt you."

He took her hand and kissed it. "Julie, my Julie. What can I do to show you how I feel—my head busting, my pulse racing. Feel."

"You're sick." She touched him, slid her hand over his chest under the shirt.

"No, I'm hurt. You'll stay? Please, Julie."

She frowned and turned her head away. She went to the table and extinguished the soldering flame. She unbuttoned her smock, took it off, neatly folded it and put it over the chair back. She slipped from her loose dress, kicked off her shoes. When she came to the bed again she was naked, unashamed, and he saw the treasure of her and the beauty. It made him catch his breath. Then he knew the part of life that was best, and he lifted his arm and she touched it. She stooped and was beside him. She kept saying, "It's foolish, it's foolish. Oh Deo, Deo, what are we doing?"

He kissed her and she came alive to his fingers with half stifled cries. Her austere, untouched façade was gone. She was alert to every nuance of his touch, active to every quiver of their muscles.

"You'll hurt yourself, *chéri.*"

They made youthful, vigorous love, and their newly merged emotions made them what they were at the moment, what they had never been before. They merged their loneliness and bitterness, and the universe dissolved.

"Yes?" he asked later.

She let her wet weary mouth remain open as she brushed his hair from his flushed face, tenderly, for the first time, and she began to kiss the bruised area on his head as if in a rite of purification.

They were still in bed in the afternoon when Dr. Alexandre came knocking on the door. He entered without being asked. In the daylight he was leaner and more blond-looking. His suit was a solid pepper-and-salt tweed, his gold-rimmed oval eyeglasses had a thin gold chain attached to his coat lapel. Under one arm he carried two bottles of wine in their straw covers, and under the other a paper bag in which were a long bread and the butt of a smoked ham and a greasy paper of brioches.

Julie made no effort to cover herself, then remembered and groped for the bed sheet.

The doctor sighed. "Incurable, both of you."

Julie said firmly, "Hand me my smock."

"How is the head, Modi?"

Deo laughed and folded his arms behind his head. "What head?"

Julie stood up, buttoned the smock and took the wine and packages. "I'd say he's strong enough to go out to dinner."

"No, I'm not," said Deo. "I feel like hibernating."

The doctor blew dust out of some glasses he found beside the easel, sniffing to be sure they hadn't been used for turpentine or linseed oil.

"He'd better stay in bed for another day or two. And not too much of that frou-frou."

While Julie emptied the paper bag, the doctor examined Deo. "Pulse a little fast, but we'll overlook *that*. It might be emotional. Any fever? Let me feel your head. Hmm . . . Breathe in, breathe out. Ever read Stendhal?"

"What are you thumping my chest for?"

"He wrote: 'The charm of Italy is like being in love.' Now lean over, I want to thump your back. Say *jeu*. Inhale. Hold a big breath. Let it out slowly. Say *jeu*. Now let me listen to your heart."

"There's nothing the matter with my heart, or me."

The doctor leaned back in the chair and folded his arms. "Cover yourself. Had any bad colds, a cough that persists?"

"I've had my share."

Julie handed around the filled glasses. The doctor took a sip.

"What kind of wine can one expect in a grocer's? Modi, do you want to be a leering old man, grow to a wild old age?"

"I don't think so. Simplicity and calmness seasoned with pleasure is enough for me."

"You will love old age, when you're older. You're well made. You're delicate yet tough, but you're weak in the chest. Come down to my office and I'll thump you again. For free, with the socialist workers I have a clinic for. I think there isn't any serious problem, but get plenty of sleep, lots of sweet country butter and red meat. And as for the frou-frou, Julie, you're no help to me."

"I'm moving in. He'll keep good hours."

The doctor nodded. "Modi, last night I saw two paintings I liked here. The boy, and the old woman with the blue eyes. I want to buy them."

"I'll trade you for the examination. My brother is the Socialist in our family, but I'll barter."

"They're worth more than a couple of five-franc visits."

"I can't take your money, doctor. And if I die of this blow on the coconut, you may also have to bury me."

Julie looked up from slicing the wedge of reeking cheese spread out on a paper bag. "You can bring some food from time to time, and Deo will give you a painting from time to time. That's practical."

"You're a practical girl," said the doctor dryly.

"I never said I wasn't. Do you like the ham thin or thick?"

"Thin, and thick cheese. Modi, you've got to look deeper into the work of others. I want you to come to the big Cézanne show when it opens. There is more to him than what you get out of him. And Matisse, daring as a man going over Niagara Falls in a tissue-paper bag, and yet succeeding. And Toulouse-Lautrec, he's not just a few tints of gaslit yellow or green."

"I'm not copying anybody."

"No, of course not. Did I suggest such a thing? Any mustard for this ham? Never mind. But you must let me show you some figures in the Ethnographic Museum of the Trocadero; there are some primitive carvings, masks, figures that will do you a lot of good. Don't become a loafer in Montmartre. I've got to get you out into the world. But first, let the head bump go down." The doctor rose, snapped back the lid of his watch for a glance and whistled. "Ah, I'm late. I'm removing four hundred francs and a tumor from a politician. I'll do it as painfully as possible." He took Julie's hand and lifted it to his lips and kissed it.

"I wish you happiness."

When the doctor was gone, Julie wrapped up the remains of the cheese and ham. Deo watched her move about the room and he felt anointed, no longer exiled to loneliness.

In the months that followed, for the first time since he left home, Deo's life became settled, almost orderly. He had a girl, and in Paul Alexandre he had a very good friend. The doctor was well known for his concern over working men's clinics and slum problems, his love of German philosophy and modern art. Deo had artists to talk to: Pablo Picasso, Henri Matisse. Constantin Brancuși with wood shavings in his wide beard. Pascin —born Julius Pincas in Bulgaria—with a whore on each arm, bedeviled by the flesh, tormented by his dreadful sensual entanglements. Georges Braque, who was also beginning to demolish forms. Maurice Vlaminck, an ex-professional bicycle rider, who smoked clay pipes and swore like a seaman, and André Derain, Raoul Dufy. All talking, grimacing, gesturing through the dense fumes of tobacco, brandy and wine, usually arguing with de Kostrowitsky, the poet-critic who called himself Apollinaire, fat, blond, a joker but also a wit.

Julie, as the spring came, continued to make her little gilt-wire objects for the shops. "Don't you think you'll catch me dependent on a painter mug."

"You earn more than I do, *chéri*. I hoped to catch some milords *inglesi*, but they didn't buy."

"Somebody has to earn the bread."

"You still don't like my paintings." Deo carefully wound his outrageously colored scarf around his neck.

Julie shrugged. "It's no worse than what the others are doing. But *real* artists? So's my behind."

Deo laughed, rolling back his head and lifting two fingers in mock blessing. "To you, Julie Fouchet, I give my grace, my love, and the hope that your eyes will open and your charm will persist." He kissed her tenderly on the cheek. "I'm going to see some strange art again with Paul. We'll have dinner together."

Julie never said, "Don't get drunk, don't get run over by a coal dray." Julie never asked him if he were faithful, if he had fights in cafés, or if dealers insulted him when he showed them work to buy. Julie was ingrown in relation to the world, placid enough, calm at all times, except at love. Deo accepted her that way, knowing if he didn't, she would pack her burner, her tools, her rolls of gilt wire, and be off. Deo had always been so sure of women, so aware of his good looks, his ability to entrance most girls, that now, with Julie, it was certainly a change.

He liked the situation. He wanted her near him; he needed her big warm body on those nights when an attack seized him, when his teeth chattered and his limbs shook. Now it was easy to shake it off—just put his head between her yielding breasts and have her stroke his naked back. "It's all right, Deo, it's nothing, *chéri*. Go to sleep . . . sleep." The deficiencies and extremes that clawed his nerve ends would leave.

Alone in the studio (Julie had gone to deliver some of her wire work) Deo began to paint quickly, to work on the canvas before him, first with a fine brush dipped in Vandyke brown outlining Julie's head and shoulders, bringing to it what he had seen in the African carvings, what had emerged from the Cézannes. He was fresh from his tour with Paul Alexandre. *Head . . . long . . . thin. Neck stretched into ritual . . . fish . . . socket and lid. Little strokes . . . freed . . . free.*

The brush flew. Deo had to paint quickly, finish off a canvas at a sitting. No staring, no thinking, no brooding. Face, neck, torso, an old chair, a scaly wall. With eyes and hands, enough there to explain all the motives of life.

BOOK II
Yellow Ocher

7

In the fall of 1908 Flinck and Baba, unanchored and nomadic, were in South America with a traveling circus, and Deo would get strange post cards showing palm trees and men on horseback twirling bolos, chasing a large frayed bird with long legs.

Julie kept the cards in a small wooden box. "Perhaps the stamps are valuable."

Deo, standing in front of his easel, was painting a picture of Julie seated in a chair with a bowl of greens in her lap, preparing a salad. He looked up. "Don't be so damn practical."

"You're not selling anything, Deo, and the market is cluttered with gilt-wire decorations. Does that make you happy?"

"I'm not hungry. Besides, happiness is the absence of unhappiness, my grandmother used to say."

"You don't eat enough. But I like to eat."

"We'll go to Pablo's tonight. He's invited us over to try smoking opium."

"You'll go alone—and don't smoke it."

Julie showed her disapproval by banging her fist on the table "It's bad for the complexion. Your skin turns yellow, and I hear you can't make love afterward."

Deo dipped his brush in emerald green and began to stipple in the background, in the manner of Seurat's pointillism.

"We can."

"You haven't smoked opium, have you?"

"I haven't been to the moon either. I'd go if I could."

He put down his palette and stood back from the painting. He didn't much care for his work of late. Groping too hard. He turned the canvas around and on its back began to outline a standing nude of Julie. The long golden-rust of her hair he got properly down, and in a turpentine wash of burnt umber he outlined her torso, the pubic area and part of her legs. He disliked doing full figures. "There is an ultimate disenchantment about feet—they come out ugly."

"For the poor, *chéri,* it's the only way to get around—on feet."

Looking at the canvas, all ocher and green, Deo rolled his head to one side and began to clean his brushes and his fingers. Julie was silent and he looked up at her. She was seated on the bed, a cigarette dangling from her lips, her head cradled in her hands. She was staring at the floor. He went over to her and knelt down and pushed her head back and looked up at her. Deo smiled but Julie didn't change her expression. He took the cigarette from her mouth and mashed it out on the floor.

"Don't throw things on the floor," she said. "This isn't a *salle d'armes.*"

He took her in his arms and kissed her tenderly. "What does it matter? This is what matters, not floors, walls, debts."

"How do you think we can last, the way things are going?"

"Something has to happen, as the peasants always say in Italy."

"Yes, I'll pack up my gear and go look for work. I hear London has a fashion in gilt-wire pins."

Deo leaned over her and began to kiss her throat and shoulders as he moved her back onto the bed. She stirred and rolled her head.

"You heard me, Deo. I'm not staying to go hungry."

He unbuttoned her blouse. "I don't hear anything but your heart. Like a regimental drum. Boom, boom, *boom!*"

"Deo!"

She was not averse to making love. She never was, and she never acted it. She always took part with enthusiasm and fury.

Julie! Julie! Deo thought. The idea of her leaving, going away, made him furious, and the full passion took over and the room and its shabby contents didn't matter. Only the seething prodigious emotion mattered.

Pablo's studio was fairly clean for a man who kept two fox terriers. A huge unfinished canvas, the *Demoiselles d'Avignon,* took one wall; two fine Hispano-Roman statues Pablo had bought from the critic Apollinaire stood on either side. Mattresses had been placed on the floor. The only light came from a small oil lamp with a red glass shade set on a fruit box. Fernande, in the colorful robe—gold and robin's-egg-blue—of a Kabuki actor, sat on a mattress, her arms hugging her knees. Max Jacob reclined, leaning on an elbow, holding a flat pipe with a yellow wood stem. Pablo and Deo sat on the floor facing him, as if waiting for an all-clarifying revelation.

On the bed a little man was sobbing, holding his face with his hands. "Oh, my poor wife, my suffering wife."

Max looked up at the man on the bed. "Pariosot, she's not poor, she's not suffering. She's dead. She never knew of your rotten marital infidelity."

Pablo agreed. "Max is right."

Max rubbed the bowl of the pipe clean with a fingernail. "Did you bring the soul of the poppy, Pariosot? It cures the melancholy of *tedium vitae.*"

The man on the bed held out a small flat cigarette tin. "It's poison."

Pablo took the tin and handed it to Max. "I was reading someplace, some American called Emerson who said: 'Tobacco, coffee, alcohol, hashish, prussic acid, strychnine, are weak dilutions; the surest poison is time.'"

Fernande giggled. "Pablo, we haven't even started smoking yet and you're floating."

Max opened the tin box. In it Deo saw a little square of tarlike substance about an inch across.

Max smiled at Deo. "The pipe is called the *yeng-tsiang* and is made of orange wood." He took up some of the black tarlike stuff and rolled a small ball of it between his thumb and first finger. "This pill is called the *gow hop*."

Pablo scowled. "We don't want the lecture, Max. Just the smoke."

Max ignored Pablo and picked up a large needle. "These needles are *yen hauch*." He placed the pill on the end of the needle. Deo could hear the fox terriers locked out in the hall scratch at the door and whine.

From the bed came more sobbing. "So young, and so much to live for. I want to suffer."

Pablo said, "Max, begin cooking."

Max looked at the tiny flame in the red lamp. He placed the needle and its pill directly above the flame by inserting it through a perforation in the glass shade. "The lamp is called *Ken ten,* Modi."

"It's good to know these things," Deo said, expressionless.

The opium sizzled as it cooked, and offered up a sweet strange smell, exotic and over-rich. Max pulled back the needle and sizzling pin, and with a strange little knife (called *tsha,* Max explained) he placed the pill in the bowl of the pipe and handed it to Fernande. She remained numbly doll-faced and took two strong pulls. Deo found the pipe being offered him. Pablo said, "Two or three deep pulls right into the lungs."

Deo found the smoke pleasant but unexciting. He passed the pipe to Max, and from him it went to the man on the bed.

Max cooked another pill. On the second round Deo felt the room stir. Shadows began to pulse and breathe, and there were Siberian wolves at the door. The little crying man on the bed was very still. Pablo's eyes were bigger, his mouth larger; the flap of heavy black hair over one eye looked plastered down. "God is suspected of liking Gothic architecture."

Time gone . . . fear gone . . . calm, calm falling . . . in long, rounding arch . . . No points . . . sharp edges. . . . Only a great eye left, waiting for redemption. . . .

Deo much later found himself looking through the pungent blue smoke at the painting on the wall. Pablo's voice was clear and firm. "It wasn't Leonardo who invented the flying machine. It was Raphael."

"It was the Wright brothers, the American cowboys," said the voice from the bed.

"No, no," said Deo, unable to lift his head from the mattress, but still staring at the figures on the canvas. "They merely reinvented it. The Greeks of Plato's time flew—how else could it rain frogs?"

Max rolled his eyes and closed them, smiling; the red lamp cast ruby shadows on Max's bald head. "Leonardo's *St. John,*" said Max, "has given me the idea that I shall one day become a Catholic. After all, my family is related to Him."

Fernande opened the robe and tried to fan her warm and beautiful face. Her eyes seemed out of focus. "One should never, Max, join a church just to enjoy the architecture."

Pablo muttered: "The *St. John* of Leonardo is fine. Ah yes, Leonardo promises you Heaven with that raised finger. But Raphael, now, he *gives* it to you. From all the open graves of the world's agony I rise, I come to confess . . ."

The figures on the canvas in Deo's vision began a slow sensual dance, pointing their pear-shaped breasts in all directions, oscillating their swaybacked buttocks, rotating their banana-shaped fingers. Someone had let the dogs in and they licked faces and peed on the legs of the furniture.

Deo fell away into a soft warm cave made of pink tissues, the inside of some body, and the sunlight there was like warm grease on his hands waiting for the birth pangs to begin. Voices dimmed, and the little red lamp became an eye that moved and blinked so he could not escape its glaring disapproval. He sighed and smiled.

The little red lamp was smoking. Its wick flared up and a black plume of smoke worked its lazy way, like a feather, to the ceiling. The Greek-Roman statues smiled at him. Max was lying on his back, his face under a weight of furrowed brow, relaxed as if by a muttered benediction. The dogs slept under the bed. Pablo and Fernande, side by side, were like some not so innocent children after secret games. There was no sound from the bed. Then a thin voice said, "For my friends' sake I shall get married again." A hiccup followed, and Deo smelled the full strength of the sickening sweetness of opium. The dried pipe and its gray-yellow ash lay on the floor. The black tar was all gone from the little tin.

Deo got slowly to his feet; he wanted to cry. He found his shoes near the screen, and carrying them he went to the door. A rug and newspapers had been pushed back against it to keep the odor of the poppy from leaking into the hallway. He kicked them aside and went out. In the stone-cold street he put on his shoes. The streets were soggy. There was a hint of dawn over the chimney pots of the roofs to the east. Deo walked slowly home, head down.

During the winter of 1908, their poverty was extreme. The few paintings Deo had sold to Clovis Sagot hung on the walls of the shop—unwanted.

They awoke in the cold of a fireless morning with only the ends of some green cheese, a few knuckles of stone-hard bread for food. Julie was in her worn work smock, her hair tied back with a gray ribbon. Deo was wearing all his clothes to keep warm. The rusty unlit stove gave off only an ashy draft. The prospects were not cheerful.

The Seine was frozen at its edges, the dispossessed died under the bridges, the café windows were misted with frost flowers, and the artists who had a few coins for a drink saved them for the dark hours when the icy world was a deep azure blue and the wind whistled in the bare tree limbs. Deo could understand how Pablo had warmed himself one winter by burning his own drawings.

It was dismal in most of the studios. Full of puzzled doubts and perplexities, the artists and their women, red-eyed from damp wood fires, their throats rasped by smoke, the very dregs of wine freezing in the bottles—when there was any wine left.

Julie's practical side came forward. Huddled in smock and blanket on the bed, she watched Deo blowing on his fingers— fingers too stiff to paint with.

"Give it up. Get some work, Deo."

"Even if I wanted to, Julie, there is no work."

"Half the Butte is filled with artists who aren't artists. All freezing their behinds, chattering away with hungry teeth of their damn art. Well, it isn't worth it. Not in suffering."

"Julie. You're a wonderfully ignorant girl—artistically."

"Damn you, I'm more of an artist than you are! At least when the tourists come back in the summer, I'll sell my wire jewelry. People will wear it proudly and say, '*This* came from Paris!' Who wants your daubs?"

"Nobody," said Deo smiling sadly. "Nobody at all. But I want to paint them. Isn't that enough? Must I have your shallow opportunism?"

"It's certainly a fine way to live."

Julie turned her back to Deo and tried to sleep. They slept a lot. It gave them a mutual warmth; it could often outweigh the pangs of hunger. There were times when for three days they didn't get out of the bed but for hurried moments, then to curl up again, their breath smoking up the cold air of the room.

Spring was late in 1909, the river gray, the trees seemed too numb to blossom.

Then one day, there was a knock at the door and Dr. Paul Alexandre came in carrying some packages and a huge bundle of firewood. Julie and Deo were in bed, too glum to get up, too hungry to think of moving. They stared at him over the blanket like winter bears from a cave.

"Up, up, you sluggards," the doctor shouted cheerfully. "I've been busy studying in London, and I thought yesterday, crossing that damn cold channel, I bet my artist friends are curled up like winter plants in the frozen ground instead of working. Up and get dressed!"

Deo rubbed his cold fingers together, touched his unshaved face. "You're not dependable, Paul. I expected you to play the raven to our Elijahs all winter."

"I've been inspecting clinics all over Europe."

The little table was filled with wine bottles, paté tins, red waxed cheeses, the silver and gold scales of smoked fish, a bread big as a cartwheel. From a pocket the guest brought out some little black sausages in oiled paper, and several cigars.

Julie was up, the blanket over her work smock and a blue unraveling sweater with long sleeves. Deo followed, winding his outrageous scarf around his neck. He threw some newspapers into the stove and began to lay sticks of wood into the ashy maw. Deo tried not to tremble. It was good to hear the flames crackle, hear the roar in the tin pipe that found its way into the wall. Good to taste the wine.

"It's been hard, Paul. I painted café signs, did some window cards for a shop, but all it brought in was just enough to tease the hunger, and not set any fire to the cold."

Julie was biting through a wedge of bread and meat.

"A girl is a fool, doctor, to hang around these types."

Paul Alexandre looked at them both fondly. "Deo, you can begin to think of doing my portrait for my office—something stiffish, in the Whistler manner but with Cézanne's touch. Frock coat, high choker collar, a well-groomed look for such a radical. Maybe some day I'll present it to the Academy of Medicine."

Deo winked. This thin, almost too thin friend; a Socialist, a follower of Nietzsche, a listener to Wagner's music. And a strange comfort to Deo; an anchor, who was himself adrift in the modern world of new forms, new revolutions planned, new processes predicted.

"I'll think about the portrait. Something juicy. Paul in a stuffed shirt." He accepted a cigar. "A regular swat."

8

JULIE WAS ALWAYS READY for a visit to the circus, and when Paul Alexandre got Deo a commission for a painting, or Clovis Sagot (still sad and still lamenting his courage in buying) took a couple of Deo's canvases away under his arm, Deo and Julie, usually after a good dinner in some little eating place on the rue Damremont, then went to a circus. The Cirque d'Hiver, or the Fernando, or the Medrano.

Pablo had made circus subjects popular with artists, and Toulouse-Lautrec had left behind many marvelous crayon drawings, done when he was locked up in a sanitarium, and he had drawn them all from memory to prove his sanity.

Deo in a cheap seat studied the faces of the clowns at the

Cirque Medrano, the wire workers, the bareback riders. Julie by his side delighted in the antics of Aubrey the trained ape, the daring of Mlle Gerva the lion tamer, and the tumbling welter of Dupin's trained dogs, dyed, like Baba, various colors of the rainbow.

The colored dogs reminded Deo of the old clown Flinck as they sat in a clashing of band music.

"I wonder where he is? Flinck is a great clown."

"Last time he wrote, *chéri,* he was in India." She gripped his arm. "It's Oberbeck's turn. I hear he's just amazing. Nerves of steel."

The lights had been turned down, a lime-colored spotlight swung high, and the band began to pump out some of Wagner's more military music.

High up on a platform was the form of a solidly overmuscled Dubonnet-colored figure with a barrel chest, overknotted biceps and well-calved legs. Tight white silk showed off a tiger-skin belt. It was all a display, Deo felt, of confident, bulging faith in living meat; all so smooth that only a vulgar artist could show such resilient mannerisms.

Oberbeck bowed coolly. He had a square Prussian head with a bump of muscle in the back of the neck. His golden hair was cropped short, *en brosse,* his fish-hooked mustache was a popular version of the German Kaiser's own. The handsome face, Deo decided, was that of an overaged choir boy.

"He's not using a net," Julie observed.

Oberbeck flexed his muscles; he had a great many of them. With a rush he leaped onto a single strand of wire, which vibrated wildly as he rode it. The applause and gasps from below went still with awe. The music died away and only the rattle of a slow-paced snare drum took up the rhythms of the highwire walker.

Oberbeck stood on one leg. He extended his arms and leaped from one foot to the other on the swaying wire. He increased the sway, balancing his body as the arc of the sway grew wider and wider. Then he fell, and a gasp of horror filled the hall. But no, as Deo felt Julie stiffen and grip his arm, Oberbeck was hanging from the wire by his arms, moving his legs back and forth in space. Then suddenly he was dangling by his knees across the wire, head down, arms extended. The row of medals pinned to his tiger skin belt dangled loosely.

The drum beat grew more intense, louder, and the hanging man went rigid. The oversized muscles grew even more solid, the buttocks hardened to stone, the breathing in that barrel chest slowed. The wire was swaying wildly now, and then the knees, which were hooked over the wire—involuntarily, it seemed, as though rigor mortis had suddenly set in—began to straighten out. Someone cried out. The drum began to shout. Now the legs were stiff and straight and the body began to slip off the wire head first.

Julie screamed. Others joined her. The drum broke off suddenly. It was a stillness worse than the bleating of shrill whistles in one's ears. The body was almost off the wire when the backs of the heels caught, and hooked. Oberbeck hung there swaying sixty feet up, held high on the oscillating wire by the slim margin of his muscled heels.

There were hysterical shouts, cheers, and the band began to play more Wagner music, of a world of gods on fire. Oberbeck grasped the wire with uplifted hands, then he let go and fell. Twenty feet below he got hold of another wire and swung himself up on a small platform. He bowed stiffly, unsmiling, the golden prongs of his mustache gleaming like temple towers in the spotlight.

Deo rubbed his damp hands together. "He's crazy."

"That marvelous ending—when you think he's falling."

"He's a brainless idiot with too much meat on the bone."

"Go soak your head."

Dupin's trained dogs came running in to tumble over the canvas floor; red, corn-yellow; blobs spinning and barking, magenta and violet, pistachio-colored and taupe.

Julie stood up. "That's enough for one night."

"There's an elephant that does the can-can I hear, and drinks beer like a German."

"I've seen enough."

He followed her quickly out of the smell of tanbark, horse litter, grease paint and the musty ammonia odor of lions and tigers. Deo, unlike Pablo, had no desire to paint this life of make-believe, of cruelty to beasts, danger to women and the dreary shop talk by caricatures of human features outlined in white and crimson.

The next day Deo expressed his feeling to Pablo as the Spaniard worked on his huge painting, which was becoming famous, or rather notorious, among the artists on the Butte.

"You paint clowns from time to time, Pablo. Why? It's all false, it's unreal. The real person is hidden."

"Perhaps it's only when we're unreal and hidden, Modi, and say, 'Look, we are false,' that we're showing something of our secret self."

Pablo stopped painting and stepped back to look at the savage idol's forms he had painted in on a woman's face.

"Max says that all the secrets of the universe, all universal ideas and philosophies, all moral and ethical concepts can . . . Do you think, Modi, there is too much red in the picture?"

"No, what did Max say?"

"Max said all that fancy stuffing which fills thousands of books, all of it could be expressed and explained by a *few* banal sentences."

"Has he done it?"

"Not Max. He's a poet, Modi. He has to keep the mystery of things. He expects to get hold of some hashish tonight. You get marvelous visions eating it."

"I don't want to get to depend on it."

"It's no habit. We can't afford it that often. Hand me the blue. I'm going to paint out the old-style head on the left. But I'll keep the bodies. The shock of mixed styles will be enough."

Deo went to see if Clovis Sagot had sold a painting. Dupin the dog trainer was at the little shop in the back drinking a blue-green wine with the art dealer. Dupin was a small man with the nose of a collie dog and the body of a greyhound in gray and black woolen checks.

He lifted the wineglass in a salute to Deo, knocked its contents quickly into his mouth, then stood up and clicked his heels.

"Ah, the friend of Flinck. We played together in a show in Panama last year. Flinck said when you get to Paris, Dupin, go see Flinck's friend, Modi, the artist."

"How is Flinck? And Baba?"

"Flinck is Flinck. They love him everyplace. Baba is passed over."

"Passed over?"

"Dupin means she's dead," said Sagot. "He never uses the word himself."

"There is no death," said the dog trainer. "There is no evil, there is no pain. Baba passed over in the Red Sea. The heat was too much for her on a P. & O. boat. Buried at sea with full British naval honors. Very impressive."

"When is Flinck coming back to Paris?"

"Bookings are easy out there, and tough to get here. He was always a hard man with a franc or a mark, or a lira, for that matter. Why don't you join us tomorrow morning? The circus is giving a party for the performers and their friends. It's really a stunt of some kind. A cinematography machine is going to take images of us in the sunlight. You've seen those little leaping photographs on a linen sheet?"

Deo said he passed the places that showed them, but he had only seen a couple.

Sagot put the cork in the wine bottle and rammed it tight with his thumb. "They'll show some there. With painted scenery. Maybe, Modi, you can get some work doing backgrounds. I know Georges Melies, who uses the Lumière machine and owns the Theatre Robert Houdin. He needs artists."

Dupin nodded and finished off his wine. "Georges is showing his *A Trip to the Moon*. Delightful. You'll come? Bring a girl, or we'll find you one."

"What do they pay to paint the backdrops?"

Sagot held up his fat hands in a negative gesture. "We'll find out."

Dupin was pushing his fantastic sheepherder's nose toward a painting of Julie on the wall. "Nice tits. Splendid pair. You imagine them, young fellow, or copy them off some body?"

"A painting isn't a copy of anything. It's a re-creation. If a thing is only a copy of reality, reality soon loses its taste."

Dupin put a thin finger to his nose and winked. "Sagot, you heard. Open the wine bottle again and pour us a round of reality."

In the open-air staging yard of the Cirque Medrano the bright sunlight flowed warm and crisp over the circus people. The clowns in their dead white makeup with red-outlined features looked like ghouls released from fairy tales into strong daylight. There were animal tamers in glistening black boots and ripe nectarine jackets hung with fraying gold braid and false medals; bareback riders and girl acrobats in tights showing pretty legs and strong calves. A long table had been set up against warm brick walls and here food and bottles made a badly composed still life. Everyone was drinking and trying to grab a bit of food or cake before it was all gone.

Deo and Julie had been introduced to the cinematographer, Georges Melies, a bald, mocking man with the mustache and little beard of a stage devil. He was waving a cane and standing behind a black box on three thin legs.

He shouted, "*Corps d'artistes!* Less eating, less drinking, more laughing, more arm-flinging for the camera. So, *so!*"

Deo watched the film maker begin to turn a crank set in the side of the black box. It didn't make much sense and Deo went to find Julie. She was by a gold and red wagon full of mangy smelly lions with Dupin, the little dog tamer, and Oberbeck, the highwire worker.

The German looked puffy and uncomfortable when fully dressed in his gray striped suit, a high collar, a plaid tie pulled through a jeweled ring. His blond hair was mostly hidden by a green velour hat snapped down on one side, the way popular Italian actors adjusted their headgear. And there was a scented pomade on Oberbeck's spiked mustache that anyone within three paces could smell.

Julie said to Deo, "Hans is an actor in the electric theater show we're going to see."

The wire worker bowed to Deo. "Such nonsense. But Herr Melies talked me into doing it. *Nein?*"

There was a shout from around the table and several plump dancers from the Paris Opéra, wearing silver stars in their piled-up hair and white tights under their flimsy robes, were turning and twisting, faking a ballet step in front of the black box and the man tirelessly turning the crank. Someone threw a wine bottle and the man cranking stopped and shouted. "We have come to the end of the film strip in the camera. Thank you. Thank you. I will show you the results in a week. You will now be remembered forever."

A girl from the Folies Bergère with a huge bosom ran up and kissed the man at the camera. "M. Melies, when can we see the electric theater?"

"Right away, right away. Inside. I've set up a projector and a screen. This way, children. Don't knock down the camera."

Everyone began to troop inside, past stalls of horses, two chained-up apes, a little black pig, and Dupin's dyed dogs.

Deo let Julie pull him into the dark interior. A white sheet had been stretched on a curtain frame in the pit where the clowns and animals usually performed. On a table twenty feet from the screen a smoking gadget of gears, lens and a short chimney of black iron was being fussed over by several people. Georges Melies pushed them all aside and began to thread some slivers of transparent celluloid through a set of gears. He wiped his bald head, arranged his little beard neatly between two fingers, and bowed, facing the circus people and their friends who were settling down with laughter and noise in the front seats.

"First I will show *A Trip to the Moon*. I understand there are some fellow artists present, but I make no excuses for the scenery in this film, which I have painted myself."

Sagot pushed himself down in a seat near Deo. "He's not a bad artist—Georges—but he needs help, Modi."

"You didn't promise him I'd paint scenery for him?"

"Wait till you see some of it. It must be amusing."

Deo saw Julie, two Folies girls, a horse trainer and Oberbeck crowd into a gilt box. Someone drew the drapes over the skylights, and Deo had a sense of malaise. The gadget on the table leaked light from a small door that was slammed shut. The smell of heated iron grew stronger, and then on the white sheet appeared a group of grotesque figures of men with false too-black beards, full of strange overdramatic gestures. It was amazing. Deo had seen a few moving-picture shows before, but rather dull ones of wagons in a street, a lady getting into a corset, a false Negro kissing a pretty girl. But now Deo sensed something special and amazing in a world of roles and symbols; not reality. This was no journalism on strips of celluloid, but a kind of art form. The scenery was painted, the action was edited into a sort of dance. The Folies Bergère girls came on to the screen pushing the huge shell that would make the trip to the moon. It was all a comic and yet heroic aggrandizement of the joy of life.

Sagot whispered to Deo. "Melies uses the Folies girls wherever he can. He says people like a good leg or tail even on a screen."

The film ran, the earth shell landed in the man in the moon's eye; strange people came to attack the explorers. It was very amusing, this special kind of world, where all the laws of nature and danger could be ignored. It impressed Deo as much as an opium dream. But of course he could not paint this kind of scenery. It would take up too much time, those large flat areas of gray and black, and the style would destroy his own idea of art; it was candy-box fantasy mixed with real objects.

The screen went steamy white and M. Melies' voice came over the metallic grind of the machine and its strange probing eye of light.

"Next, my newest entertaniment. *Long-Distance Wireless Photography*. M. Marconi has sent wireless messages over the air. I show you how I send images of people and things. Very droll, you'll see."

Deo watched new images—the Folies girls being reduced to small creatures and sent by wireless, to be received as images again and then brought to life with amusing results. Deo's eyes ached from the flickering patterns and the stale air. He pushed his way out to the yard. The wreck of the table was being brushed away by the circus handymen. There was a contagious nihilism in that film method, Deo mused. Its persistent perversity could make or destroy taste. Deo lit a small cigar, a gift from Paul Alexandre, and stood in the sunlight, smoking, hands in pockets, hearing howls of laughter from the still-darkened circus hall. On reflection, he didn't think that the films would amount to much. Best for the artist to keep away from it.

There was a crush of people as the showing ended and Deo went to hunt for Julie. Clovis Sagot was standing by the monkey cage making faces at its contents.

"Modi, look at them. They mock us—make fun of all the nasty little habits we have. And overdo them."

"I want to find Julie and get away from here. That flickering has given me a headache."

"I want you to talk scene painting with Georges."

"That's for Meissonier and Bougereau. No, I don't want to paint that kind of scenery. Besides, in a few years they'll photograph real houses and rooms. Where's Julie?"

Sagot winked at a gray spider monkey. "Glance at this one. Looks just like that fat art critic, Gerald N.N. Julie. She told me to tell you she's gone with some circus people to the Cheval Blanc. Meet her there."

Deo left Sagot feeding the monkey from a bag of shelled sunflower seeds. He felt strange, as if he were suspended between the Paris he knew and that other world invented on strips of celluloid film. Both worlds seemed phantoms existing only in the mind and eye. There was also a sense of some impending disaster here in the bright sun, in the busy day, among these indifferent people on hard streets. Perhaps his chest really was in a poor way. Paul had tapped and pounded him again and told him to be less active. The tight band across the chest didn't let up. Damn if he'd go to the Cheval Blanc and be bored by lion tamers and wire workers. He'd go home, lie down, wait for Julie to wake him with a kiss.

The sense of doom continued and Deo stopped at Druet's Café at the corner of the Place de l'Alma and the Avenue Marceau for an apple brandy. That bracer lifted the pressure from his chest. He walked on, inhaling the good weather, and after a while he found himself before Berthe Weill's shop, where Pablo's drawings and watercolors were displayed in the small window. He opened the door and a rasping bell rang its clapper of iron over his head. It wasn't much of a shop. Art objects, memories of Paris for visitors to take away. Many small things that people might buy to remember their trip to France. A wall of drawings. Deo's, more of Pablo's, some song sheets lithographed by Lautrec, some really amusing drawings of tarts in lacy underwear by Pascin.

Berthe Weill, small, dark, carrying a white cat, came forward from some wooden cave in back of the shop, looking, as usual, cryptic and at peace with the world at the same time. Foolish people said she had odd tastes in art and artists, but it was always exciting to come to her shop.

"Ah, Deo, I almost sold two of your drawings. A pair of sisters from Baltimore."

"That's in Africa, Berthe?"

"No, in the American Confederacy. Their name is Cone, the Cone sisters. One is a doctor. A real cut-you-apart medical doctor. Looks like a Foreign Legion sergeant."

Deo inspected a watercolor of a hungry family, barefooted, done in blue. A father, mother and thin child by Pablo. "It's odd how many doctors turn to art. They didn't buy?"

"No. They want to come back with Gertrude and Leo. The Jewish Americans all go to the Steins for advice when they want to buy new things. Max Jacob says Gertrude must sell kosher-killed meat in the back."

"Pablo calls Gertrude the bastard daughter of Buffalo Bill and Carrie Nation. That is why Americans are so fearful of fornication. They produce monsters. Berthe, I need paints."

"I can't spare much. Ten francs?"

Deo took the money. He'd take Julie out to the old Café de la Closerie des Lilas, next to the Luxembourg Gardens, off there at the far end of the Boulevard Montparnasse. Julie was getting bored with the places in Montmartre, getting hard to please. To keep Julie pleased he'd even endure an evening at Gertrude Stein's at times. As a descendant of Spanish Talmudists and Spinozas he sneered at German merchant Jews like the Steins.

9

Thy will is free and whole and upright
And now it would be wrong to rein it in.
Be thine own Emperor and thine own Pope . . .

DANTE's *Divina Commedia* didn't help. The mood of depression didn't leave Deo. He tried to paint in the late afternoon—after returning from the circus—but smeared up a good beginning of Sagot seated in a wicker chair rubbing his fat thumbs together.

By dusk, Julie still hadn't returned, and Deo lay down on the bed folding their only blanket over his throbbing chest. *He was eating too quickly at a* crémerie *run by a Swiss woman in the Carrefour Vavin where the space shell that was going to land in the eye of the man in the moon made a whistling sound that turned into the heavy hateful Wagner music to which that Oberbeck did his neck-breaking tricks on the swaying wire.*

Deo came awake in panic, sweating; he had lost his personal magic. He was a rational person, and Paul Alexandre, who lived in respect of all modern science and the logic of a new age of reason, had laughed at Deo's wariness of the supernatural Gypsy lore and his little Italian peasant's tricks for warding off the evil eye. Deo made the sign of the forked fingers that the natives of Naples swear is protection from sudden disaster. He sat up in the dark room. It was night. He could sense the lateness of the hour. The street noises were subdued, the ringing of bells had long since stopped.

Something was wrong. Julie was not in the bed by his side. He felt for her, an automatic gesture; he knew she wasn't there. When she was there, an aura of body heat, an orchestration of breathing, a sag in the mattress made it plain she was by his side. With trembling hands he lit the oil lamp; it was the last match and it left an odor of Satan and sulfur in the room. He drank what was left of a bottle of bad red wine, dressed and went out. In his chest, some slow assassination was taking place.

There was a white mist walking the cobbled street and a sense of frog-tasting smells coming from the river, fitting his mood of self-abnegation. Deo stood rubbing his chin. Where could Julie be? There was her girl friend Valerie, married now to a fruit huckster, living in the working-class quarter of the Place de la République. Deo walked there, being stopped twice by the police, who believed his story that his wife was in labor and he was going to get a midwife who lived near the Jardin des Plantes. He made up a little poem—we die as we are born, crying.

Deo couldn't get into the house where Valerie and her husband lived, a rookery of six stories, leaning a bit to one side, and smelling of the trade that got its living at the market among cabbage leaves, crates of spitting lobsters dying in cracked blue ice, the little blinded larks hung by their beaks and offered as pie fillings. Deo walked around in front of the house, not daring to wake up the she-dragon that lived in the basement and guarded the door. Damn Paris and its guardians.

Besides, Julie would not be at Valerie's; they had fought over something and parted snarling and with heads thrown back, nostrils flaring like racehorses. Deo walked on and found himself in the labyrinthine streets of the old Latin quarter.

He wanted a drink, his lungs were full of lumpy ice, his hands trembled and he began to sneeze. There was an all-night bistro near the Montparnasse station. There sat two hackney drivers, an old man selling anti-Semitic Royalist newspapers, two whores with damp feathered boas, all in the steam and smoke of onion soup, cigarettes and ailing plumbing, waiting out the night in the hope of some change in their fortunes.

Deo drank two glasses of Anjou wine. Someone howled a greeting at him. It was a large blond man, monstrous fat, with a small head that ended in a huge jowl, a mouth small as a rosebud, eyes tiny, set in a Japanese slant. He came over to Deo, beating night dew from his rather overpatterned cheviot jacket. He was with a tall beautiful Hindu girl wearing a red turban with several yellow feathers in it, her body wrapped in yellow folds of cloth with gold designs. A jewel was drilled through one nostril.

The blond man waved a flipper of an arm as they sat down. "Ah, Deo, a devil of a wet night. Noah looking out of the Ark saw one just like this."

Deo collected his thoughts. De Kostrowitzky was the blond man's name. Wilhelm de Kostrowitzky. Pablo said he was the son of a Cardinal in Rome and a Polish princess; a woman who spent her time with a Jewish lover named Weil—going from watering places to casinos, gambling all the time. What nonsense! Still the man did look like a grand seigneur of the Renaissance. Now he was ordering something from an apparently awed waiter.

"Have you seen Julie?"

The blond man patted his overlarge chin. "No, I haven't. But I've been showing Hatasu here the more disreputable parts of our village. She can't speak French, or I'd introduce her. Have you seen Pablo?" He waved a heavy cane with a nude Negress carved into the handle.

"Not for a few days. Listen, help me. It's Julie. She's gone."

"Don't worry. I've written a poem to Pablo's new style." He hunted in his pocket, while the dark woman smiled, showing tremendous white teeth. Her jeweled nose, her large eyes, made her exotic in the fumes of onion soup, but no one paid her much attention. She began to spoon up her soup.

The blond poet had a scrap of paper in his hand. "I'm sorry, it's the wrong one—it's a love poem. *Yvonne Lost,* by Guillaume Apollinaire. Listen to the bruised sounds:

> "Vierge au Zodiaque
> Je suis un peu braque
> Puisque je suis fou
> D'une qui s'en fout . . ."

Deo said, "It's a poem. I'm very upset and . . ."

"*Garçon,* the Ranee wants more bread. . . . How do you like it so far, Modi?"

Deo rose and put some coins on the counter. He had no time for poetry reading. "I must go find Julie."

The fat poet folded his poem and put it away carefully as he

addressed the feeding woman. "You're all bitches. All of you."
He smiled at the bistro owner. "She doesn't understand a word
I'm saying. She's from up near the Chinese border."

When the Butte boites and cafés opened for early-morning
coffee, Deo made the rounds. Somehow he was sure Julie
hadn't gone home. Near noon he returned to his studio; the
place was empty. There was no sign she had been back. Her
clothes—what there was of them—were behind the gray linen
sheet that served as her closet. He touched her work shoes, the
smock in which she soldered her gilt wire trash, the pliers, the
soldering iron, the heating jet. She wouldn't leave without
them, no more than a bride without her new rubber toys.
Where was she? Ill? Injured?

He couldn't eat and he was running a temperature. He began to pace the floor, and as he turned he walked three times to
the right in a full circle and three times to the left in another
circle. And he recited a full magic ritual of the Gros Nègres of
Haiti:

> "Oui moins p'r aller!
> Oui, moins bai ou tort!
> Moins bai ou manger."

One couldn't be too sure this was a rational logical world.
And if by rite, black mass, voodoo prescription of snake and cat
and goat he could bring Julie back, it didn't matter, he'd do it.
He placed little hope in the police, the hospital, the morgue.

The damp night journey had done him harm. He began to
cough. His throat seemed flayed. Again he went out into the
streets. A gray-brown drizzle began to polish the old stones of
Paris. He walked hunched over, hunted the bistros on the rue
de Saules where the jewelry workers drank, questioned con-
cierges near the sound of the clock tower of St. Germain des
Pres. No Julie. The police had no reports. Market workers in
espadrilles and tight sweaters smoked their dreadful last inch
of French army cigarettes and said no, they hadn't seen Julie or
anyone like her. A few clowns, still showing signs of their *ma-
quillage*, said no. Would he have a red wine with them? He
looked as if he needed a glass of wine.

Deo went on, not feeling the water in his broken shoes, the rain sopping through hat and hair. He stood outside the Catholic College of Ste Marie de Monceau, wondering why he expected to find Julie there. And when he could no longer walk, he fell down and began to weep, coughing and weeping. . . . He looked up and tried to remember a number of an apartment on the rue Fontaine, in Montmartre, where lived the shopkeeper who sometimes bought Julie's gilt wire.

He tried to move and after some time he managed to get to his feet. The drizzle had drifted off toward the Atlantic, leaving just wet air to breath, air that cut and gurgled like wine in a vat when it is turned and fermented. There were flaring yellow blooms of gas jets behind glass, and well-dressed people, and the most desirable whores having an omelette-au-rhum. He waved a wet hand at them and recited a poem of unrequited love that came to him. It seemed so good he wondered why more poets did not become feverish and write in a rain-soaked city. He tried to sing a Florentine *canzone* but failed. His voice, he had to face it, was rasped and full of strange slimes. His velveteen jacket was a rag, just an extra thick skin, an added skin that did not keep him warm, for he was shaking in illness and desire. Old St. Augustine had known: *Non ob aliud, nisi quia non licebat*—for no other reason than that it was forbidden.

Beer, thirty centimes a glass; love walking the street, twenty francs a throw. Kerosene, canvas, paint, the rent of an obscene bed; it all added up and depressed an artist. Dirty rooms in eight-story Napoleon III houses. Hundreds of artists all painting away in a *délire de grandeur,* Clovis Sagot called it—an excess of self-love.

The world was becoming hallucinatory, misted, feverish. He tried to reach an open-air pissoir, but he fell to his knees on the stones as the rain began again. Then he fell onto his face. In his mouth was the dreadful butcher taste, the salty thick feel and flow of blood. It dripped onto the wet street.

First a roaring . . . a collection of painful sounds raging in unison; then a feeling that he would never be able to rise and breathe again . . . his blood would flow away as the blood of his people had flown and been demanded since Abraham offered up his son Isaac, and God settled for a ram . . . and the torture cellars of the Church took the blood—took it black and tasting of herring and burned the donor in city squares in the name of the Son of God. . . .

He fought the return to life but at last opened his eyes. He smelled before he saw them long rows of dirty feet protruding from gray charity sheets, and the little vat of burning olive oil on the green prison-color wall that smoked in the face of the Virgin; and she, being of plaster, could not turn away from its fumes. The bitter iron taste of blood was still in his mouth, and the old nun, whose slippered feet hissed across the stone floor when she walked, bent her head over him. He moved slightly, testing with fear the delicate tension of tissues, nerves and body fluids.

"Do not try to talk."

Deo turned his head and saw Dr. Paul Alexandre and Clovis Sagot.

"You had a bad hemorrhage, Modi. Don't talk," said Paul Alexandre. "You may bring it on again."

"You're alive," said Sagot with a shake of his head. "Running around like a crazy schoolboy in the rain."

He moved his lips.

Paul Alexandre shook his head. "Not now. Later. I just gave you twelve drops of laudanum."

He took up Deo's wrist and the nun came back with a dish of steaming broth. Deo let some of the broth slip from a leaden spoon down his throat and his lungs were painful, but something—the laudanum—they had given him made all thoughts fuzzy, all pains bearable. Sagot and the nun exchanged quizzical glances. The doctor released the wrist.

"Now you must rest. I'll be back later. I know it's frightened you, Modi. I don't think it's much of a damage you have in the lung. Care. Rest. Fresh air." *Those who are weak eat herbs, St. Paul has said.*

Deo awakened to one small lamp burning in the night; he was shaking, and his teeth were chattering. He wanted to cry out, but feared the blood rising in his throat. He rolled his head in agony to see the Virgin, still smothered in the fumes of the

olive-oil lamp. His teeth clicked like old billiard balls. The
snores of old noses and damaged bronchial tubes filled the
ward; the smell of urine, carbolic, stained dressings mixed with
the shadows of the ceiling beams. The expected violent unbearable shakes did not come; the drug still held him. *Bless all
drugs, Virgin, for they shall give us release from pain; bless
that which shall soften the chains of suffering. Bless us who
suffer . . . who . . .* Outside a cart was moving between
stone curbs—most likely removing a cadaver from the charnel
house. Along the dim-lit hall beyond the ward came a nun's
winged shadow, her shuffling feet. An old priest appeared carrying the tools of the last rites, leaving behind him a small
sleepy breeze of Latin. *How comforting to build a salad of oil
and ash on the forehead of the condemned; given the body of
the Son by mouth, the blood of the Son by battered silver cup,
to be released of all cause and effect . . . all . . .*

When he awoke next, Paul Alexandre was writing on a small
official form. Deo's chest was naked and the doctor smiled.

"It's going to be all right. And don't talk." He leaned over
and tapped the chest with a stiff cruel finger and listened and
nodded. "We'll have a more detailed examination later."

Julie?

"What can I tell you? Can I quote Nietzsche to you, Modi?
'Men have ideals, women have only illusions.' There, that didn't
help you, did it? You mustn't put any strain on those lungs till
they heal."

Where?

Paul Alexandre took Deo's hand in his. "She's gone off. With
some circus character from the Cirque d'Hiver, or the Cirque
Fernando. I don't remember which."

Oberbeck?

"Yes, some such name. All muscle and shiny blond turf.
Something about them going to Hamburg or Berlin. Sagot told
me."

Gone?

"Yes. Together. Damn it, Modi—I should have waited, I
suppose, to tell this to you. But it would be worse, you straining
to ask, and building up fears and assumptions inside you."

Thank you. Deo turned his head away to stare at the unswept stone floor. Gone away. Hamburg. Or Berlin. Julie, the big German. The wire worker, the wire twister. His heart had a bone in it. Yet the pressure was less . . . less . . .

He sipped some cloudy water from a glass that was held out to him and he fell into imageless sleep again. He didn't awaken, but he must have, must have appeared awake because there were holes in the darkness through which he saw Sagot's face and heard his voice. He had been staring at the old clown for a long time before the words came through to him and began to focus into meaning. Sagot was being very earnest, and sweating and mopping his bun of a face and its little beard as he talked.

". . . clear as a boil on your tail, not that I wanted to admit it. You understand? So when Julie, she said: 'I'm going away with him'—the Boche . . . the kraut-eater—I said, 'What for? He's just a lump of pretty meat.' And she said (I laughed) she said: 'He's a real artist. I've never known a real artist before.' I was shaking like a bowl of calf's foot jelly, I can tell you, Modi. I said: 'Artist? This anatomy chart up there on a loose wire, I bet he's *babillard*—an impotent mug.' And she said: 'That's right, Clovis, a real artist. I'm tired of all those little piddling paint scrapers on the Butte, the self-styled geniuses—all itch and no francs.' Am I talking too much, Modi? I tried to explain to her a real artist has to be an artist about something big, something important, not a circus act. All right, I'll stop talking. You look better than you did when they brought you in. What?"

Sagot leaned over Deo's bed and put a hairy ear close to Deo's mouth. It was hard to get the courage to talk; suppose a red shiny flood of his life's blood welled up? He expelled air carefully and pushed it onto the vocal cords and made the proper mouth and tongue shapes. "A . . . real . . . artist."

"She was a little hysterical, you understand, Modi, like a bitch in heat at a dog show. This kraut-snapper must have dazzled her with his phony medals, his gauche biceps."

Julie had found what she wanted. Life was envenomed and there was so much of it, *if* he recovered. He wanted to scream and tear open fresh soft wounds in his lungs, drown in himself, but something selfish preserved him. He didn't want to think of going on, putting more pigment on more canvas. Yet it was true. The banal stupid easy little mottoes might just be right. Time *would* heal, time would make him forget. But he didn't really believe it yet.

"Sagot—"

"Modi?"

Sagot's breathing sounded like grease frying, and some of the patients in the row of beds made humorous sounds and one cursed.

After a while Deo sensed Sagot had gone and left some drooping flowers tied up with a red string; it would be just like Sagot, Deo thought, to steal them from some tombstone in the Montmartre cemetery.

In the next few days Deo scraped himself free of the pathology of self-pity. Still, it was not easy to go back to the shabby room where he and Julie had lived; was it a year, a year and a half? What did it matter. He was sitting in a deep chair with a blanket folded over his shoulders, sitting in the direct sunlight. Paul Alexandre was standing by the windows, his lean back to Deo, his boiled sanitary hands clasped behind him, his head rising like a turtle's out of the high collar.

"You need sunlight, clean air."

"Italy, Paul?"

"Why not, Modi? Why not? Your people are there. It's better for the cold icy months."

"If I go, maybe I'll not come back."

"Of course you'll come back."

Deo laughed. "Dead men don't come back to Paris."

The doctor turned around. "Listen, my imponderable friend. I'm not going to baby you. You have a touch of pulmonary complications. I'm even sure you have some dormant tubercular spots. But you can live to be eighty, *if* you'll take care of yourself."

"Why?"

"Why drugs? Why drinking? I'll trade you answers."

Deo didn't take up the challenge. "I'm going back to Livorno in the fall. I think I want to work in stone, carve statues. Painting I've lost confidence in. Brancuşi is right. It's a world of solid form; that's sculpture. Maybe modern painting is going to become mere décor, flat fashionable surfaces, playing with the material. But stone . . . you can't do dishonest things in stone, not often."

"You do things with any material, Modi—in flesh, in prose, in music; you can do things even with politics. But as Baudelaire said: 'To dream you must first know how.' To be an artist, Modi, first of all you must know how to keep alive. Graveworms have no genius."

Deo didn't answer.

The sun felt good on his face and shoulders.

"With everything, Paul, there must be style. I can't change my style because for me the style is the man."

"You and your damn phrases. They sound all right, but what do they mean? Learn to distrust words."

"Even yours, Paul?"

The doctor smiled and said in English, *"You can bloody well go to hell, and jolly well kiss my arse.* I'll drop by tomorrow."

10

DEO DECIDED to be out of Paris by the winter. But first he had to earn the money for the trip home to Italy. The summer of 1909 was ending in a burst of fine weather. He could no longer live in Montmartre with its memories of Julie and the time they had shared there in a life together. The numbness in the heart turned from constant pain, and while her image danced in his dreams so that he walked the night, shaking, until several strong drinks calmed him, even those memories began to dim.

When the shadows were worst, drugs helped the most. Eating hashish in the form of gray pills that he bought from some of the Turks in the gambling dens off the rue Lafitte, or the Corsicans hanging out at the clowns' bar at the Cirque Medrano. But Deo didn't like to go to the circus because of the memories of the blond Oberbeck.

The artistic move from the Butte was in progress. The new

studios were being set up in Montparnasse on the Left Bank, and there Deo went, to the Cité Falguière. He rented the same kind of room, but on the ground floor facing a dusty yard, a room with a rusting stove and a corner for his easel and art reproductions, his few clothes.

On the morning he moved in, there was a great banging next door, and Deo went out into the hall and found a big double door open across the way. A bearded stocky man was hacking away at a block of granite taking on the shape of a giant egg.

It was Constantin Brancuși, the Rumanian, as dusty as ever, the wood shavings thick in his black beard, and now mixed with bronze filings and stone chips.

He looked up, mallet and chisel in his fists.

"Damn it, Modi! The stone is flawed." He threw down the tools. "I use the clawtoothed end on it and the punch and point. But it's worthless. It's hard to steal good stone."

"It doesn't show any flaws from here."

Deo looked over the studio, and beyond it to the yard where other of the sculptor's work stood. Strange oval shapes, primitive-looking slabs with simple suggestions of lovers, knobs and screw forms, wooden carvings showing the chisel marks proudly, none of the work resembling much that Deo had ever seen before.

"You keep busy."

"I have to. Nobody buys much, Modi, so I have to pile up a lot of unsold work to impress people. Or does that lack sense?"

"How do you live? And eat?"

"You call it living? You call it eating?" He laughed. "I knock off something for a stoneyard or a wall mason."

"I moved in across the way."

"Ah, so you're here? I understand Pablo is coming down to Cité Falguière. I tell you this is going to be the place for the new art. The Butte is too romantic. It's for Americans."

"What new art?" Deo sat down on a square stone just chewed up here and there by the artist's marks, but not yet developed.

"The little cubes Pablo and Braque are working in. And Negro sculpture. It's oh-ho-ho, the stylish thing now. But it better be digested." He picked up a thin chisel and began to hammer at the stone again. "Maybe I can make something of the flaw. Look at the rotten mess of people God has to work with."

"In Italy they work stone with the *subbia, ugnetto*, chisels, and when they hit hard, a live blow, it's called the *colpo vivo*."

"You have the look of a sculptor, Modi. I always said so, remember? Something about the eyes wide apart. You never saw a crosseyed sculptor, correct? How does it look now? You'll have a drink?"

Brancuşi brought out a bottle of strong red wine and some hard bread. He filled two glasses—after blowing them clean— and in his dusty hand held his glass high. "Here's to stone and wood."

Deo drank. He picked up a chisel and the wooden mallet. "It must feel good."

The sculptor set up a fragment of sandstone. "Here, try this. Bang away. It's soft. Drive down. But try and see what lives in the stone. Every stone has something trying to be set free."

"It's very satisfying." Deo chopped boldly.

There was a yielding directness, a sense of power in sending the steel point down into the stone, driving a small valley into the sandstone. In the shape there was room for a kneeling woman, a caryatid, arms up, holding up, *what?*

"No, no, Modi. You're drawing on the stone. See not line but mass, and in the round. As if your object is making a negative mold of itself out of air."

"I need a bigger stone."

"I'll tell you what we'll do. When it gets dark, we'll go steal one. They're repairing a bridge just a few squares away. The watchman for a drink winks and looks the other way. Modi, you'll find carving in Paris better than piddling with paint."

"I'm going back home. Soon as it gets cold."

"The lungs, eh? In my country sour milk cures everything but dying. Listen, no stonecutter ever had a weak part—throwing the pointing iron, cutting away mass, it builds up the arms, the chest. You'll paw the ground like a bull after six months."

"I need more practice."

They sat drinking the raw wine, chewing on the bread till Deo left to settle into his studio.

Why not stone? he mused. Why not carvings? The painting was at a standstill. It wasn't selling. Poor Clovis Sagot, the white face whiter, was not selling anything. Perhaps, Deo felt, he could carve something to earn the train fare back to Livorno.

It didn't matter what he did as long as he worked. Since that *one* had gone off with "a real artist" it had been hard to pull his life together. That night he and Brancuşi got four very nice lengths of sandstone railing that would never fit into any bridge. The sculptor sharpened some old chisels for Deo, gave him advice for their use, and found him a good place in the yard to set up his stones.

"Just remember the good modern stonecutter doesn't destroy order, he makes it over."

"I'll try."

"Don't be tender. Treat the stone like a beautiful wild horse —spur it—teach it manners."

Deo didn't try another caryatid. He began to carve a long narrow head—his own vision of the African forms he had seen, and in the way Brancuşi cut his patterns. At the end of the third day, hammering, smoothing, choking on dust, hacking at the stone, Deo felt the style was all his own. He looked over the elongated features, the geometric treatment of the neck and throat, the sharp, defined, rectilinear volume of the nose. Yes, it was also archaic Greek he admitted to Brancuşi, and Khmer sculpture, Gothic statuary.

"But in the next head I'll make it all mean something more personal."

Brancuşi, shaking dust from his matted hair and the worn canvas overalls he wore, waved two fat thumbs at Deo. "What did I say! Born to the chisel! Crude yet, but delicate *here* and *there* with the touch of an angel's feather. *Here, there,* it's like the Greek Kores. And I see a smidgen of the stonecutters of Angkor and Rheims, but mostly I see you. Nobody else."

"I'll do a whole set of heads, all sizes in a row, like a pipe organ for a song in stones running in my head."

The Rumanian sighed. "We'll have to find a new place to steal the stone, if you set up that many to work on."

A week later, Deo, shirt off, sweating, was standing in the

yard, looking at his work. He had five unfinished heads in a semicircle set around him. He had his style now. He knew it and wiped his face. He hadn't thought of Julie for days. The heads stared up at him; strange, mysterious, delicate, strong. He rubbed stone dust from his chest.

Paul Alexandre came out into the yard, followed by a lean young man with twinkling Hebrew features—a shaved dancing rabbi, a young Elijah not yet too well fed by the ravens, Deo decided.

"Deo," said Paul Alexandre, "you're getting the color back in your skin."

"Also blisters on my hands. Look, raw meat."

"This is Jacques Lipchitz. He carves, too."

Deo held out a hand to the young man. "I've seen some of your work. Pablo showed it to me."

The young sculptor was walking around the five heads. "Interesting."

Deo laughed and the doctor was pleased at the sound and the sight of Deo's amusement. "A rotten word, Lipchitz. It's said to cover no real answer or impression."

"Perhaps, but when you're trying to discover something new in your own work, you don't like to get entangled in somebody else's visions. And when they're as good as yours are, deep down I don't want to like them. But I do, very much."

The doctor touched a polished shoe toe to a stone head. "We'll try and get the entire group exhibited in the Salon d'Automne."

Lipchitz nodded. "Why not?"

"I'm not ready yet," said Deo.

Paul Alexandre sat down on a backless chair under a poorly growing grape arbor. "The artist is usually the last to know he's ready. Degas said a man with a pistol should stand behind every artist, and shoot if he tried to go on after he's finished a work of art."

Brancuşi, hearing voices—he had the Rumanian interest in people and disliked missing anything—came out to the yard, wiping his hands on his canvas overalls.

"Ah, the doctor and Jacques. What do you think of my pupil? Damn fine boychik, no?"

Deo picked up his shirt and put it on. He began to hunt missing buttons. "I think I'll go see the Rodin statues; they might be helpful."

The Rumanian exploded with a foul horse dealer's oath in his native tongue, pulled his beard and continued to shout. "You heard him! Rodin!"

"We heard," said the doctor, winking broadly. "Rodin."

"Rodin! That man is leading sculpture down the road to ruin! Clay, mud, *merde!* He'd model in *anything!*"

"What's wrong with clay?" asked Lipchitz, giving Deo an ironic warning grimace. "Clay is good to feel in the fingers."

"It's perversion! That's what it is! A crazy manipulation of *dreck!*"

"It's the end result that counts, isn't it?" Deo asked.

"It's weak! Like modeling in straw. No vigor, and Christ, let us admit it, no grandeur! Confess, confess, no grandeur in clay!"

Lipchitz began to wave his arms, still amused, but earnest too. He wasn't letting Brancuși outshout him. "Carving directly in stone doesn't make you a god, Constantin! No! And it doesn't give you the right to claim it alone generates power, style, beauty! But let's leave beauty out of it; it's too easy a word unless you try to define it. Then it blows up."

"Rodin!"

"A great artist can give clay, plaster, even pasted paper the hard power and austerity of marble."

"Rodin!"

"All right, Rodin! What's wrong?"

The two sculptors had suddenly begun to glare at each other. Dr. Alexandre stepped between them. "Let's all sit down and smoke some sense into our heads." He handed around some of his thin black Havana shapes. The four men sat under the failing grape arbor as twilight settled over the stony yard and softened the scattered chips, the five heads, and Brancuși's weathered work pushed up against the fence. After a while, the two sculptors went off to a nearby café to argue clay and stone. The doctor took Deo out to dinner at Azon's restaurant, Aux Enfants de la Butte, on the rue des Trois-Frères.

"I can't understand why the artists are going from Montmartre, Modi. It's so fine on the Butte."

A boy passed howling editions of *L'Echo de Paris, Le Journal;* a man with an ecclesiastical face was asking a woman to observe how large was the lobster they were being served; and several Englishmen from the Académie Humbert on a café terrace were toasting either their queen or king; at the moment Deo didn't remember just who was on the throne. The street lay gorged with life, and he was leaving it all—soon.

"It doesn't matter, Paul, where the artist works. I don't think I'll come back from Italy."

"Of course you'll be back. Look how you took to stone."

"I can't start all over again on stone now. After all the years I've put in on painting? But now, I don't want to paint. Color means something too personal. It's like a hot knife in the entrails to press out a tube of red or crayon-blue."

"What's there for you in sleeping Italy? The lazy Dago land, someone called it. It's here in Paris the world is being redesigned."

"You talk, Paul, as if I'm a whole man."

For dinner the doctor ordered *endives à la monégasque* with parmesan. "You're not an invalid. Stop drinking, and let me see your eyes. . . . No sign of recent drugging. Give up this playing with drugs, Modi, and you'll survive. Survival is all."

"And the lungs—can you patch them up like an india-rubber doll when they leak?"

"They need an easy life, plenty of sleep, no debilitating wildness. Yes, the lungs will last till you die. Don't laugh. What use can they be to you beyond that? After all, plumbing is only an extension of the human anatomy. Lungs are plumbing."

Deo went on laughing. It hurt to laugh. He didn't feel he had any right to laugh. "I'll tell that to all the doctors in Italy."

"Tell me about your brother, the Socialist."

"Oh, you'd like him, Paul. He's like you, only untalented. You both feel the world can be saved by a few slogans, breaking some greedy heads, and everybody settled down to making love, breeding children for a perfectly dull and orderly world. Give me the man-eating Congo jungles."

"You make it sound too grim." The doctor poured melted butter over the steaming dish and served Deo a huge portion. "Here, clap yourself around this. It builds tissue, repairs everything. And as for a Socialist world, don't imagine it has to be grim, colorless."

"It will be. And what of the artist? Nothing helps the artist but himself, Paul. The rogues eat the dupes—the dupes reproduce to fatten the rogues."

The doctor inspected a bottle of yellow wine and poured. "Francisco Ferrer was just shot in Barcelona. A great leader of the simple people. The world is ready to burst like a rotting ulcer—or am I spoiling your meal?"

"You seem almost to welcome the blood bath!"

"When they fear change, that's a sign we are close to our goal."

"And it could be war." Deo stopped chewing and wiped his buttery chin. "Think of all the unknown Michelangelos and Goyas who died young with a rusty spear in their liver."

"War! Don't be foolish, Modi. The Socialists in every country, the trade unions, all one big brotherhood would refuse to serve. Narrow nationalism is dying. They would force an international peace."

Paul Alexandre was close to tears. "Paul, you are as much dedicated to an ideal as any patch-pants artist. I think we're all fools, but it's good to know we can cross-fertilize our foolish dreams. Can you spare a Theocritus cigar?"

"I'll leave you one, but not now. You shouldn't smoke, or—"

"I can see your international world policing us all. No love-making in the daytime, no spitting on the sidewalk."

"You're so wrong. Ask your brother."

"If I can raise the fare home, I'll ask him."

"I'll sell some of your work."

"Don't buy any more yourself. Your heirs will think you were crazy."

They talked, of how to avoid complicity in the pathetic fallacy of others, of music as thawed architecture, and they decided to go see Pablo.

Guillaume Apollinaire in Pablo's studio was larger than life almost, blonder, talking away while Pablo's two fox terriers barked and some people sat and listened. Apollinaire went on talking about *L'Art des Noirs*, explaining Negro sculpture. Deo sat drinking, getting drunk, feeling it would be sad to leave all this, trying to get drunk quicker than his rising resentments.

The painter named Vlaminck, one of Matisse's Fauves, a former professional bicycle racer, snorted, "Its all nonsense. Like de Sade's loony world."

Apollinaire rose on tiptoes, filled himself full of air like a frog. "Put it down that this man, le Marquis de Sade, who seemed to count for nothing during the whole nineteenth century, he may well dominate the twentieth!"

Deo rolled his alcohol-filled head. "I salute de Sade."

There was laughter and Pablo handed Apollinaire a drink. "What can one expect from a man whose father was a Cardinal?"

The large man made a modest gesture with his short fat fingers. "Only a bishop, please."

Deo was getting drunker; he felt the rage in himself afire at leaving all this. He kicked out at a yelping fox terrier.

"Shut up, you sidewalk soiler!"

Someone said something about the vast canvas of spurry spikiness that dominated the studio. Apollinaire waved an arm at it: *"Les Demoiselles d'Avignon*—the philosophic brothel. Here enters modern art."

Pablo and other guests began to throw hard bread crusts at Apollinaire. A thin girl with heavy black bangs hanging over a white face and protruding teeth sat down by Deo's side. "You're handsome."

"I'm crazy. Everything is spinning."

"You're drunk."

"Naturally. All life aspires to that holy condition."

"You paint?"

He showed his blistered hands. She took hold of them. "You carve?"

"I pick my nose." He pushed her aside and tried to reach the rum bottles on a table. Deo was very drunk, yet his head seemed very clear. He swung his arms wildly, knocking down a heavy wooden Negro carving.

"The new gods! The barbarians are at the gates! We greet

them and say *your* magic is *our* magic now! Nigger, Indian, Eskimo, Gauguin's native sons, filers of teeth, shrinkers of heads!"

Dr. Alexandre tried to reach him. "Shut up, Modi—don't shout."

"And if I do, oh carbolic witch doctor, I'll cough up a lung? Will my hostess mind if I commit that final nasty act; my *only* circus act?"

"That's Modi," someone shouted. Deo began to pull at objects, statues, vases, carvings, and try to toss them at the window. Some hit the glass and fell back to the floor. Deo picked up a heavy box of paints and threw it through the glass. Arms tried to hold him. The fox terriers (thinking it was a game) began to leap high into the air and snap their teeth together. Deo had a large African ebony carving of some kind and he threw that past interlacing arms reaching for him. He wanted to destroy everything. He seized canvases, packs of drawings, and threw.

"Down with art! Down with everything that is this silly game we play! The world doesn't want us, need us! And when we're dead, the dealers will chew our bones."

He was pinned down, someone crying out as he kicked at them, others hysterical with laughter, some as drunk as Deo.

That night Deo had another hemorrhage from his lungs. And two weeks later Dr. Alexandre saw him off for Italy.

The two friends stood under the bird-soiled glass roof of the train shed, a steam engine breathing harshly nearby, people hurrying for their autumnal vacations, traveling men piling up their sample cases, children wandering out on platforms soiled by nut shells, old newspapers and cinders.

Deo was paler than ever, his head sunk down partway between his shoulders. His hair was in need of cutting. Dr. Alexandre explained where to change trains, meanwhile stuffing franc notes into Deo's jacket pocket, twisting the artist's badly knotted tie into place.

"*Adieu*, Amedeo."

"*Adieu*, Paul. You are my only friend."

"No, I may be the most foolish and the most worrisome, but Pablo, Constantin, Apollinaire, they all are friends."

"When I behave."

"When you behave. Don't play the stock artist from opera or bad novels, the dirty tramp of romantic fiction *à rebours*. You've got to avoid that. It's too easy for you with your looks."

The train caller was warning loudly that the train for Italy was about to depart. Deo shook the doctor's ungloved hand, accepted the package of sandwiches, and got onto the train and stood staring on the platform. The iron pillars and steel rafters and signal arms (like the new paintings by Pablo and Braque) were cutting off the slim shape of Paul Alexandre waving *au revoir*. Deo found a seat, balanced the package of sandwiches on his knees, and looked out at the slums running past the train, the wires and poles, the gathering speed of trees and patches of faded grass overgorged on sun. He counted the years, three of them, since he had come up out of Italy, and now he was going back, down to the boot.

> And still for him the Lioness stalks
> And hunts her lover through
> The lonely walks.

The train gave a shrill silly whistle. . . .

11

THE STREETS OF 1910 were noisy, filled with spasmodic motion. There were so many more motor cars in evidence.

Flinck the old clown moved along the Left Bank of the Seine. He limped badly and supported himself with a malacca cane. A trick circus mule had kicked him in Brazil, and he had spent six months tied to boards in a tropical hell while old bones knitted slowly. He was no longer the agile popular clown. He lived here in the sixth arrondissement, in one of the foul little hotels on the rue Buci, the rent twenty francs a month; enough for a second-rate clown. He stopped at the Café Rotonde, where the artist Courbet (whom he had known in his youth) once had a studio upstairs. All that time was over, and Courbet, large, coarse, vital— What a man! Beer-guzzling, girl-loving, he was sacred now (in death) on all those museum walls.

Flinck had one gin, a habit he had picked up from the English in the Far East, and limped back to his hotel. It was good to be in Paris. He had been too long in an alien element.

Near the entrance of his hotel a shabby figure rose from the shadow of a doorway to meet him. It was a lean dark young man, the handsome face a week behind in shaves. The clothes were worn and in places marked by contact with earth and peeling walls. Under one arm was a bundle tied in greasy gray paper. The hat was black and large, but had long since lost its original shape.

"How goes it, Flinck?"

The old clown peered up; his eyes were failing but professional pride kept him from wearing his glasses in public.

"Eh, eh, who?"

"Baba will *now* perform a double somersault! Backward! From a seated position! On the chair. Landing with a rose in her teeth!"

"Ah! Modi. Modi! No! Flinck is seeing things."

"It's me, all right."

"Heard you were back in Italy."

"I was. But I just got in, third-class, yesterday."

"Come up to the room."

"A rattling train. I thought my spinal cord would dig a hole in my brain."

They walked into the dismal hotel, past the usual unoccupied people who never seemed to do much more than read fragments of old newspapers, ream an ear with a sharp finger, or chew on matchsticks. Flinck's room had just space for a low bed, a chair, and a huge pink steamer trunk, battered and worn.

"Dear boy, it's good to see you again. Flinck has had his bad luck too. Lost Baba—the saints cherish her and feed her well.

Broke a leg, was swindled by managers from Bombay to Hong Kong . . . But enough. And you, Modi?"

Deo sat down on the bed looking at his short dusty jacket, the train grime still on his hands, the shoe leather worn and about to expose his toes to the sidewalks.

"I've been living in Livorno. The family is poorer, the people are the same, unaware their life is savorless, obvious."

"You painted?" The old clown went to a narrow shelf, took down some paper bags and pulled out two golden-scaled herrings. He sniffed them, rolled his wide eyes as though he were about to go mad with desire for herring—a familiar show-stopping gesture.

"You painted a lot?"

"No. I cut stone. I've become a sculptor. I've been up to the marble quarries at Carrara. Oh, how they cut it there, virgin blocks of it, like cheese."

"Cheese?" The clown opened a bag and took out some fragments of green cheese. From below the bed he brought up a bottle of wine. And, apparently from his sleeves, came two glasses. "Join Flinck for a little food. There is bread, too."

Deo was very hungry. He began to skin a herring with his fingers. "I cut a lot of stone. I worked like the very devil. Then something came over me. Nobody I knew understood what I was carving. I became drunk. I got a hand cart. I loaded on it all my statues, and ran it down to one of the canals; Livorno has more than its share of them. And *zoom*, I dumped them all in, among the dog turds and the dead cats. *Addio.*"

"Don't fear, Modi. In hundreds of years wars will stir up the canal bottoms, and wise fools, archaeologists, will bring up your statues, the way they salvage Greek and Roman stuff today. Flinck says so."

"I believe you." Deo sighed and let out his belt a notch. "Paul Alexandre is in Switzerland, a kind of Socialist International, or something. I didn't want to appear among the artists the way I look. I wanted to borrow from you, Flinck. Sagot wrote me you were here."

"What do you want to borrow? A top hat? A rubber nose? Baba's old harness? There was an artist. Baba, sick as she was of fever, dying on shipboard. She passed out to applause, doing her swaying waltz dance. You remember?"

"I remember."

"To confess, Modi, Flinck is not working just yet. Who wants a gimpy clown? But there are a group of Japanese tumblers, the Kaburakis, comic fellows, who need someone to announce their turns in French, German, Flemish—and then Flinck will have money again. Half is yours. All is yours. Finish the rest of the other herring."

Modi rubbed his scratchy chin; it sounded like sandpaper. "I pawned my razor. Lend me yours. Maybe Sagot has sold something of mine."

"Of course. The razor is honed so sharp it could cut off the head of a cannibal king."

Deo poured water from the room's pitcher into the basin. He took out a small brown bottle and put some drops of its contents into a glass and poured wine over it. "Laudanum. I feel my shakes coming on."

"That's bad, very bad stuff, Modi. The best juggler there ever was, a Greek, called himself Amenhotep, used to sniff the white powder, cocaine, up his nose. Got the habit in Egypt. He ended up swabbing out wog privies, he who used to get fifty pounds a night in the London music halls and make the Prince of Wales roar. Don't do it, Modi."

"You're right, Flinck. The razor, please."

Shaved, fairly well washed, hair combed, in Flinck's only good shirt, Deo felt vital and alert again. He promised the old clown he'd stay with him if nothing turned up, and he went to see Clovis Sagot in his little shop.

Paris hadn't changed much, but Deo didn't want it to. The sight of Paris streets, Paris faces, the smell and sight of it was better than any drug. He'd never leave it again if he could help it; they'd have to ship him home feet first (if they could raise the money). He felt intoxicated by the city's impulsive intimacy.

Clovis Sagot was a little older, but just as plump. He was being shown some pictures by a strange young man with a wild mop of hair, an elf's face. He was dressed in a Slavic style: a pinch-waisted green jacket and frayed pants so narrow they almost seemed like tights. His high shoes lacked several buttons.

Sagot looked up. "Ah, Modi! I dreamed of you the other night."

"Good dreams, I hope. Dreams of selling paintings."

"Not *that* good a dream. I did sell two small things. Hardly worth paying you."

"I'll take it anyway."

The strange young man was unwrapping more small canvases of Russian village scenes. Booted peasants dancing on steep rooftops, old rabbis floating through wintry skies like contented birds, a Hebrew burying ground, the wild ritual dance at a Jewish wedding with the fiddler's elbows working away.

Sagot pursed his lips. "Not bad at all. But to whom could I sell anything like that, eh, Modi?"

"It's very interesting. Irresistibly simple."

"He's a Jewboy, like you, Modi. Bagall, this is Modigliani."

"Marc *Cha*gall."

He bowed like a schoolboy and shook hands with Deo with a thin poetic hand. "Sagot was talking of you. I like what he has of your work."

"Like isn't enough, Chagall. He has to sell it."

"Mine he says he can't just yet." It didn't seem to upset the young Russian.

Sagot beat his fists together. "Leave the one of the girl in white with the black gloves."

"No, that I don't sell." Chagall's French was thick with an accent hard to follow. "That's Bella, my dear fiancée. I hope to marry her."

Deo grinned. "When you sell enough paintings to send for her? Dream on, *lantzman*."

Chagall broke out in a torrent of Yiddish. "*Oi*, it's good to talk to somebody who doesn't ask me: '*Schnorrer*, have you got a potato in the mouth?' Where I come from, Vitebsk, a village the devil should own, they don't understand me, and here they think I'm mad when I show my *schoirah*."

"Everybody is mad in Paris. True, Sagot? Where are you living?"

"Where I can't afford it, in the Impasse du Maine. I need a cheaper studio."

"We'll go find Brancuşi. He's from your part, nearby anyway. Rumania. He knows every rathole for rent."

"I'm *nebich*, low in funds."

"Sagot here is a Medici in disguise. He's our patron. Correct, my dear dealer?"

Sagot beat himself on his fat cheeks and then began to probe for his purse someplace deep in his loose trousers.

Chagall smiled: "Vitebsk, I am leaving you. Stay along with your stinking salty fish."

Deo had come back to Paris because for him Italy no longer held anything of value to his own progress. It was a bewilderment and desolation to him after the bite of Paris. Italy was an *opéra-bouffe* world ready to die of its own casual insignificance. Only Paris appeared ready for that imminent moment when the direction of vision was about to change.

Of his family he could only remember the graying hair on his mother, the sadly run-down house, the poverty of his parents, the erosion of all his relatives closer to the final dissolving. Deo had wanted to give up painting, stop cutting stone, but the drive, the ache to keep working, was too strong. In Livorno, driven by that egotistic tenacity, he had continued working on his statues and heads, until that final and irresistible outburst of despair drove him to the canals. Art was treacherous as a Cardinal. No amount of Trebbiano or chianti could drive out his despair.

There had been no solemn soothing nights in Italy. There had been a great many girls, resulting in small gratitudes and large hostilities. The surge and intensity was not as strong as it had been in Paris. The emotions were essentially shallow, yet he had to admit, pleasing; the only peace he knew was in a woman's arms, his head resting between her breasts.

He had begun to think of Paris again, and in time to work toward the return journey. And perhaps he could avoid the dependence on drugs that was growing on him. They were becoming necessary to him, and he wondered, was the mere dulling of pain the essential part of experience? Perhaps our major task is not to seek happiness, but for the artist to probe all the diverse levels of consciousness. Now he was back, penniless but for some coins from Sagot. It was enough.

With the young Russian Jew, Marc Chagall, Deo found some studios in the rue La Ruche in a strange building shaped like a beehive in a garden, run down and cat-infested, close to the reek of the Abattoirs de Vaugirard. At least rent was cheap near the mooing of doomed cattle, the sight of the beasts at noon driven to the slaughter pens. It was a part of the rich flavor of the street, Deo explained. "Theocritus describes noon as being the most dangerous of all hours."

"Modi, somebody should tell the cows."

The studios had been built by a sculptor named Boucher, "a respectable descendant of the eighteenth-century painter," as he called himself. A strange hivelike structure made from timbers and forms salvaged from the Paris Exposition of 1900. There were twenty-four studios in the crazy ark, a dozen on the ground floor for sculptors and those above for painters. Brancuși was also in residence there.

Deo took a studio next to Chagall's and they soon got to know their neighbors; among them the Frenchman Léger, a stern-looking dark-haired man obsessed by cylinders and cubes. Later there came Chaim Soutine, a strange little monstrosity with great flabby lips, uncut ink-black hair. He was always complaining of his stomach. "I can't eat a bit. It *hocks* here and here."

Soutine when he arrived admitted he was from some depressing poverty-stricken section in eastern Europe. In time he grew fond of painting decaying meat; dead chickens sometimes hung on a hook in the wall, perfect models. Deo could tell the progress Soutine was making on a chicken painting by the smells let loose in the hall. Then he and Chagall or Brancuși would raid the studio and fling the decaying hen out into the yard for the prowling cats.

"It's unbearable, Chaim, what you paint," Deo would explain when the little artist came looking for his subject matter.

"It was just turning so nicely green around the *kop.*"

"Paint flowers, paint fruit," Chagall advised.

"Who can afford it? *Ba mir,* I'm no Rothschild."

"Paint meat in winter, with the windows open."

"I catch a cold in my stomach, Modi. Let me tell you my *tzaris*."

"Get out, Chaim, I want to work. Some other time I'll listen to your troubles."

It was a good place to work. All the studios were active. Deo was cutting stone, and worrying over the costs. It wasn't easy to find stone, or steal it, and when one bought it, the hearts of the limestone merchants were solid rock, without pity for a poor unsalable sculptor.

There were poets around; a strange one-armed romantic liar, Blaise Cendrars, who said he had been everywhere, and the fat critic Apollinaire, with his cane, often with his strange girl friends. One, he claimed, was a runaway nun from Poissy.

Sitting in a café with the critic, Chagall and Brancuşi, Deo shook his head. "Everybody is coming to Paris and everybody is painting."

"And why not?" said the critic, bowing to someone he didn't know. "Here at least you're not a freak; everybody is crazy, everybody is painting. The sick smell of *Les Fleurs du Mal* in the salons of the Boulevard Haussmann is gone. We make our own stinks now."

"And everyone is always talking about art!"

Deo said he didn't care too much for shop talk. "Max Jacob and the painter Delaunay in the office of Canudo, editor of *Montjoie*, trying to outtalk Gleizes, La Fresnaye, Lhote or Moreau. And Gertrude and Leo Stein and their relatives talking all the time, and worst of all reciting their strange prose."

The critic picked his teeth. "Ah, first their liver patés and then talk."

Even Sagot was talking, Pablo was talking brilliantly, Matisse rubbing his beard and making an ironic remark.

The one who didn't talk much when he got to Paris was a fellow Italian, a strange chinless young fellow, Giorgio de Chirico. Deo found him painting away, green glowing Italian architecture done over as dreams. So many lonely enigmatic figures darting down long streets that went on to vanishing points blurred by train smoke, appearing like a stage devil behind blind staring walls.

Paris was certainly full of painters, Deo reported. "As full as an egg is of meat." In Italy, he told the café groups, there had been published the *Manifesto of Futurist Painting*. Deo wanted no part of it. He was working in stone, and he didn't want to belong to anyone, certainly not to a group.

"That's good," said Apollinaire. "Stick to the *tetons* and *fesses* of the female form."

But his sculpture didn't sell, and poverty was just as bad to bear as it had always been. Deo would turn away from the stone dust and paint a few figures for Sagot, or take a bundle of drawings and make the tour of the cafés, getting a franc here and there, on a good night selling three or four drawings. There wasn't much market for his work but he kept alive. He needed alcohol, now and then drugs, and always girls. The girls could be gotten without cost, but the rest required money— money for rent, money for food, money for paint and canvas; all these could be had for so little money, and yet even these small sums seemed out of reach most of the time. Physical catastrophe threatened.

There were formidable obstacles to getting free drinks; for cadging in the cafés, one had to be an expert to bring off a glow. Deo had seen the shambling figure of a young painter pointed out as a great drink finder. He had strange dreamy eyes, a face weak, unresolved. He was painting street scenes, under the orders of his mother, a former model turned painter, a formidable beauty, or had been. She had modeled for Degas, Lautrec, Renoir and others. Her son the alcoholic was called Maurice Utrillo; he could have been the son of any of the three famous artists. Suzanne Valadon, the mother, would answer with a sly smile when asked who his father was. "They were all such great artists I'd be happy to sign *any* of their works."

Maurice had the great knack of getting free drinks. On a sad coinless night when he had had no drink or hope of getting any, Modi saw the shaggy figure of Utrillo leaning against the yellow wall of a café near the Odéon Theatre.

"You are Maurice Utrillo?" he asked.

The answering voice was timid and vague, the accompanying smile feeble. "You're Modigliani."

"I can't deny it."

"You are the world's greatest painter," said Utrillo, nodding.

Deo wasn't going to be outwitted by easy gallantry of this sort. Adaptability is essential to life.

"No, you are the world's greatest painter, M. Utrillo."

"My friends call me Mau Mau."

"The men call me Modi, the girls Deo."

"Modi, the world's greatest artist—*don't* contradict me."

"I forbid you to say that, charming as it sounds."

"I'll punch your nose, Modi, if you don't accept my word for it, you're the greatest."

"The world's ———."

They fell against each other laughing at themselves and the situation. Deo began to strip off his worn jacket. "A brotherhood rite. We'll exchange jackets."

"Yours is better than mine."

"Yours, however, is better material, Mau Mau."

They exchanged jackets and Utrillo smiled and put a shaky finger to his lips. "Let's have a drink on it. Christen the rite."

"I'm out of money. *Madre mia,* how I want to drink with you."

"Me too. I know a bistro run by an ex-policeman. He gives me a little credit. César Gay."

"I don't like *flics.*"

"You'll enjoy this mug."

César Gay's little place was cheerful. There were several of Utrillo's street scenes hung over the bar. César looked them over.

"I don't know if I can refuse a friend of Maurice's a snort."

César had a wide square body, the head of a man who took no nonsense, and you could see, Deo felt right away, he had been a terror to criminals, and still could be for all his extra fat and the iron-gray hair.

"The *dilettanti* I hate, but artists, well."

César kept pouring drinks as he talked. It was obvious he liked Utrillo and felt an interest in art. "I paint just a little myself. Nothing you would want to sell to a museum, you understand. But when Maurice's mother wants to take a bit of a fling with a new character, she leaves Maurice here. You've had enough, boys."

"Just one more, to my friend Modi."

"Just one. We let Maurice have a room here and give him paints and canvas. So he works out his keep when he lives here."

"They lock me in—that's for a fact."

"For your own good. Well, that's the last." He put the bottle away. "Keep out of trouble, boys."

They left César Gay's weaving a little. They had talked a long time about art with the bistro owner.

"The world's greatest painter, my pal Modi," Utrillo announced to the empty street.

"No, you are, remember?"

"Don't tell me such things, I don't like being contradicted, Modi. I'll report you to my friend the commissioner of police."

"You accept my valuations, Mau Mau. It's you who are the greatest."

"Say that again, Modi, my dear pal, and I'll black your eye."

"The world's ———."

They fought in the dark street, panting and circling, the way English prize fighters do, but they did each other little damage beyond a cut lip for Deo and a big bruise and scraping down Utrillo's cheek. They exchanged jackets again, and went off, arm in arm, to a café where a woman named Rose gave them some drinks on an agreement Utrillo would paint a mural on the back wall some day soon.

Again they exchanged jackets; after that Deo had little recollection of events. They came awake at dawn in the doorway of a warehouse to find two *sergents de ville* looking down at them, thumbs under their wide black belts.

"Well, it's Mau Mau again. And *à la maison,* in the gutter."

"And he has a new playmate."

Deo wiped dried blood off his nose; it felt as if it were broken. He had skinned the knuckles of his right hand. Utrillo had an eye fully closed and his chin was scraped raw.

"All right. On your feet, and trot home. What's your name?"

"He's Modi. We have made a blood brotherhood of artists."

Deo found his pockets turned inside out. "I'm ashamed. To sleep all night in the street."

"You go around with Mau Mau and you'll call the street home. You're both drunk, but move on."

Utrillo staggered to his feet. He was a fearful sight, soiled, his mouth gaping open, his arms and hands shaking. "Sergeant, please, we've the shakes, and heads like balloons. Could you spare something for two artists to have a morning bracer?"

Deo was feeling his pants. "We've been robbed. My pencils are gone. Some notes I wrote, a letter of introduction, a pocket knife, a comb, a yellow handkerchief. My estate."

One of the officers spun a coin over at Utrillo. "Here, M. Rockefeller, your mother can pay me back. But get off the street as soon as you two have had your snort."

At a shabby little *boite* they gulped two drinks and Deo looked down at his jacket. "It's yours. We must have changed again."

They parted, weary, bleary-eyed, promising to see each other again. Deo went back to his studio and sat logy and sad in a chair, biting at his knuckles. It had been a cascading night. He knew he mustn't repeat it. He was an artist. He was named Beloved of God. He had much to offer. Cadging drinks, sleeping in the gutter with a simpleton; had he come finally to that?

12

DEO, FULL OF A DREAM of unresolved allusions, came awake with a sense of some impending doom, a doom that had as yet no form or coherence. He disengaged from sleep and sat on the edge of the bed, thinking: Time falls as easy as fruit from trees. He was hungry, even sober, this morning; he must make an effort to get some money to carry him for the next few days. Perhaps, he grinned to himself, Poverty *is* the Tenth Muse. He was aware of a knocking on his door, a sound breaking the saturated silence of the room. He reached for his socks and trousers.

The door opened and the round heavy figure of Apollinaire came rushing in. Gone was the calm poised fat man. In his place was a long lugubrious face, a cuff of wild yellow hair standing up on the solid skull, and a desolation that had spread over the entire body. He flung his arms at Deo as if they were spears.

"Modi! Modi! It's been stolen!"

"Has it?" Deo asked as he climbed into his threadbare trousers.

"The *Mona Lisa! La Gioconda!*"

Deo grinned and tightened his belt. "It's a dreadfully over-rated work of art. So faded and bleached out no one will miss it."

"The Louvre is screaming, the press is thundering. You would think a king had been assassinated, a Vestal Virgin been found far gone with child."

"I don't understand, Apollinaire. What's it to you? You always talk as if the arts of the past were soggy corpses that no pyre could ever burn. You need a drink. I'll join you, as *your* guest."

"I've had several big drinks." The critic fell into a chair and began to tug at his shirt's neckband with nervous fingers. "Listen to me before they carry me off in chains to the galleys."

"They only have Devil's Island now—no galleys. You stole it?"

"Listen to me. You know Gery Pieret. No? A tramp, a dealer of bad cards, a scamp with longer fingers than any pickpocket. He's a Belgian, I've met him, I've met everybody. He's my secretary in fact. Some years ago, let me admit it, he stole two Hispano-Roman statues, a couple of little stone things. Stole them from the Louvre."

"Shame on you, Apollinaire. Rape, lies, character assassination, blacking a girl's eye, sponging meals, I expect from you, but stealing from the Louvre!"

"Don't judge me." The fat man wiped his lips, his little mouth shaking. "This false messiah, Pieret—he fascinated me, his imaginary adventures. I didn't steal with him. But I got Pablo to buy the two statues, and he's innocent. He doesn't know where they came from."

"I've seen them in Pablo's studio. But what's this about the *Mona Lisa*?"

"Pieret just stole *that!* Walked in cool as a whore talking a country boy out of his pig-buying money. Took the picture off the wall, put it under his coat and *whiff*, he's gone, and the picture is gone."

Deo shook his head and waved his hands. "Mad, mad, utterly mad."

"The worst is, Pieret only a few months ago, he stole a little Greek bust from the Louvre, this swine, and it's still at my place."

"What is it doing there?"

"Pieret has been working for me, as I said—secretarial jobs. I employed him. If they trace him as the thief, and *then* to me, and find the bust, and find Pablo's statues . . . Poor innocent Pablo has two. Oh, oh, I have such an agony in my solar plexus. I am ready to pray to St. Spiridion of Holy Memory."

"You should hold nothing back when bargaining with God."

"What should I do? Be serious, Modi."

"Warn Pablo, pray later."

"Yes. Let's go."

Deo finished dressing, took the critic down to a café to have two quick brandies, having two himself; Apollinaire was like green putty—even parting with money to pay for the drinks was not difficult, and he was usually such a frugal man, having great difficulty in getting his hands out of his pockets when a bill was brought.

At Pablo's studio all was peaceful. Pablo was alone, drawing on large sheets of paper laid on the floor, driving off the dogs with a long-handled brush when they tried to join in the work. He listened to Apollinaire's story calmly, then began to shake his fingers in a Spanish gesture of reproach, to beat his palms together and then to slap his canvas work pants on the thighs.

"How could this be? How could *I* be the victim? Look, I don't hide them—*there* they are!

Deo examined the two weathered stone figures set out on a wardrobe among old beef bones, bits of tree bark, seashells, broken sections of metal, a bicycle handlebar that Pablo had collected for some vague reason.

"They are very rare?"

Apollinaire held up a stubby finger. "We'll throw them in the Seine. Repudiate any knowledge of them."

Deo frowned. "You'll be caught. You look too guilty already. Both of you. Besides, too many people have seen them here—they can't be destroyed."

"Will you do something for us, dear friend?" the critic asked.

"Let's be calm. Let's go to a café and think."

Pablo wrapped the statues in blankets and put them away in the bottom of the wardrobe. In the streets the newsboys were howling extras on the great art robbery. MONA LISA STOLEN! The *Mona Lisa* seemed to be a national art treasure. Vast rewards were being offered.

Seated at the café, Deo read from a newspaper still damp with printer's ink. "No questions will be asked if the thief will return the masterpiece. The police expect an arrest within twenty-four hours."

Pablo leaned back in his chair and thought. On the café terrace everyone was talking of the theft. Each talker had a pet theory about it.

"Suppose we turn Pieret in," Pablo said. "We'd be heroes. Correct?"

Deo countered, "How can you explain the two statues?"

"I was holding them as a lover of the past for the Republic."

An Englishwoman stared at them over a cup of tea.

Apollinaire belched in nervous digestion. "You've had them a few years, Pablo. It's dangerous. Oh, the incurable side of existence. Devil's Island, that's all, Devil's Island. No, I'll get into a tub of lukewarm water first, and cut my veins while my friends recite my verse. It's a Roman way to depart. Don't set up any monument to me. Just see to it my books remain in print." He flung himself about in the chair as if avoiding a blow from a sword and began to pant. "Art works, the multiplicity of all possibilities, are illusionary and evil objects."

Deo snapped his fingers. "The head, Apollinaire, you have at your place! We must hide it till we also get rid of it in the river. Yes, the river is the best way after all."

Apollinaire became courageous with fear. He hailed a hackney. "To the rue Gros, and don't spare the horses."

There was only one horse, and that one gimpy and hammer-hocked, and he took the three friends on a slow ride. At Apollinaire's book-filled, picture-packed residence, they looked in vain for the stone head.

"Pieret has stolen it! Once a thief, always one. But from me—his protector, his employer!"

"Good," said Pablo. "He can have it. Have him call for the two statues at my studio."

"You don't know Pieret. He's going to do something dramatic."

Deo suggested another period of thought in a café.

Two hours later the newspaper extras were out again. The Belgian Pieret, who seemed to bear some strange grudge against museums, had taken the statue from Apollinaire's place to the offices of the *Paris-Journal*. The editor had asked for the *Mona Lisa,* but he settled for the statue, and the details of how easy it is to loot museums; it made a fine story and he promised to protect Pieret.

The statue was exhibited in the window of the newspaper, and a thundering editorial, with a sensational article, asked why a great national museum could be repeatedly and effortlessly robbed. And would a curator please call for his statue.

Apollinaire began to expel wind; he sweated so much that Pablo and Deo took him to a Turkish bath, where they sat—Apollinaire almost below the sea level of consciousness—naked and steaming in the thick creamy atmosphere, wondering what to do next. The absurdity of it all amused Deo, particularly since he was getting drunk at the critic's cost.

Pablo said, "Modi, you're not involved except with us two criminals. Go see what's doing at my studio. If the *flics* have been there, tell the lady not to talk. Say I've gone to Spain."

"And," added Apollinaire, "spread around the news that I've taken sanctuary in the Vatican, with relatives at the Holy See. I can't be touched, tell them, it's a sacred right."

Deo left them in a cloud of steam, and found that the excitement over the stolen picture was spreading. The newspaper story, the recovery of one statue, was more than a victory for official art; every citizen (even those who had no idea what the *Mona Lisa* looked like, or had ever been in a museum) had national pride in his country's possession of something valuable enough to steal. It was encouraging, Deo thought, that art can occasionally become a popular obsession.

Deo an hour later came back to the steam bath. "There is only one thing to do."

"Name it!" said the critic in nervous susceptibility, already looking loose in his skin.

"You both take the two statues from Pablo's studio to the *Paris-Journal*. Ask them to continue their fine service in recovering more art for the nation."

Pablo added, "Anonymous, of course."

Apollinaire retched. "I'm too well known. Fame is a sticking plaster."

Deo rubbed his chin. "You two better sleep here in the baths tonight. Tomorrow you can return the statues."

Apollinaire began to rub his brows. "Undone! Undone! Unbelted. Detrousered. Ruin, *utter* complete ruin."

"You need something to eat," said Deo. "Give me some money, Apollinaire, I'll send something in."

The critic in comparative tranquillity surrendered his wallet from his trousers in a locker. It was so unnatural a gesture, Pablo's eyes grew even bigger.

Apollinaire sighed, his thumbs in violent trembling. "For me nothing. A mouthful would choke me. Just something to drink, to revive me to face specters."

"Of course," said Deo. "Keep pressure off your spleen. I'll bring the drinks."

"A mild apéritif. Ask the *sommelier*, nothing in the *vin ordinaire*, a good Chablis is like medicine—to wet my mouth. Perhaps I can swallow some anchovies in oil, a few *oursins*, stuffed hard-boiled eggs. Nothing too fancy, Modi."

"I'll keep it down to a few mouthfuls."

"Today the café has *caneton bigarade*, that duckling basted in orange juice, but I couldn't eat it. *What* am I thinking of?"

Pablo winked at Deo. "In your condition you're like a pregnant woman. Give way to your whims. Indulge your digestive system. It calms the nerves, cuts the wind."

"You'll pardon me—I didn't notice. Eggs Benedict never did

me any harm, some plum *confiture*, eh? I'm mad to be thinking of eating! I couldn't digest a thing."

Deo started for the door and Apollinaire whispered, "A *petite marmite* might just get down."

There was the hiss of steam, the slap of a towel.

The next day Apollinaire took the two statues to the newspaper office; Pablo and Deo waited outside. The critic was shaved, scented, powdered, softly embedded in a pressed English-cut suit, carrying his erotic cane, an eyeglass in place. He was breathing a little rapidly and Deo had to open the door for him. The critic's vast bulk disappeared inside and Pablo said, "If he never comes out we must give a dinner in his memory."

Deo, who hadn't been sober for two days, giggled and agreed.

The delivery of the two other stolen statues added fuel to the sensation of the missing *Mona Lisa*. Journalists were coming from overseas, and senile art-collecting American millionaires were awakened in the night and asked their opinions of the theft of da Vinci's masterwork.

The newspaper editor had promised to keep the secret of Apollinaire's involvement in *l'Affaire Mona Lisa*. As August turned to September, Pablo and Apollinaire felt safe enough. The critic ate again and smiled, and if sometimes his hand shook at the thought of the horrors of Devil's Island, he pushed it away.

One day Deo was on the rue Notre Dame des Champs overlooking the Luxembourg Gardens, hunting a little place where someone had told him there was a new dealer who bought modern paintings. He wasn't too clear as to place or address, for the information had been shared during a night of great drinking. He was walking along the curb enjoying the sight of small street things, the inexhaustibility of the fecund gutter; some silver paper from chocolates, the crushed shape of an onion run over and flattened, the sweeping of some hallway fluff of carpets, a tangle of human hair ends, bits of red and yellow posters, an empty cigarette tin shining like gold in the sunlight.

Deo felt someone brush against him. It was Brancuși, his hairy frog's mouth shaking and his hair in more disorder than ever.

"They've arrested Apollinaire!"

"They have?"

"The police searched his place on the rue Gros. He's being held as an accomplice in stealing the *Mona Lisa*."

"This is serious."

"Serious!" shouted Brancuși. "He's in the Santé Prison, in solitary confinement. And you know how frightened he is of rats and small spaces."

"And Pablo?"

Brancuși shrugged. "So far I think he's still a free man. I tell you it's like Siberia and the Cossack knouts on people's backs all over again."

"No, no, Constantin, there's justice in France, a kind of crazy justice, but justice nonetheless."

"But he's guilty!"

"Then he'll need a lawyer. But he's not guilty of the *Mona Lisa*. Or is he?"

"With him, who knows?"

Paris was outraged. The bohemian artists decided that it would be wise to lay low, stay out of the public's eye, until all this blew over. The examining magistrate was a Judge Drioux. When Brancuși in his studio heard this name, he groaned a great Rumanian groan. "*Him!* He's a true shark's-head judge—right out of Daumier. It's hopeless. It's Devil's Island."

Deo could not accept that. "We must rally to Apollinaire. Pablo is drifting around in the studios, not hiding but not flaunting himself in public. A petition for justice—*not* mercy—must be drawn up and presented to the judge. Some fancy prose, and a string of shiny tophats to sign it. Real fat bellies."

Dr. Alexandre, who was present, kept slapping his hands together. "Justice and petitions. Poor Apollinaire is doomed. You remember Anatole France: 'Justice is equal for all; it is just as much against the law for the rich as for the poor to sleep under bridges.' "

Deo, who feared the police and the law, still persisted in getting a petition drawn. So had others, and at last a very impressive document on the best crisp paper was drawn up. It was signed by imposing names, many of whom did not share Apollinaire's ideas but who acknowledged his importance as a critic and a poet. Still he remained in prison as if buried alive. No sound came from the bowels of the Santé.

Early in September, Deo heard that Gery Pieret was hiding in the underworld of Marseilles, and there was a rumor that he would clear the imprisoned critic in a letter to the judge. Pieret did write a letter to Judge Drioux, addressing it as if from Frankfort. He cleared his former patron, but the judge as examining magistrate still found it all an impossible muddle.

The Catholic Royalists attacked Apollinaire under the impression he was a Jew. "Imagine a Pole who isn't a Jew!" they shouted in the cafés. "And if Apollinaire has a secretary who steals from the Louvre, he's got his greasy paw in it somehow!"

Léon Daudet, a pious animal ready to light fires at the stake, issued a statement he had *not* voted for Apollinaire for the Prix Goncourt. The police, with strange irrelevancy, began to question the critic's concierge and the neighbors. A fat police officer, belching a mist of garlic and brandy, came to see Deo. He looked over the studio and Deo standing at his easel working on the head of a girl. The *flic* pulled out a notebook and bit the point of his lead pencil with cracked yellow teeth to get at the black core of it.

"Now, this is all in line of duty."

"There is nothing I know."

"This so-called M. Apollinaire. His habits. Did he entertain little girls? *À la dérobée?* Very little girls?"

"What age?"

The policeman made a limp gesture two feet off the floor. "Little *little* girls."

"Ridiculous."

"Ah, little boys? *À l'abri?*"

"Of course not."

"Was he *outré* in any special way?"

"He is like anyone else. I can see now why anyone would at once take flight from the French police, even if he were accused of stealing only the sounds from Notre Dame's bells."

"Just remember you're an Italian. We may toss you out of the country, M. Modigliani."

At his legal interrogation Apollinaire had two lacquered lawyers, sly and dexterous in the greasy court hearing. Théry and Fraysse were their names, impressive figures in their robes, with set features, a good match for the examining magistrate. Apollinaire told his story, hand on heart, explaining that Pablo Picasso had been innocent, been imposed upon, not knowing the antiques he had bought came from the Louvre. Pablo, called the next day, denied knowing anything at all about the affairs, even to having owned the two statues at one time. Apollinaire gave way to tears, groaned out loud, and looked, Pablo later told Deo, "Like a man fallen off an ocean liner and seeing the last of her departing smoke on the horizon."

The judge seemed to sense it as blatantly obvious that the whole mess was one of those foolish things that happen in the artists' section of Paris and he permitted Apollinaire to question Pablo, who briskly confessed he had once had the statues but when he found out they'd been stolen had them taken to the paper. "I have, your honor, an obstinate conscientiousness."

The petition was now brought forward in two pairs of legal hands, read through, and a final interrogation took place. The lawyers took turns explaining: These are children, your honor, they play their little games of painting and at being artists; they are hemmed in by their own unreality. If they are guilty of anything it is being naive, and being foolish. The lawyers cleared their throats and stepped back. France, they seemed to hint, had been saved again.

The judge appeared to agree. He too suggested that these artist people were embalmed in strange ways of living and amoral doings; skilled professional thieves they were not. But where was the *Mona Lisa?* Apollinaire was happy to answer the question. "I do not know, your honor. Nor have I ever entered into any scheme to remove it."

The judge cleared his throat, looked displeased at a clerk rattling papers, and said, "The prisoner may be provisionally discharged. A definite discharge may come later."

Apollinaire's photograph appeared in newspapers that had never mentioned him before.

That night the critic sat among his friends in a café, looking much thinner in his clothes, redder in the face, making the gesture as if his short stocky arm held an invisible sword. "I have survived a menaced consciousness. I have eaten prison slop, pissed in a pail, blown my nose with my fingers, had a stone for a pillow. Do you know what it is to be alone in a stinking cell?"

"No," said Deo. "Tell us."

"It is the end of the world all pushed up into a funnel, and all they can do is pour you out into eternity. And the food! A dog's dinner twice a day, water not fit to pour down a drain. And to think there are thousands of wretches whose choice is that way of life."

Pablo said, "You must have created a few poems?"

"On my wall, scratched into that gray-green paint, were texts of desperate hopeless men. On the ironwork of the bed was the inscription: 'Dédé de Menilmontant, for murder!'" The critic looked around to see their reaction. "I have slept on the boards that held a murderer! There were also some salty verses by someone who called himself Myries the singer. I wish I'd had paper and pen to copy them. The new writers will come from prisons. Perverts are the new masters."

Dr. Alexandre smiled. "It was good for you. You look better, carry less cargo."

"I feared madness. I wept like a child. I feared I would do myself in. So I wrote verse, in my mind:

> "Oh sinister predecessors
> Who lived in my dead shell . . ."

The critic closed his eyes and went on reciting to the end of a long set of verses:

> "Oh sainted Virgin, hear them,
> Hear my poor prayers."

Pablo approved as he drew the critic's head on the table in wine. "The stay in the Santé did you good. No one is absurd when he's in agony."

"Artistically, jail is for artists," Deo added. "Oscar Wilde, Cervantes, de Sade, Casanova were famous for their jail days."

"No, no. My career is done in, my name dishonored. There

are black wings over me, the kind poor Van Gogh felt brushing his face at the end there. And I've lost my appetite."

Apollinaire moved to the rue La Fontaine. Deo helped him carry over his things. "The rent, Modi, is cheaper and my girl Marie says I need new walls. The old place had no luck. Genius is nothing, talent is dross—without luck. We're giving a party in the new place and Max is reading our hands; he is an expert in chiromancy."

"I'm sure he is. The infinitesimal proportions of a thumb can ruin empires, he claims. I've yet to find out anything Max doesn't know, except the *addition* for a round of drinks."

"You and me, Modi, we stand a chance of being expelled from France as foreigners, don't forget it."

"So a policeman told me."

"I would die anyplace else—it's all nothing out there. We should change our living places a lot, Modi. You might grow a mustache, or dress as a rabbinical student with long earlocks, pass as a *tzaddik*—learn Polish from someone. They are attacking me as a dirty translator of Aretino and de Sade. We must find out how to become naturalized."

"It's too much trouble, Apollinaire."

"Ah, Modi, I ask only for the head of a fish, two olives for food, and for obscurity and peace."

Deo laughed and shifted the two old chairs he was carrying. "On your terms, as long as you remain notorious and can talk loudly in public places."

"True. I am a vessel of vanity. Fecund, weak, vain."

The party that night in Apollinaire's new place went rather lame. Max Jacob, full of drugs and wine, took Deo's hand and looked at the palm. "You will die."

"The information doesn't surprise me, Max. If you had said I'd never die, maybe I would say thank you."

Marie, Apollinaire's girl, stuck out her hand. "Tell me, tell me anything."

"You will be unhappy in love, you will leave France, you will come back, you've burned your fingers cooking."

Apollinaire pushed out his hand. "Come, Max, no more jests.

"Oh, you will never enter the Academy, yours is a short life and fame only after your death."

Apollinaire became angry. "Your damn jokes are *not* amusing! I said you were a great clairvoyant, and you've failed."

Deo, watching the gleam in the eyeglass and the cold eye behind it, saw that Max was very serious and troubled by what he had seen in the critic's hand.

The *Mona Lisa* was not recovered for some years.

13

FOR ALMOST A YEAR Deo threw himself into his stonecarvings. He made a group of kneeling women done in limestone, caryatids based on pencil drawings and on some paintings he had sold to Paul Alexandre. His work was far from the rules of the École des Beaux Arts. Brancuşi in glee would dance like a clumsy bear around a statue Deo was carving.

"Enough, enough, no final finish. Let the original borders of the stone show, the rough iron marks for the hair. Ah!"

"It's good?"

"It's very good. But don't expect acceptance. Good art is never left unmolested."

Deo put down the mallet and chisel and wiped his face with the sleeve of his shirt. "Yes—who wants it? I don't ask much, just room, love, air, bread, wine. And what have I got?"

"A rotten mood. How's your liver?"

"Poverty, that's what I've got. My shoes are falling apart, my lungs burn. The truth is I can't go on carving much longer. The dust is bad for what's inside me."

"It's the girls and the drinking, Modi, not the dust. I'm not against it, everything is fine till you're sated. But you go beyond reason."

"Reason!" Deo got up and began to cut away at a long thin stone nose. He coughed and tossed down the mallet and the chisel.

"I need a drink. And I'm not sated. When was I drunk last?"

"I don't mark it down."

"So let's wet a spot."

"This early in the morning?"

Deo looked in reproach at the sculptor, who threw up his hands and laughed. "I'll get the bottle. I don't want it on my record that I saved anyone from disaster."

Deo carved less and less, and began to paint again. The finished and unfinished heads and statues stood weathering in the yard. Carving was too strenuous an effort, stone cost money, and the dust did make his lungs burn. He lived in dread of a red flood pouring from his throat.

Apollinaire and Paul Alexandre found Deo sitting in the mottled sunlight of the yard, his stone heads staring at him with the classical indifference he had given them. He had been out getting drunk with Utrillo the night before, and ended up in a brass bed with a Greek woman, in blue cotton stockings, whose hairiness was amazing. She had a girdle of pelt going completely around her hips. It had been like romancing an ape from the zoo.

Deo looked up, shading his usual morning headache from the direct sun.

Apollinaire with the eyes of a mesmerist, wearing a bowler hat—*un chapeau bizarre,* the doctor called it—walked on tiptoes among the statues. "You've worked hard, Modi. Yes."

"No more. I'm painting again."

Paul Alexandre nodded. "Good. I think between us we can get three of your paintings into the Salon des Indépendants."

Deo's face brightened and he screwed up his eyes to hold back his headache. "You don't just say that to get me out of my mood?"

"Of course not. We'll show your beggar woman. The cellist."

Apollinaire held up a stubby hand. "And that fine ragbag creature from Livorno. Your beggar period, Modi, will be something to pop the public's eyes right out on stems. And tonight we are treating you to a dinner and a great musical premiére. Cheer up, there's enough blue in the sky to make a Dutchman's trousers. A fine day."

"I'll take the food. The music I can leave to you two."

Paul Alexandre smiled. "It's going to be a riot. A true one. Street barricades and broken noses. This new Russian thing—called The Firebird. First performance—a ballet."

Apollinaire waved his arms. "It will break the pedants' teeth just to hear a few notes. Oh, they'll be carrying bodies through the streets tonight. The students are rallying, the stiffs with the top hats are bringing in bully boys. I tell you, it will set the gargoyles of Notre Dame to dancing."

"You're very kind to me, both of you," Deo said dryly. "To treat me to a riot."

The doctor patted his neat beard into place. "It's not for nothing. You're to begin a new portrait of me."

"You've got one."

"A good one," said Apollinaire, sitting down and wiping his vast chins with a silk handkerchief smelling of civet and musk. "But it's a picture any talented man could have done. And there is a great deal too much of Cézanne in it. Now do one that is all Modi."

"I'll try. But I can't go out tonight to a theater. I haven't any clothes, or a good enough shirt."

"At night," said the doctor, "who looks closely? And I'll give you a shirt."

"Lend," said Deo. "Poverty is a disease I have, and it's not helped by a little charity. It should be wiped out. And don't look at me with that Socialist's leer, Paul. And thanks for the shirt."

A sense of fantasy colored the night as they drove to the Stravinsky première. Deo had never heard of him, but the dinner had been fine, his skin was full of wine, the clean shirt had a starched front that made Deo proud, almost stern. The three men were smoking good cigars. The police saluted along the Promenade in the Bois de Boulogne, the Champs Elysées.

"The Russians can't paint," Deo said. "Music, yes, by the mile. Not a yard of real painterly feeling."

"But great novels," said Apollinaire. "That Gogol, that Dostoevsky. Tolstoy is too normal for me. He brushes his teeth every day. But Chekhov, there is a man who takes life in his hand and says, 'Brother, the laugh is bitter; it's not an easy world and the boots leak, and the bread is stale and full of bedbugs—but tickle each other anyway and laugh.'"

"But no painters," repeated Deo. "Rotting ikons, canvases with acres of Cossacks cutting off the *Grande Armée* in the retreat from Moscow, but no painters."

Paul Alexandre flicked ash off his cigar and tilted his opera hat to one side. "You're right, music is what they do best. In St. Petersburg I remember the concerts—voluminous skirts, Venusbergs of red velvet, the yellow lights of the *mis-en-scène,* the sound of violins—and such sturgeon!"

Apollinaire leaned back in the cab. "Some of the Russian tea merchants are collecting Picasso and Matisse. That's good taste. If you can't paint it, collect it. Correct, Deo?"

"I wish I weren't going to hear music. I'd rather see Coquelin at the Comédie Française."

The place of the ballet was well lit, the crowd was very fashionable in the best seats, and very loud in the cheaper seats. The students looked ready for a lark, and the police were standing by, their heavy riot capes draped over one shoulder, their clubs hanging from their belts. They were mostly Corsicans, and had a mean scowl and disliked students. They would be cruelly efficient if any trouble started.

Paul Alexandre had reserved good seats, and Apollinaire bowed to a great many shiny fat shirt fronts and family jewels.

"It's so good to greet a ten-carat diamond and a paunch that has been well stoked all its life."

Deo looked around at the pink and white faces, the tiers of music lovers. He felt well fed and wined; he was cosy from a good meal after so many skipped ones. He had recovered his *amour-propre.* He must find one of these society ladies for himself.

The music brought Deo to attention and Paul Alexandre pointed out the composer, who looked like an anteater with glasses. "Just like the drawing Pablo made of him," Apollinaire said.

The music was certainly strange, but Deo wondered why anyone would dislike it. The music stirred Deo, it gave him new images and patterns; he was sitting eyes closed, ignoring the dancers, bathing in this wild new sound, when the booing began. Programs began to fly through the air. Apollinaire stood up and cheered: "Bravo! Bravo! Make their hair rise!"

The boos grew louder. More objects flew through the air, not just programs, but hats and canes, even some shoes. The dancers began to stagger, to avoid being hit. Apollinaire was battling some bigot with long yellow mustaches. His collar was torn loose, and hanging behind him like a white bird.

"*Á bas!*" shouted the bigot.

"First art! Music for the new age and down with the old!"

Paul Alexandre folded his program. "Deo, you are seeing a historic event. Look at the Tartuffes scream."

"Does history have to be so violent?" he asked, ducking part of a collection of fruit rinds.

"If people object to burying the overripe past—yes."

The police came to restore order, but the crowd was too far involved in emotions. Personal fights were breaking out. It was a wonderful evening, Deo felt as they left the milling crowds, the parading students, the charging police. The slogans, some stale, some obscene, were still being shouted behind them. Most were mottos for the right of the artist to do his own work in his way. A rancid old woman at the curb was displaying Royalist literature attacking the Freemasons.

Back at the studio Deo examined a rent in his jacket sleeve and the dents in his new starched shirt front. "I'm a bit torn."

Apollinaire, his pointed shoes off, was reclining on the bed reciting to himself his impressions of the première. "Of course Stravinsky is right, just as Pablo is right, and Deo. But the fat cats a generation from now will ask how people could be so blind to Stravinsky's genius. It's easy to have a sore arse after it's been beaten for a long time. But the shock of recognition isn't given to many mortals. Of course I have it, was born with it—it came tucked in my navel. Let's go out and get some girls. A couple of dark wenches with cocoa butter on their skins. I tell you, without cocoa butter you don't know what loving can be. . . ."

Deo had picked up a sheet of paper and was drawing Paul Alexandre, who was examining a stone head.

"If I'm going to paint you again, Paul, I want that pensive

expression as if you've just discovered a new radical cure for headaches, say by cutting off the head."

"Pensive? I'm just thinking of the music."

From the bed came Apollinaire's voice. "Tonight they throw *pots-de-chambre* at artists—tomorrow they open the best wine, the good gray Volga River caviar. I've been turned down for French citizenship again, but I'll show them. When the war comes, I'll volunteer. Hero Apollinaire at the service of France. The medals, Croix de Guerre with Palms, the ribbon of the Legion of Honor, and a citizen of France . . ."

"There isn't going to be any war," said the doctor. "The people will not mobilize. The workers will not be French or German or Italian or English. They will unite into an international band of brothers."

"Yes," said Deo. "Cats will dance with dogs and the Queen of Sheba will offer herself to Sitting Bull."

Deo went on drawing. On the bed the prominent pugnacious critic soon began to snore.

Paul Alexandre watched Deo draw. "All prophets are Jeremiahs; there's no cheering for those who say human life is sacred, is worth living. Grace and style should discipline all living. It's the irascible neurotics who tell us only what's wrong. We know what's wrong. I want somebody in a delirium of joy to say what's right. Or will be right soon. Yes, things are not yet right."

Deo looked down at the drawing of the long head, the outline of the coated torso, the hands folded in front, clasped together, with the edge of white shirt cuff showing. Deo put down the paper and threw the pencil into a corner of the room.

"I'll do it better on the canvas."

"It's a good drawing, Deo. It's personal. It's Modigliani making a Modigliani drawing. Like it or not, tonight Stravinsky heard Stravinsky music, no one else's. Thousands have talent, anyone can train himself to be a fine painter, a good composer, but only a handful, a few, have anything new to say. . . . Where will you sleep? We won't get this lard-filled Mephistopheles on his feet again tonight."

"Chagall has a large padded chair. It's comfortable."

"You'll go on with my portrait?"

"If you give me a few sittings."

"I'll send you something for your cough."

"It will get better. Paul, I'm giving up stonecarving . . . it's the dust. Good night."

"Good night."

From the bed came a whistling sound, then a sudden stillness as the great bulk turned on its side, like a whale rolling. The floor was littered with his cane, top hat, shirt front and narrow cloth-topped shoes.

When Deo had brought in the big padded chair, panting— his wind was not good and his arms too thin—he set it up near the window, sat down and leaned back, his legs on the grocer box where he usually kept his palette. He fell asleep quickly, dreamed he was writing a great poem. *Morte villana di pietà nemica . . . Cruel death, pity's foe . . . ancient mother of grief, merciless judgment without appeal . . . .* And he knew it wasn't his poem but Dante's, and he came awake to hear the critic on his bed still snoring. Deo, mouth open, fell back into sleep quickly, like dropping into a well.

His three paintings at the Salon des Indépendants did not "take Paris by storm," but at least he was one of the new artists showing alongside his equally despised peers. If Deo drank too much during the following months and took hashish from time to time, and wandered with Utrillo at night into unsavory places, at least he worked. And he did have friends who admired him.

Months passed in the same dreamy manner, and in 1911 he was shocked back into the actual world when Italy annexed Tripolitania, and later de Chirico, the other young Italian painter, was accepted as one who had something to say. Now there were two crazy Italians painting, Apollinaire said.

There were many young men with earnest faces, sad mouths, and hunger, all painting away, or chopping stone, baking clay. Apollinaire was working on a book, *Les Peintres Cubistes*, and shouting that Picasso and Braque were redesigning the world.

Upstairs Soutine had a stinking bit of beef hanging on his

wall, and refused to throw it away; he wasn't done painting it.

"*Momsers,* let me work!"

These were the years everyone was later to call golden, even if in 1912 there was actually war far off in the Balkans. But the knowing ones reassured Deo it would never become a general European war. Brancuşi became expert. "The Balkans are always at war—it's the reeking goat cheese they eat."

When the gossip writers, the journalists, spoke of *les peintres maudits*—painters under a curse—they meant those who had the violent tempers, the trouble seekers, the hunters after exotic pleasures which were ruining them physically, and mentally. No one cared to write of their dreadful poverty. Modigliani was the most notorious of these, for his dissipations were extreme, his debilitating habits well known. Pascin, another member, gave the wildest parties, collected oddly assorted couples, but he was at least making money in stylish magazines from time to time, and poverty didn't gnaw at him—only possessed by deep, mind-searing depressions. Utrillo, a miserable enough figure, had a mother to seek him out now and then; Suzanne Valadon had bouts of maternal instinct when she would clean Utrillo or send him away for a cure behind one of the secret walls where the mad and the alcoholic were often mended and ironed into shape for a little while.

It was Deo and Soutine who suffered the most wretched physical discomfort of actual want, of cold, hunger, loneliness, fears in the night.

Chaim Soutine was sunk in pessimism, truculence, painting in strange El Greco colors the sterile table life of two gutted herring, bent-pronged forks, an empty bowl. He also did the faces of the starved children who worked in dives, washed up in cafés, assisted in sinister hotels. With his flop ears, his balloon lips, his dark greasy hair, Soutine was not an appealing sight. Memory of Similovitch, the Russian town he had come from, still made him shake in fear of its aberrations and meanness.

Sitting in Deo's studio, Soutine, unable to buy even a dead chicken to hang on a wall, talked on, a badly made cigarette in his fingers.

"You should see my village, Modi. It's twelve muddy miles from Minsk, in Lithuanian Russia. Filth, eleven children, and my father, a rotten tailor with a *killa*—hernia—you could hang your hat on."

"Chaim, I'm expecting a girl. Go away," said Deo.

"A girl? You talk as if that's all that matters, a *shiksa's tocus*. When I was sixteen I asked the town rabbi, Reb Hokenboken, could I paint his picture. I felt it was a *mitzva*—a good deed. His son called it an insult, and beat me to a pulp. I lay in bed a week burning up, bleeding all over. They cupped me with *bonkas*. My mother screamed and tore her cheeks in the street until the rabbi paid twenty-five rubles damages to her son. With that miserable loot I went to Minsk to study art."

"You're in Paris now. Get yourself a fat girl, smelling like your chickens, and enjoy yourself. Get drunk. Fill your windy belly. Good night."

"I can't eat or drink anything, and I haven't the cash for a *nafka*. They laugh at me."

"The best kind, Chaim, the laughers. Who wants a sour face to make love? I'm throwing you out. This lady doesn't want to be seen, you understand, very chic society, there's a husband—a banker. Jockey Club . . ."

Soutine hunched his shoulders, burped, beating his chest with an unwashed hand. "I'll go talk to Chagall, or Kisling. Among Jews I feel at ease to show my misery. Do you think I look like a Kalmuk, or a Tartar? People think I'm something from Siberia."

Deo pushed the little painter to the door. "You look dandy, Chaim. Set back your shoulders, don't be so suspicious of things, or timid. I'll get you a fat girl, don't worry. *Zaftig*."

"I'd rather have a chicken to paint. I'll do something desperate—don't think I won't."

When Soutine had gone shambling down the hall to find some other painter to brood with, Deo looked around the studio. It was as neat as it ever would be. The third painting he was doing of Paul Alexandre was facing the wall. Good. Paul Alexandre didn't approve of Deo's sensual side or his excursions among society ladies.

14

DEO WAS EXPECTING NO *vendeuse d'amour* at his studio but
a lady. There had been ladies before, of course, but this one
had flair, a grace. He had managed to provide a bottle of wine
and a half pint of apple brandy, and he didn't have to spend
anything in the cafés, which was good since he didn't have any
money. Married women were the safest, but still lacking in his
life was the great love, the woman of whom the poet said,
"Her image, that was with me always, was an exultation of
Love to subdue me." No, tonight was not for always and certainly no subduing exultation. It was a casual bit of paper
blown along the curb, as easy as the flow of water from a public fountain. Damn all poets for liars about love; dreamers of
fuzzy visions of impossible women . . .

There was a discreet knock on the door. Deo opened it and a
finely made woman in dark furs, with a veil across the top of
her face, entered. The stylish hat on her tilted head ended in a
plume of gold and bronze pheasant feathers, her skirt was fash-
ionably narrow, her silken satin undergarments made a rus-
tling sound. She walked with grace and calm. The lady smelled
of money, of private baths and good perfume. She looked
around her. "Ah, Deo, so this is where you hide. *À la sourdine.*"

"This, Paula, is where I live. I don't hide." Anticipation
began to demand accomplishment.

She lifted off her hat and veil. Her eyes were large and violet, flecked with gold; her hair was neatly coiled in pale fox-
colored braids over a high forehead. The coat slipped to the
floor. She came to him with shy assurance and they kissed.
"I'm not fearful any more, *mon cher,*" she said. "I'm not the
captive of my social position any more. I'm here; you didn't
think I'd come, did you?" You weren't really expecting any
bravery from me, were you?"

"I knew you'd come, and even sound like the dialogue in a
D'Annunzio novel."

"Don't be cruel, Deo. I've never been unfaithful to Jean before, and tonight there was the child sleeping so innocent, so pure when I left. We are so innocent, so *aimable* at four."

Deo fondled her magnificent pale shoulders, smelled the clean scented skin. He smiled at her and opened her braid-trimmed jacket, and she smiled back.

"I don't know why I'm here. I must be crazy to dare this."

"You know why you're here, Paula. To take your clothes off, to lie down in the bed, to commit adultery."

"Don't be crude, Deo. You look so handsome, you're the most beautiful man I've ever seen. I don't want you to think I let strange men talk to me in a museum. In fact I don't go to the Louvre very often."

"You went in to use the watercloset. You have wonderful skin, Paula. It's rich woman's skin. I like it, spoiled with luxury. I'm going to bite it, if you don't mind."

"Not where it will show, darling Deo. I have to go to the opera Wenesday. Oh! You *bad* boy!"

"Take off everything but the stockings."

Later—stockings off—she was drunk and very wild in the studio. They made love with the earnest endeavor of two people meeting in healthy passion, fully understanding what it was, and what was lacking. Later in the night her conscience began to sigh noisily, however, and Deo got out of bed and gave her the last of the apple brandy.

"Don't cover yourself."

Paula was magnificent in her fully matured nakedness: at least thirty-five, she glowed with a lifetime of care and good feeding. It had kept her skin healthy and her vitality eager, and up to tonight, she said unfulfilled. She was more precocious when slightly drunk and still shaking from unexpected climaxes. She kissed him again and kept moving his head back to look down at him in exultation.

"You're a beautiful object, Deo. I never knew this was why all my friends have lovers. Oh I fought it—fought it. Jean comes back tomorrow night from London, or we could meet again. But Wednesday I'll go visit my old governess, poor dear, she's crippled and I take her some old things with plenty of wear in them yet. It's a long journey and I'll reserve a room at the Ritz."

"What's the matter with here, Paula?"

"All right, I'll have the room at the Ritz but I'll come here. I just want you to have all of me you want. I want to do splendid things for you, Deo."

"You can't do anything for me, *monna mia*, but what you've been doing."

"Was I good?"

"You have natural talent, but don't be afraid to scream and cry out."

"Oh *Maître*, I'll buy a painting of yours."

"You don't have to, Paula. You most likely have dreadful taste in art."

"We own a Whistler, and hunting etchings. I think they're etchings. Deo, am I very sinful?"

"You like to think you are. But no, you're just a schoolgirl who never went much beyond dirty talk."

"Do you love me very much, Deo? I do inspire love, don't I? I wouldn't want it to be—*just* bodies."

"You're wonderful in bed, you have a magnificent body. You make me very ardent."

"No, Deo, that's so sordid. I mean, it's more than that—our destinies picked the Louvre for our meeting."

"To make peepee?"

"It's more than just a casual thing to me, Deo. To betray my husband, my little girl—the whole Delaroche family. What can I say at confession to Father Marlot?"

"Lie to Father Marlot—then go confess all to a strange priest, that you lied. *Dio mio*, I respect your religion, Paula. It's so understanding, so human."

"Deo, say you love me. That this is something strong and lasting. I'd do anything you want. Order me."

Deo was kissing her slim pale neck and her shoulders, cupping her breasts near bursting with tension, blood and muscle.

He said softly to her armpit: "All right, steal your husband's bank account, rape his safe, collect the family jewels, and we'll run away to India, China, San Francisco, the Flea Market."

"Oh don't joke, Deo! Deo! Deo!"

They were wildly entangled in a rising renewal of ardor
when there was a loud knocking on the door of the studio, ex-
actly, Deo thought, as in a vulgar stage play. Paula jerked her
head up, showing her teeth in a ghastly parody of fear, as if the
victim of a hallucination that refused to remain a bad dream.

"We're discovered!"

Deo bit into her shoulder and shook his head. "No, it must be
some drunk I know."

"Modi, Modi," a voice came through the door above the violent knocking.

"It's Jean! It's the detectives. Oh I've been a fool! The Delaroches will take my child, ruin me."

"Keep quiet. It's my neighbor Brancuși."

But Paula wasn't listening. She leaped wildly onto her fine
naked legs, jumped from the bed and grabbed a tattered drape
from the wall. She stood wild-eyed, drooling, unaware of the
thin line of spittle that fell from her kiss-bruised mouth. "To be
caught like this, and with a filthy little Jew!"

Deo did not even spare her a look of contempt as he went to
the door and opened it. Brancuși, his long nightshirt badly
stuffed into his pants, stood there barefooted.

"Modi, something terrible has happened. *Pardon,* madam,
this is unavoidable." He bowed indifferently to the hysterical
woman, her hair in wild disorder. "It's Chaim. He's tried to kill
himself, Modi. I can't get him to open his eyes."

Deo grabbed his trousers and shirt and began to dress, dancing on one leg. "How did it happen?"

"Chaim was talking strangely all night, drifting around the
studios. Then an hour ago I heard a chair fall over with a crash
in his room. It's over my studio. I think, he's not drunk—what's
he doing this late at night—then I think, the little fool . . ."

With Paula weeping hysterically, trying to unwind her tangled stockings, trying to put her shaking legs into them, Deo
ran out of the studio and up the creaking stairs. Brancuși followed, his braces dragging behind him.

"There he was, hanging from the light fixture, a bit of torn
towel around his neck!"

Soutine's studio with its absurd and shabby furnishings was

in confusion, the table overturned, a fragment of toweling still tied to the ceiling gas fixture. Soutine lay on a soiled cot, his neck bruised to a turkey red, his face white, his large carplike lips purple. His laboring chest was rising and falling in an effort to catch his breath. Deo bent down and slapped at Soutine's cheeks.

"Get me some cognac or whiskey."

"I've got some. Keep him alive, Modi."

Deo began to rub his friend's thin bony chest. He could feel the straining heart, hear the whistling intake of agonized breath. When Brancuşi was back with the cognac, they poured some of it down the gasping man's throat. He choked, but he came fully alive, struggling and gasping, and lay at last after a spasm, his face wet, coughing, looking up at them. Deo took Soutine's shaking hand in his.

"Chaim, you're a shmuck."

"A . . . little . . . bit . . . I bungled it, no? I can't even hang myself."

Brancuşi took a sip from the bottle. "Don't say that. You almost made it. If I hadn't wondered who throws furniture so wildly in the middle of the night . . ."

"I needed . . . better tools. I didn't have a rope. . . . You'd think now a bit of rope would be easy to find." He began to cough again.

It was half an hour before Soutine was calm enough to feel ashamed: "It was being lonely, it was hunger. It was the dark. It's always dark inside, but at night . . . here. . . . *Nu*, don't worry, I'm a *narr*, a fool, and you're good to me. . . . I've got friends."

"Chaim," said Deo, "You sleep. We'll talk tomorrow. Next time you want to talk, I promise I'll listen—like a *yenta*. Not throw you out."

The little figure on the cot lifted its sweating head, long dark hair in its eyes. "Deo, she came, the real lady?"

Brancuşi said, "In a red motor car with two footmen." He finished tucking his nightshirt into his pants.

"Deo, you go back to your entertaining. I'll bring up my mattress and sleep here."

"Listen," said Soutine, "I don't need a *minyen*—I'll be all right alone. I don't want to die any more, not tonight. And my neck will be stiff by morning, I'm sure."

Brancuşi nodded and tried to open the window. It was safely nailed shut. He went down to get his mattress.

Soutine kept wetting his lips. "Death tastes sour, Modi. Like poisoned sardines when you open a can that's all bumpy and bent."

"If people knew that, Chaim, nobody would die. Sleep."

Deo got back to his studio wondering about the final plunge of the spirit and the desperate courage that sends a person toward suicide.

Paula was gone. Only her smell, the scent of the furs, her underwear, her skin, the odor of their lovemaking remained in the studio; she herself had fled. Deo saw a bit of paper on the table. It was part of a pink announcement of some society musical. On it was written in shaking convent-trained handwriting, in pencil, the words, "Forgive. 2 o'clock Wednesday the Carthusian Church Boulevard Raspail *à coeur ouvert.* P."

Deo hardly bothered to do more than glance at it. He tore the note to bits and threw them into the cold little stove. The suicide attempt had shaken him badly. And yet why? What did it matter, now or later, in the senseless surge of time—time, that ultimate illusion. Time that one could not ever really touch, or feel, or take hold of. Reality was flesh. And flesh, spontaneous, unintrospective, was Paula.

Deo lay down and inhaled her residue in his mind and his room. He turned and twisted and could not sleep, thinking of her patrician insolence. Somehow, in some perverse manner, the shock of the death wish of the little man upstairs, the closeness of the thing made him—incongruous emotions—passionate and sticky with desire. He was nearly ashamed of it, but he never turned away from his private visions.

In the studios on the *rive gauche* and the *rive droite* attempted suicides, and successful ones, were common among the students and artists. As were domestic battles, fearful accidents on ancient stairs, Latin knivings. Sometimes even murder, with a trembling drunk or a drugged figure led off in handcuffs to face at some future date the "widow maker," the big knife set up at dawn in the prison yard.

*

Soutine, suffering from *la folie de la persecution,* continued to see the dark side of life, but his paintings grew in grim power. It was a time among the new artists for a merging of a vital focus on the problems of their art. Cubism, everyone in the know said, was shaking the foundations of the official Salon and the Academy.

"But they up there are entrenched," Apollinaire said. "They feel nothing. And yet one day they will tumble and take over everything of ours as their own."

Deo continued with his women, his drinking, escaping into drugs when he felt the burden of the world too much on his shoulders. But he was also entering a productive period where his art was real; as Paul Alexandre had said, "Modigliani is painting Modigliani."

Yet he sold almost nothing; poverty nipped at his heels with an unromantic snarl. Hunger, cold, lack of materials continued to be a daily problem. Only some strange unfathomably deep impulse kept him painting.

There was, as always, much talk in cafés. Talk over wine, talk over food, over the bare tables. At L'Ami Émile, Le Lapin Agile, but mostly now in Montparnasse, at La Rotonde and La Closerie des Lilas. Pablo was no longer Pablo; just Picasso, the young hero of revolution, who with Braque and Matisse led all the rest. Names on pictures were beginning to mean something. One heard of Derain and Léger, Gleizes and Kisling. Collectors listened to Pascin and his ironic talk. Utrillo was beginning to exhibit more often; his early white period, with its plaster and cigarette ash and palette cleanings mixed into his pigments for a texturing of old walls. *L'Art Nouveau* was old hat, and every week in some *café-billiard* someone invented a new school of art, a new splinter group to follow some will-o'-the-wisp variation, usually based on something Picasso had casually put down.

Apollinaire published at last *Les Peintres Cubistes,* and he became the Christopher Columbus of the new art. He had Deo take him to meet another Italian artist and got himself painted by de Chirico. He objected later, in Deo's studio, because the artist had put a hole in his portrait head.

"I tell you, Modi, it's a bullet hole," he protested. "Right through my brain de Chirico painted it."

"Is the painting any good?" Deo asked as he reclined on a sofa smoking a short snip of tobacco.

"Of course it's a good painting. Do I pose for bad ones?"

"So what does it matter if there is a hole in your head?"

"You don't understand. Someplace far back I have Gypsy blood. Suppose it's prophecy? That I'm going to get a bullet in the head?"

"See it as art, part of the composition. All prophecies are false prophecies or the world would go mad. Can you lend me twenty francs?"

"Modi, everything I have is yours—my erotic prints, my mustache wax, all but Marie. You understand I can't share her. She's small enough as it is. A morsel, but delectable. I tremble like a jellyfish when I'm with her."

"You're giving up all your other girls?" Deo tossed the smoldering fragment of tobacco into a tin pot.

"I'm not that wasteful, Modi. But my true love is also a delightful artist. One of us. Not one of those *blanchisseuses* or *grisettes*."

"Of course not. You're a man of taste."

They were strange lovers, the big blond critic and Marie Laurencin, a birdlike young girl who painted wispy pink and blue girls in pale colors. Marie and Rousseau were his new discoveries. At the Lycée Lamartine they had told Marie: "You would be better off learning to play the mandolin." But Apollinaire had met her at Clovis Sagot's little shop and fallen in love. He began to drag her around to meet Picasso and the other artists. Deo found Marie rather dull and foolish. He would listen to her prattle on at Picasso's studio and wonder how Apollinaire could speak seriously of her work: "It dances like Salome, between that of Picasso, the new John the Baptist, who cleanses the arts in a baptism of light, and that of Rousseau, the Herod of the sentiment, magnificent and puerile old man that love led to the edge of intellectualism." At least, Apollinaire delivered these lines as though he intended them seriously.

Picasso winked. "What company I'm with."

Marie lived with her mother, and she drank at times and made a bad drunk. At least there Deo could feel companionship with her.

The love affair did not go smoothly. Apollinaire, when Marie drank too much at the wrong time, would blacken her eye, and she would often hunt up Deo and Chagall and sit at a café table with them and lament her lot.

"I like writers better than painters. *Ventre-St.-Gris!* You know I read a lot, but that doesn't give Apollinaire the right to knock me about. And I bruise so easily."

"At least," said the gentle Chagall, "you inspire his poems."

"They are rather good, aren't they, Modi?"

"A little lush for me. I like the absurdities and the obscure parts best."

"A man doesn't really understand a woman, no matter how intimate," Marie said. "Take me, I love luxury, riding in the last of the fiacres. I'm proud of being born in Paris. I don't like long speeches, and Apollinaire, he gets out of bed in the middle of the night to practice some of his lines."

"Naked?" asked Chagall.

"In a long nightshirt. I don't want reproach, or advice from anyone, and I dislike compliments."

Deo, who was expecting to meet Paula, said, "We're not giving you any."

"I eat quickly, I walk quickly, I live quickly; life is a sea of breathing jade."

"Do you do anything slowly?" Deo asked, rising from his café chair as Paula appeared down the street.

"I paint slowly, very slowly. *Au revoir.*"

Deo wanted to say, "Paint slower," but he hurried off to greet Paula, hoping Chagall had enough to pay for their drinks.

She was veiled, dressed in a smartly cut dark-green silk suit, wearing a turban and some white egret feathers. She carried a rolled mulberry-colored umbrella like a cane, and leaned back on her slim heels to avoid Deo's hug on the street.

"Really, Deo, you can be more restrained in your public greetings."

He pinched her arm and hee-hawed like a mule. "Why should I? Your banker friends and the Delaroches don't stroll this way often."

"Jean is in St. Petersburg. He's working out some contract for Russian army supplies. I asked him to keep an eye open for an old Byzantine ikon."

"You're a stylish piece of tail." He licked his lips in a mocking sassy way.

"Really, I don't like that talk. I'm not a piece. I'm a lady."

"And I'm a filthy little Jew, and you *are* a stylish piece. Would you like a drink?"

"You drink too much, *mon cher.*"

"I don't drink enough. I can't afford it all the time. Come, we'll have a few brandies. Do you have any money?"

"That's what I like about you, Deo." She laughed and twirled her umbrella. "You're pure and primitive. No false manners about you."

"I am *le maître au cochon.*"

"*Mon Dieu,* no. I'd even buy a painting from you, but where could I put it? We've just done the place over in Louis Cat. Besides, Jean would wonder why I'd buy something *so . . . so . . .*"

"So mad? You could tell him art is an ornamental appendage to fashionable obscurity."

"Let's buy a bottle, Deo, and take it to your studio."

Deo slapped her on the silken rump, the tight stylish slim buttocks. "You don't want to be seen with me, Paula? You don't care for my work, and you will only drink with me in private? I don't know why I keep you around, Paula."

She wet her lips under the veil and her voice in an assertive confidence grew low and husky. "We both have our reasons."

They spent an amorous afternoon, and the brandy sank deep in the bottle. Paula was no longer apprehensive about discovery. She had become wanton in gesture and act, and was always striving for new intimate experience in the flesh, hunting, Deo thought, with the flared nostrils of sixteen generations of stag hunters for wilder jumps and faster gallops on the field of soiled linen.

When Paula left at four, Deo sat finishing off the brandy and looking at a painting on his easel. Paula was getting too confident. Perhaps he ought to begin to blacken her eye, the way Apollinaire did Marie's. But one doesn't black the eye of a Delaroche.

15

FOR ALL HIS EXCESSES, Deo was painting all the time and at full speed; neither drink nor drugs nor even women slowed him from his attacks on canvas. There were periods of addiction and remorse when he did not work, but when he recovered from some huge bout with alcohol or hashish, he was able to approach his canvas purely, devote himself to his forms and ideas. Often all his nonpainting possessions were at the Mont de Piété, the municipal pawnshop.

His work was even, and usually simplified to one figure, often of a woman, recalling the tradition of portraits by the Italian masters. The lines were clear, they said what they had to say. The work was organized to a rhythm, light laced with sinuous curves. The human body to Deo's eye was always in repose. He disliked action in art. The distortion was for poetic reasons. The neck was longer than life, the pupils of the eye usually filled the entire socket. He exquisitely elongated, making the head a bit too small for the torso. The almond-shaped eyes gleamed like jewels of blue or green. His people projected a dreamy, almost logy, melancholy, a languid glow as if sated and brooding after lovemaking. Strangely enough, even Apollinaire, who had the best eyes for his time, could not understand how anything so simple could also be sensual.

Seated at the Dôme he expanded on Deo's painting.

"It's your damn taste, Modi. You couldn't be vulgar if you tried, not in paint. No, not just taste—after all, taste is as common as whale shit."

"Painters paint, critics unbutton their lips."

"It's all in your rhythm, and you know how to hint at arabesque. And your painting of flesh. It's a secret formula, Modi."

"No, it isn't. For a bottle of wine I'll teach it to you. You can become a starving genius."

"Painting I'm saving for my old age, when I can no longer think."

"You take orange from the tube, mixed with a little vermilion, two or three yellows, edge it with a line of black or bistre, and *violà*, you have flesh."

"Other artists get mustard when they mix colors that way. Not even Dijon mustard, but some foul German mustard good only for knockwurst."

Standing at the café bar Deo smiled. "Apollinaire, you have to think a color while you mix it." He turned to the barman. "Raymond, my absinthe special."

Raymond said to Apollinaire, "You watch this. M. Modi and some society lady invented it."

The barman put a cognac glass on the bar and dripped in two drops of absinthe. Then he filled the glass with cognac. Deo picked it up, grinned and drank it in three gulps. He held out his hands, palms up, to Raymond. The barman dripped two drops of absinthe into each hand. Deo rubbed them together briskly, then cupped them over his nose and inhaled deeply, slowly, with great satisfaction.

Apollinaire whistled. "Roman, pure Roman of the late decadent period. Say between Nero and one of the pansy emperors."

Deo stopped inhaling and looked at his friend. "It took a little thought, but it's well worth it."

"You should be proud of it. Raymond, I'll have an absinthe-cognac Modigliani. *Moribus antiquis res stat Romana virisque*."

They each had two more, and some American art students from California joined them in trying the new drink. It became popular, and for a week or so threatened to set a new fashion. Then Max Jacob was inspired to create eau-de-cologne-and-ether parties on the Place Denfert Rochereau, and Deo went back to painting nudes, determined not to let the life he led away from the studio affect his work, pledged to bind his work into the stream of painting. He tried to explain it to Soutine.

"The past, Chaim, dies, yet is continuous—the best bony

parts survive, the soft stuff sloughs off. The problem of the artist is to be part of that stream, to be bone, not soft tissue."

"I think, Modi, artists should paint, not talk. Talk is for critics. And did you ever see a statue talk to a critic?"

Deo never fully explained his methods: How he liked to
scumble his canvas with an almost dry brush, his grays and
greens and yellow-whites, until he was sure of his color scheme;
how he often left parts of the canvas in an unfinished state
particularly when he was drinking heavily. His painted hands
looked awkwardly done, but they were expertly integrated
parts of the composition and took on a grace of their own.
Building up his color, grays followed by green, with hints of
bistre and black, Deo got an inner radiance. He remembered
Dante's advice, "as pale color as though of love."

Paul Alexandre, when he came to the studio to see work in
progress, shrugged aside critical opinion. "You have to admit it,
Modi, you remain an Italian painter who lives in Paris. You
work under the influence of the Sienese primitives even if your
forms are refined from primitive art, and even from cubism."

"Thank you, Paul. I have your third portrait about done."

It had turned out well. The doctor was examining the painting of himself standing against a window, one hand held over
his heart. "Perhaps to show your belief in humanity," Deo suggested. "Some Utopia to be achieved by a political system,
hand on heart."

The doctor liked it. "It's no longer me, Modi. It's the individual brought down to your patterns. But it's also me made individual by your reflections of our friendship."

"Damn if I know what you intellectuals are talking about
most of the time," Deo said.

"You're irritable. Have you been eating enough?"

"Alcohol is a food, isn't it? The potent Provençal *fine?*"

"Not a perfect food. I'll pay for the painting. Go out and
stoke up on beefsteak, English-style, lots of blood, very rare."

"I can't stand the sight of blood. It reminds me . . . never
mind what it reminds me of."

Blood reminded him of his illness, and that he was pushing
himself too hard, that he was painting at the top of his form

only by borrowing irreplaceable vitality from his meager and rapidly depleting energies. Staggering with Utrillo, his special drinking chum, from some *bar Americain*, Deo knew he was too harried and weak to think of grand compositions, of new kinds of exploratory painting. He had his original style now, and he was irretrievably tied to it.

"I must drive ahead and do a body of work before my sensibility fails."

He understood the façade on the human individuality when he painted people. He had his method; the straight line, the almost too casual pose, but it often came out true. If it was Tuscan too, as some said, full of ovals and broadly flowing curves, then so it was Tuscan, Negro, old master—all the jabber of critics smelling of ripe brie and Armagnac.

In his women Deo was painting their character, but also at times he wondered if, like the poet Leopardi, he was not hunting in the crowd of faces *per la donna che non si trova*—for the woman one never meets.

One Italian visitor looking at Deo's work, had kissed his own finger tips, then flung them upward. "Form simplified to the ghost of a caress."

"What did you expect—female Apaches?"

If 1914 was to be a climactic year—and the experts full of Calvados at Gillottes said so—for Europe and for the world, for Deo it was to produce a new champion and some warm friends. Leopold Zborowski was a young lean Polish poet in desperate exile in Paris. He had been a vocal member of the Groupe du 41e Degré, that had been formed first in the Academy in Tiflis and had spread as its members went abroad carrying their extreme constructionist poetry with them.

It was Moise Kisling from Krakow in Poland, another of the young Jewish painters, who took Deo down to meet Zborowski. Kisling was mad for the *brio* and vigor of beautiful young women, usually with red hair, a taste he shared with Deo. But he painted in a tight decorative manner, the smoothest of the École de Paris style, and while he wasn't selling too well yet, it was apparent to dealers he would soon. Kisling was a cheerful change from the grim and deeper Soutine, who had promised his friends: "I'll let you all know well in advance if I contemplate suicide again. If you can't tell friends, who can you tell, eh?"

Kisling, full of joviality and exuberance, looked over Deo's studio. "I tell you this Pole may be a poet, but he's also an earnest dedicated art dealer."

"All that Poles want, Moise, is to get their liberty and make pogroms on Jews. I don't want to meet him."

"Come down to Zbo's shop on rue Joseph Bara. I live there myself."

Deo had been drinking and was short of hashish. His handsome face was beginning to show signs of dissolution; he had stopped shaving and he had grown an unkempt beard, which was, Apollinaire said, "In the style of a sensual Christ painted by an artist who had lost the faith."

Deo allowed himself to be taken to the little shop on the rue Joseph Bara in the hope of getting money for some hashish—it was the only thing to stop his night shakes.

Kisling said, "I live over the shop and Zbo and his wife Anna live under me; not a sound ever out of them, like doves. Never a blow."

"Why the devil should I show this Polack my paintings? He doesn't even beat his wife properly. Here, you carry them."

"You mustn't treat him like a pimp from a cheap hotel on the rue Vavin. He's sensitive too."

The little shop was between the Boulevard Montparnasse and the Luxembourg. In the window, the only window, was a painting of some cuts of beef by Soutine and a pale redhaired girl by Kisling. In the doorway stood the poet-dealer.

Zborowski's face was pale-blond and pink, bearded with a kind of restless fuzz not fully hair. His blue eyes had the agony of a man who wanted to be liked and to have his dreams accepted in a world he suspected of a deficient understanding.

"Ah," he said, taking Deo's hand in his loose fingers. "I've wanted to see you here for a long time. I wanted to go to your studio, and then I felt, no, he would think I'm like other dealers."

"You mean you don't sell anything?"

"I sell a little. I take pictures around. I want some of your stone figures to place on the balcony up there. I'm sure I can sell them."

"The wind and rain will help age them properly," Kisling said.

"Can I see what you've brought? Oh, this is my wife, Anna. This is Modigliani, you've heard of him."

She was a striking woman, Deo thought, with her ink-black hair pulled back into a bun on her neck, the long perfect nose, the all-too-wise-seeming mouth. A suggestion of fidelity and nobility, able to mother the man-child Zborowski, the poet-dreamer.

"I'd like to paint your portrait," Deo said.

"Good. I'll make tea. With lemon. I baked cheese *pierogi.*"

Deo needed a drink, but he sat down inside the room behind the shop. The poet-dealer examined the two paintings Deo had brought. A sketch of a Mexican artist and of an Englishman named Haviland—done almost in Seurat's pointillism.

"Yes. That's Diego Rivera. You've caught him fat as a summer piggie. He says his breasts give milk—he must be lying, but such things can be."

"It's not finished. I don't feel so well today. I just grabbed what was handy."

"The Englishman, too, is good. But I'd like to come to your studio to see some more finished work."

The polished brass samovar in the back room began to hiss. Kisling set out the tea cups and said there was also a *torte generala.*

Zbo smiled at Deo. "I haven't even asked if you'd like me to sell your work."

"I don't mind. Clovis Sagot tries, you try. Who knows, I may be rich some day yet. So much art, so few buyers."

The tea was hot, the cake too sweet for him, and Deo sipped, feeling these were fine naive people. He balanced the saucer on a paint-stained knee and took up a bit more of the cake.

"Tell me about your poetry, Zbo. I write some too, but it's not my meat. You look like a good human being, not a translation."

"We follow Kurhenik. He invented *zaoumian*—pure spirit poetry. The new age, the new feeling. I am a disciple."

His wife handed Deo a fresh cup of tea. "But what does Zbo write about? Nostalgia, his native land, the birch trees in the snow, the grasshopper dying in the stomach of the singing nightingale."

"Now I try and sell a few pictures," said Zbo, placing Deo's paintings on a chair where he could look at them. "I support Soutine—I mean I give him a little money. I even fight my way into the stinking cell he lives in. The other day I found a pile of his paintings. He had nailed shut the window, you know, 'to keep from damaging the paintings,' he said. *What* a smell!"

"He just likes dirt," Deo said. He was shaking; he needed some hashish or his head would burst. Zbo lit a Maryland cigarette and went on with his story.

"Chaim was starving. I went out to get some food, and the crazy man, he set fire to his paintings when I was out. I had to knock him down to save a few—I mean really knock him down."

Kisling sipped his tea with dainty grace. He had the catlike quality of being at ease or making his ease anyplace. "Chaim, he's one of the old kind who in the villages beat their breasts and ask God to send them Job's boils and sufferings. Soutine paints meat now, such meat to turn the stomach of a Turk."

Zbo nodded his head. "When he's hungry, he says, he paints meat best."

Deo wiped his perspiring face, closed his protruding eyes. *I need it, need it, need it.* He said, "Take a look sometime at Chaim Soutine's terrible jaws. He buys meat, then he fasts, looking at it for two days."

"What a fanatic," said Anna.

Deo agreed. "When he starts to paint, it's with a cannibal's appetite. He puts the terror of the deed into it. On the plain table. The knife and fork he paints he doesn't even own. He tears his food apart to bits with his teeth. He drinks from the bottle. After two weeks' painting he's done as well as Rembrandt, but the meat is unfit to eat."

Anna said, "We have two rooms. Zbo, there are so many paintings now we hardly have room to live."

She can't refuse me a loan. She knows I am sick.

Deo stood up trembling. "Come and get some pictures. Can you advance me ten francs?"

Zbo sighed, beat his thin bony thigh, pursed his lips. "We should, to seal not only the bargain, but the friendship."

The wife became stern, looked closely at Deo, shrugged and went behind the curtain. When she came out, she handed Deo some coins and kissed him on the cheek.

"And shave off the beard."

"I may." He smiled, all charm again under his tautness. He clutched the coins. "We shall all be friends."

He left, damply gripping his coins. Hashish for his shakes wasn't hard to get in Paris, *if* one had the money. The police shrugged their shoulders. The rich Greeks controlled the drug traffic, and they were politically powerful—they paid for protection. Mostly hashish was handled for them by Algerians. Deo struggled to reach the cellar off the rue de Rennes where the Arabs gathered to eat with their fingers—*couscous* and mutton from heaped brass trays—and sip the forbidden date brandy. There was the stink of lakmi palm drink in the place. Deo went in past the bead curtain to a back room where a fat man in a fez was writing a letter, chewing into the end of his pen.

"Ah, Modi, we have not seen you of late. Where have you been buying?"

"Boul, I'd buy from Satan if he had the stuff. I haven't had the money." Deo let the coins roll from his fingers. "What's this good for?"

The Arab pushed the coins to one side. "Not for much. A little hashish. The heroin and cocaine that the society women use is too high for you right now. Opium is for Max Jacob, for senators, race-stable owners, the demimonde, the actors, that poet Jean Cocteau. He's white as alabaster from the smoke, but he'll outlast the healthy ones."

"Boul, shove a towel in your mouth. Get me the hemp."

From somewhere there appeared a fold of brown paper and in it a few gray pills.

"Allah give you pleasure."

"For cash, Boul."

Deo took the paper fold and went back to his studio. He lay shaking on his bed, chewing the hashish. The patina of pleasure it formed soothed him; his shaking vanished, and he floated off the bed. He had reached a peak—the final step to complete despair; he was fully addicted. Exposition and analysis were futile. Only a woman could save him. He must find one who would pull him into some kind of honest, close and warm friendship, a dependency that would still the urge he had for alcohol and drugs. Then—perhaps—he could give them up.

Never again to Mama, to rest against her body, her warmth, her milky breasts, to tug at her nipples . . . to surrender.

He was rolling over and over in outer space, he was looking for a pinpoint of light to which to move; Allah's, Abraham's, Christ's, Buddha's, Mumbo-Jumbo's. He was like the insects battering at a street lamp to be let into their destiny—a smudge of smoke and singed wings. Deo swung off; and he was orbiting faster, amid outbursts of brilliant color; then his body fell away from all tensions, and his limbs went lax. His chest was calmed and his breathing turned slow and easy. He would wake to lassitude.

The Zborowskis became Deo's family. There was warmth there, and firm friendship. He didn't mind the mild talk about his bad habits. He was at ease in the back room watching Anna sew, or cook *Karp po Polsku,* or he'd just sit and talk about poets and Paris and pots. He painted Anna again and again. He painted Zbo, poor tired worn-down Zbo. He wasn't a dealer, he was a peddler. He carried bundles of paintings the way the fezzed Algerians carried their rugs. Zbo invaded the haunts of collectors, of the rich, of the fashionable. He hung around hotels where visitors registered. Zbo shadowed industrialists, smugglers, actors, anyone who should own a Modigliani, a Soutine, a Kisling, a statue by Zadkine, a nude by Pascin, a little whimsy of lovers by Chagall with heads on upside down, kissing as they floated in the wine-colored sky.

Modigliani became Zbo's favorite. But this young unknown Italian didn't sell, he told Anna. It was a shame.

Zbo with a crucified expression came home at evening, tired, dusty, the bundles of paper-wrapped paintings still under his weary arms.

"Nothing today again . . ."

Deo, having coffee and croissants with Anna, grinned. "We didn't expect any sale."

Zbo patted his wife's arm and she felt his forehead to see if he had fever. "Did you eat anything?"

"I may have. I was waiting for Monteuz, the big steel industrialist. I know if he sees Modi's statues, he'll buy them. He's rich as a pig in the turnip patch, and with all the war talk . . ."

"The statues are getting rained on, windswept and aging neatly on the balcony. I'd dislike to see them moved to a rich clean place."

"Don't mock, Modi. He'll buy them, someday." Deo saw Zbo was nearly in tears. He put an arm around the Pole's thin back. "We'll go and have dinner at the Chez Rosalie. I've promised Utrillo to help him paint the walls there someday soon. I think I can get credit for our meal."

"Anna," Zbo asked in panic, "are we that low in funds?"

His wife nodded her head and showed an empty hand. "And there's nothing in the little china jar."

Deo picked up some sheets of paper. "I insist. Dinner as my guests. *Bistecca,* salami, *cacciucco.* I'll draw the guests, and if they don't buy, Rosalie will put the drawings on the walls till they sell. Madame, your furs, jewels and the red shoes."

Deo loved the Zborowskis, and if there was hope for him, perhaps it would bloom here. If not, one day at a time, one crisis at a time, would seem less of a problem with their help.

Chez Rosalie on the rue Campagne-Première was a modest restaurant. Rosalie was large and wary, with intense luminous eyes, and she greeted Deo and the Zborowskis with a stern grin. She had bills to meet too.

"No more drawing, Modi. I've a cellar full of yours, and of others. Even the rats are getting tired of nibbling on them, believe me."

"We'll have the soup, an Italian meat course, fish in season, the little pancakes, the red wine." He patted her firm arm and pinched the skin of the elbow as if asking for an amorous answer.

"Artists!" said Rosalie, as Deo put his face near hers and fluttered his lips at her cheek in a kissing sound: "Don't try to talk me into being a bigger fool than I am."

Deo kissed her warmly on a corner of her firm mouth. "*Grazie!*"

At the table Deo looked into the thin red wine. "She's not making it up about the rats. I once saw a rat in the kitchen back there with a bit of one of my drawings in his mouth. But don't fear, Anna, the kitchen has been repainted and a tin floor put down."

Zbo peered into his soup. "Someday they'll hunt these cellars for your drawings, and all they'll find is rat litter."

Deo nodded. "Utrillo says they'll cut out the walls he's painted for the café owners some day. Rich Americans will come, he says, with their own saws, and they will offer thousands of dollars and get right down to cutting out the walls in their Yankee drive. Of course he's drunk when he dreams this—but it's a good dream."

Deo began to draw the patrons, and when Utrillo himself came in, hands in pockets, staring around, Deo drew him too.

"Well, Mau Mau, how's the street painting?"

"Oh, the paintings are very good, but I haven't caught the attention of buyers yet."

Zbo said, "Sit down, Maurice."

"Well—I'm not hungry, but—"

"Have a drink," said Deo. "Rosalie, another bottle of this army horse brine."

"You don't pay and you insult it. *Carissimo,* this is the last bottle for you."

"*Chi lo sa?*"

Utrillo rubbed his hands together and accepted the filled glass and they all toasted each other. Zbo said, "It's only a little time to wait. Paris will be full of buyers. And they'll buy only the new artists."

Deo said, "I have been reading some Czech writer. He says: 'The messiah will appear only when he is no longer needed; he will arrive the day after his arrival; he will not come on the last of the days but on the day after the last.' And where will he come? To the Zborowski Contemporary Galleries, of course."

"No, no, the messiah must come to all the dealers," said Zbo. "I'm not greedy."

"You're not greedy," said Utrillo. "I like that in a man. When I was locked up in that place for my own good—behind walls, you know—I came awake one morning and the inmates had found my color box and they were pressing the colors out of the paint tubes. Red, yellow and brown, and crying out, 'Ah, strawberry, and orange and chocolate!' It was fearful to watch them gulping the stuff down. I thought I'd go even loonier than I was. Then I thought, why be greedy, Maurice, I said to myself—to them it is strawberries, oranges and chocolates."

"Didn't they get sick?" asked Anna.

"That's the only time they pay attention to you in those places—when you're sick. They all had their stomachs pumped. They threw up all over the doctor's office. It was a painting, a big mixed omelette of a painting. Oh, pardon me, you're eating."

Deo refilled the glass. "Just have another glass, Mau Mau, before you go. As a favor to me."

"I will, if you press me this way. Oh, Modi, let me have that drawing of the girl you just made. From the couple in the corner. He's holding her hand. At this stage he still gets her things. I know a customer when I see one."

Deo laughed. "And they say you're a simpleton, Mau Mau. Yet how well you blend impulse with sensitivity."

"Oh, I am simple. That way you see things other people miss."

Zbo rubbed his nose in an absent-minded gesture with the back of a spoon. "You know, this Maurice, he's a great painter, don't ask me why."

Deo smiled at Anna. "Mau Mau proves a great artist doesn't need brains. Just a hand, an eye, a nervous system, and a fool's idea people may care for what he's doing."

Utrillo was back, offering Deo some coins. "He loves the drawing, Modi. And she wants you now to do one of him. They're from Lyon. He's a bookkeeper. They're on their wedding trip—been married two days."

Deo blew a kiss at the bride, nodded to the bridegroom, and

began to draw. "Tell Rosalie the rats will have to chew the old drawings tonight. I'm paying for the dinner. A commission . . ."

It was Zadkine, the Russian sculptor, who first mentioned La Belle Anglaise to Deo. Saturday morning the artists from Eastern Europe and their friends would gather in Brancuși's studio; it was the most roomy, and there they would talk of the horrors of their past, yet with nostalgia for the gefilte fish of their mothers, of the high holidays wearing their *tallis* and ritual fringes.

Soutine sat in a corner complaining of what the pickled sour tomatoes and stuffed derma had done to his digestion; a frayed cigarette hung on his swollen lips. Chagall talked of village weddings and bar-mitzvas and the Friday-night candles and *cholla*, white as marble. Pascin didn't come often, but if he did, he would gossip of worldly things; rich bankers and junk dealers in Prague and Vienna and Berlin, and their daughters fat as roasting geese, ready for the wedding canopy. And Kisling remembered wedding feasts and the old grandmothers, in a circle, dancing. Deo was amazed at their nostalgia for their dismal villages and their fearful childhoods.

They all claimed to dislike their past, and yet they salvaged bits of it. Deo himself no longer mentioned the family connections to Spinoza, nor proved "historically" that Moses was an Egyptian and not a Jew at all, that Jesus had the calm mind of a rabbi.

Zadkine, not given to memories, smoking his clay pipe, took Deo to one side while Brancuși served a native dish—onions, dipped in a tacky cheese mixture—that was his own fearful secret.

"Deo, you must meet La Belle Anglaise. She's not beautiful the way you like them. But the thin English girls have an elegance—the nearer the bone the sweeter the meat, they say. Not that she's truly skinny."

Deo said he disliked the English for the South African war. Besides, Paula had been four months in St. Petersburg and was home again.

BOOK III
Burnt Umber

16

DR. PAUL ALEXANDRE held the thin pale wrist and looked down on the damp handsome head. All the grand oaths, all the fine words could not help much. Here was his friend, ill-used, sick, most likely a genius and yet desperate for the simple needs, driven to stronger and stronger ways to calm his nerve ends, to blot out his miseries. Where were the great healing powers?

The eyes opened, staring dully. The lips were dry and the man wet them slowly with his tongue. When he spoke, his voice was rasped and he had difficulty in getting out the words.

"Oh, it's you, Paul."

"Some day it will be the Angel Gabriel."

"You damned romantic."

The doctor held back an eyelid and peered down on the large dark eye, at the tiny red veins.

"You need someone to take care of you, Modi."

"I can't afford a housekeeper, and my love of the moment, well, she doesn't want to break with her social duties."

"You need a wife."

"I'll speak to Chaim Soutine. He knows a *schadchan,* who will find me, for a fee, a fat junk dealer's daughter with a rich dowry. Will you come dance at my wedding?"

"Go back to sleep. I've left some medicine."

Deo closed his eyes. "A wife . . . a nice fat . . . little wife."

The street sounds of Paris were to Deo like an articulate oboe. The rubber-horn burps of the auto cars, mixed with the *clop-clop* of what were still the best horses (soon to die in fearful horror in the mud of Flanders under shell fire), the hiss of hurrying feet passing and repassing on what Deo thought of as French history; these slabs of slate and sidewalks had seen a new ironic king ride in ("Paris is worth a Mass"), had thundered to the marching women who were going to visit a palace (and slaughter the Swiss Guard), had been scarred by cannon that helped blow down the Bastille (or perhaps those marks were just caused by waiters dragging out the little iron tables every spring).

Paula was late. He stood beyond the transepts and buttresses of Notre Dame. Deo had no watch, but he could tell by the rooks flying against the wind, landing in the trees by the church, what time it was. They always came at this hour. Like the actresses in their hobble skirts for *la promenade hygienique* —the walking of their little dogs. Paula was very late, but Deo did not worry. They were casual, indifferent lovers, living in separate worlds, coming together like those fish he had read about in a book Max Jacob had—fish that mate as they pass at full speed. It was not love, it was not true affection. What was it? Habit? A kind of shared perfection, like playing the violin well, but not caring for the tune. Yes, a fine little wife would be the better answer. True love and simple poverty.

A young girl with a plain Norman face was bowing to Deo. She held out a note to him. "You are Deo?"

"I am Deo."

Another bow and the note was pushed at him by red, work-scrubbed hands. He took the note and the girl was gone on clumsy shoes before he could ask her anything. Twice Paula had sent this maid to cancel their meetings.

The note was short: *"Au revoir, mon cher.* For good this time. Jean and I go to Washington to join the Embassy there for what may be four years in these troubled times. *Adieu au serieux."*

The dubious gentility of the casual note seemed a poor jest.
It had some ludicrous incongruity about it.

It was a mad mixed-up world, he thought, looking at the
patina of pigeon-droppings on the church over the way, and
beyond over on the right bank the sycamores near the Pont de
l'Alma. Something was certainly wrong with the world. There
were more soldiers; the headlines in the newspapers, which he
rarely read, were taller. And people were being sent places,
their faces knotted seriously, like constipated sheepdogs. There
was something attached to the note, a Jeanne d'Arc medal. He
rubbed it. Gilt, not even gold. AD MAJOREM DEI GLORIAM the
raised letters spelled out. Usually he responded wittily to experience, now he felt melancholy.

Deo wandered down to a bistro where the artists often came
in the afternoon for a hasty drink. Utrillo was there staring into
an empty glass. Deo held up the medal to him.

"You know about these things, Mau Mau. Is it worth two
drinks?"

"Please, Modi. Don't talk that way. She's my favorite saint.
Jeanne d'Arc. To trade *her* for drinks! No."

"How thirsty are you, Mau Mau?"

"Like sand in my gullet. But I can't trade Jeanne."

"All right, she's yours. You have the proper respect for things.
Some day you'll be very respectable, and bored by it all."

"Not a chance."

Neither of them got a drink that afternoon.

Life was empty without Paula. He saw her later in a smooth-
paged magazine, standing at the rail of a ship, wrapped in furs,
by the side of a fat little man with a bigot's eyes and a clever
mouth. . . . *The Count and Countess Delaroche leave to join
the French purchasing mission in Washington. The Countess is
the former Pauline Juliette Valcour.*

Soft voices lost to sound, the slow stir of unflexed naked legs.
But there were other girls for Deo and other drunks and other
times. The summer was warm, and the news headlines grew
taller. Diplomatic manners were deteriorating quickly.

One night Deo got very drunk and slept most of the next

day. A knocking at the door awoke him. "Enter. The door's not locked."

Paul Alexandre came in, followed by the sculptor Zadkine. They stumbled over a collection of old paint tubes in a low wooden box.

"Somebody light the lamp," Deo muttered into his pillow.

Paul Alexandre found a match and set a flame to the dirty wick. "You've been sleeping all day. And the room smells it."

"I've stopped working. A contrition of ideas and ideals . . . Besides, don't leave too much to the dealers."

Zadkine said, "I don't see any new work."

Deo sat up and tapped his forehead. "Up here in the deeper stratum of the mind. Working things out. Is there any wine in that bottle?"

"Empty," said the doctor. "Modi, I've got to go to a military medical conference near the Swiss border. I was thinking if trouble starts, perhaps you'd better be back in Italy."

"No, I'm fine here. Where you hang your heart, that's home. It's the best I can think to say with a headache. I need a drink."

Zadkine said, "There's a big party planned. Come along."

"I'm in no mood for parties."

"Shave, wash. You'll meet La Belle Anglaise at last."

"Don't keep shoving your long-toothed English bitch at me."

"She's named after your favorite poet's lady love."

Deo's eyes opened wide. "Beatrice?"

The doctor nodded. "And her last name is a battle. Hastings. She writes poems. But the English haven't had a good poet since Shelley. I leave out Yeats; he's Irish."

"Beatrice Hastings? It sounds like some grim old governess in black cloth, with whalebone stays and a cameo pin over tits as big as walnuts. No."

Zadkine grinned. "I think you're coming, Modi. Food and drink."

"No, I never knew a girl named Beatrice."

"She knows you. Saw you at Rosalie's place one night, full of hashish and brandy."

"Of course not. When I take hashish, I don't need brandy."

"And I introduced you to her at the Rotonde only last week."

"Was I sober?"

"Who's to know?" asked the doctor.

"You invited her, Modi, to see your work."

"I don't remember. I must have been very drunk."

"You showed her your copy of Lautréamont's *Maldoror*."

"A peculiar work to show an English lady."

Zadkine smiled. "Mrs. Hastings is strangely English, and strangely not *too* English."

"Mrs. Hastings?"

"But there is no Mr. Hastings. Come on with us, Modi. She lives behind a little court, with a flower garden in the rue du Montparnasse."

The doctor sighed. "Sounds dreadfully English. Society woman. No Mr. Hastings. Good clothes, I suppose?"

"She likes whiskey," said the sculptor.

"Beatrice likes whiskey," said Deo. "Dante's Beatrice liked whiskey. But of course she can't be Dante's Beatrice, can she?"

He was attracted, but only by the name. The rest of it sounded too outré, even for him. There was a genteel inanity about it all.

"I'm not going out."

"You should, Modi," said the doctor. "Out of Paris."

"It's like asking me to get out of my skin. Why?"

"For your own good."

"For my own good."

"Yes."

"Tell me, for my own good."

The doctor looked at his double-lidded old watch. "I still think, Modi, you should go back to Italy."

"What kind of trouble do you expect?"

"There will be no trouble. There is just a lot of talk."

"What's happened?"

The sculptor moved his shoulders in indifference. "Somebody shot a fat archduke and his wife someplace nobody ever heard of."

Paul Alexandre snapped his watch case shut. "I'll be gone a few days. If you decide to go home, my office will advance you the fare. Against a picture, of course."

Deo got up out of bed and began to pour water over his aching head direct from the pitcher. He sputtered, shivered, groaned and rubbed his thick soaked hair.

The English in Paris were divided into two groups, he told the sculptor. "There are those who have gout, breathe through their mouths, have been to 'Injah,' are surrounded by maiden sisters and aunts who dress in damp wool. These have some money; the men go to the brothels to watch, the women sit and knit and read Jane Austen. The other kind of English have big feet, long teeth, wear thick glasses and are in Paris as humorless students of Art, Music, and Literature—all in capitals. The young itchy women wear batik scarfs, have bangs cut low on their foreheads, and are absolutely wonderful in bed, Apollinaire says. Their skin is mild and cream with a tint of peach added. They make stomach noises while in passion, for which they blush, and they are always brewing tea on spirit lamps, which they spoil by adding a blue milk. Their bite is rarely poisonous."

Beatrice Hastings was nothing like either of Deo's descriptions of the English in Paris. The flat was on a good but not too fashionable street. The staircase was fairly clean. The room Deo entered was covered in a yellow, Second Empire wallpaper, like a novel by Zola. There were several blue landscapes painted by people Deo had never heard of. The mottled marble fireplace had a good collection of coal burning on its grate. Deo smelled a cat, a fine face cream, old toast, well-printed books, aired clothing. The curtains on the windows were of lace. There were copies of *The London Illustrated News,* an *avante-garde* magazine called either *Blast* or *Blow* (Deo never could remember which), some dexterous drawings by someone who signed himself *John.*

In the middle of the party Zadkine introduced Deo, while Paul Alexandre wandered toward a man in tweeds chewing sea crackers.

The Englishwoman took Deo's hand in hers. "It's just going to be a small gathering. Some people canceled. The channel train was late."

A lean young man, folded up like a carpenter's ruler, sat by

the fireplace. He wore a hairy Shetland jacket and kept saying,
"Oh, jolly, really jolly," as he looked up from some handwritten
sheets he was reading. He held a glass of Scotch whiskey all
evening and sipped from it, and no one bothered to talk to
him.

Beatrice Hastings, Deo saw, was no great beauty. Her ears
stuck out from either side of her well-shaped skull. Her dark
hair was parted in the middle and flew back behind her ears to
be caught there in some fashion and held captive. The chin was
long and sharp, bursting with character. The eyes were close
together, the nose fine and long. Deo found her fascinating,
desirable as no woman had been desirable for a long time. His
amorous faculties were at their most creative.

"You'll have a drink? Whiskey?"

Deo accepted the whiskey. He accepted several whiskeys. It
had a medical smell he didn't care for, but it bit properly into
his entrails. Beatrice sank down on a sofa covered with a patterned tropical cloth. She had good legs, her body was well
made. Deo sat down facing her, admiring her with the unanes-
thetized parts of his brain and body.

"I like your painting. I'm going to buy one."

"I'll give you one," he said from his unencumbered heart.

"I can afford to buy it, thank you."

"Why are you so crisp with me, Mme Hastings? I don't often
offer a painting."

"You need the money. That's why. Be practical."

"Since when is a poet giving advice on being practical?" Deo
swallowed his drink and she refilled his glass. "I wish I could
read English properly. You write poetry, I hear."

"How would you know?" Her voice had that edge of firmness
and authority he liked in some people.

New couples came in and Deo sat sipping whiskey, watching
the man by the fireplace go on reading the manuscript, still
observing out loud, "Oh, I say! No, *really!*"

The whole tapestry of the party took on form. The people
were French and English; one American in a stringy yellow
beard, a Hindu who carried two watches ("never the twain
shall meet"), and two girls with heavy hands, who wore long
jet earrings and kept talking of clay, the kiln, the glaze, and

high firing for crackle, bringing out the edges of form to catch the light. ("The Greek pots, you know, frightfully overrated.") They were from the Slade School, Deo found out, over for three days. ("To see the new things. You been here long, Mr. Mo-dig-liani?")

The place was filled with people, the overflow was standing out in the hall, a girl holding a glass and a man leaning against her, one hand flat against the wall, talking very earnestly. Women with pendulous breasts were quoting G.B.S. In the main room itself people sat cross-legged on the floor and someone had put a log on the fire; it was becoming very warm. Deo wasn't really drunk. He was feeling mellow and indifferent to the talk about the Balkans, cubism, Joseph Conrad, Georgian poetry and Bunny Somebody, who was playing tennis in Santa Barbara. Deo had been to hundreds of studio parties and this one was like all the others, only it had an Oxford accent, and Scotch whiskey had an exuberance of power.

Deo went to hunt up the hostess and found her between kitchen and bedroom. She was nodding to a fat man with a large nose on which were balanced very tiny gold-rimmed eyeglasses on a black ribbon. As he spoke he gyrated belly and buttocks.

"Beer, beef and a return to the days of yeoman, miller and castled grace, Mrs. Hastings. Medieval England was a paradise. Every man to his own place, every place passing from knighted father to spurred son. Tip the cap to my liege lord, the lord bows a ribboned knee to the orb-and-sceptered king, and the king kneels to the Holy Father, the Pope. I ask you who would want more, or better?"

Beatrice seemed a bit glassy-eyed. Deo took her arm and turned her away from the speaker. "Isn't there any fresh air?"

The large man wiped his damp straggling mustache. "And the glorious bannered guilds, the swinging gilt signs, and real smoking virile manure, cowshit—if I must say so, Mrs. Hastings—not this artificial stuff they mix up from chemicals. Nothing tastes like it did when I was a boy when things were grown in . . . I say, Mrs. Hastings . . ."

Beatrice was gone from the large man's line of vision. She was leading Deo through a little low door in the damp kitchen out onto a wedge of open roof. Below them Paris glowed and twitched; the hum of traffic was muffled, but there. They leaned together on a smudgy railing feeling the geographical spread of the night.

Deo said, "That's better."

"You don't like my friends?"

"You don't either, Mrs. Hastings."

"I suppose not. I do dislike all this surface felicity."

"All this talk to prove the behind is a baroque form. I'll be back tomorrow. I want to paint you, Mrs. Hastings, with your hair pulled back that way and your ears sticking out."

"You don't like the way I look?"

"I like it very much, Signora Inglese." He tried to pat her hand.

She put her arms behind her back and teetered back and forth on her heels. "You have a very dreadful reputation, and you are destroying yourself."

"What do you care what my reputation is? What do I care what yours is? You might even be a very rotten poet."

"You wouldn't know. You haven't got the ear for English."

Deo imitated Paul Alexandre's English. *"Bloody awful mess, what?"*

She laughed, and he liked the way she laughed. No subterfuge, no falsification. "Why do people always pick on a phrase like that as being so English?"

Deo turned and took her in his arms. "You wanted to meet me, La Belle Anglaise. I'm here." He kissed her hard on the mouth and she neither helped nor resisted. The burdens of individuality seemed to fall from them. He felt her back under his lightest touch—it was hard and muscled. He bunched her ribs between his strong fingers, applying pressure, and slid his hands down to her flanks.

She moved away from him as if keeping her emotions out of range. She was very calm and expressionless. Her skin had colored. Even here in the semidark of the rooftop he could sense the flush in her cheek and see the rapid rise and fall of her breasts. Certain mutual revelations seemed about to be released.

"You could begin the painting tomorrow at ten o'clock."

"We're standing on the edge of a great deep, *amore mio*."

"You're drunk, you know, so I think we'd better talk tomor-row."

"That's one of my bad habits. I drink. I have others. I hate being ordered around even by one so *simpatica*."

"Trim your beard, or cut it off. And clean your fingernails."

She turned to walk away. He grabbed her arm. "Don't you think I know what I want, and how much I want it?"

"You don't show it."

He said, "I don't give a damn for sophisticated talk."

"I want the best of you," she said.

"And perhaps there isn't any best of me? I'm too late for you maybe."

"I've been trying to meet you for some time."

He could see the way it hurt her to say this, and the way she chewed with her long teeth on her lips, as if she were plunging a knife into her own flesh to admit this much.

"You're very honest, Mrs. . . . ah . . . Beatrice."

He was drunk, but he had been drunker, and he could con-trol himself from getting too crude and wild—at least he would try. "It's all going to be fine, *amore mio*. You've become human and you've talked. You do make good poetry; what you said is poetry. Just don't feel lovers are shadows of people making pri-vate spectacles of themselves."

He patted her hands, and they were cold and he rubbed them.

She said, "You're much too sure of yourself."

He kissed her hands. She stood there, head down, body very straight, not slumping (she had been educated at a strict school, he thought; no slouching, no biting fingernails, fifty strokes of the hair every night with the brush, and never get caught with another girl in your bed.)

Beatrice leaned her feverish forehead against Deo's chest. "I've got to go back to the party. It's all right, darling."

She left him there in the dark, and Deo rubbed his beard. *What* was all right?

Good as Deo's paintings had been before, there were those in his intimate circle—Zbo, Sagot, Picasso—who felt that with his portraits of Beatrice Hastings Deo entered his maturity as an artist.

They studied each other on a warm summer afternoon, the repeated clauses of household noises muted in the building, and the rug she sat on, a Veronese red, patterned with scattered books and literary reviews.

There had been not much talk. He was painting her, and it was going well. The English girl had not responded to his ardent advances, for all the intensity of their first meeting. Instead of passion they had words, he bristly as a mastiff. He did not want to talk with Bea.

"For my Italian, Bea, has to be translated into French, and you would have to absorb it in your British mind, and bring back to me your ideas in *your* French for me to take back and reclothe in Italian images."

"But why all that long way around, Deo?"

"In love I think in Italian, not French."

The first painting day's rebuff sent Deo trembling to hashish. He crisped and smoked his mind; he lay on his bed later and saw inside the building; in every studio slept the artist, each hung in a progressive atrophy, like fruit on his own personal vine. The Genesis and Exodus of love and bodies grew hazy; hashish soothed away the carnal and temporal lusts and left Deo at morning chastened with needs of more human proportions. At the second sitting for the portrait they merely stared at each other.

At the third sitting he put down his brush, ready to risk everything. He went toward her, wanting to say that to enter love is like coming into a sheltering cave, but she just looked at him as if fearing injury and ingratitude. The little vein in her forehead throbbed and her hands were tightly rolled into fists at her side. He carried her into the bedroom, assuring himself that she wanted to be taken like a fortress, by storm.

She was marvelously made, rewardingly naked. The pink English body, the small tight breasts, pleased him, also the length of leg, almost too long for the body, and the way she rolled her head on the long neck. And when he covered her in a flow of body against body, she began to move her limbs like a recalcitrant child.

They made love with ease, their passion rubbing the surface of their merged consciousness. The room seemed to Deo filled with the sound of their breathing, and the colors of sensuality: rose madder, bitumin and violet. She lost the sense of a social misdemeanor and bit him on his shoulder, and when the great falling together had roared in their ears, Deo was suddenly aware that to lovers bodies murmur like echoes in a seashell.

They slept in the replaying dreams of their passion, images overlapping, and they came awake slowly as if delaying a fresh meeting. Still they did not speak to each other. They could feel a vibration like a discernible pulse beat, and they smiled and showed they had for each other the urgent glow of the young carnivore.

It was dark outside when they were again aware of the shrill quartertones of the city birds settling down for the night. They lay in each other's dampness, short of breath. From Bea came a continual vocal breathing like sea tide. Deo continued in a state of copious extravagant persistency, until at last they fell into a sleep again in the cast shadow of the exhausted oil lamp by the bed. For Deo love was like the hashish—welding the waking and dreaming world. He reached for the girl and hurt her in his grip, and he neither knew nor cared that she did not protest. Deo felt the pain was good for her, and someplace, he knew, in the back of her senses was the thought that there was punishment and sin, and that one could not really escape them by living in Paris, by seeing them as disintegrating social myths.

They slept till noon. Deo cooked the breakfast. He was very good at it, he explained, when he could afford the shopping.

She lay pink and slim in the bed, her hair loose and tangled, the tips of her ears red, and rings forming under her dark eyes from the continual assaults of lovemaking.

"You stay in bed, *ma chère*. The English like tea in bed, I hear."

She was not much given to smiling, feeling life serious, but she grinned now. "But I'll have coffee, Deo."

"You want the kippers, Bea, or the bacon?"

"No, no, just some toast and marmalade. Let me do it." One naked leg hunted the floor.

He pushed her back and put his arms around her. "Bea, Bea, don't just this morning do anything, but what I tell you. I have the *viva forza* for us both."

She let herself fall back on the pillow, forced herself to rumple his uncombed black hair, made herself forget the old teachings of sin and damnation that she was sure she had outgrown. "You are too handsome, Deo, too sensual. You'll ruin everything that comes near you, Deo."

"Including myself, *senz'altro*." He laughed and showed all his fine teeth. "What's wrong with burning out in a big burst of flames like an exploding star? That reminds me, the coffee is boiling."

They ate by the window, wrapped in light robes, Deo enjoying the Japanese pattern on his; it had been a gift, Bea said, from an aunt in Kent whose family were tea planters somewhere in the Far East.

Deo wanted to enjoy her, to look at Bea, to place her hair in order, to kiss her long slim toes, to be vulgar and raucous with her, but he knew all that would take time. Bea did not leap into passion and its byplays; she was like the English ladies shown in the magazines in their frilly bathing suits at Brighton, putting one toe gingerly into the tepid sea.

She said, "We'll paint today."

Mrs. Hastings, her background, remained a mystery. Mr. Hastings, if he had ever existed, remained in the void. Her poems also did not seem to exist; what she quoted always seemed to be from poets of the past. She had a small income, not much, from some fusty source in London. Her look was controlled and cold in public, very proper; no one dared act familiar with her. She had a crisp personal authority, and was conventional in her habits, but for her whiskey, and her ménage with Modi.

There were times in her private physical pleasures when Deo wondered, Had she really capitulated to him? Or was this merely a side of Paris she expected? Her clothes were smart, without being of the moment; one felt that she really was a society woman.

She shared the poetry of Dante Gabriel Rossetti with Deo. They recited the sonnets of *The House of Life* together.

"The blessed damozel leaned out
From the golden bar of Heaven . . ."

"That's fine, Deo, for one who knows no English," Bea said.

"It's the sounds I like. You mean he really threw his only copy of these poems into the coffin of his wife, just before they buried her?"

"His grief was extreme, Deo. Very extreme. But his mood didn't last. He had friends, much later, dig up her coffin and bring him the moldy manuscript."

"Ah now! I understand him! A *true* artist."

They fought their first battle over the merits of Dante and Milton.

"My dear boy, your Dante was a mean little peasant who still belonged to the middle ages."

"Your Milton was a stinking blind old man, forcing his daughters to read to him, cruel to his wife. A rotten Puritan, hating life!"

"Your dirty little—"

They were drinking whiskey. They rushed at each other. Neighbors had to come in to separate them. Later they bathed each other's bruises and talked like lovers and acted like lovers. They read less poetry after that.

17

To LOVERS much of the outer world does not exist, Deo explained to Bea. He refused to brood over the war talk, the mobilizations, the screaming headlines, the spike-headed pictures of the Kaiser, the Tsar reviewing six-foot-tall Cossacks, the house of Hanover shooting grouse in Scotland. Better to talk of *la bella maga d'amore* and to go on with one's work.

Mornings Deo painted, afternoons he was with Bea, overwhelming her with a passion beyond any boundary she might have set up about love and emotions. Later, in her lapidary French, during a speculative calm, she lectured him on the condition of his clothes and his habits, his abilities. She also tried to channel his ardors into a kind of timetable of hour and place.

He would laugh wildly, drive her into a frenzy and then a betrayal of her controls with kisses, caresses and venery. She lay in the dazed contentment of well-sated satisfaction. He bit her earlobes and laughed at her protests.

"Few human activities, Bea, have any respect for middle-class ideas. Don't think we can love by the clock or the calendar. Like ten o'clock painting, noon a plain lunch and not too much wine."

"You do drink too much."

"Two o'clock the nap for one hour in separate beds, four o'clock tea naturally; and horror, after dinner exposing one's body, naked, on a meal of boiled beef and brussels sprouts, then heavy wool nightgowns, teeth in a glass of water, visit the w.c. and open the window."

"Deo, Deo, I'm not trying to pattern your life, but—"

"Once a week sexual contact approved by the Archbishop of Canterbury. Or twice a month, if over thirty; a polite fornication with mouth closed, eyes lowered—all blessed by the Church of England. Undressing in the dark, of course, and feeling under the night dress as if hunting a hot potato mislaid between one's legs!"

"No, no, darling."

Bea began to laugh at this picture of herself, and she grabbed Deo and kissed him, and they made love without any British sense of degradation; time was amputated, the clock was handless. When Bea's sense of duty, or guilt, came alive after passion, she would force him back to his studio, while she wrote down in pale-blue ink certain private thoughts. She would work on her poems, go shopping for drapes ("the English drape everything"), speak of British pride and British courage and the faith and destiny of the English to settle the affairs of the world.

"Maybe, *ma chère*, the sun never sets on the British flag because God doesn't trust it in the dark."

"Really, Deo!"

To Deo her character was mysterious. Bea had rebelled against the straight post-Victorian England, had fled to France, had enough income in Paris to do what she wanted. Yet, in the core of Beatrice Hastings, Deo suspected a reserve that led right back to all she had escaped from.

When she became too demanding for order in Deo's life—for better, cleaner work habits, for respectability ("You mustn't pinch my bum in public"), he would get drunk with Utrillo, or would wander off to adventure with Apollinaire, who was suffering a final or near-final break with Marie. ("I tell you, Deo, we men go on paying off all our emotional debts with love, receiving or fighting kisses. We are sleeping partners, packed two by two on creaking springs, into sea tombs of our makings. I fear the winey intimate darkness of love at the bottom of the aquarium—for that's where the great destroyers lurk —bearded like the *mons pubis*, ready to swallow us alive and kicking.")

When Deo, after an escape, came back to Bea, bedraggled and worn, she would make firm her mouth and look at him with what he called that grim British look of Wellington at Waterloo. She forgave him and forgave him and forgave him, and cleaned him and salved him and loved him.

Once, revolting against too much correction, he went back to hashish, and she found him in a desolate house with dreadful people. She refused to see him when he recovered. For a week Deo sat alone in a dimensionless despair, too proud to go back to Bea unwanted. He could no longer work; the drug, the alcohol, only pressed him deeper into sunken misery. He found Bea in the park, seated, a firm arched back, smoking a cigarette. She was watching the children's games, the colors of the nurses and their charges.

He came up and stood beside her, wondering: Are the objects of our affection worth all the agony we suffer when with them?

"In the spring the flowers and children come up together, and it's very beautiful."

She looked up at him, her face suggesting she had come through an emotional crisis, a kind of fever.

"You're too shadowy and insubstantial, Deo. Go away."

He sat down and took her hand and kissed it. "I will hurt you again and again, but always remember, I do love you."

"Is that enough, Deo?" the pale contralto voice asked, and her eyes looked away from him.

"It's all there is. The rest are manners, poses—none of *that* matters between two people."

She said softly, as if ashamed of her passion betraying her, "Shall we go to my place?"

"No, to my place."

Bea with a kind of devout forbearance threw away the cigarette. They walked to Deo's disordered studio and were reunited in the *sotto voce* muttering of their desires and need for each other. Later they went out to the Restaurant Namur and devoured, as young hungry lovers will, a great deal of food. Duck-egg omelette, *topinambours* with snowflower roots. Deo bought Bea with his last franc some *muguets*—wild lilies of the valley. Bea gave a tattered *clochard* a coin. As they walked there were crows shrilly protesting on the Place de l'École Militaire, and horsemen with plumes in blue uniforms galloping, and people were waving newspapers and cheering.

"Oh!" said Bea, looking at a newspaper headline. "We are at war."

On the café *terrasses* excited men were drinking coupes of champagne. The whores had gathered under groups of fluttering flags, at the Sélect, on the rue Vrain, and were singing Mistinguette's song: *J'en Ai Marre*. Already the city seemed full of raw new soldiers in badly fitting sky-blue uniforms. No one was sweeping the streets of horse litter, discarded newspapers (PEACE HOPE DIMS) and crumpled cigarette packages.

That night Bea closed the windows of her bedroom so they could not hear the orgy of celebrating over quick and easy victories. In the dark she said, "Oh, my darling, our world has started to decompose."

"Never our world, *ma chère*—always *their* world, and they're welcome to it."

But soon the old way of life seemed to dissolve around Deo like a ghost at cock crow. Kisling came to Deo's studio carrying an already broken suitcase and an armful of old magazines.

"I'm going to join the French Foreign Legion. You may ask why now?"

"Why now?"

"I'm going, that's all I'm sure of."

"You must be mad. The war will be over in six weeks, the experts say. Christmas at most."

"War experts are like art experts—turds. I've brought you some magazines. Everybody is going into the war. Chagall wrote me from Berlin, where he's been showing his work. He's going back to Russia, back to Vitebsk. He must be home already if the Germans didn't grab him."

Deo flexed his fingers, cracked his knuckles. "With my work I can't make any heroic and stupid gestures. What about Soutine, Apollinaire?"

"Chaim they think has stomach ulcers. Him they don't want. Apollinaire, he's talking of going into the artillery. The big guns he wants."

"What's he, a Pole, or an Italian? He doesn't have to go to war."

"Apollinaire, he's saying he's Chinese now, the son of the old Empress and a Negro Cardinal. He'll get in. He'll talk his way in. But to get out talking doesn't help."

"He should remember that bullet hole in the head de Chirico painted."

"So, goodbye, Modi."

When Deo was alone, he could only feel his head bursting. He went out to the cafés; drinks were not hard to get now. Everyone in the invigorating thoughtless ecstasy of war was standing treat. The streets were full of milling uniformed men; tailed coats of the Crimean wars, the little kepis stuck full of dead flowers, callow recruits drunk and vomiting everyplace. The old sods were pinching the girls and showing the bayonets they were going to stick up the arse of the Crown Prince Willie. A rash of flags was appearing everywhere; tarts were doing so well that hotel rooms were being rented in many districts only to old customers. The act of generation engrosses men who fear death in battle.

The blare of military music filled the city—and so did red faces screaming devotion and great deeds. Hysterical respectable women were clinging to strangers in a total abdication of all sense. No one had yet heard a shot. Smelling of mule sweat and fermenting wine, smoking and shaking, their rubber horns blaring, the taxis carried officers in well-tailored uniforms making the rounds of the brothels with baskets of brandy and hothouse fruit.

Picasso sat with Max Jacob in front of a café. He was tearing little paper figures out of a newspaper, making them stand up as little bulls, picadors, matadors. He looked up as Deo came over and slumped into a chair.

"No hero's colors for you, Deo?"

"Not yet. Is it true about Apollinaire?"

"The full fat hero? Sending wires to all his friends, organizing impromptu entertainments. For him this war is another holy crusade. He'd fight on either side, I think."

"Picasso, what are you going to do in this war?"

The Spaniard shrugged. "There were these two men who both lived through the harrowing days of the French Revolution. They met after the bloody days. One asked, 'What did you do during the Terror?' The other said, 'I survived.' Modi, we must survive. We're seeing the end of the nineteenth century."

Max Jacob nodded. "Yes, Apollinaire always said that the nineteenth century would last till the first big war of the twentieth. It's very depressing. Are you painting, Modi?"

"Yes. No matter what's happening, we've got a trade, haven't we?"

"I suppose so," said Picasso. "Our war is bigger. Who else but artists dare new experiences, unestablished sensations?"

Deo went to find Bea. She was not home but had left the key for him on the molding over the door. He let himself in. The room with its rows of English novels, its burnished tea things, the smell of lavender that scented her underthings in the big chest, was pure Bea—even the odor of Bea herself in her silver-backed hair brush and comb, in their heavy ornate patterns and the letters in Old English, *B.H.* It was herself, mercuric, voluble and proud, that dominated the little flat. Deo sat by the window, looking at the platinum-gray sky; already the weather seemed full of threats. He was sleeping when Bea came in and she sat watching him till he awoke and tried to focus his eyes. His mood was of touchable softness, like velvet.

"Have you been there long, Bea?"

"A little while. You're so defenseless when you sleep. A little bad boy."

"Everybody is a bad boy and going to war. All the French artists are called up. Braque, Léger, Derain, *all* the rest."

She came into his outheld arms. "You're not going. You mustn't."

"If I were British, would you say that?"

Her long nose, expressive of temper and sensitivity, twitched. "I don't know. It's dreadful. All the young Oxford boys are rushing back from vacations in the south of France. They say the Germans are on French soil."

"It's only dirt, that soil, full of the dead of a thousand useless wars. What good did it do them to cheer abstractions? A mouthful of clods."

"Let's not go out tonight, Deo. It's too gay out there. Too unbelievable."

They could hear all night the cheers and the drunkards, the shrill cry of amused and screaming women, registering in treble and higher.

In the days that followed it was best, Deo found, to stand in the street with a free gift cigar dangling from one's lips and listen to all of them talk. The Germans had wheeled their armies to encircle Paris. The British were landing their troops to move inland. All the French retreats were presented as brilliant moves to lure the bestial Germans forward to their doom. Businessmen like scuffing stoats and ferrets made their profits decked in flags.

German cavalry was reported near Paris, and at lunch Deo said to Bea, "The Germans are on the Marne."

Bea nodded and bit her lips together on a *mirabelle*—white plum. Her long English face was drawn and serious in all its pliant finely bred features. "I had a letter from London. They expect Paris to fall."

"Don't you want to run?"

"No, of course not, Deo. It's not real yet."

An old man reading a copy of the *Mercure de France* began to shout: "We'll defend Paris with a rampart of our dead bodies!"

Two waiters led him away. Deo said, "He's too old to be called up. They're the real bloodthirsty ones, the ones with hernias and official jobs. I need a very strong drink, Bea."

She wanted to say no, but she didn't. And when he left her, agreeing to meet her later, Deo was humming a popular tune and bowing to the soldiers who shoved him off the sidewalk.

"The world is your herring—eat it, tail and all."

In his studio a well-tailored major with polished boots was standing at the window. He turned slowly around and Deo saw it was Dr. Alexandre, looking tired and unhappy.

"Not you too, Paul!"

"Yes—me too."

Paul Alexandre seemed ashamed of something. He ducked his head to one side and gestured as if to shake off the question.

"And why not? I'm in charge of an army medical unit. A complete rolling hospital."

"But *you?*"

"I'm a doctor. I wanted to see you, Modi, before I left."

"But where are all the Socialists protesting this war? Where are the workers of Europe, the unions, the internationals that would never permit this war?"

"Deo, it isn't that simple. Perhaps it is a betrayal of all we talked about." Paul seemed too taciturn. "Yes, I suppose it is."

"And talked and talked, Paul. There could be no war, all men are brothers and there are no narrow national borders for the truth."

"I remember what I said. I'm still a Socialist. Believe me. My ideals haven't changed. But after this war, the good life will come and—"

"They said that of every war. Chagall is in Russia. I hear Pascin is going to New York. And you, Paul, you have put on that uniform, and . . ."

The doctor seemed very sad. "Yes. There was no place to go but into the army when called up. Deep down, Deo, I'm still a

Frenchman. And much as I love Wagner, Schiller, Heine, Nietzsche, Dürer, they're not the ones who are encircling Paris, are they?"

"Yes they are, but it doesn't do to talk sense at this time. When do you leave?"

The doctor was staring at his own image in the window. "At four. This is not the end of our friendship."

Deo and Bea went to the railroad station to see Dr. Alexandre off. The war was drawing closer and closer as the Germans advanced on Paris. The city was in a numb trance, crouched and waiting while the Germans rimmed it in.

The railroad station was being propped up by sandbags. No one was removing the debris of the army trains leaving in packed confusion from all platforms. A sadness in the late summer air seemed to brood over the soiled glass shed roofs, and the soldiers, seen as fathers of families, pale clerks, pimply and callow slum dwellers, were all in their itchy army uniforms, carrying deforming packs and rifles ending in cruel thin-edged bayonets. Whistles, the smell of steam, shouts, a melodious sob filled the station.

Paul Alexandre, trim and calm and well pressed, a leather dispatch case under one arm, stood by the side of an old International-Europa carriage repainted white and decorated with a large red cross.

"We're moving up to the battle as soon as medical supplies are loaded."

Bea looked around her, at the pushing, sweating men, packing into compartments already too full, at the hurrying figures of greasy train crews. Several cannon were being clumsily loaded onto a flatcar. Everywhere there were signs in schoolboy script, with arrows and stars, identifying various military service units. Several priests passed carrying cases filled with items for the last rites.

Deo watched the pigeons; not at all upset by the activity below them they came hunting tidbits in the fearful mess piling up on the platforms.

"Who will be left to care for painting? And in this madness isn't painting another form of madness?"

The doctor smiled. "Of course not—and we'll come back. And painting will go on. After all, this is Paris. Man does not live by bread alone."

Deo shivered. "You quoting the Bible?"

"We'll hold on the Marne and then push them back."

Deo was confused. "*We? Them?* It doesn't sound like you, Paul."

The doctor shook his head. "The dreams are over. Bea, cheer him up."

"Take care of yourself. There isn't much else to say."

A train whistle began to shrill; a nerve-tearing chord—the cloud of pigeons fluttered their wings and a mauve dust cloud formed. Panting, heavy-burdened men in uniform with the faces of unhealthy office workers began to run along the platform, mouths open, their feet unaccustomed to the heavy army boots slipping on the concrete platforms. A dusty train began to pull out, its windows burdened with worried faces and unhappy mouths going off to war. The seething ill-conducted business of the platforms proceeded.

Bea put her hands to her ears. "I seem to hear the guns going off."

Deo said, "Guns this close? Hear them?"

"You may be," said the doctor, saluting a group of male orderlies beginning to load bundles of stretchers into the hospital cars. "I heard them last night when the wind shifted. A steady roll of thunder." He pressed Deo's arm. "Goodbye, good friend. If we never meet again . . . but that's nonsense."

Deo said, "You're a fool, Paul. What's the war to you?"

"When I've fought it, perhaps I'll know. Have a drink for me." The doctor kissed Bea's cheek and hurried off toward a car where men were battering, with a great pushing, a case of medical supplies too big for the doors.

"There's nothing to say, Bea."

"Nothing worth while."

Deo and Bea turned away. In the street in front of the station the first wounded men Deo had ever seen were lying on the pavement on stretchers, their unshaved faces glazed with pain, staring at the indifferent sky while someone kept lighting cigarettes in blue lips that did not feel them. Some youths with bandaged arms and plaster leg casts were being helped into taxis, aided by nuns in white bearing crests of some holy order Deo couldn't make out.

The wounded, he noticed, no longer seemed to belong to the people in the streets. They were mistakes, the pitying faces of the citizens seemed to say, that should be hidden away with shame. Yes, Deo agreed, away from the sight of men and women. As if they had committed some fearful crime. He knew what it was. They had permitted themselves to be mutilated in a barbaric ceremony on a destroyed field.

Deo saw that Paris was changing too. The glass of the lamp posts was being painted black, sandbags were being piled around shop windows, heavy curtains were being hung in doorways. Prices were going up on everything. The shopkeepers shrugged off protests.

"What's all this for?" Deo asked Bea as they walked past warehouses being filled with cases of goods.

"The zeppelins are coming, everyone says. All lights are to be covered or turned out if they appear."

"What can they do?"

"Drop explosives," said Bea. "It's all so out of *Alice in Wonderland*, isn't it?"

In the days that followed the zeppelins did not come. The zigzag slaughter at the Marne went on. Someone suggested moving troops to defend Paris by taxis. Then came the fearful hours when they heard the guns battering at the horizon, sounding like the belches of demented monsters, and Paris waited.

The tide turned. The Germans failed to take Paris.

There was celebrating in Paris and the ringing of great bells to thank *Le Père Éternel*—and the first casualty lists were posted up. Women in black went to mass for the soul of some departed. Deo didn't paint. 1914 was to be the year when he did very little work. He sat and smoked too much, drank too much, needed Bea too often; the germinating completion of oneself in another. In the nights as winter came, the lovers' arms turned into delicate antennae, and their longings were often exhausted before fulfillment. Meanwhile, the newsboys ran loudly by with newspaper extras of imaginary victories.

Paris the first winter of the war found Picasso in a sad state. He had been separated from Fernande for a couple of years; his new love had been Eva, whose nickname, Ma Jolie, he had signed to many cubistic paintings. And Eva had just died.

Deo found Picasso living in a studio on the rue Schoelcher, overlooking the Montparnasse cemetery. It was not a cheerful view, Deo decided, and Picasso was not a cheerful man. Apollinaire in uniform came in and waved an arm at Deo. "The brass monkeys are coming indoors. What a cold!"

It was freezing in the studio; coal rationing had already begun. Picasso was bundled against the cold in several coats and wore a woolen scarf.

"Our hero," he said, greeting Apollinaire. "Blue is a sad color."

"We are all sad," said Deo, rubbing his red chilled hands. "Apollinaire has lost a girl and found a new one. I have one and I don't know if I can live through the experience. And *you* . . ." He gestured toward the cemetery, stone-bone-white in the chill weather outside the studio window.

"You forget the war," said Picasso, sketching Apollinaire in his uniform. "Braque is with his regiment; he left from Avignon. Max is unfit for military service, but without your talk, Apollinaire, his ideas are usually nonsense. He became a Catholic, you know, in February."

"Max, the grandson of a rabbi?" asked Deo.

Apollinaire smiled. "A man can't have too many religions. All are good for one thing or another."

"You know about the camouflage?" Deo asked. "You invented it."

Picasso nodded. "The guns on the Boulevard Raspail look like one of our rejected exhibits. It's depressing, Europe drowning someplace out there in a sea of mud."

"What can we do?" asked Deo.

"Begin to eat each other," said the critic. "Make knife handles out of the bones of our friends who fall. I myself carry enough for a full set of piano keys."

Picasso looked up from the drawing that Apollinaire, aware of the honor, was now sternly posing for. "We can paint. We have to paint."

Deo did not answer. He sat very still and thought if he held his breath, the world would go away, but was it worth the trouble?

18

THE MOURNERS' BENCHES MULTIPLIED, but the Germans never got to Paris. The French held for the second time at the Marne, the British dug in and began to drown in the muck of Flanders (whole generations of them dying, Apollinaire said, under poor generals that were still fighting in the manner of the Napoleonic wars). Bea could not at first grasp the stupidity and the dreadfulness of the conflict. It all seemed doomed to absurdity. Only the wounds were real.

Paris grew shabby, grew dark after sunset. The zeppelins came a few times and blew up a household here and there. Big Bertha was fired on the city from sixty miles away on schedule, so that one could set one's watch by the huge gun—only Deo still had no watch.

Uniforms, medals, crutches, bandaged heads filled the cafés. The French soldiers that marched off to the slaughtering pens were older, the sky-blue uniforms were exchanged for field mustard. The maimed and the blind, the limping and less disfigured began to move about Paris, to sit in the sun and feel for lost limbs.

For Deo it was a chaotic period of drying up. Paintings, it would seem, were the last thing anyone wanted. Zbo could move nothing. Sagot said he could sell post cards to the soldiers but not paintings. From Italy Deo got only bad news; a time of trouble there too, the agony of war moving closer to the Livorno family, destroying a cousin here, blowing up an uncle in the Alps, sending out a nephew to some desert to addle his brains into madness.

Only a line from Dante made sense: *Come t'e picciol fallo amaro morso.*

The rains were cold, the sky, Deo saw, was like fat congealed on a dirty plate. The war settled down that winter to a long line of graves full of living men, running from the English Channel to the Swiss border. It had become a series of horrors called trenches, where men lived in excrement, mire, unburied dead; dug in underground and facing each other across corpse-filled no man's lands. Here they would stay, Deo felt, for years, for decades, while everyone read casualty lists. In Paris, even by promise and perversity, one could not live, so how could one paint? There was still hashish to be had, only the price was higher.

He sat in his studio smoking the last Maryland cigarette he had left. The canvas had been on the easel a long time. It was some Gypsy girl; he didn't remember just where he had met her or started the painting. He took down the painting and turned it to the wall.

He inspected his room as he had done a hundred times. Two cracked panes of glass in the window frame and no chance of replacing them. A yellow wallpaper faded to some dun hue that showed old nails, stains too obscene to think about, facing reproductions of Italian paintings he had brought with him from Italy—how long ago: here an arm by Michelangelo, there a head of Titian's; hawknosed, whiskered, modeled in the paint of a master.

He turned away and saw the iron cot, the gray crumpled linen, the blue blanket too thin for these winter nights. Some paint-stained clothes hung on nails, and along the walls at the floor line a piling up of unsold paintings, some half finished. A box nailed to a wall held an empty wine bottle, the tail of a herring, and one crust of bread too hard to gnaw on. The rusty iron stove was unlit. The water in the pitcher and basin needed changing. The oil-lamp shade was cracked.

Deo had no desire to paint. The tacky cigarette stub was too short to hold. He threw it into the cold stove and got his orange and yellow scarf and wound it around his neck, the way, he supposed, the Egyptians must have wound their mummies after a good bath of pitch and brimstone and sneezy spices. His hat was black and old, and the brim had no courage left in it. He went out into the street, passing some whores on the second floor, laughing in doorways with some Negro soldiers from the Cameroons who were very drunk. Their faces were delicately tattooed and scarred with amazingly fine scrolls and lines. They were making lewd suggestions to the whores, one of whom un- buttoned a soldier and said, *"Le garde mort ne se rend pas."*

In the street Deo shivered. There was no painting and, of late, no comfort in Bea; his pleasures with her seemed an evil byplay among all this misery, this foul exploiting of nations and people, and the sight of the rich fat ones making such a good thing out of war supplies.

Where could he go? Where could he hide? He could become part of the madness; the rabbit hiding among the hounds; the little fish that actually lived inside the jaws of the shark.

Perhaps he had been avoiding life, the painful common part of it outside the little games of marking up canvas, paper, chip- ping into stone. Art was, of course, the biggest, silliest madness of all. It had no reason to be, no philosophy, and since the camera had come along, served no needed purpose as a record- ing of history or society. That Herr Doktor Freud Appollinaire talked about; he had called art a little game played by short- lived mortals while waiting to be destroyed by nature, and so wanting to leave something like a dung beetle's ball, or a sponge's spine, or a coral's lime skeleton—leave something called art.

Deo had tried almost everything at least twice. Why not war? To take the thing one hated, to join what was stupid, an insanity that would in the end leave a planet sterile and empty —why not? *La farce est jouée.*

Deo knew what he wanted to find. A stained stone building with the faint smell of horses that had died a century ago at Waterloo, and some later at Sedan; an old remount depot with its windows bricked up and the courtyard full of American fliv- vers, each one the color of elephant hide and carrying the in- signia of the Foreign Legion. The Legion was not any more in its romantic desert uniform, at least not as shown by the new recruits standing along a row of old horse-watering tanks, hold- ing rifles outdated fifty years ago.

Deo went up a dirty stone staircase spotted by sunflower-seed husks, torn-up letters and bits of red carpet. The recruitment office was full of scarred desks, tobacco smoke, the smell of sweat and feet.

A little soldier with a foxy face and the blue eyes, yellow hair and neckless head of a German was stamping some papers, a smoldering ceramic pipe hanging from one corner of his mouth.

He looked up at Deo. "You want to join up?"

"Some of my friends are in the Legion."

"We're all friends. Weren't you in the general mobilization?"

"I'm an Italian."

"An ally." He turned to shout at a square man seated behind him, working a typewriter with two stubby fingers. "Gebhart! Get me form L-2."

Deo sat down in a chair pointed out to him.

"Name, father's name, mother's maiden name? Catholic, Protestant, Jew, Moslem? Occupation?"

Deo answered. The little German looked up. He turned to the square man. "Gebhart, an artist!"

"Muck off, I've got this frigging report to get done."

"What do you paint?"

"Pictures; heads, portraits."

"You do any nude ladies? Gebhart, he collects them. He's a dirty old sod. Here, take this paper to the medical officer. One flight up. Room 6. Good luck, artist."

Room 6 was narrow, long, and had many canvas screens. A lean beanpole of a man with red hair, a large bony nose and teeth with spaces between them was thumping a naked boy on the buttocks. "Into your pants and across the courtyard. Take these papers to Sergeant Wasserman."

From the smell Deo judged the doctor was drinking medical alcohol with water.

Deo wondered why he was there, and he re-counted his reasons while the doctor, his white robe soiled with tobacco stains and machine oil, looked into the mouth of a middle-aged man with a great mustache. "Ah, no back teeth. Well, you don't need them. The army food is prepared by the best chefs in Paris—from Maxim's and Café Voisin. Melts in your mouth.

Take these papers across the courtyard to Sergeant Wasserman."

Deo found himself standing in front of the doctor, who took another sip of his mixture. "Damn it, weren't you told to take your clothes off?"

"No, I wasn't."

"Shuck them all off. Keep your socks on. Your feet clean?"

"Yes, they are."

"That's a relief. The damn French never bathe." The doctor lit a dark-brown cigarette while Deo got out of his clothes. Behind him several more men had appeared, carrying papers. The doctor ignored them and looked at Deo and listened to his heart and thumped his chest. He frowned.

"Cough."

Deo coughed. The doctor grabbed him by the testicles, pressed, and said, "Cough!"

Deo coughed. The doctor released him and again listened to Deo's chest.

"You been to a doctor lately?"

"Dr. Paul Alexandre. He's a friend of mine."

"Major Alexandre? What he say of your lungs?"

"Congestion at times."

"Spit blood?"

"Sometimes. But not lately."

The doctor shook his head and began to mark up Deo's papers with a large purple-ink word: REJECT. Under it he wrote in smaller text something Deo couldn't read.

"What do you do?" There was an old sardine tin the doctor used as an ashtray, and he shook ash off his cigarette.

"I'm a painter."

"Get off the ladder—away from house paint. It's full of lead. Your lungs can't stand it."

"I'm an artist."

"*That* kind of painter?" He pushed a new bit of paper at Deo. "Here, show it at the gate—to get out. You paint landscapes?"

"Heads, nudes."

"Can't use them." He slapped a little fat man in a friendly gesture on the bare buttocks. "You bend over ten times. Your truss bother you?" He turned to Deo. "I have all the nudes I can stand here. But a tree is something. . . . Now jump up on your toes twenty times. Hop it!"

Deo walked slowly down the stairs. On the official form in purple ink he read: REASON FOR REJECTION FOR MILITARY SERVICE: *Medically unfit for training of field service. Dr. Josef Lubowski.*

Deo seemed to be coming out of a bad dream. ("Get off the ladder.") He walked away from the old barracks with a quick step. Had he really been mad enough to want to go to war? That mass insanity of barbarous games at the death of the human race. For what? Politics, trade, national slogans, questions of boundaries, pride of princes, greed of merchants: the special national emblems of double eagle or farting lion or addled hawk one lived under? What foolishness.

He went over to César Gay's bar almost on the run and said to César, "This is one of those times when I need an absinthe-cognac to survive—as artist to artist I swear it."

"On credit?" César put two drops of absinthe into a glass, added the cognac and watched Deo drink it. Then he put two drops each into Deo's hands, and while Deo sniffed up the absinthe he served another customer. Deo held out his hands again. "Once more."

"A new trick?"

Deo rubbed the added drops behind his ears. "It was a close thing, César."

"What happened?"

"Something I tried to do."

"You did what?"

"I found myself doing something I didn't want to do."

"That happens, Modi."

"I nearly went over to the real enemy."

César put away the absinthe without any comment.

"I almost got off the ladder."

He found the steel in Beatrice Hastings; the hardness of her character, so English, yet so feminine, he supposed.

"I don't see, Deo, where you are so badly off," she said to him.

"I have no money, I have no dealer who can sell a painting."

"The world is fighting to survive, to fight off these Huns."

"Forget the filthy Germans; they always make trouble. Isn't there any other way to control them so the world can go on living?"

Bea was very British at those times, feeling so right, so superior to the French, who were moving numbly, placidly, slowly to the front lines, raw columns of men with wild mustaches and unrolled leggings, carrying long loaves of bread and wine bottles. And dying, not so placidly, in the mud by the hundreds of thousands, while Deo heard of the graft and dirty politics that went on behind them. The new rich appeared in fur collars, smoking cigars, and the fat cats in favor made fine speeches at munitions plants, and the offal called army supplies became big business—in billions of francs—in Paris.

Deo in 1915 was depressed by the evil pattern the war settled down to, to what it was to be, he feared, for the rest of the conflict. Paris was the leave town, a sin city; "Sodom and Gomorrah in pink tights," Max Jacob called it. A weathered, unpainted roaring military camp by day, a brothel by night, thousands of dives, cellars, clubs, hotels, circuses, ballrooms and alleys, all designed for one basic purpose. Women were the prime objective of the soldiers, women perfumed and dressed in silk for the Allied officers, anything female available for the foot soldier, hot with a fearful lust, ashen with the terror of death only a two-day army pass away. Alcohol and gambling were almost as strong a way to deaden the pain of awaiting annihilation as flesh. Deo, drinking a deadening brandy with a soldier, sensed, even smelled this fear.

He read Machiavelli on war: "Bitter foes today, sugared darlings tomorrow, kissing and scratching in a breath."

Better to work. Deo began to paint again, and he painted with a fury, not the war, not the gray poverty of those who did not partake in graft or grow rich on military supplies, or the legal murderers, the generals and their staffs. He painted his girls, his friends; those that were left; he drew children, couples. He was at his prime painting, and if he drank more and used hashish with a recklessness that tried to dull these bitter days, it did not affect his work, nor his poverty. He had a lot of poverty. "Leave it to a Jew to grab a lot of something around."

There were times when he sold his overcoat—the overcoat that Bea had gone to such hardship to get for him in the second winter of the war, bribing, smuggling, paying a bonus to a busy tailor. He sold the overcoat one day in a bitter snow to a passing factory worker, and for two days he lay in a dank cellar smoking poppy until they threw him out, shoeless, and only the bitter weather saved him from losing his shirt and trousers.

Beatrice Hastings, looking grim and serious as Florence Nightingale, took him in, bathed him and returned Deo to normal life.

He sat listlessly, in a catatonic state, wearing a robe, in Bea's flat, a cigarette smoldering in his fingers, and she stood at the fireplace and looked at him, shaking her head like a female Jehovah in British tweeds.

"Don't you want to live?"

"Everything wants to live, Bea. But on its own terms."

"You've got to earn life."

"No flatulent English school mottoes, please. I feel very ill."

She knelt down by his chair. "You're destroying our love, Deo."

"Love can't be destroyed. I read it some place in an English novel. Galsworthy, I think."

She stood up sternly in that crazy English integrity and pride he disliked. She said as if shaking a finger at a small child, "Don't give me any of the kind of talk that's popular among your bohemian friends."

"We don't talk like this."

"Do they ever try to keep you from drinking, from those horrible drugs?"

"No, that's why they are my friends."

She lowered her head. "Am I your friend, Deo?"

"You try to be." He looked up at her and he saw she hadn't forgiven him, but that she was excited and ready to go to bed. He took pity on her. That night they lay in each other's arms and the alarms of a German plane over Paris, the marching of a regiment past the house, the long grind of gear-tormented army convoys trucking to the front did not intrude on their bodies or their minds.

When Bea was unrestrained, there was also a seepage of her self-confidence. In the morning she was tender and kind. They went at noon to the park. There were rows and rows of blind and broken soldiers laid out in the first wan spring sunlight. It was harder to find a place to eat without meeting drunken military faces and their loud and shrill women in dirty dragging petticoats.

Anxieties tormented all their friends. Zbo and Anna were having a hard time of it. Deo and Bea sat in the back room of the Zborowskis' and hoped the stew smelling of bay leaves would turn out well. Meat was hard to get, the vegetables were usually frozen and potatoes black and rotten.

Zbo had grown thinner; the gold of his hair had turned a commoner yellow. He found fewer and fewer prospective customers.

"Pascin is a great man in New York," Anna said, stirring the stew. "He's bought a double-breasted American suit, he wrote us, and he chews gum, and sleeps with coal-black girls in a place called Harlem."

"Is he painting?" Deo asked.

Zbo began to lay out the plates and cutlery. "He's working for some fashionable magazines. Says he's going to become a Yankee citizen."

Bea lifted a fork to see if its prongs had been properly cleaned. "Imagine Pascin as a Yankee, a Puritan."

Deo watched Anna ladle out the watery but savory-smelling stew. "That far Pascin will not go. He'll paint a pair of lacy drawers on the Statue of Liberty and teach Mme Woodrow Wilson to do the can-can."

"Kisling is in the Foreign Legion. He says the food is terrible and *traif*, and the officers wear girdles. But it's a brave group of men. Chagall? He's painting in his Russian village, Vitebsk; even the Tsar wouldn't trust a gun in Chagall's hands. The group here is breaking up fast. Braque in the army, Léger, everybody has been called up. Soon Modi and Picasso will be the only working artists."

Deo laughed and began to spoon up stew, taking big bites of the gray and gritty wartime bread. "That *yenta* Gertrude Stein is going to drive a Model-T ambulance. She's the most dangerous man in Paris, behind a wheel."

Bea sniffed as if she suspected a bad odor, but Deo knew it wasn't the stew; it was the name Stein. Bea did not worship at the large flat feet of La Stein.

The front door opened and soon a huge figure in a wrinkled uniform came into the back room of the shop.

Deo leaped to his feet. "I've seen everything! Here comes Father Mars! Apollinaire!"

The soldier saluted with the wrong hand as they crowded around him. He said, "Noncommissioned officer de Kostrowitzky now, of the 70th Battery."

"No!" said Zbo. "Now France is really in trouble. *You're* an officer?"

"At the moment an acting corporal. But an NCO living with my 75s; a beautiful weapon, as sweet and strong as some of my poems. A jolly little rapist with a snout of phallic grace."

Deo spun the big man around. "What a uniform! Spurs, gaiters, baggy breeches, sloppy tunic, kepi, belt and holster. You have a gun in there?"

Apollinaire shook his head. "I carry peppermint-stick candy in the holster. At thirty-four, for me, food is more important than weapons."

Deo said, "You have a new girl, we hear."

"Yes. The other, Lou—it's all over; my ardor, my devotion left Lou unmoved. The new one—I picked her up on a train near Nice. It looks eternal and destined. Now I also have my horse to love, which I fall from regularly, and the gun carriage is very troublesome on my tender stern. I tell you war isn't to be enjoyed any more."

Anna asked, "You'll have some stew."

The big man sighed. "It's kind of you to ask a fellow Polack."

Anna set her bowl down before him. He ate with vigor. "The best chefs in the army go to the generals, naturally—the staff are all constipated—and we get canned beef marked: *Mexico*

1861. It's touching historically, but when you open a can of it, unbearable. Even the Africans will not eat it, and they collect German ears and fingers, and castrate almost everyone they capture. There will be a lot of terrors in Germany."

The critic polished the bowl with a shard of bread, swallowed and looked about him with a happy greasy mouth.

"So what is new in art?"

"Nothing," said Deo. "No one cares if it lives or dies."

"Ah no—you should see the big guns, the ships at the bases, the flying machines. Rare cubism now! Painted in Picasso's and Braque's shapes. Camouflage, they call it. It's a moving gallery of art, done on steel, in deadly sport. Art may die out on canvas and in the galleries, art for the next century may be machines, motors, functional shapes, and what we call artists, just junk gatherers, picking up auto fenders and bicycle wheels and calling the dismal stuff art."

Bea asked, "Have you been to the front?"

"Easter day, *cannonier-conducteur* Guillaume de Kostrowitzky—they don't recognize the Apollinaire—left the Nîmes training camp for the northern front. Paris papers please notice. It was a dazing experience, moving along the banks of the Rhône with my comrades. I was made a corporal near the front. As someone has already said: 'War is too important to trust to the generals.'"

"And poetry?" asked Deo, accepting an army cigarette.

"Of course. I've been writing better than ever." He plunged a hand inside the tight uniform and pulled out a booklet bound in blue covers with military emblems on them. He flipped the pages, printed by some vile gelatine office process in a violet ink, much smudged. "Only twenty-five copies were printed on squared writing paper. The flyleaves are sheets from the *Bulletin des Armées de la Républic.*"

Deo took the booklet. "*Case d'Armons.* I like the title."

"Twenty-one poems written at the front." He saluted again.

"Where to now?" Zbo asked, beginning to clear the table.

"Traveling on military matters, just staying overnight in Paris. I must see Picasso. I hear his new girl is dead. I brought him a copy of the poems."

Deo rose. "I'll walk you over."

Bea stiffened. He took Apollinaire's arm and the two walked out into a street rumbling with army lorries. Apollinaire looked about him.

"Shabby, yes, run down at the heels like a tart walking the pavements, but it's still Paris, Modi. Still the Chinese-jade arsehole of the world. The big prize. What's with you? You look like rat poison."

They walked along, Deo with his hands in his pockets. "It's like this, Apollinaire. I have three choices. I can kill myself, a natural desire in all human beings when cornered. Or starve here. I mean slowly, day to day, living off scraps at Zbo's, and they have nothing accepting a little from Bea, whose income from England is cut way down. Or going back to Italy, and it's a uniform and a gun there. Bad lungs or not, you know that."

"What does all this matter, Modi? If you're painting."

"But painting for what? For who? And why? I see the whole world running over with blood. When I'm sober enough our whole culture has come to the end of its rope. Everything is falling apart, and everything is turning brown. The very paper in the window there, the rooftops, even the stones underfoot are crumbling away. Soon it will be an empty planet, growing cold, the sun dead, and nothing will whirl or spin, and all we've done worthless."

Deo stopped and shivered. He rubbed his brow and his lips. "You think I've gone crazy?"

"No, Modi, I've known for a long time this is an age of decadence, but see it all as the farmer sees it—when the world turns to manure it's a time to plant new seeds. You're desperate, but that's the condition of man. Survival and seed time is the new slogan."

"I can't go on in 'the deep dark night of the soul.' It isn't the hunger, or lack of courage. Drink less, drug less—sound advice. But there's a feeling I'm settling for so little. As they say at the stock brokers'—I'm settling for ten cents on the dollar. If I only had the courage to walk off a bridge. But then I think, it's a shame to wreck myself so soon when nature will take care of it later. And I want to say a little more, do a little more. Then it's cold in the morning, the bottle is empty, the bread stale and everybody is in uniform. Do I sound banal?"

"There is always love. . . . What is love to me? It fails me and I seek again. Modi, perhaps it's the being in love that's the only hope there is."

"You enjoy the looking, me the finding."

"There's this English bit, Bea—I've watched her. Her eyes swim when she looks at you."

"Bea? Yes, she loves me. But she doesn't accept me. There is another man she loves—one who wipes his feet on the mat, bathes more often, combs his hair, sits home evenings listening to Elizabethan ballads, admires the poems of limp-wristed boys. She thinks she can turn me into that man. I had hopes, I had such desperate hopes, Apollinaire, this time it was the all, the everything. But instead, it's only a course in manners, a lecture on the relationship of gentlemen and ladies. And when the lecture ends? A wild flinging aside of clothes to wallow in the lower emotions, and later, little regrets for being so fully degraded and human. It isn't easy to be loved."

"Of course not. If it were, just think how happy everyone would be, how perfect this world would look. And, Modi, who wants a perfect world? The novelists would have no adultery to write about, the poets would have nothing dark and brooding to tear apart like a fly, and artists would all paint boxes to hold chocolates. It's better this way, not perfect, lamenting, hurt, able to pity, certainly to feel pain with love; offering our throats to some woman's razor-edged passion. Telling her, 'Cut, cut, *ma chère.*' "

The critic wiped his nose with blunt sagacious fingers. "Now you cheer *me* up, Modi."

"You've got your poems, a new girl, you like the stir of battle."

"I shiver too—I fear the evil eye. I keep thinking of that painting de Chirico did of me with the circle like a bullet hole in my head—right *here.*" The big man stopped and held a finger pointed at his temple, like a pistol. "Just *here,* a very common wound at the front."

Apollinaire took Deo's arm and they went along against a

tide of Greek, Italian and English officers, who were moving curb to curb down the street as if Paris was a conquered city.

19

THE SITUATION with Bea was unbearable. She was shiny and steel-hard most of the time. He could make no impression on her ideas, her manners, her social patterns. She found him soft, and persisted in her attempts to mold him into her version of the artist as a companion. Deo, outraged, would disappear on drunken bouts, would find other girls. He would entertain soldiers in a mist of cheap tobacco and spilled cognac, peddle a drawing, trade his tie or his shoes for a drink.

"Arm yourself against the Puritans," was his café battlecry.

In the end Deo would find himself again under Bea's unamused stare, and the worst of it was she stopped slanging him, correcting him. Bea merely gave him her "iceberg look," she cleaned him, fed him, and enveloped him in inarticulate disapproval.

"Damn you, Bea, don't look so smug, so right."

In despair he longed, after their lovemaking, for a long anonymous sleep, a blankness of inner desolation where small amenities were retained and one didn't have to wake up to a cold Paris, a mistress with a long, lugubrious, British, self-righteous face.

Sleep was his brief sanctuary against cold and hunger, against another surrender to drugs, against vacant staring at empty canvases.

But, in fact, he was painting better than ever, even selling a few drawings at the Rotonde, passing them out with a gesture of a millionaire presenting shiny dimes to children.

"Vulgarize your prophets," he said to a buyer of a café drawing, "and you don't have to crucify them."

He took his fees with the limp wrist of a man amused at the world.

The coal merchant Lemmonnier refused the drawings, holding up his black hands to his soot-soiled face. "Pay for your coal. No, no, M. Modigliani, things can't go on like this."

"I need to keep warm."

"I'd rather feed my children coal than your drawings."

The little rusting studio stove remained cold. Deo's hands turned blue and he couldn't paint till the weather changed a bit.

The concierge let Deo warm himself at her stove on those nights when the birds froze in the trees. "It's just too bad, seeing a fine young man like yourself getting into such dreadful habits."

"You're so right, Mme Morabeau."

"It's getting colder outside."

The coal merchant Lemmonnier took pity and again extended credit, and the corner café let Deo carry home some scraps of food in a copy of the *Echo de Paris*. (THEY SHALL NOT PASS! VERDUN STANDS FIRM—GERMAN DRIVE HELD.)

Art was beginning to move again. So many people in wartime Paris—not with the best of taste—wanted a painting to take back from the city. Deo was hopeful; wore his faded corduroy suit and his thin colorful muffler, took to a checked shirt and red belt, and painted away when he could get materials and canvas.

More poet than dealer, Zbo continued hopeful. For some years Deo had sold a painting now and then to a dealer named Paul Guillaume, a sharp-faced man always wreathed in tobacco smoke, a dark felt hat pulled over to one side of his lynx-like head. A wise one, a knowing one. Guillaume began to say among the dealers: "Modigliani, I might do something for him."

He was a supercilious man, full of self-conceit, articulate, petulant, with a greasy love for art. ("A perfect dealer," Apollinaire said.)

Deo thought often of Italy, but reports from home were worse than ever. His brother Giuseppe Emanuele was now a Socialist pacifist, "Not an easy thing to be," he wrote Deo from jail.

Deo could boast of one collector of his work, "I have a single admirer and he's blind."

He was not totally blind, this old man named Leon Angeli living on the rue Gabriel, but nearly so. He was a ghostlike little man, usually wrapped in old sweaters, following with a weak but wary step a long cane around his cluttered little apartment that smelled of fried fish and spilled wine. When Deo was desperate, he would drop in on his admirer with a painting and the blinking old man would try and see it and then run his hand over it.

"Ah, ah! Yes, nice thick paint." His red-rimmed eyes would tear and the pale-yellow eyelids roll up like a curtain.

"You'll buy it, M. Angeli? I need to pay the coal merchant."

"I have so many," the old man gestured with his cane. "Yours, others."

The walls were hung with unframed canvases, more were stacked among the blind man's bundles, his collections of pots and pans, empty bottles.

"I'll take ten francs, M. Angeli."

"Someplace I have a few francs . . ." The old man fumbled his way to a tall Empire bookcase and began to claw through the novels of Balzac, hunting each one with splayed fingers and dropping it to the floor.

"I thought I put away a few francs."

"Can I help you search? Try the Zolas. The *Nana.*"

"No, no. I can tell by the feel if I have the right volume. You ever read Voltaire?"

The Zolas yielded no franc notes.

"You are collecting a lot of art, M. Angeli."

"The law of averages never changes."

"I suppose not," said Deo, picking up volumes of Dumas.

"I'm bound to strike a winner among you painter chaps now and then. A real genius—a high-priced painter someday. The more I own of young fellows, the better the chance to hit a real top runner or two."

"Certainly. Very clever, M. Angeli."

"Ah!" The old man was fingering a large book bound in half morocco.

"You've found it, M. Angeli!"

"No, a shirt collar I thought lost. Yes. It's here! The francs. Are there ten or twenty?"

"Only five francs, M. Angeli."

"I am sorry. I can't buy today."

"You can owe me the rest," said Deo, thrusting the painting at the old man.

The blind man pushed it back with his cane and began to shout, to thrash around him with his long arms, knocking over bottles, a small bronze statue of a lion. "No, no, I owe no one. I never borrow. I never lend. I'm *not* buying today."

Deo was already at the door, clutching the francs in his hand. "It's the full price, M. Angeli. You owe me nothing!" He shut the door, hearing the old man moving around his personal debris like a crab caught in reeds.

There were not enough blind art collectors, Deo told Utrillo, whom he had invited to spend the results of the sale.

Drunk that night, Deo became quarrelsome, obstreperous. He broke a bar mirror, he insulted an American Red Cross officer by asking of her menopause when she questioned his intake of alcohol. He walked up to a group of Russian officers who were throwing pieces of hard bread at a waitress and shouted, "I'm a Jew and you can all go to hell, you lousy pogromist Slavs!"

A colonel of the Tsar's Imperial Guards with a drunken face nodded and said:"*Jid, Jid,*" and spit between Deo's toes. Deo slapped the colonel's chops and was pulled to safety by Utrillo and others before more damage could be done. Deo's lungs bled that night.

The next day he and Utrillo were drunk again. Utrillo began on sight, in the streets, to kick pregnant women in the stomach ("They spawn like salmon!"). They were both arrested and taken to the police station.

Sergeant Lescot shook his head at the sight of them. "Back again, my old customers? Paint or jail?"

Deo, nursing a sore mouth, a darkening eye, said, "We'll paint."

Sergeant Lescot had a back room at the station where he kept canvas, brushes and tubes of color. He was interested in art and an artist arrested for anything short of rape, murder or treason was permitted to paint a picture and be set free. There were times when the police station looked like an art gallery.

Deo set up a canvas in the chilly back room and watched Utrillo attack a surface, outlining a picture of a walled garden and street. Deo started to draw in a portrait of a Gypsy girl he knew. In an easy self-confidence the two friends painted.

"How's the war going, Mau Mau?"

"It's still on out there. My mother is off someplace with a soldier." Utrillo mixed a bright green.

"Noble of her. A good Frenchwoman."

"She married this one."

"One can carry a good thing too far, Mau Mau. Have you any lake blue?"

"Try this green I just mixed—apple-green."

"That's a fine street you're painting."

"I'd do better, Modi, if I had my picture post cards with me."

Deo stepped back from the image of the Gypsy girl he was painting. "No one can say the French Republic isn't helping its artists. Let's make every jail an art studio."

"You think the war will ever end?"

"*Magari,* of course not, Mau Mau. It will last a hundred years. People may end up in the year 2016 living in caves, eating mice and fighting their wars with stones. You have any kind of yellow?"

"Sorry, I just used the last drop."

"Never mind. My mouth hurts, my eye hurts, my lungs hurt."

Deo threw down the brush and lifted the painting. It was a quick sketch but it was a good one. He felt miserable and desperate. His head ached and he knew Bea would find him before the night was over and she would primly give him her glacial look. She would drag him off like a female spider to her den, first to prepare him for sacrifice by making him feel his faults, and then she would mate with him in grim self-abandonment. *Mah!* What a life.

"Mau Mau, you don't like girls?"

"I don't dislike them. There was one big-titted girl, Suzanne's model. Big all over. She was warm to the touch—like a fever.

Her skin tasted like honey, and furry armpits. But no, I don't need them like you do."

"You're a lucky fellow, Mau Mau. A simple mind, natural, pleased by a bunch of grapes in a bottle, and in need of little. A genius who can work from post cards. Never oblique or subtle. And a drink solves everything."

"Not a drink. Drinks. I'm thirsty."

"We'll sign these *if* Sergeant Lescot gives us a drink. If not, no signing. You'll be firm?"

Utrillo nodded and wiped his paint-stained fingers on his shirt. "It's a good world when you come to think of it."

"It's a good world," said Deo, "when you don't think about it."

Deo heard Bea's voice from the front room of the station-house, and Sergeant Lescot's answering tone. Somehow Bea always knew when Deo was in trouble, and he wondered if the police were in her pay. The English, Max Jacob had said, are *so* skilled in their use of bribery; they use it like a favor conferred.

Wordlessly, Bea came into the back room, striding along as if going to the greengrocer's; wordlessly Deo put his hands in his pockets and walked out; wordlessly Bea followed him into the street, and caught up with him. He pushed her against an iron railing.

"Get away from me, you Cockney harpy. I didn't send for you."

Bea remained silent; only her eyes were wide with outrage. Her nostrils flared, but not a word was proffered.

Deo punched her in the side. Soundlessly she caught at her breath. Deo waited till she straightened up, and he said softly, "I am sorry."

Not a moan, not even the consolation of a curse. Hating each other they walked down the street, side by side; neither was happy and neither was alone. Loneliness, Deo thought, fills more beds than love.

The complacent and naive years of peace for Europe were far behind—irrelevant memories. The great war ground into 1916 and Deo began to feel he was walking through a fearful

public drama in which one had no real role, only the detachment of the onlooker who is the historian, perhaps, but never
the actor. Paris was shabbier than ever, but livelier too, as it
became the leave town, the playground, the place soldiers
came to from the mud and disaster of the rotting trenches; they
came to get drunk, to seize love, to sit and drink a Courvoisier
and what passed in those days for wine. The women they
hunted—women in dark cloche hats—smiled with their teeth
showing, teeth that grew longer and sharper as the war went
on.

He could not gear himself to the time, or participate by vicarious bystanding. Deo's poverty was abject to the point
where he would appear at some friend's flat late at night
carrying a battered suitcase full of rags. The time for pride, for
any remnant of gentility was past.

"Anything at all for these. Twenty francs, ten francs, five.
I've had nothing to eat for two days."

"Modi, what the devil do I want with your broken suitcase,
those unwashed rags?"

"You want me to keep alive, don't you?"

"Come in, and have a drink."

There was always someone good for a drink if one waited
long enough. But food, shelter, heat, those were the insoluble
problems.

Still he had three dealers now—Zborowski, Sagot, and Guillaume—and occasionally a painting was sold. And Deo was
paid for a drawing now and then sold at Berthe Weill's little
shop. She was thinking of giving Deo a show of his paintings of
nudes.

Berthe Weill lived among her cards and her drawings, while
soldiers looked over her stock for something to send home. She
managed to find space for a few artists she felt had more than
just promise. In the shop's percolated opaque light, some good
canvases were hanging.

The idea of a show of his nudes pleased Deo. He was thirty-
two, but he felt older. Time for a show.

"At twenty, Berthe, everyone has talent, but who has anything at fifty?"

"Let us just worry about today."

"I'll never reach that far. Fifty—it's like thinking of being twelve feet tall."

"You've done some fine nudes. Do seven or eight more. I'll give you the show."

"It seems a good idea. Let them look at the flesh as an artist sees it, let them stand around and see the body presented with the decorum of an archbishop smiling at a choirboy."

"You talk when you should be painting. I'll frame them neatly and we'll make it a good show."

Deo smiled; he still was a charmer. *É così giovane e parla bene* when not in his drunken angers. Yes, he could always quicken a female heart when he put his mind to it.

"You share it too, Berthe, this vicarious kick of knowing life is extended beyond ourselves, often by the bodies of women. I'll paint you a set of nudes to knock their eyes out on stems. Now advance me enough for a few glasses of Armagnac."

"You can talk a statue down off his horse."

Deo had become talkative, always shouting and arguing in cafés and studios, making trouble, breaking chairs, getting his face smashed from time to time. He was losing control. It was Bea, damn her—the ethereal and martyred Bea. Always he was just about ready to break with her and yet he was always going back. But she and the drink and hashish were ruining his nervous system.

Why should he shatter furniture, set fire to the drapes? Howl his denigration and condescension? He shook his head and stood on the street corner by the little shop, nodding to himself; if he kept this up, he'd begin talking to himself. He went to drink the Armagnac on Berthe Weill's small advance.

After a few reprehensible days—somehow he had embarked on a series of drunks—he found himself in his studio with Soutine pressing a cold wet rag to his head. He looked up and pushed away the rag, revolted by his inept frustrating habits.

"Chaim, have I got *tzaris*."

Soutine grinned, his big frog-mouthed grin. "Paint it out."

"I could have a show of nudes."

"Nudes I never paint. Dead meat, yes. Live *nafkas* I can't handle. You'll be all right? Who punched your eye?"

"I'll be fine. Bea hasn't come around?"

"I don't think so."

"It's not right, Chaim. I want true tender love. I want a kind of woman that doesn't exist. " He sat up and lay down again at once. Standing up would have to come later in the day. "And you know why? I've created an image out of poetry, and where can I find it?"

> "*Tanto gentile e tanto onesta pare*
> *La donna mia quand'ella altrui saluta . . .*"

"I don't understand this spaghetti talk, Modi."

> "My lady looks so gentle and so pure
> When she is greeting others by the way . . ."

"That what you want? I like them with muscle, *zaftig*."

> "That the tongue trembles and remains mute
> And the eyes which desire to see dare not look."

"Very cheerful, Modi. Better work on your painting. I've been doing chairs and people myself. Who can get meat? That's for the officers, the *fastunkina*."

"You may get to like it alive."

The nudes Deo began to paint were not a new departure, but rather an extension of forms he had become interested in. He used the young girls from the cafés; his charm always assured him a model. Best of all he found Zoie, a little milkmaid who would come to him after delivering her heavy buckets of the pale fluid that was wartime milk, after serving behind the counter in a creamery. She always smelled pleasantly of cheese and sweet country butter.

Zoie reminded him of Italy, of places and colors and sounds from his early youth. After a painting session he sat alone in his only chair, smoking a cigarette, dreaming of the Isles of I Galli on the Tyrrhenian Sea, in sight of Positano and of Capri, there on the Sorrento peninsula where he had walked as a young artist, dusty and sunny—brown and glowing with purpose, looking for life, themes and love.

It was fine there, no crazy war, no Senegalese or Somali tribesmen in uniforms pushing you off the sidewalk. But perhaps war had come down hard on the Italy he remembered, even harder than here in Paris. War was always going on in Italy, going back to the Romans as during the time the Emperor Vespasian had taxed the privies with the remark, "Money does not stink."

Deo put out the cigarette butt. It certainly doesn't when you don't have it. If he only had rich patrons, like the artists Ingres and Rubens, who were sponsored by the Jesuits. But Deo shook his head; no, he didn't want patrons with power. He smiled in memory of Rome; the cafés and the interiors of churches all gold mosaic and green faïence, and then there was the husband of his landlady, that *cornuto*—who had threatened to knife Deo. *Mah,* those were the days.

Campagna oxen dragging marble past the Farnese Palace, the loud pleasures of art students howling under nocturnal fireworks over the Colonna and Odescalchi palaces and the whole world was younger, and only a bit more innocent.

Deo hunted another cigarette and failed to find one. Perhaps he'd go back to Italy after all when the war ended—settle down, cure himself outside and inside, marry some fat barefoot girl smelling of olive oil and outdoor sweat, and get himself a crop of *bambini.* He laughed; fat chance of any of that working out. He turned back to the nude painting.

BOOK IV

Ivory Black

20

ZOIE THE MILKMAID, posing in the nude for Deo, was shy and frightened of Paris. She had, she told him, come from a farm near the Swiss border and was saving her money for a dowry, to go back and marry a pig farmer.

"*Le maître au cochon,*" Deo said, mixing a pale color.

Zoie always took her clothes off while staring at Deo with a worried expression. She had a very young body, round with adolescence. Deo painted her with a flickering neat line in a diffused light of his own invention; he did not care for natural or scientific light in painting. He treated her flesh on the canvas to subtle modulated transitions of heavy pigment. In a larger version he drew her directly and boldly with his brush. Nudes against brown backgrounds seemed the most successful. He tried to catch it without coercion or simpering.

After posing, Zoie stepped into her petticoat, cupped her firm little breasts in her hands and stood staring at the painting.

"M. Deo, that's me?"

"Of course it's *you,* Zoie, seen through *me.*"

"It's rather sweet, don't you think?"

"I do, Zoie. But then you are sweet."

"And people will hang me like that on their walls?"

"They'll have to. You'll bowl them over. Even museums

someday will have Zoie in all her skin in their halls, painted by that early-twentieth-century master A.M. You're immortal. We both are immortal and more."

"I don't feel it."

He kissed Zoie's cheek and slapped her tight little rump. She shook her head. "You know what I said, M. Deo, when I said I'd take off my clothes for you?"

"That you were saving that for the bridal night."

"Where I come from the old women examine the bedsheets the night after the marriage, and if there isn't any blood, the husband beats the wife and throws her out into the village street. There is much disgrace."

"Zoie, you have nothing to fear. I agree with Dr. Johnson, 'Maidenheads are for plowboys.' Now get back on the sofa. I want to do the right arm over."

"This Johnson is the horse butcher that also has the market restaurant in Les Halles?"

"A distant relative, most likely. Strip. Back on the stand. Don't move!"

The nudes Deo painted were sensual, but they had the kind of modesty and decorum of the best landscapes. Picasso got through to the special quality of these nudes at once.

"You've become a classic, Modi, that's what's happened to you. There is purity of concept here, for all its erotic content. You suggest the moments after a shameless abandon of loosened passion, as if it's all been done in the next room."

"You don't miss the feet?"

Picasso laughed. "You're like a film director, Modi. Now in the flickers they move the camera in close, so you see only heads, bodies, never the unnecessary parts. That's what you've done, moved in closer."

"Thank you. Now I know. To tell you the truth, women's feet usually are very ugly. Except in Italy where they go barefooted and smell of cow muck."

"I may go to Italy, Modi. I'm living in a small country place in Montrouge and the war is depressing me. All the dying, everything gray. Jean Cocteau wants me to go with him to Rome."

"He has a Baudelairian bleat, but good opium."

"Erik Satie has written some music, Jean says, and Serge Diaghileff has his Russian Ballet there. At least it will be different. Don't you miss Italy, Modi?"

"I miss my mother too, but I can't live with her. I don't often miss Italy. Would you live in Spain?"

Deo walked up to a painting of a seated Zoie in just her thin white slip.

"Classic?"

"That's right, Modi. I wish Apollinaire, that brave lard of a soldier, were here. We'd drink a toast to your new classic nudes. There's nothing as beautiful as a nicely turned ass, is there?"

"Let's drink to that. If you'll buy."

The painting of the nudes brought closer Deo's desperately unsatisfactory relationship with Beatrice Hastings. Bea still insisted on looking over his paintings. One day, she came to give him a sweater as protection against the early spring chills. She pursed her lips and marched around the displayed canvases of the new nudes.

"You're telling the world your secret."

"I don't think the world cares, Bea."

"Is it like this for us?"

"No. We have words and touches and dark and liquid movements, but these paintings are things I've never found in life."

Bea went up to him and pulled on one of his earlobes. "Poor dear Deo, in love with a dream. Isn't the little girl in the slip enough?"

"She's just a model. Works in a creamery near here. She's very innocent—and untouched."

Bea looked at him and went away, unbelieving and unsmiling. Deo lit a cigarette and sat down and looked at his painted harem; the most perfect things, he mused, the finest ideas and truest, most tender emotions in the world don't exist except when set down on paper, on walls, on canvas.

What had Soutine said one day? "It is taught in the Talmud that life is a turning wheel; who is on top today will be on the bottom tomorrow, and everything is repeated in that manner." Deo looked out of the window in a sudden burst of despair;

birds were showering down on the trees like feathered confetti, pots of oleander bloomed on window sills.

Deo tossed away the cigarette and had a drink of chianti smelling of paraffin. He went down into the streets of soldiers, of posted casualty lists, of women in black sobbing for men who had once beaten them, holding onto children that seemed all eyes, with cropped flea-bitten heads and matchstick legs. Drink and venery had won the war. No matter what the fat cats said they were fighting for, no matter how sacred the field mass and the flinging of holy water, the fat voices of the politicians, or the proud stance of generals relaxing their prostates— the war was being fought for a few days' leave in Paris to get drunk and connect with some woman.

Deo decided one could not disengage gracefully from this world. He got drunk that night on the proceeds from a drawing and broke a table in a café, punched an Englishman in the mouth, cutting his hand on the protruding teeth. The war was now inside of him, and raging Modi was no mocking Voltairian, Apollinaire had said.

He leaned against a building to think it out—it was greasy with the stains of how many women pushed by how many panting soldiers against the rough bricks? Deo's head spun and he wiped blood from his bruised lip against blood from his cut hand. All around him in the embodied world of sound and smells were the calls of the hunt. The great braying hunt for women, for a few hours' intimacy before going back to the long brown graves in the mud, to the last twitch beyond the sandbags and the firing step; to twitch, not in passion but in the death rattle, in the evacuating expectancy of suddenly ending up as splattered shreds dangling from rusting barbed wire.

Hallways smelling of creosote, the Palais Royal station with couples eating each other's noses in farewells, signs of *Gouvernement Français* proclaiming Victory just ahead, dripping plane trees and store windows on the rue St. Michel, and drunken officers with shoulder pips, swagger sticks and good boots vomiting in the yellow mist around the street lamps.

There was a *café-billiard* on the Left Bank where Deo went sometimes to make drawings of the officers of the Allied armies. If they were in a good mood and full of brandy, they would often give him some money for a pencil sketch. Just before it got dark was best for selling officers portraits, before they became sodden and maudlin with drink, before the whores and *vendeuses* and false *grisettes* had stripped them of their army pay.

Deo was going along to a café, passing the big couturiers on the Place Vendôme, his drawing pad under his arm, moving along a narrower street. An old man, in a fifty-year-old uniform, made up as a toy soldier, was beating a drum, while on its hind legs a little brown mongrel dog, also in a toy soldier's uniform, was marching around with a small toy gun strapped to its front limbs. The old man's face was painted boneyard white with big red circles on his cheeks and the end of his nose. A curly mustache, copied from a playing-card king, was pasted on his upper lip.

He was marching with a slight limp on one spot of sidewalk —bobbing up and down, up and down—singing an old song:

> "Comme je veux je peux
> Tu peux, je veux
> La façon que tu plaise!"

No one was paying too much attention to the performance, and no one dropped any coins into the tall patent-leather soldier's hat the old man held out to the passing crowd.

Deo went up to the performer. "Flinck, it is you?"

The old clown, thin and worn, turned the empty hat upside down and clapped it back on his painted head. "Oh, it's Flinck, all right, Modi."

"You have a new dog."

"You can't call it much of a dog. It's not the great Baba, eh?"

"No, it isn't, Flinck." The little brown dog was staring up at Deo, its tongue out.

"But then, Modi, face it, this isn't the great Flinck any more either." He looked down at the little dog and shouted, *"Mori, bis.* Encore!"

The little dog just stared and kept his tongue out.

"The war is hard on everybody, Flinck. On painters too."

"You still smear, eh? Make the pictures?"

"I do. Nobody really wants the paintings, but that's all I know how to do."

"It's a crazy nihilist war. All wars are crazy, but look around you—except for the dying and the hell of living in the trenches, men like the war. Look at them gobbling up the girls, with all their teeth showing, and smelling so richly of the bistros. You make Paris the scene of war and battle and they'd never go home."

"Flinck, you're a genius. Take the killing away, make it a game, keep it a big party, and you've solved everything. Flinck, you belong in the government with a mistress on the rue Bonaparte. I'd like to treat you to a rabbit paté, a bottle of wine, but as you see . . ."

"You're not looking well. Modi, you never did take Flinck's advice. Excess in everything, eh, for you?"

"You're talking like a father."

The old clown's strangely painted face seemed a travesty of pain and pity and tenderness for all its gaudy surface. He fluttered his fingers in their white gloves in a comic gesture. "Everybody has a second father. And a clown makes a good one because you can say he isn't for real, he wasn't given me by the *Père Éternel*. Get rich and hire Flinck for the job. Flinck now must go back to work, Modi."

The old clown began to do a comic jig that was a parody of the rigid army drill, and the little dark dog barked and got up on his hind legs. A melancholy lambent glow illuminated the street as soldiers and girls, officers and nurses in capes—the whole busy night traffic of Paris at war—continued the grotesque ballet of a desperate hunt for pleasure.

"*Au revoir, mon cher* Modi," shouted the old clown.

"*Au revoir, mon père*," said Deo.

Painting the nudes helped Deo, invoked a period of calm, a kind of physical and moral convalescence. It did not last, but Deo was thankful for the respite; he knew he was long past the point of no return. He was doomed, and while waiting for whatever was to come, he painted. Existence was more inter-

esting if one had a grievance against society—but never against
life.

Deo missed Apollinaire, who had been a kind of jolly balance wheel, whose grand rambling sentences were so tasty and
often so wise. For Deo talk was not a cleansing thing as it was
for Apollinaire; it only left Deo with a raw throat and regrets
later that he had made a spectacle of himself in public.

Apollinaire had been made a sergeant. From Damery, near
Épernay, the critic wrote: "I sleep very little and only have to
stretch out on the ground like the poor buggers I command and
I fall asleep at once. It is fantastic how much one can endure."

On March 9, 1916, Apollinaire was made a citizen, a French
national, only two years after he had applied for the honor.
Deo and his friends celebrated in Paris in a dingy café where
wine could still be bought at a reasonable price. Deo made the
first toast, overheated, laughing, snapping fingers for attention.

"To M. Wilhelm de Kostrowitzky, known to us with affection
as Guillaume Apollinaire, a French writer by choice, a lover by
desire, a friend with a large heart, now a citizen of this boun-
teous republic."

Picasso stood up, his dark eyes large with mirth. He held a
bit of paper in his hand. "I have here the police report sent to
the commission that at the front awarded our friend his cher-
ished citizenship. I read: 'From the national point of view he
has never been the subject of any report which could lead him
to be considered suspect.' End of report. Let us cheer."

Soutine and Brancuși banged their glasses on the café table
of warped old oak.

"Citizen de Kostrowitzky! France salutes you with a fart!"

Deo in worn brown velveteen and a Basque cap motioned
the waiter to bring more wine.

Nearly a week later Deo was sitting at Gillotte's sketching
some unbuttoned British pilots drinking Calvados and *fines*. He
had already sold three sketches. The smoke was thick, the air
bad. Max Jacob came in, his eyeglass missing from its usual
place on his left cheek, his worn suit pressed but darned in
several places. He walked over to Deo and put an arm on the
artist's shoulder.

"Something terrible has happened."

"What?"

"Apollinaire was dreadfully wounded on the 17th."

Deo dropped his pencil. *"How* badly?" He felt his hands tremble, the taste of copper fill his throat. First Braque badly hit, now Apollinaire.

"In the trenches at Bois des Buttes. A shell fragment went through his rotten tin hat and into his skull."

"He's alive?"

"He was evacuated to the hospital at Chateau Thierry. And now he's reported at the Val-de-Grace here in Paris. Do you mind if I finish your drink? This bit of German *schrecklichkeit* has upset me."

Apollinaire was in Paris. He lay in a narrow iron bed in a miserable dirty room filled with a long row of other fearfully wounded men in other iron beds. He was pale, his head a balloon of bandages. His features appeared bloodless to Deo, as if carved out of the end of a church candle. On a night table lay a steel helmet with a ragged hole in it, and a copy of the *Mercure de France,* torn and black with dried blood.

The pale eyes of the critic rolled around to get Deo and Max into focus. The big body did not move. When he spoke, the voice was thin and seemed unrelated to the splendid head.

"A dirty bit of business, what?"

"Don't talk," said Deo. "You caught a bad one on the noodle."

"I was reading that newspaper when *whoosh* like a bee passing."

Max nodded and tried to read the headlines in the mangled newspaper.

"I went on reading; I didn't think I was hit. Then suddenly my blood just poured out."

Apollinaire closed his eyes and shook his head. "That blasted de Chirico. He's in touch with the other world. But why this exorcism on me, his friend, his defender?"

Two hospital orderlies passed carrying a shape concealed in linen. Another soldier, held up by two nuns, hobbled along, groaning the most horrible obscenities into the sisters' ears. It was, Deo thought, a scene from an unwritten play at the gates of Hell.

Apollinaire opened his eyes. "I swiped a look at my medical report. Head wound from a shell splinter, from the scalp to right temporoparietal, grazing the outer table." He recited it almost proudly. "Fancy medical talk, what? No brain injury, but these dog gelders, what do they know?"

"Any pain?" Max asked.

"Antitetanus serum, patches of rash. The wound is five centimeters by four centimeters. Very giddy at times, chaps. I get an impression, a suggestion I'm falling through the floor. Just sinking through it."

"It's nothing," said Deo. "I get that after a few drinks."

The cheerfulness left the poet and critic. He wet his lips, the small mouth seeming more out of scale than ever on the large head. "It's a dirty business all around. Man is betrayed everywhere."

A large bony nun was tapping Deo in the small of the back. She had a harsh dry voice. "That's enough. No more visiting."

Max pulled up the bedsheet on the big chest of Apollinaire. "We'll be back. Anything you want, we'll get it."

"Within reason," whispered the wounded man. "Did you see the helmet? Amazing . . . *that* de Chirico."

Deo took the nun aside. "Sister, how badly hurt is he?"

"That's for the doctor to say. They want to trepan his skull— open it up."

"But why? It's an amazing brain. It must not be hurt."

"His giddiness is bad, and there's prolonged granulation and dirt in there."

Max sighed. "His enemies have already said that."

Deo began to gag on the smell of stale blood, urine and decaying flesh. He ran toward the big double doors.

21

His life with Bea reached a strange climax. He wanted this affair resolved, yet he dreaded the moment. Happiness had been lost, like music in a dream.

There were many fancy and wild balls for the war effort, to raise funds for buying amputees cork limbs, to support the Red Cross, buy flags, rebuild shelled houses, feed refugees, to host and honor an ally. Bea liked to appear at these balls in some new stylish gown, acting like a duchess, but her checks from England were coming later and later. Finally, there was one ball for which she could not afford a new gown.

She said to Deo as they sat in her flat drinking whiskey, "I can't go to the ball for the Italian ambulance fund tonight. I have nothing to wear."

"It doesn't matter. There will be smoke, music, fat generals, bad wine, poor food. And we have no money for more whiskey."

"I want to go. I want to feel happy without feeling guilty."

"So we'll go." Deo was not in a cheerful mood.

"I haven't a new gown. My money hasn't come."

"There's a war on, everybody tells me when I need something. Wear your black faille dress. It's a stunner."

"It's been seen too often."

Deo was drinking the last of the whiskey. "Put it on. Go ahead!"

Bea looked at him, then turned, surly and cool, and went into the bedroom. She came out in the black faille, marching like a smart shop mannequin, showing neither exuberance nor friendship.

"You see, utterly impossible."

"Just stand still."

"Whatever for?"

Deo found a box of pastel crayons in a window seat. Taking

up a white one, he began to sketch an arabesque design of flowing patterns on the cloth.

"It tickles," Bea said. "What the devil are you doing?"

"Stand still and you'll see. Why not paint *on* a woman for a change? Nothing awesome like the Apocalypse—just, say, flowers. Yes, flowers."

Deo picked up a fistful of colored sticks. Swiftly he began to draw amazing flowers on the black cloth, from Bea's neckline to the hem of the dress. The dark material took the pastels well. It was a beautiful and altogether original creation.

Bea said, "It's wonderful. But it will all brush off, soon as I move."

"Don't move."

"I'll have to someday."

"I'll fix it. Just stand still—*still*, damn it."

"Control your foul temper, my dear boy."

But she was not angry. She had grown wilder of late. The war had done something to the prim Mrs. Hastings. Some of her inner experiences were being articulated. The war excited her.

Deo covered her yielding belly with pastel designs—he worked up toward her cupped breasts. He laughed at her and howled like an Indian. "Oh ho! Oh ho. *Sans blague!*"

"Not now, Deo. Finish the dress."

He gripped her around the knees with one hand and flexing the cloth finished off the bottom of the dress. He banged his head against her hips with impudence.

"Don't move."

"I wouldn't dare spoil it. It's so exuberant."

"The belle of the ball . . ."

He turned and rummaged in an old paint box. He found a small tin of fixative varnish and a tube used to blow the fixative over charcoal drawings to keep them from smudging. He set the tube to his lips, one end in the tin can of fixative. Blowing hard, Deo began to cover the dress and its designs with a spray mist of thin varnish.

"It's cold, Deo!"

"It will harden and dry in a moment. Not a flower will be smudged."

She ran her hand through his hair. "My crazy Deo. A genius."

"Don't say it like that." Their incompatibility of temperament was ready to clash again.

Bea smiled. "I'm going to give you my last five francs to get us something to eat at the ball buffet."

"It's nothing designing this. I always said those prancing fashion queens were frauds. Anybody can do it, but not as well as this, of course."

The ball was a wild one, filled with rumors of great victories on the Western Front. A statesman had made a speech. The large ballroom was packed with colorful banners, officers limping or whole, women escorted or alone, men in evening dress, *agents de police, inspecteurs.* A band played Offenbach and Elgar, then South American music. People drank. Bea's dress was a great success.

"Let's dance." Bea was looking down on a moving flood of uniforms, gowns, medals, people coming and going, faces green-orange under the lights behind pink crepe paper.

"I'd rather have a drink." Deo waved to a little Japanese artist at the buffet.

"You're tight now on the last of my whiskey."

"How English of you, Bea, to remind me what I drank is yours."

She stepped on his toes and smiled enigmatically at a beaming officer in the uniform of the Garde Royale.

"Ah, Mrs. Hastings. How charming, how daring. How *chic.* Yes, *chic.*"

"Deo, you know Eric. He's a sculptor."

Deo bowed with a mocking gesture. He didn't think much of the big Scandinavian sculptor, even in uniform. They all did big muscled sexless monuments, these northerns, in their clean prosperous studios.

"You'll dance, Mrs. Hastings?"

"I'll dance."

"I'll be at the buffet," Deo said.

The music grew louder, aided by gourds and brass. At the buffet Foujita, the little Japanese artist with the horn-rimmed

glasses and the protruding teeth, treated Deo to several large
and strong drinks.

"What a Dubonnet-colored light this war casts, Modi."

On the floor some were dancing an intricate tango. Bea and
Eric were almost amorously locked together. People were
cheering them on. Deo could see Bea's coquetry and Eric's red
flushed face. The fat back of his neck was the color of un-
cooked pork.

A café owner to whom Deo owed money stood at the buffet
sipping pale wine. "Well, I must say the English are letting
themselves go. Mrs. Hastings, she wearing any underwear
under that strange dress?"

Deo turned back to the bar.

"It's almost," said the café owner, "like in one of the dives
behind the Opéra. Look at them twist and turn. Audacious,
no?"

Foujita put a hand on Deo's shaking arm. Deo's protuberant
eyes were staring wildly at the two dancers.

Foujita hissed politely: "Maybe you'd better take her home."

"To hell with her! And all the English. To hell with William
the Conqueror, Nell Gwyn, Lord Wellington, David Copper-
field *and* King George!"

"I say," said an English officer in the uniform of the Black
Watch standing at the buffet.

Deo pushed the officer aside. The drink, Bea's dancing, Eric's
gripping hands on her naked back, the moving flowers on the
black cloth, all seemed to pump pure acid into his groin. Deo
let out a roar and charged onto the dance floor with the little
Japanese close behind. The overhead lights were like hot
grease.

Deo pulled the dancers apart. Eric raised his fists but some
fellow officers grabbed him. Bea screamed, "Let go of me! Let
go, you rotter! You filthy rotter."

Deo struggled to grab her. A necklace broke—beads flew in
all directions. Foujita stepped in between them. "No, no, *not*
here."

"Get away, little man."

"No. You hit me, Modi, I give you the damnedest jiu-jitsu
lesson you ever saw."

"*Cortigiana!*" shouted Deo.

Men were pushing at him and he felt himself dragged and carried through the garish halls and to the front doors, where he was flung out into the night. Bea followed, not waving her arms, but her face white, her eyes round and filled with terror, and yet arrogantly in control of herself.

"You madman! You drunken savage!"

He reached for her, but he was too drunk to catch hold. Bea began to run down the street. One of her shoes came off, but she kept on running. Deo swayed and saw his flowered design round a corner.

"*Ritornerò domani,*" he shouted. "*Sans blague!* I'll get you tomorrow."

He turned to face a group of howling urchins holding up newspapers and wilted flowers for sale.

"*Sans blague! Sans blague!*"

"Get out of my way, you stinking brats."

"*Sans blague!*"

He moved off, hands in his hair, escaping their insults.

He could not sleep. Alone on his studio bed he suffered shame for his rage. To behave so badly; he, the leader of a school. What school? What leader? What art? The devil devour Bea. He would end it now. She was too strong for him, not at all the perfect, tender love; that kind would never come to him. What a foolish dreamer to act the itchy wet-faced schoolboy and let himself be carried into tantrums like this over a wriggle on a dance floor.

Deo feared his temper, which was becoming stronger and more uncontrollable. He must cheer himself up, talk to somebody, but he was still too unsteady to get out of bed. He had wanted to go see what Soutine was doing, to sit with him and talk of miserable Jewish villages among dreadful murderous peasants, and the High Holidays in a muddy world of rutted roads and cold fields, and the blood-red velvet cover of the Torah in rotting village *schuls* and the singing of *Am Yisroel Chay.*

No, it wasn't for Deo, all this bitter nostalgia. There was just an artist in the dark, lying, waiting to sober up, waiting for morning to go and beat Mrs. Hastings black and blue.

He began to sing softly *Torna a Sorrientu,* and when he had sung all he could remember of the words, he sang a little louder *O Mare Chiaro.* He liked the old Naples street songs; they always cheered him up even when hungry.

He grinned in the darkness. . . .

The next day Deo went around to her place. Bea had been drinking. They wept in incomprehensible joy and fell into each other's arms. After a few drinks, however, they were fighting again.

"Help! He's killing me, he's murdering me!" Bea shouted over the sound of breaking furniture.

The neighbors shrugged. It had happened too often.

"The Italian is at it again."

"The English slut is no better. Soon they'll make it up with cooing and biting, and come out, arm in arm."

For two days they fought, drank, made the rounds of the cafés. They ate a lunch of omelette, Vichy, peaches; on credit— borrowed and begged. Bea refused to take off the flower dress. At the Dôme, the Rotonde, the now soiled and torn dress was her banner of indifference to Paris.

"I'm going back to London."

"Don't say it if you don't mean it."

On the third day, at last, the long overdue check came from London. Deo felt defeated; now she could mock him again with money in her hand.

Bea sobered up, bathed, put on a tweed suit. She looked at Deo, still sodden and soiled, and shook her head.

"This is the end, Deo. We've had it, and it's done."

"You only say that because you have money. What would I do if you leave me?"

"You'll paint."

"What makes you so sure?"

"You're a painter, aren't you? Paint!"

Two days later Bea ran away from him. He banged on her door until an old woman with a broom in her hand shook her head.

"She's gone. Books, drapes, everything."

"When?"

"This morning."

"Where did she go?"

"She didn't say. But she sent her big suitcase back to England. A travel service picked it up."

Deo walked away shaking, rolling his head.

Zbo found him brooding and told him he had sold a painting, but Deo didn't care. He took the money and got drunk. He began to hunt Bea in the Red Cross halls, in the English eating places. He haunted the railroad station where the trains left for the English Channel. More soldiers, more wounded. All began to look to Deo like Apollinaire with the hole in his skull.

He had an idea. Deo phoned Cook's from the station, and affected his most charming voice.

"Hello? This is the Sagot Art Gallery. We have a painting Mrs. Beatrice Hastings wants us to send over to her. Our delivery boy has just been drafted into the army, and he took the address with him. Can you give me Mrs. Hastings' new address? She's sent some luggage to England through you. I fear this painting may be held up in customs if we try to ship it to her."

"Ah yes. The address is Hotel Model, 235 rue de la Gaité."

Deo hung up and stood breathing hard. His chest was filled with burning charcoal heated to an amazing degree. He found the place, a small hotel. He managed to get her room number by the ruse of the fictional painting. The hotel was, in peacetime, a clean respectable place, full of English university people, now given over mostly to British officers, judging by the shoes and boots outside the doors.

He knocked on the fumed-oak door of Bea's room. There was no answer. He knocked again. He heard someone stir inside. Far down the hall a scratchy gramophone was playing music from *H.M.S. Pinafore*.

"Bea!"

No answer.

He began to bang like a madman. "Bea, I know you're in there."

The door remained closed. Faces in shocked disapproval began to appear at other doorways. Deo began to hammer with his fists on the oak. "Open the door, damn you! Open the door!"

He was weakening. He was suddenly sober, hollow, deflated. He fell against the door and tried to dig his fingernails into it. Everything was lost—everything was gone. A slow assassination of his body and mind seemed to be taking place.

"Bea, Bea," he whimpered like a child.

He felt hands on him. He pulled free. He sank to his knees, mouth against the door. He must commit this final act of humiliation and leave.

"Bea," he said, "if you don't want to ever let me in, slip me some money so I can get drunk, really drunk."

He was impressed by this final abject gesture.

There was no sound behind the door. Now the arms were dragging him down the hall, past English faces, English mustaches, English smells of shaving lotion and wet Burberrys, past English magazines held in pink boiled hands. . . .

They turned Deo loose on the sidewalk, warning him the police station in the rue de la Gaité was nearby. He walked off and buried his hands in his pockets and found some money, the remains of what Zbo had paid him for the sold painting. There was one deep, *deep* escape route. The smoke. Escape Bea, escape the sight of Apollinaire's broken skull, escape from everything as long as he had the price of the smoke. Some called the smoke the Dream Made True. What did it matter as long as one could move for a time into another universe.

He began to walk slowly toward the place of release. No. First to tell Apollinaire about it all. At the hospital they only let Deo wave to the wounded man. They were, they whispered, going to operate on the skull. Deo turned away and left. He had to escape any intricate reflection of himself and Apollinaire, his head banged open like a tin cooking pot.

Deo left the world. He resigned from the human race the moment he left the hospital. He knew he was dead; a delightful sensation he told the old Algerian woman in the opium smokers' flat where he bought the pipes. At last tranquillity came, brought on by the first pipe and his own exhausted spirits. He lay in a long narrow room, somewhere near the Deux Magots, on a filthy rug. Peace appeared with a shell of indifference as thick, as hard as a deep-sea turtle's shell—it protected him.

Every artist is his own ancestor. I am beyond the fear of wounds, the agony of hunger and cold, neglect, the wrong kind of love, man-eating women, beyond shattered helmets. And skulls they chop open to sort out the brains and label the parts —this tender bit of sweetbreads is for Beauty, and this neat bit of gray matter is Sexual Love. Oh, here is a fearful fellow; look at the size of his Poetry Gland, and where could you find anything shaped like this lobe full of Art?

The old woman, her flesh pierced by gold ornaments, went by, swishing at buzzing flies, ignoring the smoldering heaps of rags that were men deep in escape. Deo smiled, his eyes closed . . . *We walk a well-traveled labyrinth that is not a puzzle, only a trap. Apollinaire's face appeared; his skull was unbandaged, the raw wound dripped a purple fluid—a Cardinal's, an emperor's, essence—more sacred than blood.*

"I have the paunch of a marsupial, Modi, and in it I carry our final mortalities," said Apollinaire. "Two lumps of brie cheese, one of my baby teeth, an aphrodisiac made of tiger bones, and the first chapters of a new book asking: Why molest God? He is as unhappy as we are. . . ."

Deo tried to answer as two girl dancers came in, their faces veiled, their pudenda exposed to the yellow rising smoke.

Apollinaire clapped his hands.

"Absurdity may be the essential human condition," the critic shouted, his wound streaming, his fat body wriggling in time with the dancers' rotating bellies.

The old woman bent down and put a fresh opium pipe in Deo's mouth; he took three long pulls of the sweet poison into his lungs. *The image of Apollinaire began to shake like a reflection in stirred pond water. The dancers pulled off their veils, and they were both Bea, and one said, "Don't touch me," and the other, "Take me now—hurt me."* The images dissolved as everything dissolves if one waits long enough. . . .

22

A MAN CAN BECOME A RUIN just like a church, Zbo said to his
wife. Not just disorder and squalor but an enigmatic loneliness
as in their friend Modigliani, that drugs and alcohol could only
numb for a little while. A full falling away of the purpose, the
habits that had kept him alert, kept him proud. The messianic
formulas by which Deo held together his life seemed to have
gone slack to the point of dissolving. He was still handsome,
with the dark luminous eyes of a Caravaggio, but drawn and
lean, worn and sick. Impecunious, improvident, he roamed the
studios, the streets of the Carrefour Vavin neighborhood, still
innately convinced of his genius, but changed.

He was becoming not just notorious, but even a little famous.
Zbo was selling a painting from time to time for as high as four
hundred francs. Deo could still paint, could still, as he said,
relight his flame when he placed himself at the easel. Slowed a
bit, not as daring as when Bea had driven him toward his best
art, but he could work.

He never had any money left over; he spent as soon as he
collected, then was shabby on the stairs of the rue Muller, beg-
ging a drink in the rue Pigalle or the rue Damremont, passing
with a wink the tombstones in some little burying ground,
laughing into the palm of his hand, as if he had suddenly made
some great penetration of the secret of the universe.

Picasso had gone to Italy to paint scenery for the Russian
Ballet, Chagall was now important. New powers were arising
in Russia; the Eastern front had collapsed, and there were
names like Trotsky and Lenin. Deo vaguely remembered them
at the Dôme, a few years back, drinking a cheap wine and talking a lot with their hands, pulling on their little goatee beards.
Soutine was still malodorous in his filthy studio but painting
like a star-crossed angel. The rest? It was too hard to think of
them all.

1917, and there was talk of the Americans coming in, but

Deo no longer cared to remember the war. Paint and many windows were gone from the house fronts. Food, coal enough to keep warm, were not to be had, and the *Bulletin des Armées de la République* was a collection of fairy tales by official fiction writers. Great mutinies had broken out in the French armies. Only the casualties were real, the long lists of names, the girls and women with snotty kids, all in black, too hungry to cry, too weak to protest the great crimes on the chalk plains of Champagne. The gendarmes moved them quickly on their way. In many regiments every tenth man was taken out and shot by general orders.

Apollinaire had never fully recovered from his operation; his center of vitality appeared affected. He lost weight; he always threw off a grimace of pain in the middle of some heated debate; his memory at times seemed to fail; he went into strange moods. He was still in uniform, a leather patch over his wound under the army cap, serving in some government office, in danger of being sent back to the front, where the slaughter went on like a ritual.

Sitting in a café where nothing tasted like anything used to taste, Deo and Apollinaire sipped the raw wine from the carafe in front of them and looked over the sunny day, the green trees, the summer air.

"I am ardent again, Modi, and inclined toward seduction."

Deo stirred a finger in the red wine in the glass. "It's just motion. Without love it's like pig-breeding."

"There's a model, Modi, says she's had a child by you."

Deo made a grimace, one of his scowling ones. "Thérèse? Suzanne, tasty as *antipasti misti*? Lili? Helène? Moue? I don't remember. But I'm not the father of any of their children. Half the French army and part of the marines perhaps, but not me."

"She says it's yours, Thérèse, or Suzanne, or Lili."

Deo poured out the last of the wine they could pay for. "I shall never fall in love again. Wine is my destiny. Not love."

"Tell me that in your old age. You and me, we shall make art and love a long time to the sound of tambourines."

"No, no, I'm run down like a cheap clock. I have only a little bit of my brain left."

"Enough to read something good about your painting?

You're carrying on the battle of the individual with society—refusing to come to terms with the bourgeois world."

"Only a little bit of brain left."

"I'm going to leave you soon, Modi. I'm being picked up by a
very beautiful woman in a wonderful autocar. Mlle B."

"I feel the end is near. Not enough brain left to butter a crust
of bread."

Apollinaire brushed his uniform, adjusted his leather patch.

"Oh, she drives me mad. So jealous. She says she'll never see
me again if I go courting anyone else. And I'm so dreadfully
inconstant."

"You think it matters that the Americans are really coming?"

"They have to come. They are vital barbarians—crude, rich,
and very innocent. How can they avoid coming over to tell us
how to run our world? They have an extraordinary capacity for
other people's business."

"They buy paintings."

"To decorate their log cabins. They have killed off the In-
dians, Modi, and the buffalo, and they seek adventure. I fear
we shall win the war after all."

"Is that bad? I can't sleep nights thinking of all the dead, all
the fancy fools with fancy talk who had them killed, all the
senseless reasons why they are fighting. But to lose a war can't
be good."

"Naturally winning a war is bad for us, Modi. Only defeated
people get desperate enough to create new art. The best corre-
lation of eye and hand grows on disaster, on débâcle. *Ah.*"

"Ah?"

"Mlle B. I'll tell you a secret. I hear she has three breasts—
three perfect breasts. Says it runs in her family.

"You don't know for sure?"

"Today I find out."

Apollinaire had risen and like a turkey cock was preening
himself, adjusting his uniform. A large black closed car pulled
to the curb. A liveried chauffeur held open the door with the
tiny gold and red monogram on it. In back a slim woman with
a veiled face sat well back from the light; only a small pointed
chin—like a shark's fin cutting water, Deo thought—showed.

Apollinaire rolled his eyes at Deo, swung his cane in an arc and walked toward the car purring and exhausting blue smoke. He entered the car and it drove off in a reek of rationed gas. Deo sat hunched in thought at the café table, wondering why men went on with this woman hunt, this adventuring with perfumed bodies, strange bath powders, mouths smelling of toothpaste and coffee, flesh loose or taut under restraining silk and rubber.

Bea had disappeared into England and no sign of life issued from the island—no letter, no gossip ever came back about Mrs. Hastings. But for the portraits Deo had painted of her, the nude drawings, Mrs. Hastings had not existed. No one ever produced one line of her poetry.

It was all gone and almost all healed over, but it had left its ridges of angry flesh, its scars that itched and ached in bad times. Deo looked around in the day's sun for someone to buy him another drink. Only the weather was kind.

He should, he decided, go sketch again from the nude. There was a school on the rue de la Grande Chaumière. The fee was small, the model often very good. . . . For a landscape artist it was not at all a bad day—all those damn green trees.

For several days he worked on his drawings. Deo saw her sketching over the shoulders of the one-armed soldier who was drawing the model with a heavy untalented charcoal line. It was the third time Deo had seen her. She was the reason he kept returning to the sketch class. She appeared magnificently sensitive, had a stately neck, features delicately flowing rather than modeled. She was small-boned, she was modest, she had light-brown hair worn down over her narrow sloping shoulders in two long heavy braids. She was called Noix de Coco—Cocoanut—by the rude young boys in the class, because of her perfect oval head. Her friend, the big bold girl with the mahogany-colored hair worn in a huge Second Empire chignon, was called, in the easy banter of the American bars, Haricot Rouge —Kidney Bean.

They were both untalented. Noix de Coco drew with great care and rubbed out her mistakes slowly, with a frown. Haricot Rouge drew swiftly, boldly, covering up all her mistakes with a lot of messy curly lines. She also avoided hands and feet in hard-to-draw positions. She said it didn't matter, she was training to paint on china.

The windows of the sketch class were open; there was the orchestral buzz of summer insects. The model was a big healthy animal—some apache's *môme*—showing her flanks to about a dozen members of the sketch class. M. Bauvette, the instructor, was ingesting a *pot-au-feu* and two large brandies in a corner behind a stack of drawings he had no intention of looking at.

The model stretched, slapped her overripe buttocks with the sound of a pistol. "The hour? Same time tomorrow, M. Bauvette?"

"Eh? Yes. Students please don't leave any papers behind you."

The pupils began to look over their sketches, compare drawings, talk of the evening, hunt for cigarettes.

Deo closed the blue covers of his sketch pad. Noix de Coco and Haricot Rouge collected their drawings, their pencils and charcoal sticks, dusted their fingers and went out side by side. Deo watched them walk. All he knew about the girl was that he was madly in love with her; he didn't dare speak to her without the danger of frightening her back to some respectable home. Her name, he found out from M. Bauvette, was Jeanne Hebuterne.

"Modi, please, she's no pimp's tart from the Caveau des Innocents."

"I was just admiring her drawing."

"She has *no* talent."

Deo was in a talkative mood by nightfall on the terrace of the Rotonde. Saucers piled up, rug peddlers were denied, and Soutine kept nodding and agreeing without saying anything. Several artists and their girls at nearby tables kept repeating in amusement with an unmelodious hooting: "That's so right, Modi. Tell them. Tell them!"

He had been drinking, but not too much. He was articulate with love.

"I've reached the time, have become aware of the lengthening shadow, and I tell you, perhaps happiness is not mediocrity. An artist should paint and not worry about his troubles. Now take me, I'm about ready for pre-sanctity. Don't laugh, you swine. *Garçon*, another of these miserable Pernods. As for me, I shall not have a disreputable senility in any monotonous future. Chaim, are you listening?"

Soutine flopped his face down on his hands and grinned with his large lips. "You *nudnik*—what are you saying, Modi?"

"I am saying, like the hermit crab the artist must build his own house, from the debris of the past, and as some writer once said, 'Our doubt is our passion, and our passion is our task!' *Garçon*, where the devil are you?"

"Modi, don't drink any more tonight. You know how wild you get now when you're drunk."

"Ah, Chaim, I talk and you don't listen, and you don't understand. I am a *tzaddik*, a wonderworker. Alcohol itself is a form of creation, a low form, to be sure, but a little art form, nonetheless. It keeps the clock striking in the back of your head. *Garçon!*"

"You'll get wild. *Oi vey*—the police will lock you up. What are you trying to prove, that you can drink up all the booze in the universe? Look who's coming. Haricot Rouge, the porcelain painter, and Noix de Coco."

Deo lifted his head and smiled. "Her name is Jeanne Hebuterne and she is the great love of my life."

Soutine cocked an ironic eye and lifted his shaggy eyebrows in wonder. "You *momser*, again?"

"Never like *this*."

The two girls came onto the terrace of the café and sat down at a table near a shaded light. Jeanne was shy and avoided staring at those around her.

Deo said, "I've asked about her. She comes from the parish of St.-Medard. Her parents—the father is in the wool business—think she has artistic talent. They think there is money in it."

"Has she any talent?"

Deo made a small grimace and did not touch his fresh drink. "She plans to try to get into the École des Beaux Arts, but she has no talent, just wonderful little hands that hold the chalk as if it were an angel's feather."

"You know her well?"

"I've just asked about her, that's all."

Jeanne sat stiffly at the edge of her chair. It was clear she did not often go to cafés. She looked younger than her nineteen years as she touched Haricot Rouge's sleeve. "Is this where all the real artists come?"

"That's right, Jeanne. There are worse *boites de nuit*. I like to come here for an hour or so. The studio gossip gets around. You meet people."

"Thank you for bringing me. But I must go home soon."

"We'll have a little white wine. It's very mild."

Some giggling models at the next table waved to them. "Ah there, Haricot Rouge, how are the picnic plans going for next Sunday?"

Haricot Rouge nodded. "It's going to be amusing. One of the chaps is bringing his flute; we'll rent a boat."

A model with a gold front tooth turned to Jeanne. "You coming along, *mademoiselle?*"

"No, I have to go to mass."

"I didn't know anybody from the studios ever went to church much."

Jeanne blushed and sipped her white wine. Her honey-colored hair hung in two heavy plaits over her flat chest. To Deo staring at her she was a child. Her demeanor showed how out of place she felt on the café terrace.

Foujita, the little Japanese artist, came over to Deo's table.

"Marvelous night. You can hear the trees breathe. You don't like trees, Modi?"

Soutine said, "He's stopped talking. Was going like a steam engine. But now Modi is in love. He's actually shy. Think of it, Fujee, the stud stallion of the Left Bank, sighing like a schoolboy."

"Soutine," said Deo. "You're better company when you don't talk."

"Oh, *mademoiselle*," said Foujita, bowing across to the two girls. He waved. "How are you?"

Jeanne smiled. "Very well, thank you."

"Ah, so—good."

Deo snarled at Foujita. "She's a nice girl; don't try any of your Oriental erotic tricks on her."

The little Japanese's eyes went wide behind his thick glasses. He bowed and hissed, "Ah now, Modi, you have fleas in your brain. But if you want to, I will be happy to give you some satisfaction for your anger behind the café." Deo swallowed his drink at a gulp, threw some coins on the table and left the terrace.

Soutine said softly as he arranged the coins in a straight line on the marble tabletop, "He's been acting odd all evening, and when he saw your friend Noix de Coco come in, it was like a stone fell on his head. He says he's in love with her."

Foujita said, "It's a madness. It's called *musth* when it happens to bull elephants; you have to chain them up till it's over."

Jeanne had finished her wine. She rose from her chair and arranged her gloves on her fingers. "I must be getting home. Thank you for bringing me here. Who was the very handsome one who just left? He's been to the sketch class several times."

Haricot Rouge frowned. "Modigliani. A crazy Italian painter. Stay away from him. He has a rotten reputation with women. He's crazy. You saw how he suddenly got up and went off grimacing like something from the Medrano Circus."

"He's like a Greek god, I mean the statues you see in the museum."

"I'm happy I don't see him that way. I'll meet you in class tomorrow, Jeanne. I'll stay on and have another drink."

Jeanne quickly departed; her father was strict about her getting home before nine. The house on the rue de la Montagne Ste-Geneviève was a respectable one, her father always told her, and while she had a brother who was an artist, and she had talent, there were people involved with art, she was told, whom one couldn't trust. Home was where she would put on her little blue apron, her father would pull on his beard, bow his head over the table and say grace. Then they would eat the good food her mother helped the cook prepare. And if she had any sense, she would never think of the handsome Greek god again. At the school Haricot Rouge always tried to protect her, called her one of St. Ursula's virgins, and approved of the flat-

heeled shoes she wore, and the fact that Jeanne used neither
powder nor lipstick.

None of this had anything to do with the way she thought
about the hot-eyed young Italian after she said her prayers,
kneeling in her rough linen nightshirt, then getting into bed
and just before falling asleep having the strangest visions and
blushing at them . . . his dazzling black hair shimmering with
a luster like a Phidian helmet.

The next day she was working on a drawing of the model in
the sketch class, rubbing and altering her drawing, making a
correction, a *repentir* as the artists called it, when someone's
hand appeared against the white of her paper like some stage
magic.

"Let me show you, *mademoiselle*, how to draw a line so it
doesn't sag or get grubby and mean."

"If you please," she said, very softly, lowering her head as if
trying to bite her own collarbone with shyness.

His hand took the stick of charcoal. "Now, always see it first
in your mind, with the eyes closed. Then again look at the
model. Then down on the paper, *so*. No scrubbing, just glide
the line on. Boldness is all, with a direct unaffected style."

She looked at the simple, powerful outline he made of the
model, all detail abolished and everything recreated, monumental, yet with great charm. She became at once convinced of his
genius, then frightened by his closeness.

"*You* take the charcoal."

"I could never do it."

"Take it."

She took the charcoal stick and he held her wrist very firmly,
and there she was—*drawing!* She laughed from fear and
shame, a silvery kind of little girl's laugh, showing all her small
perfect teeth. Then she blushed and her stomach rumbled from
nervousness. *Oh, mon Dieu!* "You make it *so* easy."

"Of course. It is, once one has the confidence."

"I'm Jeanne Hebuterne."

"How do you do, *mademoiselle*," he said formally, very seriously. "I am Amedeo Modigliani. I am very much in love with
you."

"Oh, dear, how wonderful. I mean . . ." She lifted a hand to her face. "Oh, dear, why should you be?" She began to laugh hysterically.

Haricot Rouge said, "You're going to pee in your pants, Jeanne."

Deo said, "Can we take a walk during the next posing break?"

"Of course, if you want to."

"Damn," said Haricot Rouge, breaking her pencil point.

"You're very trusting, Jeanne," Deo said. "Don't be." He pressed her hand. "I'll meet you outside."

Jeanne nodded, her hand shaking too much to use the charcoal.

Jeanne's parents, Deo, Haricot Rouge, the students of the sketch class, all had the wrong impression of Jeanne. She was actually a very strong personality, whose shyness covered the firmness of her own convictions and certain stone-hard traits that gave her an inner character that might have shocked those who thought they knew her very well.

At an early age she had refused to let her mother dress her, but scowling in her baby fat had attempted to get into her own clothes. She disliked the color yellow, and because she had very pretty legs and feet, to curb her vanity she wore dark cotton stockings and low-heeled shoes. She hid little bags of peppermint sweets all around her room, and ate them secretly with great feelings of guilt after she put out the lamp, aware she would never qualify for true sainthood.

She trusted God, the Virgin, Jesus, Marshal Foch, the President of the Republic, the Pope, her father, the art of Degas and Ingres, and the man who fed grain to the deer at the zoo.

She was very well read—liked Balzac, disliked Dumas—preferred books where the lovers suffered in a strange stilted language and the authors didn't waste too much prose describing sunsets. Jeanne was very hard and well-muscled for all her size, but nothing marred the smooth neat surfaces of her limbs. She was sure the modern world was full of mediocrity, that love would come when she found someone whom she could help because he was fully unaware of his own abilities, and that he would admire her for her spiritual qualities. He would also appreciate—not too grossly—her fine little shape, which she inspected in her mother's dressmaker's mirror, before which she paraded nude when the family went to the country weekends. Until told otherwise, at a convent school, she thought love was made through the navel.

Jeanne was very level-headed in most matters, and she doubted she had the true artistic skill in art her family hoped for. She rarely lied, but when she did, she overdid it and invented too many fascinating details. Jeanne wondered how actresses had the courage to march around so boldly on a stage. She had a passion for peeling oranges.

Apollinaire, fully uniformed, sat in the Zborowskis' kitchen stolidly finishing off a plate of *Karp po Polsku*. He wiped up the sauce with a chunk of bread and fed it into his small mouth, chewed hard and pushed back his chair from the table.

"So there is the pretty picture, the rogue turned by love into a cooing dove. It's enough to turn one's stomach, no reflection on your food, dear Anna, dear Zbo, but Modi's like a mooning calf over this girl. Anna, dear, the peppercorn and bayleaf were just right in the *carpe Polonaise*."

"It isn't like Deo," said Anna, "to feel this way about a girl. He's *usually*—" She tossed her shoulders and began to clean the table as if aware a respectable woman couldn't express just what Deo was to most women.

Zbo pulled on his beard. "He's deeply serious, or thinks he is. Is that enough to ask from love?"

Apollinaire lit a dreadful-smelling length of thin black cigar and polished his *medaille militaire* with a thumb. "He acts so stiffly, so without humor—as if he's found the secret of life. He makes no sense, he stares into space, the way characters perform in very bad novels, where the lovers never go to bed in full view of the reader. And I don't think he's laid a heavy finger on the girl. This isn't the Modi we know and love."

Anna set down a bowl of beet soup with barley. Apollinaire laid aside the cigar and polished his spoon on a corner of the tablecloth and began to eat.

"Ah, Anna, where did you get the dried mushrooms, and the

kvas? Modi should be here helping me eat this instead of mooning away, sighing like a steam engine. In love, I have found out something Modi will never learn. To commit oneself completely, to love at first sight, is betting on the long shot in a very questionable horse race."

Zbo lit his pipe and puffed smoke slowly toward the ceiling. "To believe in love this way isn't the crime you're trying to make it appear."

23

THEY HAD BEEN WALKING and talking for hours in an exquisite reciprocity of emotions. It was getting dark and around the Place de l'Observatoire they were lighting the few wartime street lamps. Deo and Jeanne sat down at the foot of the monument commemorating a certain Captain Garnier who conquered and explored the Mekong River regions.

There was the sound of night insects, the final cry of the last playing child dragged indoors from the park, the marrow-shivering hoot of a barge on the river, a heavy thumping of army lorries grinding along someplace in the darkening twilight toward some grotesque destination.

But at the monument there was a great calm. He held her hand. He had told her everything. How he drank, took hashish and marijuana, about his terrible rages, and his numerous and unhappy love affairs. Deo told Jeanne that he was bringing up blood from his lungs, that he was not selling enough paintings to keep a wife, that he was a Jew. He might be sent back to Italy, he said. His whole life, until now—this moment—was nothing, nothing. But he loved her, and she would have to decide. He would make no gesture, force no issue between them.

"In love, Jeanne, the servitude of one enslaves both."

She took his hand and held it to her heated cheek and kissed it. "Oh Deo, I know so little. What do I know of life? Only what the convent sisters taught me, what the priest said, what my mother advised."

"All that is behind you, Jeanne, if you come with me. You're like Columbus now, facing the unknown, the deep drop over the edge of the world, perhaps."

She looked up at him calmly, feeling the chemistry inside her and what it was doing to her skin, her fingers, the tips of her little breasts.

"We were never taught much about Columbus."

They sat huddled in the irradiated air of their own passions at the base of the weathered monument, arms around each other. "Ah, to spit in the eye of time, of history, Jeanne—that's the trick! To be only you and me. It's not easy. All those people out there in Paris who feel we owe them something—all those streets and houses with rooms, doors and walls that feel we belong to them in some ways. It's not easy what I'm asking, Jeanne. I'm asking for all of you. It's a short life even for you. An English lady I once knew used to quote something . . . 'as perish as the summer fly. Head without names, no more remembered.' She was full of things like that."

"I don't think I like that poem, Deo. Do you know any others?"

"They all seem too sad:

> "Brightness falls from the air
> Queens have died young and fair."

"Is that also from the English lady? Is she one of those you told me about? The bitches?"

"Yes, and you're right about the poems. Let me tell you of the things that are mine, Dante's *and* mine. From his *La Vita Nuova*. You don't understand Italian? Of course not. This is my own translation:

> "When first the glorious Lady of my thoughts
> Was made material to my eyes . . .
> At that moment I tell the truth
> That the spirit of life
> Which had been living in the secret
> Chamber of the heart
> Began to tremble so violently
> That the least pulse of my body
> Shook me instantly . . ."

"I must be getting home," said Jeanne, primly aware that Deo was becoming very excited; he was trembling.

"Jeanne!"

"I'll see you tomorrow."

He let her go after a redundant adieu, the little schoolgirl with the swaying braids, her green-and-black marble-paper portfolio tied with the black laces under one arm. He had for the first time in a long while a sense of actuality. His past, and his fatalistic preoccupation with it, fell away. He was drawn to this girl the way a convert is drawn to the smell of incense. He would work better, he would really have that exhibition of his nude paintings. He and Jeanne would develop an immunity to the venom of the outer world. The devil take fame; posterity is something we pass in a coma, anyway. Life is *now*, under the fingernails, itching the scalp, and perfection in art may be nothing but a disguise for some entirely irrelevant sense of guilt. No, no, he told himself, after drinking a few *vin rosés*—hurrying back to his studio—he would now, fully, do his best to make a life for himself.

Deo stopped in front of a shop where they sold surgical supplies, trusses, braces, paunch supports, crutches, bandages. A plaster woman wore all the appliances at once, like an advertisement for a catastrophe. Deo beat his brow with a fist. His vision, how could *he* give it substance in fulfillment. He was so unworthy of Jeanne, worn down, aware of the slowness of hope.

So young, so pure. On the rue Grenelle he looked at himself in a shop mirror. How he had fallen away to the thrusting bones. His once handsome face was drawn, lined, puckered with dissipated flesh, punctuated by eyes that had seen horrors and imagined worse. He turned away from the mirror. He had never seen himself so clearly, or with such shocked disappointment.

After a quick Pernod-and-anisette, he decided he must spare this girl. Let her unripe dreams slumber within her girlish contentment. In his charnel house she would only decompose, as he had. Slowly he walked homeward, aware of nothing in the night outside his own misery and memory. *"Desponsamus te, Mare, in signum veri perpetuique dominii,"* he recited. We take

thee to wed, O Sea, in witness of true and everlasting do-
minion.

In a dark doorway smelling of cats he kneeled and blurted
his penitence.

> *Padre del Ciel, dopo i perduti giorni,*
> *Dopo le notti vaneggiando spese . . .*

Father in Heaven, after my misspent days, After my nights
wasted in vanity . . . Petrarch's lines came pouring back as he
rose and ran, his teeth chattering.

> Henceforward with your might and help I turn
> To a new life and finer endeavors,
> So that my fierce enemy is put to scorn
> After spreading his snares in vain!

Deo stumbled over a street barrow left unattended in the
dark, kicked over a rubbish can, and somewhere a half-
mocking voice across the street hailed him.

"Hey you, Modi! What's the hurry? The *flics* after you?
Modi, I've got a bottle! *L'art pour l'art!*"

Deo ran on, ignoring invitation and slogan, stumbled up to
his studio, and now the dreadful enemy that had hunted him
down for so many years was at its most fierce; the shaking was
so bad he could hardly find the wardrobe drawer where he had
a pill of hashish hidden away for just such an emergency. At
last he held the gray dust-colored pill in the trembling fingers
and threw it into his gaping, sobbing mouth.

Deo paced his room, back and forth, panting, the sweat
pouring from him. Soon he could hear his own breath soften
and the trembling first went from his legs, then his arms, and at
last the great weight came toppling from his head. The band
across his chest was torn off. He wept in relief, in self-pity, and
continued to walk. He must not sit or lie down for at least
another ten, fifteen minutes. He hated his body for betraying
him once more.

When at last Deo threw himself on his unmade bed, he was
limp and numb. The whistling sound of his breath subsided,
and his chest calmed. Biting into his forearm he drifted into
sleep.

Galerie B. Weill
50 rue Taitbout Paris (9me)

EXPOSITION
des
PEINTURES
et de
DESSINS
de
MODIGLIANI

du 3 decembre au 30 decembre 1917
(*Tous les jours sauf les dimanches*)

On the right of the sheet of paper was a nude drawing of his, reproduced sharply—and the text was set with taste, in fine type. Jeanne took the announcement from Deo's hand and looked at it; first she frowned, then she smiled and pointed to the dates.

"They forgot the capital letters."

"That's modern design. No *grand farceur.*"

"I'm so proud of you, Deo."

"My first true show. Zborowski helped me arrange it with Berthe Weill. Nudes. I've been working on them. The rue La-fitte will sing, Berthe's gallery will shine!"

"Shouldn't we give out the announcements at all the cafés and restaurants?"

He kissed the top of her round head. "Did Goya do it, or Michelangelo spread around his own announcements? Of course not. It's like kissing the Pope's ring *en déshabillé.*"

"You're as fine an artist as Goya and the rest."

"I'm better for only one reason. *I'm* alive, *they're* dead."

"Yes!"

"Even the district gendarmerie know Modi is alive."

She laughed and took his hand. He was so comfortable with her; and yet how could he explain to her that his love was so strong it had to keep them apart. It was nonsense to think like this and certainly Jeanne expected and wanted more. Even schoolgirls, even young girls of nineteen, who had been to school in a convent, had bodies under their starched petticoats, and emotions that drove them.

Jeanne was pouting as they stood under the monument, arms around each other, she ready to go home to the family house, the family dinner, her father's voice saying grace—and finally to sleep in her clean and lonely narrow bed.

"Deo, don't you love me *that* way?"

"What way are you talking about?"

"I want to adore you, I want to be part of you."

"You are, you are, *ma chère*."

"I know. But the poetry and the walks and close contact, being with you—it makes a girl, well, physical. I want *everything with you*."

"What do you know about *everything? Everything* is not all rose petals and soft voices and looking at a moon and smelling flowers from a chaise-longue stuffed with goose feathers."

"I know."

"No, you don't know." Abruptly, he pulled his hand away from hers.

She lowered her head. "I hear. I listen to others talking. And . . ." She looked up at him. "I want. I want very much. If I'm yours, I want *everything*."

"Don't talk of what you don't know, Jeanne. It's nothing the way you schoolgirls imagine."

She stamped her little foot against the ground. "I'm not a child. I know . . . I know . . . I know. But Deo, it's what love is, and there can never be anyone else for me but you."

"Jeanne, I'll walk you a little closer to your home. Your family may get worried."

"Let them worry—I've been obeying them too long."

Hand in hand they walked, Deo with his grimace of brooding worry and she looking up at him, wide-eyed, expressionless, hurrying to keep up when he forgot her steps were shorter than his.

"You mustn't talk that way about love, Jeanne, to anyone but me. It's flattering. It's good to hear. I must admit that. But you're too young and I'm too old."

"That's not so!"

"Not just by years, by living. You're shiny and new, like a fuzzy chick. I'm an old tomcat, worn and scarred. My limp is bad," he tapped his chest, "and my gravestone is in here."

She ran off, her shoes kicking up gravel. "Tomorrow?" he shouted after her.

She turned and nodded, then she ran on. He held out the announcement of his show, offering it to her, but she ran without looking back.

There was a quickening sense of expectancy and almost of hope in Paris. The Americans were coming into the war. Their pink-faced officers in their boots and Sam Browne belts, their tight khaki uniforms so badly cut by French standards, amused the café sitters.

"Even a war," Apollinaire said in Brancusi's studio, "should have *chic*. To die for one's country in baggy pants destroys the illusion of one's sacrifice."

Apollinaire was not in a good mood. His head still bothered him, the wound under the leather patch ached. He was still in danger of being shipped back to the front, and he was thinking of marrying one of his girls. "War makes one submit to natural forces."

And Deo had asked him to get up early and come and see the show of his nudes at the gallery before it opened to the public.

At eleven o'clock in the morning Apollinaire sat sipping a wartime cup of coffee. "I am just turning over in my sleep for the first time. Do all those in the street always get up this early?"

Deo wound his orange scarf around his neck. The December air was cold, and outside the day was bright as crystal. "There are twenty-four hours to a day, you should meet them all."

"Too bad you're not a cubist, Modi. You understand I can't follow all the esoteric preoccupations artists have with paint. But I'll go see your exhibition."

Zborowski came in blowing on his gloveless fingers.

"I've had the announcements passed out. I've bought the last bottle of Polish brandy in the city. Real slivovitz, Constantin. This is the birth of a great reputation we'll see."

Brancuşi smiled. "Slivovitz!"

Apollinaire gazed at the coffee grounds at the bottom of his cup. "I'll have one more cup, and put some of the plum brandy into it."

Soutine staggered in like a clumsy bear, unwashed, his hair in wild disorder, his eyes still sticky with sleep. "You should see the American soldiers. Callow farm boys but *so* healthy. They tell me they eat meat *every* day. I talked Yiddish to some from Brooklyn. What accents! And they take their mother's tit till they're four or five."

Apollinaire finished his coffee and brandy and the party started for the rue Lafitte. If Paris was pleased by their new ally, the U.S.A. (Eeu Ess Hay), the artists had long since gotten over the excitement of war. Some, like Braque and Apollinaire, had come back fearfully wounded, others still lay in the trenches, or piddled and fumbled along behind the lines. Those in Paris had gone back to painting. There was a feeling of hope and a rising interest in art. Painting or not, Paris was the home of modern art, and many strangers passing through the city were alerted, and often bought paintings to take back with them.

"*Sans blague,*" Deo shouted as they walked around sand-bagged buildings and parks of army transport. "Feel the forms crumbling around us. The new will win in the end."

"And become old," said Soutine, blowing his nose in a very private way with his fingers.

Apollinaire was in a good mood, beating his thin cane on his leather military leggings. "The time is past for evasions, chaps. We're out in the open now. The war is unimportant. We must destroy the querying eyes of the pirouetting whores—the fashionable dealers and critics."

Zbo looked around. "You want to give me heart failure? Don't say such things as the war isn't important."

"To win a war is of no value because there will be other national or political wars for the same foolish reasons. Somebody doesn't like your grandmother's nose, or someone is selling a pound too much of what you want to sell yourself in some lousy market place. But in art there is always a long period of waiting and then a break through into no man's land, a fruitful senescence—are you listening, Modi?—that transcends the reality of stylish forms, the mortal annihilation of flesh and . . . Modi, what's the crowd in front of the gallery for? You said this was a pre-opening show."

There was certainly a crowd of people in the rue Lafitte around Berthe Weill's shop.

Zbo shaded his eyes to look. "They don't look like art lovers, more like *café-marc* drunks."

Soutine agreed. "Bistro loafers, street boys and women in bedroom robes who came out to shake the broom in the street."

Deo had a sudden gut-burning sense of disaster. He ran ahead and pushed his way into the crowd of gaping riffraff. In the window were four of his best nudes—oils, pinkly glowing in the cold crisp light. Two policemen were standing, legs apart, in the doorway. Berthe herself, very pale, was with a short fat captain of the gendarmerie. He was shaking his head and tossing his hands into the air with the air of a busy man doing his duty while being annoyed by gadflies.

Deo panted forward, elbowing, pushing through the crowd, the pressure of bodies, pulling his scarf free from around his neck.

"Berthe! What's happening here!"

"Ask this creature." She was near to tears, but determined not to cry.

The captain, his porky jowls escaping over the uniform collar, pivoted his whole body around to face Deo, as if he could not move the head alone.

"Who is *this?*"

"The creator of the paintings. M. Modigliani."

"So," said the captain. "Just what we'd expect. A foreigner, a bohemian."

"What's happening?"

"I have to inform you, M. Modigliani, that a citizen of Paris, a Frenchman, has protested the showing of these revolting paintings and has lodged a legal formal protest with the police."

"Revolting! *Protest!*"

At his back Deo felt Apollinaire moving and pushing back the crowd with his cane. A staccato barking of voices filled the street.

The police captain stuck a thumb under his wide black belt and nodded, trying to look fierce and shocked. "An order has been issued to remove without delay from public exhibition all examples of this work." He pulled out a paper and began to read from it: "All examples on public exhibition of this intolerable offense to public morals are to be removed."

Zbo was screaming in a high Polish voice. Apollinaire was demanding armed resistance, street barricades and a rising up of the population. Deo's blood steamed, his breath was trapped in his throat.

He saw Berthe's white drawn face and heard her words as if coming from far off. "There is nothing I can do, Deo. The paintings will be removed from public exhibit."

"My exhibition! My first true exhibition . . . " Deo turned to fight his way through the crowd, to escape the hands and arms of his friends. He broke free, swimming in air, aware only of a sky that hung without mercy.

24

HE WAS VERY YOUNG. Outside the window was an interminable expanse of Italian sky. The night light, a wick in a little bowl of oil, was smoking. Someone had told him the Grand Dukes of Livorno in Tuscany had given up their residence in the city, and Mama had pointed out to him the crowded Venezia Quarter where their palaces had once been. They were cruel and given to a touch of *morbidezza*. When he grew up, he told Mama, he would live in a big palace among the Turkish mosques, Albanian churches and the synagogues of the Jews. He would have a boat at Piombino, where the last of the grandsons of the Bonapartists came to make the sacred trip to Elba.

But he wouldn't be a merchant or stock jobber, maybe a cadet at the naval college and go walking Sundays by the statue of Ferdinand I in the park with its diluted hues of green while the band played music from the *Cavalleria Rusticana*.

The little night light flickered and made strange smoky creatures appear on the ceiling. If he called out for Mama, she would come to him barefooted, with her big breasts and earnest face, and Papa would be angry in the big oak double bed. It was best to withhold the dark fears a little longer and soon the menacing sky outside would turn the purple of the inner skin of a grape and the night would be done with and the day would exist under a splendid perpetual blue.

But he couldn't wait. If he lay here any longer alone he would grow up and go away from the family and end up in a far place; dreadful things would happen to him. He wanted Mama, wanted to press close to her, bury himself against her body, hold and smell and feel the safety of her.

"*Madre!*"

Now there would be a waiting, then a solid set door banging and a lacy flutter of drapes in the sudden draft. And in the garden the umbrageous stone-pines creaked in the wind.

"*Madre! Mamma, Mamma mia!*"

Nothing happened. No one came. No warm arms, no soft yielding comfort came down the interminable stretches of hallway.

"*Mamma mia!*"

He was shrill now, in panic. The little gilt thread of flame in the night light began to shiver and shake; it also lived in fear. It turned from yellow to orange and then to angry red and began to fade like a whisper. A narrow column of soot-colored smoke drowned the flame. He lay rigid in inky darkness. He screamed. The dark would bring on the secret second face of things that he dreaded.

"*Madre!*"

Warm, womanly arms caressed him.

"Don't, Deo, don't scream any more."

He held her close, feeling safe, calm, comfortable, a firm protection against the night's terrors.

"You mustn't scream, Deo. Everything will be all right."

He looked up and Mama was younger than he had ever remembered her. More like a girl than a woman. She made a deprecatory gesture to show the insignificance of his fears.

"*Mamma mia . . .*" he sighed. "I had such a terrible dream."

"It doesn't matter," said Jeanne, cradling his head against her body. "You had us all crazy with worry. Where have you been all day?"

Deo stared open-mouthed at Jeanne. He shook his head as if to shake dust from it, to clear the evidence of his own senses.

"I thought perhaps you'd come back here and I ran here and you were on the bed having a nightmare and screaming out. Oh Deo! Deo! We have each other, for what it's worth. The rest doesn't matter."

He closed his eyes and held on to her. "Doesn't matter? Of course it matters. But not now. I'm all out of rage. Oh Jeanne . . ."

"I am not leaving you tonight."

"Your family . . ."

"I told them I might stay with Haricot Rouge."

"You'd better go. I'm not sane. I can go raving mad any minute. Go away."

"No, no." She rubbed his cheek. "You mustn't fight anything, not even me, Deo." She released him and stood by the bed fumbling with her dress.

"What are you doing, Jeanne?"

"I'm taking off my clothes."

When she came to him, she was naked and small and perfect. But she filled his room, his blood, his addled thoughts. In pleasure and pain, they merged in this ultimate thing.

He said from under her mouth, "No, no."

She answered with a long sigh of happiness and he relinquished the world to its own futility. Only the passion mattered, and the blood, the muscles and signals of nerve end to nerve end. It seemed the better way to let things happen, and he gave her hesitant responses until, with a savage thrust of pent-up emotions, he made Jeanne a woman. Her cry of pain was loud, Deo thought, as they lay in each other's arms, but like a shout of victory. She stayed the night.

He called her his wife. She neither objected nor demanded a formal ceremony. They were in love and for both it was the most genuine deep-felt kind of emotional experience. On his part he knew no matter what the past had been, no matter all the others whom he might or might not have loved, with Jeanne he was certain of understanding, of a haven that was peace. But beyond that he knew, unstable as he was, he should not look any further, nor need to. He hoped for a halt to the progressive deterioration of his mental and nervous faculties. That he would be unfaithful to Jeanne worried him. He lived by his frayed nerves. His health was shattered, he was spitting blood in secret when Jeanne could not see it.

There had never been enough sales of his pictures to keep him in food, in clothing, in warmth, all at the same time. Now there were two of them to provide for and hard times grew harder. But his great disappointment over the exhibit had lifted. Under Jeanne's influence his shaking bouts were reduced. He drank less, and was less frequently driven to hashish.

At first, Jeanne would go home every night to her parents' house. Finally there came the inevitable bad moment when Jeanne's parents found out about their daughter and her iconoclast bohemian lover. Deo never could get her to talk in detail about what went on in the respectable fourth-floor flat of her family. Just that her mother wept and her father ranted. They did not approve; they suffered. They closed the fumed-oak door on their daughter, severed her from family. They remained baffled. The church, the orthodoxies of their good frugal life, a middle-class adhesion to their political ideas, had not prepared them for their daughter's new way of life.

Deo was painting when Jeanne came to the studio carrying a big bundle of her clothes wrapped in a sheet. He went on mixing a special golden brown of umber and chrome yellow, and she set down the bundle on the bed.

"This is the way it's going to be, Deo."

"It's good and it's bad." He looked down at his paintbrush. "I want you here more than anything I can think of, but I don't know how we'll live."

"You'll see. You'll be famous, and rich."

"Ha! When Zbo sold a painting and was lucky at playing poker a few months ago, what did he do? He took me and

Soutine and Foujita for a crazy trip to the South of France. To hunt up patrons, his *idée fixe!*"

She came up from behind him and put her arms around him. "It did you good, that trip. You saw the sun."

"The whole thing was a disaster. A delirium."

"You met Renoir."

Deo snorted and threw his brush down. "Poor old bastard. Rich, in his own villa, everything around him the size and color of money. And his hands all deformed. Chair-bound, whittled down to a wrinkled monkey. That was his reward. And he said to me, 'I hear you're a painter too, young fellow.' So I said, 'Yes, I paint.'"

"Deo, he didn't intend anything mean. He just doesn't keep up with the new things in Paris."

"He showed me a lot of his naked women. Like sides of pink beef, but of course lushly well painted. Then he asked me, 'You brought something of your own for me to see? Well, let's see it.'"

"It was kind of him."

"Perhaps. And Zbo almost fell over himself rushing to get the paintings we had left in the hall. The old monkey looked at them and said, 'Young fellow, you paint with a feeling of joy.' I almost pulled on his beard. As if joy alone matters in painting, as if any artist can say yes or no to life—and paint only joy."

"You're getting excited again, Deo. It's bad for you."

"The old lecher. He said to me, 'Paint the way you make love, as if the painting is a woman. I spend days and days caressing the backsides of the nudes in my pictures.' And he leered."

"Not everybody has to paint for the same reason, Deo."

"I couldn't stand any more of this drivel, this spiritual insolvency. Zbo was trembling as if I was about to pick up the monkey, wheelchair and all, and throw him through a window. I went to the door past the old man's paintings, and I turned, my hand on the doorknob, and in case he was also a little deaf, I shouted: 'M. Renoir, I happen *not* to like backsides!' Then we came back to Paris. Penniless."

Jeanne laughed. She had the tight solid ability of seeing the funny side of things. She could be happy and pleased at even a slight amusing suggestion of a flaw in the human comedy. She was not boisterous or loud in her pleasure at something she enjoyed.

"Deo, don't you see how amusing it is. He is so famous and rich, and what are you two talking about—the buttocks of girls."

"*La dolente strada*—the doleful road of flesh? No. I wanted to shout that idea and interpretation must take precedence over the mere sensual."

"So? In the end, on the museum walls, both of your works will hang side by side; let the critics decide."

"I'm not convinced to let you move in. Christ, why should I care how he paints?"

He stood up, hunted out the snipe-end of a cigarette in a tin box, lit it slowly. He fought down the cough in his throat and stood at the window, his back to Jeanne. "Stay, *ma chère*."

She began to unpack her bundle. "I have sheets, I have towels, I have knives and forks. My Aunt Hortense left them to me. I didn't bring the bird and the cage."

"Thank you. Birds I hate and they make a mess. Did you know birds long ago were all reptiles?"

"My school album, the little lace cap I made when I was ten. My silver hairbrush. Look, J. H. engraved in gold."

"We'll be able to pawn it when we're hungry for a dish of *saucisses* and *choucroute*."

"My sewing kit. Oh, Deo, say you're happy I'm here!"

"I am very happy." He turned to look at her. She came up to him and put her arms around him and kissed him first on one cheek, then on the other.

He said, "If I don't say much to you, it's because words mean little—I've said too much to too many girls—and I don't want to say anything insincere to you."

"I will tell you something very fine, Deo."

"How fine can it be, to let you live like this! No food, no comfort. Sometimes even no studio if I'm behind in the rent. I've had a dozen of these places. All alike. The same rusting iron stove, sometimes the windows were bigger, sometimes the ceilings were lower. Once I even had a piano. A real piano with a Spanish drape on it. The landlord said it wasn't worth moving; a music student, some Dutchman, had committed suicide, leaving the piano for his rent—it gave an air to the studio, the landlord said. Besides, he couldn't sell it—moths were in the felt keys. No, be clever, repack and go home. They'll take you back."

"I can't go back," she said. "That's the fine part of it."

She was giggling and burrowing her head against his chest. He looked down at her and lifted her face with a hand on her little chin.

"What is that fine part?"

"You can't send me home any more."

"Why not?"

Very low, her robin's-egg blue eyes opening very large, she said, "Oh Deo, *we* have made a baby!"

He patted her hair, and he smiled and for the first time he felt fully relaxed, more relaxed than even drugs could make him. He felt as if this news had resolved the contradictions of his nature. When he spoke, his voice was thick with feeling.

"A *bambino*. Oh no, Jeanne!"

"Oh yes. Oh *very* yes."

She took his hand and moved it down to her stomach. She was soft and smooth to the feel under the cloth; her muscles moved and there was life to her, and now also life in her.

Deo felt exalted, and in that part of him that had racial roots he felt favored by God, truly named Amedeo. For a few moments they stood holding each other close, aglow with the moment, and the feeling of warmth and fulfillment that held them, for all the squalor of their surroundings. The cynical city, the stone streets, the depraved pleasures of its visitors, the greedy drive of its people, all were very distant and unimportant to this love and this consequence of that love.

"Fortunately," Deo said, "It will not be winter for a long time yet."

The Americans were in the war now by the hundreds of thousands and the sadness would soon be over, people said. It was the waiting that Deo had no patience with, waiting for the battle sounds to die away, for his child to be born. He no longer cared that his reputation as a painter was growing. The grim irony of poverty, all the nasty little nuances of squalor still surrounded his life with Jeanne. He wondered at those artists able, Esau-like, to barter their birthright for a mess of fashionable trash.

One evening the ear-numbing pizzicato of a summer rain drumming on the roof drove Deo out for a drink. Afterward, when it was very late, he did not go home but wandered over to the rue du Montparnasse, where the working people lived. Someplace there lived his friend Jacques Lipchitz the sculptor, now married. Deo stumbled up the stairs and began to pound on a door. Soon all over the building voices frayed with anger began to shout to let them sleep. It was a bleary-eyed Lipchitz who opened the door, blinking like a rabbi-faced owl.

"Modi, are you crazy? It's three in the morning."

"St. John of the Cross's 'dark night of the soul'. *Sholem aleichem.*"

"Come in. Don't stand out there."

Lipchitz lighted an oil lamp. Stone figures stood around the studio, and Lipchitz' wife Berthe rose from the bed and got into a robe.

Deo bowed. "I come to offer my very late congratulations on your marriage."

"You picked a devil of a time for it and months too late."

"I really came for your copy of Villon. Ah, now, there is a poet. I must read him in my sad state. Poets, children and artists never lose some of their innocence."

"This late? And you're drunk."

Deo began to claw books out of a small bookcase near the bed. "You have Baudelaire, Mallarmé, Rimbaud. All of us doomed by the hostility of the passing crowd. We all have too much of a—don't you think, a sulky inconstant beauty, to be really accepted."

"They're accepted," growled the sleepy sculptor. His wife lay down again and closed her eyes. Deo threw himself into a creaking armchair, clutching an open book.

"I can't sleep, I can't. I keep thinking, shall we perfect the world, *or* demean it? Ah, here's a juicy bit: You listening?

"Men, brother men, that after us yet live
Let not your heart too hard against us be
For if some pity of us poor men you give
The sooner God shall take of your taken pity . . ."

"Modi, you're very drunk. The *chutzpah,* waking us up to read Villon. Get out of here. Go home.

"I die of thirst at the fountain's edge
I am hot as fire and my teeth all chatter
I am far from my own country
By some fire I shiver all aflame
Naked as a worm . . .
I laugh in tears, and hope with no hope
I take comfort in mean despair . . .
I am strong without strength or power
And have no pleasures
Eagerly welcomed
And rebuffed by all . . ."

"All right, stay—but shut up."

Berthe, the sculptor's wife, lifted her nose above the sheet. She whispered to her husband. "The *meshuggener* has gone to sleep?"

Lipchitz nodded and examined Deo slumped deep into the chair, his eyes closed, mouth open.

"He'll sleep till morning in his condition."

"Come to bed, Jacques."

The sculptor lowered the oil lamp's wick and got in beside his wife. Deo slept, hugging the open book of poems to his chest. From time to time he coughed softly but without wakening. . . .

Near morning the end of sleep was near and a line stuck in Deo's throat:

Car chassée fut comme une souillon
De son amour hayneusement.

For he was driven
From his love with humiliation.

Later he opened his eyes to murky sunlight. The dampness of the day before was gone. A little table was set with dainty care; Berthe was a good housekeeper. The sculptor smiled at Deo.

"You sober?"

"I'm sober. Is that a good condition?"

Berthe Lipchitz handed Deo a cup of coffee. "You'll feel better after you drink this. Do you always cough so much?"

"No. Sometimes I cough harder." The coffee, hot and strong, bit into Deo and he revived and shook his head. "It's always Judgment Day when I wake up. I'll never make old bones."

Lipchitz grinned. "*Shikker* philosophy. Modi, what would you charge to paint Berthe and me?"

"For a friend, almost nothing."

"Not nothing. We'd like a painting of us two together. A belated wedding picture."

"Ten francs a sitting and a little alcohol."

Deo got some paper from a pad on a side table and began to sketch with a thin pencil line. When he left, he said, "I'll be back tomorrow with some canvas and paints."

He had borrowed five francs in advance on the painting to carry back to Jeanne.

She looked worried when he came in. "Oh Deo, I don't like to be alone at night, not now."

He kissed her cheek with rough affection. "I was out drumming up work. A portrait pair. Not a great deal of money, but from a modern master working in stone. Lipchitz."

She felt his jacket as she nuzzled her head against his chest. "It's still damp. You slept in it."

He agreed and began to dig out tubes of color from an old paint box. "Tonight we'll dine in style. I don't get a portrait commission every day."

She knelt down by his side as he threw away used-up paint tubes.

"We'll be able to have the baby with us if you keep working."

"I hope so, Jeanne. Yes, of course. This poverty can't go on. It mustn't. Soon, soon, I'll be getting a thousand francs a painting. Zbo, Sagot, all say I'll be famous in a matter of months."

He patted her arm. She smiled at him and pushed his long black hair out of his eyes.

"It seems such a shame you have to struggle. We want so little, and that little is so hard to get."

"You should have been a Greek thinker, Jeanne. Maybe they're right. Man is an intruder who has violated the order of the universe and made chaos. And man is a reed—but as Pascal said, a thinking reed, hungry or not. Have you seen any scarlet or yellow umber? I'm almost out of paints."

"That's all there is in the box."

"I'll paint a door for Zbo in his place and borrow the tubes of color."

"You'll eat something, Deo?"

"Berthe will find something for me. Her dowry was a feather bed—lucky Lipchitz. And don't look at me that way. I'll have a few drinks, but I never get too drunk when I paint."

He went out cheerfully, lugging paint box and canvas. Jeanne sat down to repair his pants. Deo's clothes were worn, but he liked them to be clean and whole. She was happy. Deo was right; life is unique, untransferable and precious. She winced as the baby inside her kicked. She leaned forward on her arms and began to breathe through her mouth. The kicking stopped.

25

THERE WAS a fastidious shyness about the Lipchitzes. But the sitting for their portrait had gone well.

Deo looked up from the canvas. It was done. The sculptor in a blue turtleneck sweater and a brown jacket, and his wife painted in the lower-right-hand corner of the canvas, his arm on her shoulder. Deo had done just her head and a white lace collar. In the background was painted a suggestion of a window and a wall. Enough. With a brush he lettered LIPCHITZ across the top of the painting and in the window space he wrote out *modigliani.*

Deo had been taking a good pull now and again on the bottle of brandy since one o'clock, and he had to sit down to finish the painting.

He looked up at the sculptor and his wife.

"It's done. Not *soignés* types—but solid."

The couple looked at it, nodding their approval.

"But you only made ten francs, Modi. It was done in one sitting."

"I can't drag out sittings just to make money. I'm not Sargent, thank God."

Lipchitz looked at his wife. They had hoped Deo would sense he could take a few days; they actually were sitting only to give him a chance to earn a little money.

"I try and finish things at one sitting. I may not last a long-drawn-out job."

"Look, Modi, for you it's fine. But I'm a sculptor and we in our trade like a little more building up of forms, of substance."

"You want me to work it up?"

"If you don't mind."

Deo took another drink. "If you want me to spoil it, I'll go on with it."

"It's perfect, we admit. But do a little more on it," said Berthe Lipchitz.

"If you insist."

Deo took the canvas away with him. He did nothing to it for two weeks, then added some lines and an area of paint work and brought it back to the Lipchitzes. They paid him for a few more sittings and the sculptor hung the work on their wall.

"Someday, Modi, it will be in a museum."

Deo growled, "In that case I'll send them a full bill for a thousand francs."

"Anything else we can do?"

Deo nodded. "Teach me that village song you sang while I painted."

"Which one?" asked the sculptor.

"You know, the one about the cradle. The lullaby."

"*Unter dem kind's veegele?*"

"That's it, and tell me all the words I don't know."

The sculptor looked at his wife and lifted an eyebrow. "So now I'm a Yiddish street singer?"

"Go on," said Berthe. "He wants to sing it to Jeanne."

"She'll know even less than you about the words."

"Just *sing.*"

> "*Unter dem kind's veegele*
> *Shtate a goldene tzeegele*

> Under the baby's cradle
> Stands a golden kid.

"It's not effective in translation."

"Go on."

> "*Dus tzeegele is gefooren handlen*
> *Rozhinkess mit mandlen.*

> The kid went off to trade
> Raisins and almonds.

> *Rozhinkess mit fygen—*
> *Dus kind vet sluffen un shvygen.*

> Raisins and figs—
> Baby will sleep quietly."

"I'll remember it. And I thank you. Raisins and almonds."

Later when he sang it to her and explained the lullaby, Jeanne liked the little song very much. "But what is a little goat doing under the cradle?"

"French farmers keep the livestock in the house sometimes, don't they?"

"But their livestock don't deal in raisins and figs."

"And we don't have a cradle. I must get a basket someplace, when it's needed."

Deo got no more orders for portraits. Jeanne was his only anchor to reality. The coughing grew worse, and bringing up blood no longer annoyed him. It was part of the ritual now. The fall of 1918 had brought great excitement to Paris as victory neared, but it also upset the lives of the artists as everything was thrown into the last final effort to end the war. The

Germans were disintegrating all along the Western Front. The Russians had made a separate peace, and from there Chagall wrote the new slogans: All power to the Soviets; Peace; Bread and Land—but there were little canvas and paints for the artists.

Jeanne was near her time. Heavy, slow of movement. Their poverty was abject. She refused to let her family know of her condition. Deo painted desperately—café signs, lettered posters—but there was little of this work to be had. Deo's disquieting rages began to return. To earn something he was painting a dining-room door for the Zborowskis.

"One of my best nudes. The trick is to catch the nonchalant grace of pride in one's body."

Anna Zborowski watched Deo outline the drawing on the yellow wood of the door.

"It's fine work, I agree, Deo, but is it suitable?"

"Where, Anna, would the human race be without nudes? No place. Reproducing by fission or sitting on eggs." He began to cough. "There's no malice in a nude."

"But this is a dining-room door."

"It will hint of good things to eat. The skin of a roast duck, red lips going to a wine bottle or a plate of Polish beet soup."

Deo looked up and saw Anna Zborowski's doubt. He put down the brush. A coughing fit overcame him when he tried to talk. He took out a handkerchief and turned away from her. When he turned back to look at her, he seemed so thin and haggard she wanted to take him in her arms.

"How is Jeanne?"

"Any moment now, I should think, by the looks of her."

"You'll stay to lunch? It's just some cold pike in aspic, a little pastry."

"I'm not really hungry."

"Try to eat something."

Deo sat toying with his fork and the fish. Zbo came in with a package of paintings under his arm.

"Ah, Modi, a good morning." He blew his nose, kissed his wife, scratched his head.

"You sold something?" Deo asked.

"It's not done that way. First you talk, you explain, you soften them up. The next day they often write or phone, and we make a deal. And Jeanne?"

"Any moment."

"Ah, some are born, and some are in need of repair. Apollinaire is not in good shape."

Deo dropped the fork. "Apollinaire? Haven't they opened his skull enough?"

"I just met Picasso. He says our friend is very bad. Since getting married to one of his girls—even that hasn't helped poor Apollinaire. That wound cut down his vitality. And now, it's something in the lungs. They're full of water. Who knows what doctors can find."

"I must see him," said Deo. "Of all the people alive he would resent dying most."

"It's mostly just a bad cold," said Zbo as his wife set a plate of soup before him.

In the streets Deo found there was more talk of victory, gossip of Armistice in the crisp November air. He found Soutine and Utrillo at a bistro drinking the cheap red wine and happy to be able to afford it as the assimilation of news items and rumors went on all around them.

Utrillo asked, "What's this peace they're talking about, Modi?"

"You know there's been a war on?"

"You don't think I'm a simpleton, do you? Yes, you do."

"When they near the end of a war and have killed off all the best young men, they talk of peace. Have you heard about Apollinaire?"

"Yes." Soutine nodded. "Bad lung congestion, weak bronchial tubes. Then on top of *that*, influenza. Everybody in Paris is getting it. I feel sick myself. I've caught it."

Utrillo grinned. "Drinkers never catch anything. If your liver is floating in alcohol, no germ can touch you. Have I got it? Has Modi got it? No. We have beaten the medical men. Now on Soutine maybe dirt works the same way. You're the filthiest artist in Paris."

Deo moaned. "I must go see Apollinaire."

"Oh, he's too sick for visitors," said Soutine. "Picasso told me

Apollinaire is deep in fever and keeps yelling out to the doctor, 'I want to live! I want to live!' "

Deo made his mad grimace—more and more it was becoming a second set of features for him. "He's been too busy with his damn career; a member of Association of French Writers, the Union of Artistic Press, working at the office of the Ministry of Colonies, writing for the *Europe Nouvelle,* and for what? Tolstoy said it for all of us."

Utrillo looked around the bistro for someone to buy him another drink. "What did he say, this fellow Tolstoy?"

"How much land does a man need?"

"How much?"

"Six feet, either way, and he's ripe brie cheese for the worms." Deo got up. "Where is Apollinaire living? The same place?"

"Yes, down from Paul Guillaume's gallery. You know, the blue-painted house."

Without saying goodbye, Deo moved down the street. He thought of Apollinaire, the Pope of cubism. For Deo, he was like a father who was also an older brother. He hastened his steps, but this only brought on the cough, a hacking like a seal's bark. He stopped and leaned against a building till the fit passed. He arrived too late.

In death, Apollinaire was even more monumental than in life. He was hugely inert, ponderously passive, immensely and obscenely cold on the narrow bed. The cramped bedroom, smelling of illness, Armagnac and coffee, was lit by candles, and over the bed was a particularly unconvincing crucifix made of brass and wood. Deo crouched in a corner of the room, his hand to his mouth. The terrible raw scarlet scars on the corpse's head showed through his close-cropped hair. The waxy eyelids were lowered, and his small mouth was pursed, as in life, with enthusiasm and a suggestion of frivolous wit. But that must have happened after death. For Guillaume Apollinaire had feverishly lamented his dying and protested the unfairness and the vulgarity of death.

Deo's head buzzed. Now the room was crowded with people. Picasso and the ballet dancer whom he had recently married and whom they hardly knew. Vollard the dealer, and Jean Cocteau, and Max Jacob, who was assuring everyone in a stage whisper that he would remain with the body for the next few nights. He quoted someone: "The world is an arena which friendship alone makes tolerable."

Deo turned away and left the room. His friend was gone, only cold clay was left, with a mask that was already dissolving. He managed to get drunk before dark, and went home to Jeanne, holding her hand all night and refusing any comfort. She was so big with child that moving was difficult to her. She was, less her burden, *so* small. In the morning Deo told the woman in the flat below to keep an eye on his wife. He went out and got drunk again. He didn't know how many days he did this, but on the terrace of a café he opened his eyes and heard wild singing. Newsboys were shouting:

"WAR ENDS! WAR ENDS! GERMANS ASK FOR ARMISTICE!"

There was no trouble getting drinks that day; everyone was standing treat. American soldiers were making love to some whores on the staircase of a house down the street as if this were a spontaneous natural expression of peace.

Long lines of men and women, hysterical and with mouths open, filled the paper-choked streets. Lorries, taxis, private cars became entangled in clogged boulevards. Emotions were subject to no limits. Several crimes were committed during the celebrations. Women were willingly outraged in public parks, and the police began to gather in those whose heads they broke with their clubs. That night, every light in Paris was lit. Eructations of brisk wind stirred the torn paper in the streets. A victory ball was organized.

In their room, Deo sat with Jeanne as she began to feel violent movement. They held hands and looked down at the frenzy of peace that roared up from the city. On the horizon they were firing guns.

"They shouted like this when war broke out," said Deo. "They always shout and jump about before and after people die. It's tradition, I suppose."

"I'm happy our child will be born into a world at peace."

"And I hope with some comfort, and with something to eat."

Jeanne put her head on his shoulder. "You are happy, Deo?"

"I could be happy. I have a wife, I'm about to have a family.

And you keep asking me to say it—so here it is: I've never had love before, not the way we have it."

"I didn't think it would be this satisfying, Deo. I've never regretted anything. Not even the big things that trouble us."

"The drinking? The hashish? The mean temper, the pushing, and rages I get into?"

"It's all only a small part of it, and you do try, you *do*."

"Only sometimes." He closed his eyes. If he talked any more, he would begin coughing again and start a hemorrhage, and he knew now how precious life was, how tender and vulnerable, and how one had to husband it—like a cheap toy.

On the 13th of November, Apollinaire was buried. The church of St. Thomas Aquinas was stylishly packed. A Mass was sung, and there was a long procession of friends, and others who came to be seen. Wounded officers, men from his company were present, hushed, Deo felt, as if in a new boudoir. The press, the colonies, the military government of Paris, *all* sent representatives. Deo stood in the candle smoke among those who didn't push forward. He was depressed by the mummery, the official medals, and boozy faces fortified with Calvados. There are times, Apollinaire had once said, when one must carry one's sanity in one's teeth, like a mother cat her kittens. This was such a time.

The mortuary at Père Lachaise; where the 237th Territorials, in full uniform, commanded by a lieutenant, paid the dead man a last official honor. The hearse was swamped in flowers. Deo had read the names on the wreaths and sheaves; the *Mercure de France* and other publications. Max Jacob escorted the widow and the poet's old mother with her large orbiting eyes.

The Picassos, Paul Guillaume, Léger, Derain, a personage from the Académie Goncourt who spoke with low but impassioned eloquence.

Picasso had time to whisper to Deo, "Just like Apollinaire to die beyond his means."

Picasso was very depressed. For many years, Apollinaire had been his closest friend. Deo drifted away, thinking that in los-

ing Apollinaire so much was lost. The fat poet had tasted everything, touched everything, found something everyplace, and
had always laughed loudly. He had lived on paradox and now
—as Picasso implied—he was being buried in the same style.
He had been wounded by love, abused by enemies, mocked by
the respectable, and now would end up most likely the victim
of a cult. Apollinaire would have liked his own burial, Deo decided, and would have quoted himself:
"*J'irai m'illuminant au milieu des ombres . . .*"

On the 29th of the month Jeanne Hebuterne gave birth to a
daughter after a difficult labor at the Tarnier Maternity Clinic
in the rue d'Assas. Deo, coming into the charity ward, found
Jeanne pale, her damp hair rebraided, and by her side in a
fragment of blanket a red-faced bit of meat that showed a large
toothless mouth when it yawned.
"You are all right, Jeanne?"
"I am all right, Deo. Do you like the daughter we made?"
"She looks like a skinned cat."
"She will grow beautiful and tall, and we will be proud of
her."
He kissed Jeanne's hand, her ringed eyes. "You must have
suffered so. What will we call her?"
"Whatever you want." She smiled at him, pale, so tiny, so
intense, but also so tired for all her exuberance.
He said, "We'll call her Jeanne too."
Jeanne nodded and closed her eyes, not letting go of his
hand. The newly named child yawned again and its mouth
closed slowly. . . .

With peace came a kind of pathological letdown in which
the nation licked its wounds and the survivors looked at each
other and marveled at how they had aged, or survived. Picasso
had settled down in marriage with his Russian ballet dancer of
the luminous agate eyes; he was wearing collars now and
speaking of *his* flat and *his* collectors, and the likes and dislikes
of the society in which he now belonged. With Apollinaire
gone, the old comradeship of the painters never reformed

along its old lines. They still met at exhibits and parties, but they were middle-aged now—Matisse, Bonnard, Rouault—and hard at work.

Deo could not adjust to the peace; it was harder even than war for him to see the sudden animation of the city being re-painted and repaired. And the new invaders, as the twenties appeared on the horizon—travelers, peacemakers, king-break-ers, tourists, Americans and Italians who were staying on after the war. And the sound of the first jazz heard publicly in Eu-rope. The dead were forgotten, Deo felt, except by the sad women in shabby black. Captured German guns rusted in the parks for a few months and then disappeared. So many young artists that Deo remembered were dead, in Alsace, Belgium, Créancy, the Flanders plains, Verdun. Braque, too, had been badly wounded in the head. Pale survivors did not want to talk of their horrors when they came out of the hospitals. There was no real peace, Zbo said, only a precarious grouping of confer-ence tables marked "reserved already for the next war."

Montparnasse was blooming in this postwar shrillness. Deo, walking along, a cigarette butt hanging from his lips, saw new galleries opening, men with rich-fed blood in their faces—the new *condottieri* and *conquistadores*—looking at canvases. But although he was already well known, Deo pointed out to Zbo, his fame didn't sell enough paintings to keep him and Jeanne, or little Jeanne, in food and shelter. What hurt Deo like stab wounds was that they had to send the baby away to an Italian couple who grew vegetables for the Paris market. There was no income to keep the child alive. Their hole of a room on the rue de la Grande Chaumière was hardly fit to live in, let alone paint in, or to raise a child. They would all starve to death, and little Jeanne with them. The Ambrosis were good peasants who wanted children of their own, but couldn't produce them. It was better for little Jeanne to have the good country butter, heavy-yolked eggs, solid hot food, than to live off greasy news-papers holding rotting potatoes fried in horse fat.

But it was flesh of his flesh and of Jeanne. He was Jew enough to feel the horror of destroying a family. He could not face the agony of going home, but he had to or Jeanne would collapse. The baby, now several months old, was kicking up her heels in the padded basket she lived in. Jeanne was seated in a chair, staring at the splintered floor.

Deo came and stood behind Jeanne and put his arms around her shoulders.

"You can go with little Jeanne. The Ambrosis will be happy to have you stay for a few months."

"No, Deo, I couldn't live without you. I know that. It tears my heart to give up Jeanne so she can live. But to give you up, Deo, no matter for how long or short a time, is not possible." Her eyes were dry and serious as she lifted her head to look at him. "That would kill me, or I would kill myself."

"That's foolish talk. It's just a little time to wait. Everybody says the twenties will be running with milk and honey for artists. People are already hoarding my paintings and trading them among themselves. Just a little longer, *ma chère*, just a little while, and Jeanne will be back with us, and you'll be wearing diamonds, even in your nose, the way the ranees do in India. Why, I'm . . ."

There was a knock on the door and Deo went and opened it. A middle-aged, large-faced Italian stood there, his crisp curly hair touched with gray. His arms and legs were large and clumsy, his skin the healthy color of a man who worked out of doors.

"*Buon dì*, Signor Modigliani, you have not changed your mind?"

"No. *Buon giorno*, Luigi. This is my wife and this is the *bambina*."

Jeanne did not look up at the introduction. She sat firmly unmoving in the chair. The big man wiped his flushed face with the back of the cloth cap he was holding. He walked slowly—as if treading on eggs—up to the basket and the baby. "Ah, from *gente* of good stock. A little pale, a little thin, but Bianca and myself we'll have her rosy and dancing."

Jeanne said, "She doesn't walk yet."

"*Non importa*, she will be treated like something from the womb of the Virgin herself, forgive me, *padrona*."

He stood looking at the pale listless baby, and Deo made his fearful grimace and picked up the basket and handed it to the man. Deo could not talk. There was a bone crossways in his chest and he lived the terrible moment to its bitterest end.

The big man, inarticulate, stood there confused, shy, worried and sweating, not knowing what else to say. *"Peccato,* it has to be. And now I must get back to the farm and Bianca. To you two, *a domani."*

Deo found his voice. *"Arrivederci. Fai a modo."*

Jeanne said nothing, and the big man bowed to her, *"Grazie mille,"* and went out with the basket.

As the door shut, Jeanne suddenly leaped to her feet and flung herself at it with the despondent cry of a stricken animal. Deo grabbed her and pulled her back. She fought him, scratched his face, kicked at his shins, a shrill senseless cry issuing from her throat. Her face was distorted with grief and one of her long braids came undone. "No, no! *No!"*

Deo tightened his grip. Jeanne began to sob in a trembling desolate voice, then went limp; she felt so light in his arms, a street sparrow with thin bones and a beating little heart.

"Amore mio, she would have died here. Starved as we're starving."

She nodded. "I know, I know."

"It's a dreadful day. But when we see little Jeanne again, she'll be fat and rosy and very round."

"If we see her again." All of woman's pity and suffering was in Jeanne's face, and he wondered how the human race had been able to survive all its troubles. He pleaded with her to lie down on their rickety bed, and he lay down with her and put his arms around her. She lay very still, and Deo recalled Balzac: "Sinai and Golgotha are not here nor there. The angel is crucified everywhere and in every place."

Jeanne stirred and rolled her warm teary face against his cheek. "We'll make another baby for ourselves."

"Sleep, Jeanne, sleep."

And St. Paul had held that women, by their nature, are without souls. He pressed against his wife's stricken body, and knew that without her love, without her presence, he could no longer live. They were more now than the quivering wing-beating of love making, the overstimulated embraces of the bed. Deo had come into love, and in a disintegrating world this was his good fortune. Man is usually alone in his misery.

Jeanne slept. Tears, crystal-clear, were poised ready to fall from the corners of her eyes. With a finger Deo touched them and carefully rubbed them dry in a gentle rotating motion on her soft cheeks.

BOOK V

Blue Lake

26

"GARÇON, *a round of brandy for myself and my friends. No,* mon Dieu, *you don't think Modi can pay? I can't, but we're the guests of this American. Thank you, sir. I'm only a little drunk, but I shall do better, eh, Zbo, before we get up.* Dio vi benedica *. . . So you were in the war? Office of Supplies, how fine . . . you regret missing action . . . ah, well. It isn't over, the war, you know . . . just the fancy fools in power taking time to regroup and make bigger machines.* Di grado in grado. *The energy to act, you know, does not explain the action, I always said. . . . Well, if I didn't, I should have said it before. . . . Yes, I'll have another glass. . . . In this world I sink as naturally as a drowning man in water. In this new peace, this world of so much disaster, my experiences are no longer my own. I feel extremely disposable. None of us did in the early days, did we, Chaim? But our center of gravity has shifted— oh, I'm sensitive to balance—it's no longer within reach. From now on new voices will manipulate all existence. You think you've got the answer, sir? That's fine. But here, on this ragbag of a Europe, our private acts soon will no longer belong to us. It will be done by manipulating buttons you fine Americans are so busy inventing. Weak brandy, sir, isn't it? Never drink water . . . sir . . . Believe me the domination of the apparatus is*

*coming—even in art—all art will be made of war salvage, junk
and* merde, *and the critics will cheer.* . . . Il n'y a pas à dire.
. . . *Life has become a large-scale plan of battle for the individual . . . without innocence, personal guilt or pathos. The
image, sir, of I and You will vanish—the time of the anti-hero,
the anti-artist and anti-art art will be the true glory; for the
individual will be unredeemed.* . . . *Did you know Spinoza,
that lens-grinding bastard, was a relative of mine? I say it without any lousy pride, what the devil, who can pick his grandfa-
ther's nose? An old Jewish joke, sir.* . . . *But at least, you, me,
Zbo, Chaim, we were all once people, now everything becomes
anonymous.* . . . *Dada will rule the next hundred years and
be rediscovered as the true anti-art in sculpture; the blindfolded
painter, the garbage can will be the natural geniuses—our life
will be painted on a whorehouse glass door and shattered and
then framed at cocktail parties.* . . . *Is it true, sir, that the
buffalo are all dead, and that Buffalo Bill was a fraud?* Il va
sans dire. . . . *Don't mind me . . . sir . . . I drink quickly
and thank you . . . another glass. Disorder will replace reason. Everything that is individual will go, has to.* . . . *the de-
light of cutting across the grain will be outlawed. Everyone will
breed for happy bondage; slogans, the false song of science,
torture will be normal, and anti-art . . . to collect, not to create . . . the museum is the perfect tomb. Objectives will be
the only goal—the individual nothing. Irresponsible freedom,
the only creative force, is doomed.* . . . *You wouldn't, sir, want
to meet some lusty girls?* Il tempo buono viene una volta sola
. . . *I mean, no, I suppose not . . . with three children and a
wife in Boston. Is she fat . . . do her—? I beg your pardon,
sir . . . How vulgar of me.* . . . *You haven't their pictures on
you . . . too bad.* . . . Garçon, *another set of drinks, naturally.* . . . *As for me, I am fortunate in dying at the proper
moment. The world* inside *us all has been eaten up by the
world of* matter. . . . *You know the way a starfish gobbles up
the fat soft oyster after forcing open the shell . . . I used to
watch it being done when I was a boy . . . in the blue rock
pools near Naples.* . . . *Oh, don't mind Chaim, he has a tender stomach.* . . . *Imagination will soon be a secondary activity . . . like making a bigger fountain pen or taller noise.* . . .

*The self does not endure—only an image of self. I sell you my
secret for a drink, sir . . . didn't know that, did you? The future we face, it has to destroy all images—only now there are
no old idols left to smash, so man, no longer free from matter,
will destroy the last true image, himself . . . even in art. . . .
Who's waving his arms! Who's shouting! All right, I'll sit
down. Where was I . . . A world in which the image no
longer exists* behind *or* within *change . . . now I ask you what
is left? The cause, the pursuit—wild game or little girls . . .
the right side, the wrong side, never the individual . . . he is
done for. . . . So who will be left to starve in attics . . . to
distill experiences? Believe me, the world was once our own
idea—our will, our desire. Now look at it . . . a marching
order to the moon. I mean that as a metaphor, I think—the
moon is beyond reach. . . . Wasn't it better, as Lord Byron
said . . . an English society bitch once read it to me as we—I
beg your pardon, sir—as we made love on her Second Empire
bed . . . 'I was my own destroyer, and will be my own hereaf-
ter.' Excuse my accent; English doesn't come easy to my mouth.
. . . Garçon, another round of saucers. . . . You only pay for
those we drink—clever, non? Every man his own Prometheus
was what the world once was. Our only obligation was to shake
the fat ones awake from time to time and shout in their ears:
You're alive! . . . Take your hands off me, Zbo . . . I'm not
going to fall down . . . I'm sitting . . . oh, I'm not sitting?
Help me up, sir. . . . Soon everything human will be deballed
by science. . . . You know why Justice is always shown blindfolded . . . because she's crosseyed, that's why. . . . Where
was I . . . I love you, sir . . . so clean, so earnest, so brave
. . . you smell so innocent. I love all things American . . .
Mutt and Jeff, the Captain and the Katzenjammer kids, Har-
vard, chewing gum, Voodrow Vilson, tin lizzies, bazball, toilet
paper; oh, you have asses, such soft asses, admit it . . . eh? Just
one more glass . . . can't hurt me. . . . Sensibility now can
only be lived secretly in our shifting consciousness . . . so you
see, sir, the readymade clothes of the future . . . of the new
wars, the new slogans, will never fit. . . . The non-art art and
the scientists are the betrayers of the world . . . a new stink, a
new wet windy sound, a new way to get to die faster. . . . Sci-*

ence is the true Antichrist . . . Chaim, you chacham, sage, don't stare so . . . I am a tzaddik, a wonderworker, I am science-proof . . . just look at me . . . would you trust a machine in my hands, or a revolution, or an empire? Of course not. . . . What . . . you want to buy a painting . . . I'm pleased to hear that. . . . Paint you, sir? It's a kind offer . . . but I'm a little too shaky just now . . . these days . . . being a seer and seeing the future so clearly, it's shaken a man up a bit. Another drink . . . no . . . I couldn't refuse . . . so why refuse me . . . I mean . . . a man isn't a swine to swill alone. . . . What . . . what's the time? Time is an invention . . . it doesn't exist. . . . Catch me a bottle of time . . . My hat, garçon . . . didn't have one? I confess it freely, don't shoot. . . . I'm drunk . . . low-down, gutter-high goddam drunk . . . drunk . . . I give you this world as a gift . . . there's another universe swinging by in a moment and I'm jumping on . . . don't try to stop me . . . get your filthy hands off me . . . goodbye . . . and arrivederci . . . *to equals* . . . arrivederla . . . *to superiors* . . . and au revoir *to . . .*"

"Help us pick him up."

27

TIME WAS no longer inexhaustibly fecund. For Deo it passed almost unnoticed. He was hardly aware of 1920 looming up. If asked the date suddenly, he would just as soon have answered 1906, 1914, as 1920. He seldom even painted now. The world seemed composed of specters. And when Zbo or Paul Guillaume came to him with some favorable review of his work, he would push them aside and ask, "You'll stand me to a couple of drinks?"

He was more inexplicable, uncommunicable. He wanted no one around but Jeanne. When drunk, all others were antagonists and deprecators. Jeanne was enough. This talk of art and artists, of markets and critics, no longer mattered. He was worn and thin, and the drinks and the hashish on which he survived made his dreadful grimace madder than ever. Often he had no idea he was wearing his grimace and Soutine or Zbo would point it out to him.

"You're frightening people."

"I'm frightening myself. I've somehow mislaid myself. Buy me a drink."

The violence of his own temperament made him an outcast. He was not permitted into many cafés where he had in the past broken mirrors, smashed chairs, destroyed glassware and crockery.

When the White Russian refugees came to Paris with their silken rags and some family jewels hidden in their frayed underwear, they were as violently anti-Semitic as they had been in the wonderful days of the Tsar. Deo, in his rages, would seek them out in their own nightclubs and cafés, and stand in the smell of borscht and *kulebiaka* listening to them curse the world's indifference, their own bad fortune, and that Jew Lenin.

"*Zdrahf-stvooy-t'eh.*"

Sometimes they offered Deo vodka and hors d'oeuvres while he recited Dante or Baudelaire. But there was often the moment when a drunken Deo would rise, beating his fists together like cymbals, and shout, "I'm a Jew! You rotting stinking anti-Semites!"

"*Jid! Jid!*"

Shashlik and *blini* hot from the fire were flung at him, but he never backed down until thrown out on the sidewalk bloodied and bruised.

"Swine!"

"*N'eh zuh shtuh.*"

The old police doctor Molet examined Deo after one of these fights at the Zakuska café. The doctor pressed on Deo's torso and ribs, listened to his breathing, examined his eyes, took his pulse. He sat back under the lonely yellow bulb in the ceiling of the back room where bicycles were kept.

"You're a sick man, Modi. Why fight? You need a favorable climate to survive. Like Italy. Lots of rest, extra nourishment."

"Dr. Malot, you have a cigarette?"

"Ah, you see? Smoking. Also drugs, alcohol, cold studios—it's not the right treatment for your lungs."

"No, it isn't. But it's too late to change."

Dr. Malot moved closer. "Listen to me. I suspect you may have a dormant tubercular meningitis. It can develop for months, even years, with only a few visible symptoms. You must get into a hospital, take tests."

"With what? You offer me illusions, Dr. Malot. I make my own."

"This tubercular encephalic disorder, if I'm correct, has done things to you that may seem mad or unexplainable. Haven't you been puzzled at your own actions, reasonless actions at times?"

"What actions?"

"Modifications of yourself, of your personality, Modi. You're extremely irritable at times? You break things, smash furniture? You have violent outbursts of great rages, angers. You are unsociable. I just have to look up your police records to prove to you I'm right."

Deo closed his eyes and leaned his aching head on his hands. "I don't say I'm neat or sociable. But I'm drunk or drugged when I act that way."

"Not always. You withdraw into yourself. Tell me about your aches. You have visual, even auditory disturbances?"

"I get the shakes, my teeth chatter. Things move. I hear sounds."

Two policemen came in, took their bicycles and left. The doctor offered Deo his cigarette case.

"I can only advise you, Modi. I don't say I'm right in what I think may be the matter. But you get like a madman when you're roused. Here, smoke if it calms you."

"*Merci.*" Deo lit up and inhaled.

"Doctor, can't it be my poverty, my hunger? My rage at what I see and can't get others to see? I haven't any bread to take home to my wife. And she's pregnant again. We haven't seen our little girl for a year. What's the answer, Doctor? But to booze, drug and shout."

Deo was shaking and he held his fists tight under his armpits. "You're right, Doctor, I'm a wreck, and it's obvious my nerves are shattered. Maybe there is a morbid irritation in my brain, maybe I say to myself it's all worth it. Stupid, isn't it? Life is for living, not for art. *Morbus et Genius* you doctors might call it."

"We might, Modi, we might. Put your shirt on and go home. I'll give you a salve for your bruises. For the rest, some would suggest prayer; I never, myself, found prayer as good as a clinic and a clean hospital bed."

"You're wrong, Doctor." Deo inspected his cigarette end. "The church is smarter, it lets the aches and the visual madness and noises pass for miracles. It would be a fine jest, Dr. Malot, if they were right and we with our logic were wrong. St. Modigliani. No, I don't see myself in so high a station . . . a halo, a bottle of cognac in one hand and paintbrush in the other."

Deo stepped on the cigarette and buttoned his shirt and then turned in the doorway. "Oh, Doctor, if you're right about the thing you said, the symptoms that could take months to develop, that's *our* secret?"

"I was only guessing, Modi. You may be just a terribly wild man under drugs and drink who has to make noises and break things. All I ask, don't do them in our police district. Get drunk and shout elsewhere."

"Optimists drink to confess, Doctor, nihilists to forget."

He wished he had begged for another smoke. He refused to look at the day. It was too funereal. The sycamores and lime trees on the avenues were bare and black in the winter wind. An art dealer in his doorway, the *sale cogot*, was smiling at him; the window held one of Deo's *nus harmonieuxs*.

The art he and Picasso and Matisse and the rest were doing was being accepted, the critics were giving them solemn absolution from the sins of heresy and schism; they would become the old salon in their turn—the accepted academy—and other wild young men would pull them down.

He did not feel tranquil, consoled by or fortified with faith in his art; that could come to those who would be here when he was dead. For the present the will doing the work of the imagination, that was enough. His mind was drifting again . . . someday it would just wander off, leaving him headless.

He must go back to the studio and somehow find enough money to keep them alive.

Deo proved the doctor was right late the next afternoon. He and Jeanne were coming back from a fruitless trip to sell some of his drawings. A note had been left with Jeanne, an address where some American visitors were living; they wanted to buy some drawings. Jeanne had lost the note, and had guessed at the address. Of course they had not found the house. Passing the Luxembourg Gardens, the black grimace on his face, Deo was in a furious temper at the lost hope for food or drink.

"Come along," he shouted at Jeanne. "Come along."

"I'm all out of breath."

"It's your fault we're on this fool's errand, ruining our shoes, working up an appetite—for what?"

He grabbed her arm and began to drag her along. She protested, "Deo, please, you're hurting me."

He seized one of her braids and pulled on it in a senseless fury—then he banged her body hard against the iron railing. She fell, her shabby clothes fluttering in the cold wind. It all happened like a nightmare oversteeped in allusions; he knew now he could not stop his rage, that he had no control of himself. The doctor had been right; he was a madman, reasonless, unrelated to his true feeling.

"Deo, what are you doing?"

She warded off his arms and picked herself up and ran. He watched her move, ungainly with child, on her worn flat shoes, her shawl trailing, the braids flying behind. He let out a roar and followed, but as he ran he began to sob, and when he was weeping and shaking, she stopped and waited for him.

He could hardly drag his feet. He felt unfocused, his mind contaminated. Her melancholy eyes held forgiveness.

"Jeanne, I'm very very ill. I'm mad."

"No, of course not. You're highstrung. Things affect you. I annoy you with the stupid mistakes I make. Losing that address."

"No." He put an arm around her. He could feel her shaking in the chilly weather, and the pulsebeat in the wrist he held. "No, we mustn't do this to each other. I know I've banged you around before. But it has to stop."

"Let's go home, Deo."

Arms around each other, the winds like mandolins in the bare tree limbs, they walked slowly toward a cheerless, fireless, foodless room. He could just see the sunset of old silver and blemished bronze over the trees. His fingers twitched on Jeanne's shoulder as overhead the raucous cries of cold birds settling for the night were like illusions in a dream he could not fully understand.

"We'll get into bed, with everything we own piled over us. We'll live out the winter like bears in a cave."

"I heard if you sleep a great deal," she said, "you don't get as hungry."

In a newfound elation they moved on slowly, holding on to each other.

There was in Jeanne a strength and a quality that grew stronger as their condition grew worse. She had a way of looking at Deo, very wide-eyed, with just a tiny smile in the corner of her mouth, and then looking quickly away, as if caught in an uneasy shameful act. She insisted, as long as they had polish, that Deo shine his shoes no matter how broken the leather. And usually she did it for him. She ate slowly when they had food, taking small bites, chewing placidly, and when she was very hungry, her throat would go taut and her muscles stiffen, but she never complained. She could perceive Deo's moods before he did.

Jeanne had a great fear of direct light in her face, but unlike most women did not draw back from a bug or a mouse, and would hunt and mash them with a small worn broom they had inherited until Deo roared with laughter. She often hunted nonexistent bugs.

She sewed badly, but insisted she was as good as any seamstress, and would spend hours darning, patching a shabby garment only to have it split as soon as someone put it on.

She had the habit of looking into space, mooning for long periods of time, then coming to as if out of a trance, and smiling wildly, still not in full control of her senses. She was very quick and bright in dealing with people. From her father, she told Deo, she got a good business sense, and she could be raucous in a shop, demanding full measures when they had enough money to buy food.

Jeanne was startlingly ignorant of the true facts of space or distance and history or science, Deo discovered. She had a marvelous storytelling gift and sometimes when without food or coal they would lie in bed for days and she would repeat to Deo all the stories and fairy tales of her youth. Her skill was amazing and she could have been a charming imaginative writer.

She was very frugal with string and old paper, none of which served any useful purpose, but if they managed to have bread, she would crumble up a good portion of her share and set it out on the windowsill for the birds. If she had milk, she fed the alley cats, and Deo had to remove by force a nest of newborn kittens from under their bed; Jeanne had taken in a pregnant one-eyed cat during a rainy night.

Jeanne, Deo came around to thinking, was neither shy nor weak, nor did she fully accept many of the problems of their life together. She could raise her voice in anger at some art dealer dickering to cheapen one of Deo's paintings. She had a marvelous art sense and understood fully what was going on in Paris, and just how good a painter Deo was. For all her tiny size she could wrestle a pair of buckets of water up three flights of stairs and scrub a floor. But as their second child quickened within her, she had to give up trying to keep their dreadful room as clean as she could get it.

She had a habit of suddenly making little bright remarks to cheer Deo up. ("Let's shout: 'Open Sesame—we want to get out.'") For all her hard lot she was never really depressed so long as Deo came home nights. She placed high confidence in love, and did not dream of any other way of life being possible for her.

Her voice was very beautiful when under control, and she had one little dark tooth that she tried to hide from Deo by a crooked smile, head turned to one side. She was unique, and Deo knew it and adored her; she dreaded his strange rages when he was brutal and cruel to her. She forgave him without looking like a martyr, or sniffling in self-pity. Once she clouted him with the broom and thickened his ear.

Jeanne had great faith in prayer, but never showed any sign of it in Deo's presence. She prayed when alone, whispering softly as if not asking a favor, but explaining something from one person to another.

January ended in a freezing blue cold. The streets were almost deserted but for people on errands, deep in their coat collars, their red noses steaming. Deo and Jeanne had retreated to their bed. From time to time Zbo and others had sent them a basket of coal, but now they had none left. Kisling and one or two admirers of Deo's work had provided some tins of sardines, but the little oily fish were all consumed.

For four days they had lain in bed under everything that could hint at some warmth: old rags, drapes, their spare garments. It was dark in the room, the oil for the lamp was long since used up. The wind whistled through the rattling window panes and formed glacial pockets in the corners of the darkened room.

Deo hardly moved; only the sound of his labored breathing showed he was alive. Jeanne moved with great effort, her ballooning pregnancy tender to the slightest touch. She was not too clear in her mind as to what was happening to them. *We stand at a window, wondering at the strangers outside. . . .* But as long as Deo gripped her cold fingers with his freezing hand, it was enough.

A great unutterable weariness was on them, but they were not in pain. Deo could dimly see through his fever the stained ceiling and certain Bosch-like patterns on it; if he could only read them, all the tragic implications of life would be clear. But he could not focus either his eyes or his mind. For four days now they had lived on cold water and a last crust of bread.

He wondered if they would ever leave this bed. There was a damp burning in his lungs and a kind of exaltation was raging inside him. The cold burned like flame and he burrowed closer to Jeanne. The tragic débâcle of their lives seemed right and proper and very wonderful.

He wanted to explain how much more they felt than other people, how much closer they had come to some gemlike flame of mutual understanding that cleansed everything that was wrong . . . how they were above the predatory, destructive appetites around them . . . how . . . art . . . was even above those tired subjects birth, death and the godhead. In the faraway silence of empty streets would one day come voices to say *good* of his work. One transcends all by art. How right Van Gogh was: Painting never pays back what it costs.

He could not voice any of it out loud, and he was no longer able even to think of it clearly. The images were dissolving and the fever was growing. He felt warm and wanted to unburden himself of the coverings. His strength failed and he could barely hold Jeanne's fingers.

The room grew colder, the wind blew harder, and the window frame rattled and made the sound of large wooden teeth chattering.

There was a knocking on the door. First earnest and even, then in fear, loud and irregular. Zborowski's voice came through from the other side of the door.

"Modi! What's the matter in there? Modi, is anything wrong?"

In the hallway a fearful blast of polar air was coming up the staircase. Zborowski and Kisling stood at the door, scarfs around their coat collars, staring at each other, listening for an answer.

Kisling rubbed his cold hands together. "I haven't seen them in days."

"What have they lived on?"

Kisling put his shoulder to the door. "Modi, Jeanne!"

Zbo added his weight. "Break it down!"

Others appeared on the landing. The concierge with a blanket over her frowzy head and some other faces, one still chewing a lump of bread.

"What's happening here?" screamed the concierge.

"Something's wrong," Zbo shouted back.

"There's maybe nobody home there. Crazy artists!"

"No, there must be. Modi!"

Kisling rubbed his aching shoulder. "It's a damn solid door. Have you a key, madam?"

"Of course not."

The man chewing the last of his bread rubbed his sooty face. "If you want it busted in, stand back."

"You're not juggling sacks of coal now, Victor," shouted the concierge. "That's a valuable door!"

The huge frame of the coalman drove at the door. It creaked, held. Then again he put his strength to it. The lock tore out with a sound of protesting metal and wood and the door banged back with a heavy thud.

The bed was like a burial mound. Under the rags two forms could be made out. Scattered everywhere in the freezing room were empty sardine cans.

Zbo turned to the people pushing in.

"Somebody get a doctor."

The bedclothes were stained with fish oil.

28

HOW FINE IT WAS to be well and healthy again, to be able to search out all of one's life. Sometimes the ideas of the individual and of his setting get lost. Deo was very happy. It was so warm and the yellow sky hung low enough to touch, and he recalled the lisping sidewalk theology of childhood games, and his mother calling him in from play: *"Vieni quà, Deo, come va?"*

"Non c'é male."

He no longer feared an old voice smelling of stale black, "Remember you are a Spinoza."

He turned away from things past. The light was ticklish as velvet, and when he opened his eyes, the large room full of sick men in beds spun in a mechanical orbit. He felt his nerve ends respond to moving skin, the soft antennae of hair. His senses were wide open. The seashell murmur of fever in his ears, the carbolic and stale-feet smell, the peeling walls and the dirty ceiling told him he was in the pauper ward of the Hôpital de la Charité. He had been there before.

A bearded doctor was looking down at him through great magnifying lenses that turned into gold-rimmed eyeglasses.

"You're very sick."

Deo did not answer.

"Do you want a priest?"

Deo shook his head. "Jeanne."

"You're most likely contagious. We can't let anyone in."

Deo didn't fully understand why they had to put a pound of lead on each of his eyelids, fill his stomach with broken glass. "I kissed my wife goodbye . . . we agreed . . . on eternal happiness . . ."

It was dark again, a whistling ear-breaking darkness. He felt someone touch him, the bite of the hypodermic injection. He escaped into a blue-hydrangea world by a sea of wrinkling silver. A wind smelling of *pasmata, vino santo* was blowing out of the Alps, a wind that the natives over the *passito* wine called "a wind that will not blow out a candle but kills a man."

He was painting his own portrait, almost his last picture, a worn-out, dark-haired man, lean of face, a fancy scarf around a thin neck, the palette in hand, brush ready (in the wrong hand in the mirror), a man neither disheveled nor frivolous. From nowhere to nowhere. Sleep is our goal. The doctor's face came back clearly, porcine nose commanding a ludicrous physique— the nurses were moving a canvas screen around the bed. It was a fine painting. . . .

He tried to speak. . . . *Art itself is no god . . . only a tool . . . show life wonderful . . . totally phenomenon . . . from the sad songs I rise, the secrets of the inner eye . . . Testify. . .*

But no words were coming out. His mother would understand why he must tell them. His mother reading, he on the floor, listening: *The magic spring was guarded by a giant in the deep mountain cave. When asked if you could drink of the spring, he told you, "The price is your right eye."*

The doctor pushed up one eyelid and looked deeply into the blind staring pupil.

Lips parting . . . listen . . . dry fever-blistered lips . . . bend low around the bed all of you . . . a low fierce whisper . . .

"Italia . . . cara Italia."

Dante lingered only a moment in the gathering dark:

> Cruel death, pity's foe
> Ancient mother of grief,
> Merciless judgment without appeal . . .

The doctor closed the eyes and drew the gray linen sheet over the beautiful dead face.

There was a wire from Rome on Modigliani's death (dead he was no longer Deo, or Modi), from his brother Emanuele, the Socialist deputy: BURY HIM LIKE A PRINCE.

The body was taken first to the mortuary at La Charité. The consuming illness continuing after death had molested the flesh and it was no longer the beautiful man. Jeanne, pale, silent, intense, fought off the doctors and the nurses. She was large, ready to bear; she remained firm-lipped and determined.

"I want to see him."

"Like this?"

The doctor wiped his brow, swung his gold-rimmed glasses off his nose, and motioned them to let Jeanne in. The gray room, the single green-yellow light, the shape, sheeted on a cold slab of brown stone. Some hands tried to keep her from going closer. She shook them off, went and bent over the wounded, festered face. No battle could have inflicted worse damage.

Kisling came up behind Jeanne and held her upright. She turned in fury.

"Alone! Alone with him!" she shouted. Kisling released her. Jeanne cried out over the body, a terrible root-tearing scream. Then she knelt, to embrace.

"Alone. Alone," she sobbed.

Her father, serious, pious, unforgiving, opened the door to Jeanne. He said nothing. Her mother wiped her tears and stood back among the satinwood and buhl.

Jeanne went up to her room and looked down on the city, the streets, the Place de l'Observatoire where they once met, all so familiar since childhood.

Yesterday they had let her say goodbye to the dead artist.

Life went on, but senselessly. They said a bed was ready for her again in the Tarnier Clinic where his child would be born. A lot of life still to be lived; it stretched away to the horizon beyond the rooftops.

Clumsy in her heaviness Jeanne stepped up onto the window sill and launched herself into space.

In the studios and on the café terraces, at the zinc counters of the bistros and along the streets there was talk and shaking of heads. *Both* dead now. The waiters at the Dôme and the Rotonde heard a great deal of philosophy about the brevity of life, the futility of human endeavor. In the rue Campagne, the rue de la Grande Chaumière they were already repeating legends, engendering myths of the wild and raucous artist, Amedeo Modigliani.

The journey was not yet over. The hospital wanted to get rid of the painter's body. Friends collected money, opened subscriptions. There was enough for a casket, some flowers, a hearse, three carriages, a grave.

In the echoing stone hospital courtyard the coffin was placed in the hearse. There were many mourners: artists, the curious, models, dealers, drinking companions. Emanuele Modigliani, a stouter, darker version of his brother, with a stern political mask gone limp, stood alone, in loose black, weeping openly in the Italian manner.

Kisling, Zborowski joined him; they were to head the long line of mourners. The hearse moved slowly toward the Père Lachaise cemetery. The cortège of mourners drew respect. The policemen were saluting, thinking how often they had brought him in for disturbing the peace, or fanned his behind with their capes during one of his wild nights.

By the cemetery gates stood an old man with a wet red nose, holding a tray of folded paper fortunes. On his shoulder a red and green parrot perched. He was a shabby old man, waiting for someone to offer a coin to let the parrot pick a fortune from the tray. As the hearse passed, he took off his battered hat, crossed himself and said aloud: "Never mind, Flinck, that you forgot for a moment he was a Jew."

The three carriages were filled with sprays of dying flowers, ornate wreaths. As the hearse entered the cemetery, Zborowski turned to Soutine behind him, blowing his nose in the bitter cold.

"Tomorrow we do this all over again for Jeanne." He sighed and looked up at the hard blue sky.

The carriage wheels crunched with a grinding sound onto the cinders of the cemetery drive. The day continued bright and brisk.

For a fee slipped into his hard dry hand, the attendant at the cemetery of Père Lachaise brings you up to the stone with these now-weathered words cut into it.

AMEDEO MODIGLIANI
pittore
La Morte lo colse
quando
Giunse alla gloria

Death struck him as he reached glory.

THIS BOOK WAS SET IN

CALEDONIA AND PALATINO TYPES,

PRINTED AND BOUND BY

H. WOLFF BOOK MANUFACTURING CO., INC.

IT WAS DESIGNED BY

LARRY KAMP.